BITTERSWEET

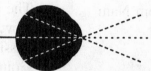

Also by Danielle Steel

Mirror Image
His Bright Light: The
   Story of Nick Traina
The Klone and I
The Long Road Home
The Ghost
Special Delivery
The Ranch
Silent Honor
Malice
Five Days in Paris
Lightning
Wings
The Gift
Accident
Vanished
Mixed Blessings
Jewels
No Greater Love
Heartbeat
Message From Nam
Daddy
Star
Zoya

Kaleidoscope
Fine Things
Wanderlust
Secrets
Family Album
Full Circle
Changes
Thurston House
Crossings
Once in a Lifetime
A Perfect Stranger
Remembrance
Palomino
Love: Poems
The Ring
Loving
To Love Again
Summer's End
Season of Passion
The Promise
Now and Forever
Passion's Promise
Going Home

DANIELLE STEEL

BITTERSWEET

DOUBLEDAY DIRECT LARGE PRINT EDITION

Delacorte ▤ **Press**

This Large Print Edition, prepared especially for Doubleday Direct, Inc., contains the complete, unabridged text of the original Publisher's Edition.

Published by
Delacorte Press
Random House, Inc.
1540 Broadway, New York, New York 10036

ISBN 0-7394-0286-2

Manufactured in the United States of America
Published simultaneously in Canada

To Tom,
for the bitter
and the sweet.

with all my love,
d.s.

Never settle for less than your dreams.
Somewhere, sometime, someday, somehow,
you'll find them.

Chapter 1

India Taylor had her camera poised as an unruly army of nine-year-old boys ran across the playing field after the soccer ball they had been heatedly pursuing. Four of them collapsed in a heap, a tangle of arms and legs, and she knew that somewhere in the midst of them was her son, Sam, but she couldn't see him as she shot a never-ending stream of pictures. She had promised to take photographs of the team, as she always did, and she loved being there, watching them on a warm May afternoon in Westport.

She went everywhere with her kids, soccer, baseball, swimming team, ballet, tennis. She did it not only because it was expected of her, but because she liked it. Her life was a constant continuum of car pools, and extra-curricular activities, peppered with trips to the vet, the orthodontist, the pediatrician when they were sick or needed checkups. With four children between the ages of nine and fourteen, she felt as though she lived in her car, and spent the winters shoveling snow to get it out of the garage and down the drive-way.

India Taylor loved her children, her life, her husband. Life had treated them well, and although this wasn't what she had expected of her life in the early years, she found that it suited her better than expected. The dreams that she and Doug had once had were no longer relevant to life as they now knew it, who they had become, or the place they had drifted to since they met twenty years before in the Peace Corps in Costa Rica.

The life they shared now was what Doug had wanted, the vision he had had for them, the place he wanted to get to. A big, comfort-able house in Connecticut, security for both of them, a houseful of kids, and a Labrador retriever, and it suited him to perfection. He left for work in New York at the same time every day, on the 7:05 train out of the Westport station. He saw the same faces, spoke to all the same people, handled the same accounts in his office. He worked for one of the biggest marketing firms in the country, and he made very decent money. Money wasn't something she had worried about much in the early days, not at all in fact. She had been just as happy digging irrigation ditches and living in tents in Nicaragua, Peru, and Costa Rica.

She had loved those days, the excitement, the challenges, the feeling that she was doing something for the human race. And the occasional dangers they encountered seemed to fuel her.

She had started taking photographs long before that, in her teens, taught by her father, who was a correspondent for *The New York Times*. He spent most of her childhood years away, on dangerous assignments in war zones. And she loved not only his photographs, but listening to his stories. As a child, she dreamed of a life like his one day. And her dreams came true when she herself began freelancing for papers at home while she was in the Peace Corps.

Her assignments took her into the hills, and brought her face-to-face with everything from bandits to guerrillas. She never thought of the risks she took. Danger meant nothing to her, in fact she loved it. She loved the people, the sights, the smells, the sheer joy of what she was doing, and the sense of freedom she had while she did it. Even after they finished their stint with the Peace Corps, and Doug went back to the States, she stayed in Central and South America for several months, and then went on to do stories in Africa and Asia. And she managed to hit all the hot spots. Whenever there was trouble somewhere, for a while at least, India was in it, taking pictures. It was in her soul, and in her blood, in a way that it had never been in Doug's. For him, it had been something exciting to do for a time before he settled down to "real life." For India, it *was* real life, and what she really wanted.

She had lived with an insurgent army in Guatemala for two months, and had come up with fantastic photographs, reminiscent of her father's. They had won her not only praise internationally, but several prizes, for her coverage, her insight, and her courage.

When she looked back on those days later on, she realized she had been someone different then, a person she thought of sometimes now, and wondered what had happened to her. Where had that woman gone, that wild free spirit filled with passion? India still acknowledged her, yet she also realized she no longer knew her. Her life was so different now, she was no longer that person. She wondered sometimes, in her dark room, late at night, how she could be satisfied with a life so far removed from the one she had once been so in love with. And yet, she knew with perfect clarity, that she loved the life she shared with Doug and the children in Westport. What she did now was important to her, as much as her earlier life had been. She had no sense of sacrifice, of having given up something she loved, but rather of having traded it for something very different. And the benefits had always seemed worth it to her. What she did for them mattered a great deal to Doug and the children, she told herself. Of that, she was certain.

But there was no denying, when she looked at her old photographs, that she had had a passion for what she did then. Some of the memories were still so vivid. She still remembered the sheer excitement of it, the sick feeling of knowing she was in danger, and the thrill of capturing the perfect moment, that explosive split second in time when everything came together in one instant in what she saw through her camera. There had never been anything like it. If nothing else, she was glad she'd done it, and gotten it out of her system. And she knew without a doubt that what she had felt was something she had inherited from her father. He had died in Da Nang when she was fifteen, after winning a Pulitzer the year before. It had been all too easy for India to follow in his footsteps. It was a course she couldn't have altered at the time, or wanted to. She needed to do it. The changes she had made came later.

She returned to New York a year and a half after Doug had gone home, when he had finally issued an ultimatum. He had told her that if she wanted a future with him, she had better "get her ass back to New York" and stop risking her life in Pakistan and Kenya. And for only a brief moment, it had been a tough decision. She knew that a life much like her father's was out there for her, maybe even a Pulitzer like his one day, but she knew the dangers too. It had ultimately cost him his life, and to some extent his marriage. He had never really had a life he cared about beyond the moments when he risked everything for the perfect shot, with bombs exploding all around him. And Doug was reminding her that if she wanted him, and any kind of normalcy, she was going to have to make a choice sooner or later, and give up what she was doing.

At twenty-six, she married Doug, and worked for *The New York Times* for two years, taking photographs for them locally, but Doug was anxious to have children. And when Jessica was born shortly before India turned twenty-nine, she gave up her job at *The Times,* moved to Connecticut, and closed the door on her old life forever. It was the deal she had agreed to. Doug had made it very clear to her when they got married that once they had children, she had to give up her career. And she had agreed to do it. She thought that by then she'd be ready. But she had to admit, when she left the *Times* and turned her attention to full-time motherhood, it was harder than she expected. At first, she really missed working. In the end, she only looked back once or twice with regret, but eventually she didn't even have time for that. With four children in five years, she could barely keep her head above water or take time out to reload her camera. Driving, diapers, teething, nursing, fevers, play groups, and one pregnancy after another. The two people she saw most were her obstetrician and her pediatrician, and of course the other women she saw daily, whose lives were identical to hers, and revolved only around their children. Some of them had given up careers as well, or were willing to put their adult lives on hold until their children were a little older, just as she had. They were doctors, lawyers, writers, nurses, artists, architects, all of whom had given up their careers to tend to their children. Some of them complained a lot of the time, but although she missed her work, India didn't really mind what she was doing. She loved being with her children, even when she ended the days exhausted, with another baby on the way, and Doug came home too late at night to help her. It was the life she had chosen, a decision she had made, a deal she had lived up to. And she wouldn't have wanted to leave her children every day to continue working. She still did the occasional rare story close to home, if she had time for it, once every few years, but she really didn't have time to do it more often, as she had long since explained to her agent.

What she hadn't known, or fully understood before Jessica was born, was just how far from her old life it would take her. Compared to the life she had once led, taking photographs of guerrillas in Nicaragua, and dying children in Bangladesh, or floods in Tanzania, she had had no idea just how different this would be, or how different she would become once she did it.

She knew she had to close the door on those early chapters of her life, and she had, no matter how many prizes she had won, or how exciting it had been, or how good she was at it. In her mind, and Doug's especially, giving it up was the price she had had to pay for having children. There was just no other way to do it. Some of the women she knew could juggle work at home, a couple of her friends were still lawyers and went into the city two or three days a week, just to keep their hand in. Others were artists and worked at home, some of the writers struggled with stories between the midnight and four A.M. feedings, but eventually gave it up, because they were too exhausted to do it. But for India, it was impossible. There was no way to continue her career, as she had once known it. She kept in touch with her agent and had done local stories from time to time, but covering garden shows in Greenwich had no meaning for her.

And Doug didn't even like her doing that much. Instead, she used her camera as a kind of mothering tool, constantly making visual records of her children's early years, or taking photographs of her friends' children, or for the school, or just playing with it as she did now, watching Sam and his friends play soccer. There was no other way to do this. She was bound and chained, set in cement, rooted to her life in a thousand ways, visible and otherwise. And this was what she and Doug had agreed to. And what they had said they wanted. And she had lived up to her end of the bargain, but her camera was always in her hand, at her eye, or slung over her shoulder. She could never imagine a life without it.

Once in a while, she mused about working again once the kids grew up, maybe in another five years when Sam was in high school. But that was inconceivable to her just now. He was only nine, Aimee was eleven, Jason was twelve, and Jessica fourteen. Her life was a constant merry-go-round of activities between them, after-school sports and barbecues and Little League and piano lessons. The only way to do it all was if you never stopped, never thought of yourself, and never sat down for five minutes. The only respite

she had from it was when they went to Cape
Cod in the summer. Doug spent three weeks
there with them every year, and the rest of the
time he commuted on weekends. They all
loved their Cape Cod vacations. She took terrific photographs at the Cape every year, and
got a little time for herself. She had a darkroom in the house, just as she did in
Westport. And at the Cape she could spend
hours in it while the kids visited with friends,
or hung out on the beach, or played volleyball
or tennis. She was less of a chauffeur at the
Cape, the kids could ride their bikes everywhere and it gave her more free time, especially in the last two years, since Sam was a
little older. He was growing up. The only
thing she wondered from time to time was
how grown up she was. Sometimes she felt
guilty about the books she never had time to
read, the politics she had lost interest in. It
felt sometimes as though the world beyond
was moving on without her. She had no sense
anymore of growth or evolution, it was more a
question of treading water, cooking dinner,
driving kids and getting from one school year
to another. But there was nothing about her
life that made her feel that she had grown in
recent years.

India's life had been virtually the same for the last fourteen years, since Jessica was born. It was a life of service, sacrifice, and commitment. But the end result was tangible, she could see it. She had healthy, happy children. They lived in a safe, familiar little world that revolved entirely around them. Nothing unsavory or unsafe or unpleasant ever intruded on them, and the worst thing that ever happened to them was an argument with a neighbor's child, or a trauma over lost homework. They had no concept of the loneliness she had felt as a child, with one constantly absent parent. They were unfailingly ministered to and cared for. And their father came home every night for dinner. That was especially important to India, as she knew only too well what it was like not to have that.

India's children lived in a different universe from the children she had photographed two decades before, starving in Africa, or jeopardized in unimaginable ways in underdeveloped countries, where their very survival was in question daily, fleeing from their enemies, or lost to natural aggressors like illness, floods, and famine. Her children would never know a life like theirs, and she was grateful for it.

India watched her younger son pull himself from the pile of little boys who had cas-
caded on top of him as he scored a goal, and
wave at his mother.

India smiled, the camera clicked again,
and she walked slowly back to the bench
where some of the other mothers were sitting,
chatting with each other. None of them were
watching the game, they were too busy talking. This was so routine to them that they
rarely watched, and seldom saw what their
children were doing. The women were just
there, like the bench they were sitting on, part
of the scenery or the equipment.

One of them, Gail Jones, looked up as
India approached, and smiled when she saw
her. They were old friends, and as India
pulled a fresh roll of film out of her pocket,
Gail made room for India to sit down. There
were finally leaves on the trees again, and everyone was in good spirits. Gail was smiling
up at her, as she held a cardboard cup with
cappuccino in it. It was a ritual of hers, particularly in the freezing cold winters when they
watched their kids play ball, with snow on the
ground, and they had to stamp their feet and
walk around to stay warm as they watched
them.

"Only three more weeks and then school's over for this year at least," Gail said with a look of relief as she took a sip of the steaming cappuccino. "God, I hate these games, I wish to hell I'd had girls, one at least. Life defined by jockstraps and cleats is going to drive me nuts one of these days," she said with a rueful smile as India smiled at Gail in answer, clicked the film into place, and closed her camera. Listening to Gail complain was familiar to her. Gail had been complaining for the last nine years about giving up her career as a lawyer.

"You'd get sick of ballet too, believe me. Same idea, different uniform, more pressure," India said knowingly. Jessica had finally given up ballet that spring, after eight years, and India wasn't sure if she was relieved or sorry. She would miss the recitals, but not driving her there three times a week. Jessica was now playing tennis with the same determination, but at least she could ride her bike there on her own, and India didn't have to drive her.

"At least ballet shoes would be pretty," Gail said, standing up to join India as they began to walk slowly around the field. India wanted to take some more shots from a different angle, to give to the team, and Gail walked along beside her. They had been friends ever since the Taylors moved to Westport. Gail's oldest son was the same age as Jessica, and she had twin boys Sam's age. She had taken a five-year break between them, to go back to work. She had been a litigator, but had quit finally after she had the twins, and she felt she'd been gone too long now to ever consider going back to her old law firm. As far as she was concerned, her career was over, but she was older than India by five years and, at forty-eight, claimed she no longer wanted to be trapped in the court-room. She said all she really missed was intel-ligent conversation. But despite her com-plaints, she occasionally admitted that it was easier just being here, and letting her hus-band fight his daily wars on Wall Street. Like India, her life was defined by soccer games and car pools. But unlike India, she was far more willing to admit that her life bored her. And there was a constant sense of restlessness about her.

"So what are you up to?" Gail asked ami-ably, finishing the cappuccino. "How's life in mommy heaven?"

"The usual. Busy." India took a series of

photographs as she listened distractedly to her. She got another great shot of Sam, and even more when the other team scored a goal against them. "We're leaving for the Cape in a few weeks, when school lets out. Doug can't come up for his vacation this year till August." He usually tried to take it before that.

"We're going to Europe in July," Gail said without enthusiasm, and for an instant India envied her. She'd been trying to talk Doug into it for years, but he said he wanted to wait until the children were older. If he waited much longer, India always reminded him, they'd be gone and in college, and going without them. But so far she hadn't convinced him. Unlike India, he had no real interest in traveling far from home. His adventuring days were over.

"Sounds like fun," India said, turning to look at her. The two women were an interesting contrast. Gail was small and intense with short dark hair, and eyes that were two burning pools of fiery dark chocolate. India was long and lean, with classic features, deep blue eyes, and a long blond braid that hung down her back. She claimed she always wore it that way because she never had time to comb it. As they walked side by side, they were two very striking women, and neither of them looked anywhere near forty, let alone a few years past it. "Where in Europe are you going?" India asked with interest.

"Italy and France, and a couple of days in London. Not exactly high adventure, or high-risk travel, but it's easy with the kids. And Jeff loves going to the theater in London. We rented a house in Provence for a couple of weeks in July, and we're going to drive down to Italy, and take the kids to Venice." To India, it sounded like a wonderful trip, and worlds away from her lazy Cape Cod summer. "We'll be there for six weeks," Gail went on. "I'm not sure Jeff and I can stand each other for that long, not to mention the boys. After ten minutes with the twins, Jeff goes crazy." She always talked about him the way people did about irritating roommates, but India was always sure that beyond the grousing, Gail actually loved him. In spite of evidence to the contrary, India believed that.

"I'm sure it'll be fine, you'll have plenty to see," she said, though being trapped in a car with twin nine-year-old boys and a fourteen-year-old for extended periods of time didn't sound like India's idea of heaven either.

"I can't even meet a handsome Italian, with the kids along and Jeff chasing after me, asking me to translate for him." India laughed at the portrait Gail painted, and shook her head. It was one of Gail's quirks, talking about other men, and sometimes more than just talking. She had confided to India frequently that she'd had several affairs in the twenty-two years she and Jeff had been married, but she had surprised India by saying that in an odd way, it had actually improved their marriage. It was a form of "improvement" India had never been drawn to, nor approved of. But she liked Gail enormously, despite her indiscretions.

"Maybe Italy will make Jeff more romantic," India suggested, slinging her ever-present camera over her shoulder, and glancing down at the small, electric woman who had once been a terror in the courtroom. That, India found easy to imagine. Gail Jones took no nonsense from anyone, and certainly not her husband. But she was a loyal friend, and in spite of her complaints, a devoted mother.

"I don't think a transfusion from a Venetian gondolier would make Jeff Jones romantic. And the kids with us twenty-four hours a day sure as hell won't help it. By the way, did you hear that the Lewisons are separated?" India nodded. She never took much interest in the local gossip. She was too busy with her own life, her kids, and her husband. She had a handful of friends she cared about, but the vagaries of other people's lives, and peering into them with curiosity, held no magic for her. "Dan asked me to have lunch with him." At that, India cast a glance at her, and Gail smiled mischievously at her.

"Don't look at me like that. He just wants some free legal advice, and a shoulder to cry on."

"Don't give me that." India was uninvolved in the local scandals, but she was not without a degree of sophistication. And she knew Gail's fondness for flirting with other people's husbands. "Dan has always liked you."

"I like him too. So what? I'm bored. He's lonely and pissed off and unhappy. That equals lunch, not a steamy love affair necessarily. Believe me, it's not sexy listening to a guy complain about how often Rosalie yelled at him about ignoring the kids and watching football on Sundays. He's not in any condition for anything more than that, and he's still hoping he can talk her into a reconciliation.

That's a little complicated, even for me." She looked restless as India watched her. According to Gail, or what she said anyway, Jeff hadn't excited her in years, and India knew it. It didn't really surprise her. Jeff was not an exciting person, but it made India think as she listened. She had never actually asked Gail what, in her opinion, *was* exciting.

"What do you want, Gail? Why bother with someone else, even for lunch? What does it give you?" They both had husbands, full lives, kids who needed them, and enough to do to keep them out of trouble and constantly distracted. But Gail always gave India the impression that she was looking for something intangible and elusive.

"Why not? It adds a little spice to my life, just having lunch with someone from time to time. And if it turns into something else, it's not the end of the world. It puts a spring in my step, I feel alive again. It makes me something more than just a chauffeur and a housewife. Don't you ever miss that?" She turned to India then, her eyes boring into hers, much as they must have done cross-examining a defendant in the courtroom.

"I don't know," India said honestly. "I don't think about it."

"Maybe you should. Maybe one day you'll ask yourself a lot of questions about what you didn't have and didn't do, and should have." Maybe. But to India, at least, cheating on her husband, even over lunch, didn't seem like the perfect answer, far from it. "Be honest. Don't you ever miss the life you had before you were married?" Her eyes told India she wouldn't tolerate anything less than full disclosure.

"I think about the things I used to do, the life we had before. . . . I think about working . . . and Bolivia . . . and Peru . . . and Kenya. I think about the things I did there, and what it meant to me then. Sure I miss that sometimes. It was great, and I loved it. But I don't miss the men that went with it." Particularly since she knew Doug appreciated all that she'd given up for him.

"Then maybe you're lucky. Why don't you go back to work one of these days? With your track record, you could pick it up again whenever you want. It's not like the law, I'm out of the loop now. I'm history. But as long as you have your camera, you could be right back in the fray tomorrow. You're crazy to waste that."

But India knew better. She knew what

her father's life had been like, and theirs, waiting for him. It was more complicated than Gail's perception of it. There was a price to pay for all that. A big one.

"It's not that simple. You know that. What am I supposed to do? Just call my agent tonight and say put me on a plane to Bosnia in the morning? Doug and the kids would really love that." Even the thought of it was so impossible that all she could do was laugh at it. She knew, as Gail did, that those days were over for her. And unlike Gail, she had no need to prove her independence, or abandon her family to do it. She loved Doug, and her kids, and knew just as surely that he was still as much in love as she was.

"They might like it better in the end than you getting bored and crabby." It surprised India to hear her say that, and she looked at her friend with a questioning expression.

"Am I? Crabby, I mean?" She felt a little lonely at times, and maybe even nostalgic about the old days now and then, though not often anymore, but she had never become seriously dissatisfied with what she was doing. Unlike Gail, she accepted the point to which life had brought her. She even liked it. And she knew the children wouldn't be small forever. They were already growing up rapidly, and Jessica had started high school in September. She could always think about going back to work later. If Doug let her.

"I think you get bored, just like I do sometimes," Gail said honestly, facing her, their children all but forgotten for the moment. "You're a good sport about it. But you gave up a hell of a lot more than I did. If you'd stayed with it, by now you'd have won a Pulitzer, and you know it."

"I doubt that," India said modestly. "I could have wound up like my father. He was forty-two when he died, shot by a sniper. I'm only a year older, and he was a lot smarter and more talented than I was. You can't stay out in that kind of life forever. The odds are against you, and you know it."

"Some people manage it. And if we live to be ninety-five here, so what? Who will give a damn about it when we die, India, other than our husbands and our children?"

"Maybe that's enough," India said quietly. Gail was asking her questions she almost never allowed herself to think of, although she had to admit that in the past year it had crossed her mind more than once that she hadn't done anything truly intelligent in years, not to mention the challenges she'd given up. She'd tried to talk to Doug about it once or twice, but he always said he still shuddered to think of the things they'd done in the Peace Corps and she'd done after. Doug was a lot happier now. "I'm not as sure as you are that what I would be doing would change the world. Does it really matter who takes the pictures you see of Ethiopia and Bosnia and on some hilltop, God knows where, ten minutes after a rebel gets shot? Does anyone really care? Maybe what I'm doing here is more important." It was what she believed now, but Gail didn't.

"Maybe it isn't," Gail said bluntly. "Maybe what matters is that you're not there taking those pictures, someone else is."

"So let them." India refused to be swayed by her.

"Why? Why should someone else have all the fun? Why are we stuck here in goddamn suburbia cleaning apple juice up off the floor every time one of the kids spills it? Let someone else do *that* for a change. What difference does *that* make?"

"I think it makes a difference to our families that we're here. What kind of life would they have if I were in some two-seater egg-crate somewhere crawling in over the trees in bad weather, or getting myself shot in some war no one has ever heard of, and doesn't give a damn about. That *would* make a difference to my children. A big one."

"I don't know." Gail looked unhappy as they started walking again. "Lately, I think about it all the time, about why I'm here and what I'm doing. Maybe it's change of life or something. Or maybe it's simply the fact that I'm afraid I'll never be in love again, or look across a room at a man who makes my heart leap right out of my chest looking at him. Maybe that's what's driving me crazy, knowing that for the rest of my life Jeff and I are going to look at each other, and think okay, he's not great, but this is what I got stuck with." It was a depressing way to sum up twenty-two years of marriage, and India felt sorry for her.

"It's better than that, and you know it." At least she hoped so, for Gail's sake. It would be terrible if it wasn't.

"Not much. It's okay. Most of all, it's boring. He's boring. I'm boring. Our life is boring. And ten years from now I'll be nearly sixty and it'll be even more boring. And then what?"

"You'll feel better when you go to Europe this summer," India said kindly, as Gail shrugged a shoulder in answer.

"Maybe. I doubt it. We've been there before. Jeff will spend the entire time bitching about how badly they drive in Italy, hating whatever car we rent, and complaining about the smell of the canal in the summer in Venice. He's hardly a romantic figure, India, let's be honest." India knew that Gail had married him twenty-two years before because she was pregnant, and then lost the baby after three months, and spent another seven years after that trying to get pregnant, while fighting her way to the top in her law firm. India's life had been a lot simpler than Gail's had been. And her decision to give up her career had been less agonizing for her. Gail was still asking herself if she'd done the right thing nine years after retiring when the twins were born. She had thought that she'd been ready to do it, and it was obvious now that she wasn't. "Maybe having lunch with other men, and having an 'indiscretion' with them now and then, is my way of compensating for what Jeff will never give me, for what he isn't, and probably never was." India couldn't help wondering if her affairs only made her more dissatisfied with the life she was living. Maybe she was looking for something that didn't exist, or wasn't out there, not for them at least. Maybe Gail was simply unwilling to admit that, for them, that part of their lives was over. Doug didn't come home from the office with roses in his arms for her either. But India didn't expect that from him. She accepted, and liked, what they had grown into. As he did.

"Maybe none of us will ever be madly in love again, maybe that's just the bottom line here," India said practically, but Gail looked outraged.

"Bullshit! If I thought that, I'd die. Why shouldn't we be?" Gail looked incensed. "We have a right to that at any age. Everyone does. That's why Rosalie left Dan Lewison. She's in love with Harold Lieberman, which is why Dan isn't going to get her back. Harold wants to marry Rosalie. He's crazy about her."

For an instant, India looked startled. "Is that why he left his wife?" Gail nodded. "I really am out of it, aren't I? How did I miss that one?"

"Because you're so good and pure and such a perfect wife," Gail teased. She and India had been friends for a long time, and were each the kind of friend the other could rely on. They provided each other with total acceptance, and India never criticized her for the men she slept with, although she didn't approve or fully understand why she did it. The only explanation was that Gail had a kind of emptiness that nothing seemed to fill, and hadn't in all the years that India had known her.

"Is that what you want, though? To leave Jeff for someone else's husband? What would be different?"

"Probably nothing," Gail admitted. "That's why I've never done it. Besides, I guess I love Jeff. We're friends. He just doesn't provide much excitement."

"Maybe that's better," India said thoughtfully, mulling over what Gail had said to her. "I had enough excitement in the old days. I don't need that anymore," India said firmly, as though trying to convince herself more than her friend, but for once Gail was willing to accept what she said at face value.

"If that's true, you're very lucky."

"We both are," India affirmed to her, wishing she could make her feel better. She still didn't think that lunch with Dan Lewison, and men like him, was a solution. Where did that lead? To a motel between Westport and Greenwich? So what? India couldn't even imagine sleeping with someone else. After seventeen years with Doug, she didn't want anyone else. She loved the life that she and Doug shared with their children.

"I still think you're wasting your talent," Gail prodded her, knowing full well it was the only chink in India's armor, the only subject on which India occasionally dared to ask herself pointed questions. "You should go back to work one of these days." Gail had always said that India's talent was so enormous that it was a crime to waste it. But India always insisted she could go back to it later, if she wanted. For now, she didn't have the time or the inclination to do more than the occasional story. She was too busy with her kids, and didn't want to rock the boat with Doug. "Besides," she teased Gail, "if I go back to work, you get to go out to lunch with Doug. Do you think I'm that stupid?" They both laughed at the suggestion, as Gail shook her head, her eyes dancing with amusement.

"You have nothing to fear. Doug's the only man I know who's even more boring than my husband."

"I'll accept that as a compliment on his

behalf," India said, still laughing. He certainly wasn't exciting, or even colorful, but he was a good husband, and good father. That was all she needed. He was solid, decent, loyal, and a good provider. And besides, no matter how boring Gail thought he was, India loved him. She didn't have the lust that Gail had for intrigue and romance. She had given all that up years before, and before Gail could say anything else, the whistle blew and the soccer game ended, and within seconds, Sam and Gail's twin sons had come thundering over to them.

"Great game!" India said, smiling broadly at Sam, relieved in some way to be out of the conversation. Gail always made her feel as though she had to defend herself, and her marriage.

"Mom, we lost!" Sam looked at her with disdain, and then put his arms around her and hugged her just a little too tight, as he dodged the camera swinging from her shoulder.

"Did you have fun?" India asked, kissing the top of his head. He still had that wonderful little-boy smell of fresh air and soap and sunshine.

"Yeah, it was okay. I scored two goals."

"Then it was a good game." They began

walking to the car with Gail and her boys, who were clamoring to go out for ice cream, and Sam wanted to join them. "We can't. We have to pick up Aimee and Jason." Sam groaned at the prospect, and India waved at Gail as they got into their van, and India slid behind the wheel of her station wagon. It had been an interesting conversation. Gail certainly hadn't lost her touch at cross-examination.

And as India started the car, she glanced at her son in the rearview mirror. He looked tired, but happy. There was dirt all over his face, and his blond hair looked as though he'd combed it with an eggbeater, and just looking at him told her once again why she wasn't climbing through bushes in Ethiopia or Kenya. She didn't need more than that dirt-smeared face to explain it. So what if her life was boring?

They picked up Aimee and Jason at school, and headed home. Jessica had just walked in, there were books all over the kitchen table, and the dog was going crazy wagging his tail and barking. It was life as she knew it, as she had chosen to live it. And the thought of living it with anyone but Doug depressed her. This was exactly what she wanted. And if it wasn't enough for Gail, then she was sorry for her. In the end, they all had to do what worked best for them. And this was the life India had chosen. Her camera could wait another five or ten years, but even then she knew she wouldn't leave Doug to go trekking halfway around the world to find adventure. You couldn't have both. She had figured that out years before. She had made a choice, and she still thought it was a good one. And she knew that Doug appreciated what she was doing.

"What's for dinner?" Jason asked, shouting over the frantic barking of the dog and the clamoring of his siblings. He was on the track team at school, and starving.

"Paper napkins and ice cream, if you guys don't get out of the kitchen and give me five minutes' peace," India shouted over the din, as he grabbed an apple and a bag of potato chips and headed to his room to do his homework. He was a good kid, a sweet boy. He worked hard at school, got good grades, did well in sports, looked just like Doug, and had never given them any trouble. He had started discovering girls the year before, but his greatest foray into that realm had been a series of timid phone calls. He was far easier to deal with than his fourteen-year-old sister, Jessica, whom India always said was going to be a labor lawyer. She was the family spokesperson for the downtrodden, and rarely hesitated to lock horns with her mother. In fact, she loved it. "Out!" India shooed them all out from underfoot, put the dog outside, and opened the refrigerator with a pensive expression. They'd already had hamburgers twice this week, and meat loaf once. Even she had to admit that she was lacking inspiration. By this point in the school year, she couldn't think up any more creative dinners. It was time for barbecues and hot dogs and ribs, and time on the beach on the Cape. She settled on two frozen chickens, and stuck them in the microwave to defrost them, as she pulled out a dozen ears of corn and began to clean them.

She was sitting at the kitchen table, thinking about what Gail had said that afternoon, sifting it as she did sometimes, trying to decide for herself if she had any regrets about her lost career. But she was still convinced all these years later that she had made the right decision. Besides, it was a moot point anyway, she told herself, there was no way she could have continued traveling around the world as a journalist, or even working locally, and still have done the right thing for her children. She owed this to them. And if Gail found her boring as a result, so be it. At least Doug didn't. She smiled, thinking of him, as she put the corn in a pot of water and set it on the stove, and then took the chickens out of the microwave, put butter and spices on them, and put them in the oven. All she had to do now was put some rice on the stove, make a salad, and presto magic, dinner. She had gotten good at it over the years. Not fine cuisine, but fast and simple and healthy. She didn't have time to make them gourmet meals with everything else she did. They were lucky she didn't take them to the drive-thru at McDonald's.

She was just putting dinner on the table when Doug walked in, looking slightly harried. Barring a crisis at the office, he usually came home promptly at seven. Door to door, it was a twelve-hour day for him, or slightly longer, but he was a good sport about the commute, and he kissed the air somewhere near her head, as he set down his briefcase and helped himself to a Coke from the refrigerator, and then looked over and smiled at her. She was happy to see him.

"How was your day?" she asked, wiping

her hands on a towel. There were wisps of wheat-colored hair framing her face, and she never thought much about what she looked like. She was lucky, she didn't have to. She had clean, healthy, classic looks, and the braid she wore suited her. Her skin was good, and she looked about thirty-five instead of forty-three, with a long, slim figure that looked well in shirts and turtlenecks and jeans, which was the uniform she wore daily.

Doug set down the Coke and loosened his tie as he answered. "Not bad. Nothing exciting. I had a meeting with a new client." His business life had been uneventful for the most part, and when he had problems, he shared them with her. "What did you do today?"

"Sam had soccer, and I took some pictures for the team. Nothing terrific." As she listened to herself speak, she thought of Gail, and how dull she accused their lives of being. They were. But what more could she expect? Bringing up four kids in Connecticut was hardly glamorous, or fraught with excitement. And India couldn't see how Gail's illicit activities could change that. She was kidding herself if she thought that made a difference, or improved things.

"How about dinner at Ma Petite Amie

tomorrow night?" Doug offered as she called the kids in to dinner.

"I'd love it," she smiled, and within the next millisecond chaos erupted in the kitchen. But they always enjoyed their meals together. The children talked about their day, their friends, their activities, while complaining intermittently about teachers and the amount of homework they'd been given. And Aimee blew the whistle on the news that a new boy had called Jessica three times that afternoon, and he sounded really *old*, like maybe even a senior, and Jessica looked daggers at her. And for most of the meal, Jason provided them with entertainment. He was the family clown, and made editorial comments on everything. Aimee helped her clean up afterward, and Sam went to bed early, exhausted by his soccer game and the two goals he'd scored. Doug was reading some papers from the office by the time India finally joined him in their bedroom.

"The natives seem to be keeping you busier than usual tonight," he commented, glancing up from the report he was reading.

There was a staid, solid quality that India had loved about him right from the beginning. He was tall and lean and lanky, with athletic good looks, and a boyish face. At forty-five, he was still very handsome, and looked like a college football hero. He had dark hair and brown eyes, and was given to tweeds and gray suits for work, and corduroy pants and Shetland sweaters on weekends. And in a quiet, wholesome way, India had always found him very attractive, even if Gail did think he was boring. And in many ways, he was the ideal husband for her. He was solid and reliable and unflappable, generally, and fairly reasonable in the demands he made of her.

She sat down in a big, comfortable chair across from him, and tucked her legs under her, trying to remember, just for an instant, the boy she had met in the Peace Corps. He was not so very different from the man she sat across from now, but there had been a glimmer of mischief in his eyes then that had enchanted her at the time, when she was young and filled with dreams of daring and glory. He was no longer mischievous, but he was decent and reliable, and someone she knew she could count on. Much as she had loved him, she didn't want a man like her father, who was never there, and risked and eventually lost his life in the pursuit of his wild, romantic notions. War had been romance to him. Doug was far more sensible than that, and she liked knowing she could count on him to be there for her.

"The kids seemed a little wound up tonight. What's up?" he asked, putting his report down.

"I think they're just excited about the end of the school year. It'll do them good to get to the Cape, and get it out of their systems. They need some downtime, we all do." By this point in the school year, she was always sick to death of her car pools.

"I wish I could take time off earlier than August," he said, running a hand through his hair, thinking about it. But he had to oversee some marketing studies for two important new clients, and he didn't want to leave town prematurely.

"So do I," India said simply. "I saw Gail today. They're going to Europe this summer." It was pointless to try and talk him into that again, she knew, and it was too late to change their plans for this summer anyway, but she would have liked to. "We really should do that next year."

"Let's not start that again. I didn't go to Europe till I finished college. It's not going to kill them to wait a couple of years to do that. Besides, it's too expensive with a family our size."

"We could afford it and we can't cheat them of that, Doug." She didn't remind him that her parents had taken her all over the world when she was a baby. Her father had taken assignments wherever he thought it would be fun, at vacation times, and taken her and her mother with him. The traveling they'd done had been a rich experience for her, and she would have liked to share that with their children. "I loved going with my parents," she said quietly, but he looked annoyed, as he always did when she brought up the subject.

"If your father had had a real job, you wouldn't have gotten to Europe as a kid either," Doug said, almost sternly. He didn't like it when she pushed him.

"That's a dumb thing to say. He had a real job. He worked harder than you or I did." Or you do now, she wanted to add, but didn't. Her father had been tireless and passionately energetic. He had won a Pulitzer, for God's sake. She hated it when Doug made comments like that about him. It was as though her father's career was meaningless because he had earned his living with a camera, something that seemed childishly simple to her husband. No matter that he had lost his life in the course of what he was doing, or won international awards for it.

"He was lucky, and you know it," Doug went on. "He got paid for what he liked to do. Hanging out and watching people. That's kind of a fortuitous accident, wouldn't you say? It's not like going to an office every day, and having to put up with the politics and the bullshit."

"No," she said, a light kindling in her eyes that should have warned him he was on dangerous ground, but he didn't see it. He was not only belittling the heroic father she revered, but he was casting aspersions on her own career at the same time, who she was, and who she had been before they married. "I think what he did was a hell of a lot harder than that, and calling it a 'fortuitous accident' is a real slap in the face." To her, and to her father. Her eyes were blazing as she said it.

"What got you all riled up today? Was Gail off on one of her tangents?" She had been, of course. She was always stirring the pot in some way, and India had said as much to Doug before, but the things he had just said about her father had really upset her and had nothing to do with Gail. It had to do with her, and how Doug felt about the work she did before they were married.

"That has nothing to do with it. I just don't see how you can discount a Pulitzer prize–winning career and make it sound as though he got a lucky shot with a borrowed Brownie."

"You're oversimplifying what I said. But let's face it, he wasn't running General Motors. He was a photographer. And I'm sure he was talented, but he also probably got lucky. If he were alive today, he'd probably tell you the same thing himself. Guys like him are usually pretty honest about getting lucky."

"For chrissake, Doug. What are you saying? Is that what you think of my career too? I was just 'lucky'?"

"No," he said calmly, looking mildly uncomfortable about the argument he had inadvertently backed into at the end of a long day. He was wondering if maybe she was just tired or the kids had gotten on her nerves or something. Or maybe it was Gail's rabble-rousing. He had never liked her, and she always made him uncomfortable. He thought she was a bad influence on his wife with her constant complaining. "I think you had a hell of a good time doing what you did for a while. It was a good excuse to stay out and play, probably a little longer than you should have."

"I might have won a Pulitzer too by now, if I'd stuck with it. Have you ever thought of that?" Her eyes met his squarely. She didn't really believe that, about the Pulitzer, but it was a possibility certainly. She had already made her mark in the business before she gave it up to have children and be a house-wife.

"Is that what you think?" he asked her, looking surprised. "Are you sorry you gave it up? Is that what you're saying to me?"

"No, it's not what I'm saying. I've never had any regrets. But I also never thought of it as 'playing.' I was damn serious about what I did, and I was good at it . . . I still am. . . ." But just looking at him, she could see that he didn't understand what she was saying. He made it sound like a game, like something she had done for fun before she settled down to real life. It wasn't "fun," al-though she had had a good time at it, but she had risked her life repeatedly to get extraordi-nary pictures. "Doug, you're belittling what I did. Don't you understand what you're saying?" She wanted him to understand. It was important to her. If he did, it made what Gail had said a lie, that she was wasting her time now. But if he thought what she'd given up was unimportant anyway, what did that make her? In some ways, it made her feel like nothing.

"I think you're oversensitive, and you're overreacting. I'm just saying that working as a photojournalist is not like working in business. It's not as serious, and doesn't require the same kind of self-discipline and judgment."

"Hell, no, it's a lot harder. If you work in the kind of places my father and I did, your life is on the line every second you're working, and if you're not careful and alert constantly, you get your ass blown off and you die. That's a hell of a lot tougher than working in an office, shuffling papers."

"Are you trying to make it sound like you gave up a lifetime career for me?" he asked, looking both annoyed and startled, as he got up and walked across the room to open the can of Coca-Cola she'd brought him. "Are you trying to make me feel guilty?"

"No, but I should get a certain amount of credit at least for my accomplishments. I shelved a very respectable career to come out here to the suburbs and take care of our kids. And you're trying to make it sound like I was just playing around anyway, so why not give it up? It was a sacrifice for me to do that." She looked at him intently as he drank his soda, wondering just what he did think about her career now that he had opened Pandora's box. And she didn't like what she was seeing in it. It was a real disregard for what she had done, and given up for him.

"Are you sorry you made the 'sacrifice'?" he asked bluntly, setting the can down on the little table between them.

"No, I'm not. But I think I deserve some credit for it. You can't just discount it." But he had, that was what had upset her so badly.

"Fine. Then I'll give you credit. Does that settle it? Can we relax now? I had a long day at the office." But the way he said it only made her angrier, as though he was more important than she was. He picked up his papers again then and was obviously determined to ignore her, as she looked at him in disbelief at what he had said to her. He had not only discounted her career, but her father's. And the way he had said it had really hurt her. It was a lack of respect that she had never felt from him before, and it made all of Gail's comments that afternoon not only real, but valid.

She didn't say another word to him until they went to bed that night, and before that, she stood for a long time in the shower, thinking it all over. He had really upset her, and hurt her feelings. But she didn't mention it to him when she got into bed. She was sure he was going to bring it up himself and apologize. He was usually pretty aware of those things, and good about apologizing when he hurt her.

But he said not a word to her when he turned off the light, and he turned his back and went to sleep, as though nothing had happened. She didn't say good-night to him, and she lay awake for a long time, thinking about what he had said, and what Gail had said to her, as she lay beside him, and listened to him snoring.

Chapter 2

The next morning was chaotic, as usual, and she had to drive Jessica to school, because she'd missed her car pool. Doug never said anything to India about their conversation the night before, and he was gone before she could even say good-bye to him. As she cleaned up the kitchen, after she got back from dropping Jessica off, she wondered if he was sorry. She was sure he would say something that night. It was unlike him not to. Maybe he'd had a bad day at the office the day before, or was just feeling feisty and wanted to provoke her. But he had seemed very calm when he'd spoken to her. It upset her to think he had so little regard for everything she'd done before they were married.

He had never been quite that insensitive about it, or quite as blatantly outspoken. The phone rang just as she put the last of the dishes in the dishwasher, and she was going to go to her darkroom to develop the pictures she'd taken the day before at soccer. She had promised the captain of the team that she would get them to him quickly.

She answered on the fourth ring, and wondered if it would be Doug, calling to tell her he was sorry. They were planning to go out to dinner that night, at a fancy little French restaurant, and it would be a much nicer evening if he would at least acknowledge that he had been wrong to make her career sound so unimportant and make her feel so lousy.

"Hello?" She was smiling when she answered, sure now that it was he, but the voice on the other end was not Doug's. It was her agent. Raoul Lopez. He was very well known in photojournalism and photography, and at the top of his field. The agency, though not Raoul, had previously represented her father.

"How's the Mother of the Year? Still taking pictures of kids on Santa's lap to give to their mommies?" She had volunteered at a children's shelter the previous year to do just that, and Raoul had not been overly amused by it. For years now, he had been telling her she was wasting her talents. And once every couple of years, she did something for him that gave him hope she might one day come back to the real world. She had done a fabulous story three years before, on abused children in Harlem. She had done it in the daytime while her own kids were in school, and managed not to miss a single car pool. Doug hadn't been pleased but he had let her do it, after India had spent weeks discussing it with him. And, as in the past, she had won an award for it.

"I'm fine. How are you, Raoul?"

"Overworked, as usual. And a little tired of getting the 'artists' I represent to be reasonable. Why is it so impossible for creative people to make intelligent decisions?" It sounded like he had already had a bad morning, and listening to him, India was hoping he wasn't going to ask her to do something totally insane. Sometimes, despite the limitations she had set on him for years, he still did that. He was also upset because he had lost one of his star clients, a hell of a nice guy and good friend, in a brief holy war in Iran in early April. "So what are you up to?" he asked, trying to sound a little more cordial. He was a nervous, irascible man, but India was fond of him. He was brilliant at pairing up the right photographer with the right assignment, when they let him.

"I'm loading the dishwasher, actually," she said with a smile. "Does that fit your image of me?" She laughed and he groaned.

"Only too well, I'm afraid. When are those kids of yours ever going to grow up, India? The world can't wait forever."

"It'll have to." Even after they were grown, she wasn't sure Doug would want her to take assignments, and she knew it. But this was what she wanted for now. And she had told Raoul that often enough for him to almost believe her. But he never gave up entirely. He was still hoping that one day she might come to her senses, and run screaming out of Westport. He certainly hoped so. "Are you calling to send me on a mission on muleback somewhere in northern China?" It was the kind of thing he called her with from time to time, although occasionally he called with something reasonable, like the work she had done in Harlem. And she had loved that, which was why she kept her name on his roster.

"Not exactly, but you're getting close," he said tentatively, wondering how to phrase his question. He knew how impossible she was, and just how devoted to her children and husband. Raoul had neither a spouse nor a family, and could never quite understand why she was so determined to flush her career down the toilet for them. She had a talent like few he had known, and in her case he thought it was a sacrilege to have given up what she had been doing.

And then he decided to take the plunge. All she could do was say no, although he desperately hoped she wouldn't. "It's Korea, actually. It's a story for the Sunday *Times Magazine*, and they're willing to put it out to someone freelance, instead of a staffer. There's an adoption racket in Seoul that's going sour. The word is they're killing the kids no one will adopt. It's relatively safe, for you at least, unless you ruffle too many feathers. But it's a fantastic story, India. Babies are being murdered over there, and once it runs in the magazine, you can syndicate the story. Someone really has to do it, and they need your pictures to validate the story and I'd rather it be you than anyone else. I know how you love kids, and I just thought . . . it's perfect for you." She felt an undeniable rush of adrenaline as she listened. It tugged at her heart in a way that nothing had since the story in Harlem. But Korea? What would she tell Doug and the kids? Who would drive her car pools and make dinner for them? All they had was a cleaning lady twice a week, she had done it all herself for years, and there was no way that they could manage without India to do it all for them.

"How long are we talking about?" A week maybe . . . maybe Gail would agree to cover for her.

There was a pause, and she could hear him suck in his breath. It was a habit he had whenever he knew she wouldn't like his answer. "Three weeks . . . maybe four," he said finally, as she sat down on a stool and closed her eyes. There was no way on earth that she could do it, and she hated to miss the story. But she had her own children to think of.

"You know I can't do that, Raoul. Why did you call me? Just to make me feel bad?"

"Maybe. Maybe one of these days you'll get the fact that the world needs what you do, not just to show them pretty pictures, India, but to make a difference. Maybe you could be the one who stops those babies from getting murdered."

"That's not fair," she said heatedly. "You have no right to make me feel guilty about this. There's no way I can take a four-week assignment, and you know it. I have four kids, no help, and a husband."

"Then hire an au pair, for chrissake, or get divorced. You can't just sit there on your dead ass forever. You've already wasted fourteen years. It's a wonder anyone's still willing to give you work. You're a fool to waste your talent." For once, he sounded angry with her, and she didn't like what he was saying.

"I haven't 'wasted' fourteen years, Raoul. I have happy, healthy kids who are that way because I'm around to take them to school every day, and pick them up, and go to their Little League games, and cook them dinner. And if I'd gotten myself killed sometime in those fourteen years, you wouldn't be here to step into my shoes for me."

"No, that's a point," he said, sounding calmer. "But they're old enough now. You could go back to work again, at least on something like this. They're not babies, for chrissake. I'm sure your husband would understand that." Not after what he'd said the night before. She couldn't even imagine telling him she was going to Korea for a month. It was inconceivable in the context of their marriage.

"I can't do it, Raoul, and you know it. All you're doing now is making me unhappy." She sounded wistful as she said it.

"Good. Then maybe you'll get going again one of these days. I'd be performing a service for the world if that was all I accomplished by calling."

"For the world maybe, although you flatter me. I was never that great. But you wouldn't be performing a service for my children."

"Lots of mothers work. They'd survive it."

"And if I didn't?" She had the example of her own father dying when she was fifteen. And no one could tell her that couldn't happen, particularly with the kind of stories she was known for doing. The one in Korea would have been tame in comparison to the work she'd done before she was married.

"They'd survive it too," he said sadly. "I won't send you on the really hot ones. This one in Korea is a little dicey, but it's not like sending you to Bosnia or something."

"I still can't do it, Raoul. I'm sorry."

"I know. I was crazy to call you, but I had to try. I'll find someone else. Don't worry about it." He sounded discouraged.

"Don't forget me completely," she said sadly, feeling something she hadn't in years, over the assignment she had just turned down. She really wished she could do the story in Korea, and felt deprived that she had to turn it down. Not resentful, just bitterly disappointed. This was the kind of sacrifice she had been talking to Doug about the night before, and that he had discounted so completely. As though what she had done with her camera for all those years, and giving it up for him and the kids, meant nothing.

"I will forget about you one of these days if you don't do something important again soon. You can't take pictures of Santa Claus forever."

"I might have to. Get me something closer to home, like the piece in Harlem."

"Stuff like that doesn't come around very often, and you know it. They let the staffers do it. They just wanted something more important out of that piece, and you got lucky." And then, with a sigh, "I'll see what I can come up with. Just tell your kids to grow up a little faster."

And what about Doug? How fast was he going to "grow up," if ever? From the sound of it the night before, he didn't really understand that her career had been important to her. "Thanks for thinking of me anyway. I hope you get someone terrific to do it." She was worried now about the Korean babies.

"I just got turned down by someone terrific. I'll call you again one of these days. And you owe me on the next one."

"Then make sure it doesn't require my presence at the top of a tree in Bali."

"I'll see what I can do, India. Take care of yourself."

"Thanks. You too," and then as an afterthought, "I just remembered, I'll be in Cape Cod all summer. July and August. I think you have that number."

"I do. If you get any great sailboat pictures, call me. We'll sell them to Hallmark." She had actually done that a couple of times, when the kids were really small. She'd been happy with it, and Raoul had been furious. As far as he was concerned, she was a serious photojournalist and shouldn't be taking pictures of anything or anyone unless they were bleeding, dead, or dying.

"Don't knock it. They covered my kindergarten costs for two years, that's something."

"You're hopeless."

They hung up after that, and she was upset about the call all day. For the first time in a long time, she felt as though she was missing something. And she was still looking glum when she ran into Gail that afternoon at the market. Gail was looking happier than usual, wearing a skirt and high heels, and as India approached her, she noticed that Gail was wearing perfume.

"Where have you been? Shopping in the city?"

Gail shook her head with a wicked grin, and lowered her voice to a conspiratorial whisper. "Lunch with Dan Lewison in Greenwich. He's not quite as devastated as I expected. We had a very nice time, and a couple of glasses of wine. He's a sweet guy, and after you look at him for a while, he's actually pretty attractive."

"You must have had more than a couple of glasses of wine," India said, looking at her unhappily. Even hearing about it depressed her. What point was there in having lunch with him? India just couldn't see it.

"What are you looking so down about?"

It was rare for India to be in such poor spirits. She was usually pretty "up" about everything. She was always the one telling Gail to cheer up, and assuring her that their life was just "peachy." Now she looked anything but, as she chatted with Gail, standing next to the produce.

"I had a fight with Doug last night, and my agent just called me with an assignment in Korea. Apparently there's some adoption racket where they're murdering the babies that don't get adopted."

"Christ, how awful. Be grateful you didn't have to cover that one," Gail said, looking revolted. "How morbid."

"I'd have loved doing it. It sounds like a terrific piece, but it would have taken three to four weeks to hang around and get the story. I told him I couldn't do it."

"Nothing new there. So why are you looking like someone died?" She had gotten to India the day before, in a way she never had in earlier discussions, and Doug's comments, and the call from Raoul, hadn't helped any.

"Doug made a lot of dumb comments last night about my career being sort of a plaything, a toy, and it was no big deal that I gave it up. There's something about earning your living with a camera that makes everyone think they could do it if they wanted to be bothered." Gail smiled at what she said, and didn't deny it.

"What got into Doug?" Gail knew they didn't fight very often, and India looked particularly upset as she told her.

"I don't know. He's not usually that insensitive. Maybe he had a bad day at the office."

"Maybe he really doesn't get what you gave up for him and the kids." That was what India was afraid of, and she was surprised herself to find that it really mattered to her. "Maybe you should make your point by doing the story in Korea." Gail tried to provoke her into doing it, but India knew better. She knew that would be driving the point home a little too firmly.

"Why should the kids have to suffer because he hurt my feelings? Besides, there's no way I could leave for a month. And we're leaving for the Cape in three weeks . . . I can't do it."

"Well, maybe you should do the next one."

"If there is one. I'm sure Raoul is getting

tired of calling me and having me tell him I can't do it." He hardly ever called anymore anyway. There just weren't many stories that suited her particular limitations.

"Doug will probably come home with an armload of flowers for you tonight, and you'll forget all about it," Gail said, trying to look reassuring. She felt sorry for her. India was bright and beautiful and talented, and like many of them, she was wasting her life cleaning out the barbecue and driving car pools. It was a waste of an extraordinary talent.

"We're having dinner at Ma Petite Amie. I was looking forward to it, until he got me all riled up."

"Drink enough wine, and you'll forget all about it. Which reminds me, I'm having lunch with Dan again on Tuesday."

"I think that's a dumb thing to do," India said bluntly, putting a box of tomatoes into her basket. "What's that going to do for you?"

"Amuse me. Why not? We're not hurting anyone. Rosalie is in love with Harold, and Jeff will never know, and he'll have my undivided attention for six weeks in Europe." To Gail it seemed like perfect justification, but to India it didn't.

"It seems so pointless. And what if you fall in love with him?" That was a whole other issue. If what Gail wanted was to be madly in love again, one of these days it might happen. And then what would she do? Dump Jeff? Get divorced? To India, the risks just didn't seem worth it. But on that score anyway, she and Gail were very different.

"I'm not going to fall in love with him. We're just having some fun. Don't be such a spoilsport."

"What if Jeff were doing the same thing, wouldn't you mind?"

"I'd be bowled over," Gail said with a look of amusement. "The only thing Jeff ever does at lunch is go to his podiatrist, or get his hair cut."

But what if he wasn't? What if they were both cheating? To India, particularly in her current mood, it seemed pathetic.

"You need to get a haircut, or a mani-cure, or a massage or something. Do some-thing to cheer yourself up. I'm not sure giving up a story about dead babies in Korea is something to get so depressed about. Get de-pressed about something that would be a shame to miss, something fun . . . like an af-fair. . . ." She was teasing her then, and India shook her head and grinned ruefully at her.

"How can I love you, when you are the most immoral person I know?" India said, looking at her with affectionate disapproval. "If you were a stranger, and someone told me about you, I'd think you were disgusting."

"No, you wouldn't. I'm just honest about what I do, and what I think. Most people aren't, and you know that." There was certainly some truth to that, but Gail went a little overboard both with her point of view and her honesty about it.

"I love you anyway, but one of these days you're going to get yourself in one hell of a mess, and Jeff is going to find out about it."

"I'm not even sure he'd care. Unless I forgot to pick up his dry cleaning."

"Don't be so sure about that," India assured her.

"Dan says Rosalie has been sleeping with Harold for two years, and he had no idea until she told him. Most guys are like that." It made India wonder suddenly if Doug would suspect if she were having lunch with another man. She liked to think so. It was one of the many things she believed about him. "Anyway, I've got to run. I have to take the kids to the doctor for checkups before we leave for Europe. They're going to camp as soon as we get home, and I haven't even filled out their health forms."

"Maybe if you stayed home for a change, you could do it at lunchtime," India teased her, as Gail waved and hurried off to the checkout counter, and India finished buying what she needed for the weekend. It was certainly not an exciting life, but maybe Gail was right. The assignment in Korea would have been a very depressing story. She would have wanted to come home with an armful of Korean babies to save them from getting murdered when no one else would adopt them.

She was still in a somber mood later that afternoon when she picked up the kids and drove home. Jason and Aimee had friends with them, and they all made so much noise that no one noticed that she wasn't talking.

She fixed a snack for all of them, and left it on the kitchen table when she went to take a bath. She had called a sitter that afternoon, and she was going to put dinner together and rent videos for them. For once, India had some free time on her hands, and she luxuriated in the bath, thinking about her husband. She was still upset about what he'd said the night before, but she was just as sure he must have had a bad day at the office.

India was wearing a short black dress and high heels, and her long blond hair was looped into an elegant bun when Doug came home from work. He fixed himself a drink, which he did sometimes on Friday nights, and when he came upstairs, he looked happy to see her.

"Wow, India! You look terrific!" he said, taking a sip of his Bloody Mary. "You look like you spent all day getting ready."

"Not quite. Just the last hour of it. How was your day?"

"Not bad. The new client meeting went pretty well. I'm almost sure we got the account. It's going to be a very busy summer." It was the third new account he was in charge of, and he had commented to his secretary that afternoon that he'd be lucky if he got to the Cape by August, but he didn't say anything about it to India as she walked toward him.

"I'm glad we're going out tonight," she said, looking at him with the same wistful look she'd had in the market when she ran into Gail, but unlike Gail, Doug didn't see it.

"I think we need a break, or some fun, or something."

"That's why I suggested dinner." He smiled, and took his Bloody Mary into the bathroom with him to shower and change for dinner. He was back half an hour later, wearing gray slacks and a blazer, and a navy tie she had given him for Christmas. He looked very handsome, and they made a striking couple as they stopped on their way out, to say good-night to the children. And ten minutes later, they were at the restaurant, and on their way to a corner table.

It was a pretty little restaurant, and they did a lot of business on the weekends. The food was good, and the atmosphere was cozy and romantic. It was just what they needed to repair the rift of the night before, and India smiled at him as the waiter poured a bottle of French wine, and Doug carefully sipped it and approved it.

"So what did you do today?" Doug asked as he set down his glass. He knew before she said anything that her day would have revolved around the children.

"I got a call from Raoul Lopez." He looked momentarily surprised, and not particularly curious. The calls from her agent were rare these days, and usually unproductive. "He offered me a very interesting story in Korea."

"That sounds like Raoul." Doug looked amused, and in no way threatened by the information. "Where was the last place he tried to send you? Zimbabwe? You wonder why he bothers."

"He thought I might agree to do the story. It was for the Sunday *Times Magazine,* about an adoption racket that's murdering babies in Korea. But he thought it would take three or four weeks, and I told him I couldn't do it."

"Obviously. There's no way you could go to Korea, not even for three or four minutes."

"That's what I told him." But she realized as she looked at Doug that she wanted him to thank her for not going. She wanted him to understand what she'd given up, and that she would have liked to do it. "He said he'd try again with something closer to home, like the piece in Harlem."

"Why don't you just take your name off their roster? That really makes more sense. There's no point leaving your name on and having him call you for stories you're not go-

ing to do anyway. I'm really surprised he still
bothers to call you. Why does he?"

"Because I'm good at what I do," she
said quietly, "and editors still ask for me, apparently. It's flattering, at least." She was
groping for something, asking him for something, and he wasn't getting the message from
her. In this area at least, he never did. He
missed it completely.

"You never should have done that story
in Harlem. It probably gave them the idea
that you're still open to offers." It was obvious
to her as she listened to him that he wanted
the door to her career closed even more
firmly than it had been. And suddenly she was
intrigued by the idea of opening it, just a
crack, if she could find another assignment
near home like the one she'd done in Harlem.

"It was a great story. I'm glad I did it,"
she said, as the waiter handed them the
menus, but suddenly she wasn't hungry. She
was upset again. He didn't seem to understand what she was feeling. But maybe she
couldn't blame him. She wasn't even sure she
understood it. Suddenly she was missing
something she had given up, for all intents
and purposes, fourteen years before, and she
expected him to know that, without having

explained it to him. "I wouldn't mind working again, just a little bit, if I could fit it into everything else I'm doing. I've never really thought about it for all these years. But I'm beginning to think I miss working."

"What brought that on?"

"I'm not sure," she said honestly. "I was talking to Gail yesterday and she was harping on me about wasted talent, and then Raoul called today, and that story sounded so enticing." And their conversation the night before had added fuel to the fire, when he dismissed her career and her father's like just so much playtime. All of a sudden she felt as though she needed to validate her existence. Maybe Gail was right and all she had become was a maid, a short-order cook, and a chauffeur. Maybe it was time to drag out her old career and dust it off a little.

"Gail always is a troublemaker, isn't she? . . . . What about the sweetbreads?" As he had the night before, Doug was dismissing what she was saying, and it made India feel lonely as she looked at him over her menu.

"I think she's still sorry she gave up her career. She probably shouldn't have," India added, ignoring his question about their dinner, and thinking that Gail probably wouldn't be having lunch with Dan Lewison if she had something else to do, but she said nothing to Doug about it. "I'm lucky. If I go back at some point, I can pick and choose what I do. I don't have to work full-time, or go all the way to Korea to do it."

"What are you saying to me?" He had ordered for both of them, and faced her squarely across the table, but he did not look pleased by what she was saying. "Are you telling me you want to go back to work, India? That's not possible and you know it." He didn't even give her a chance to answer his question.

"There's no reason why I couldn't do an occasional story, if it was local, is there?"

"For what? Just to show off your photographs? Why would you want to do that?" He made it sound so vain, and so futile, that she was almost embarrassed by the suggestion. But something about the way he resisted it suddenly made her feel stubborn.

"It's not a matter of showing off. It's about using a gift I have." Gail had started it all the day before, with her pointed questions, and ever since, the ball had just kept rolling. And his resistance to it made it all seem that much more important.

"If you're so anxious to use your 'gift,' " he said in a mildly contemptuous tone, "use it on the children. You've always taken great pictures of them. Why can't that satisfy you, or is this one of Gail's crusades? Somehow I feel her hand in this, or is Raoul getting you all stirred up? He's just out to make a buck anyway. Let him do it using someone else. There are plenty of other photographers he can send to Korea."

"I'm sure he'll find one," India said quietly as the pâté they had ordered was put on the table. "I'm not saying I'm irreplaceable, I'm just saying the kids are getting older, and maybe once in a while I could do an assignment." She was beginning to feel dogged about it.

"We don't need the money, and Sam is only nine, for heaven's sake. India, the kids need you."

"I wasn't suggesting I leave them, Doug. I'm just saying it might be important to me." And she wanted him to understand that. Only the day before she had told Gail how little she cared about having given up her career, and now, after listening to her and Raoul, and Doug belittling her the night before, suddenly it all mattered. But he refused to hear it.

"Why would it be important to you? That's what I don't understand. What's so important about taking pictures?" She felt as though she were trying to crawl up a glass mountain, and she was getting nowhere.

"It's how I express myself. I'm good at it. I love it, that's all."

"I told you, then take pictures of the kids. Or do portraits of their friends, and give them to their parents. There's plenty you can do with a camera, without taking assignments."

"Maybe I'd like to do something important. Did that ever occur to you? Maybe I want to be sure my life has some meaning."

"Oh, for God's sake." He put down his fork and looked at her with annoyance. "What on earth has gotten into you? It's Gail. I know it."

"It's not Gail," she tried to defend herself, but was feeling hopeless, "it's about me. There has to be more meaning in life than cleaning up apple juice off the floor when the kids spill it."

"You sound just like Gail now," he said, looking disgusted.

"What if she's right, though? She's doing a lot of stupid things with her life, because she feels useless, and her life has no purpose.

Maybe if she were doing something intelligent with herself, she wouldn't need to do other things that *are* pointless."

"If you're trying to tell me she cheats on Jeff, I figured that out years ago. And if he's too blind to see it, it's his own fault. She runs after everything in pants in Westport. Is that what you're threatening me with? Is that what this is really about?" He looked furious with her as the waiter brought their main course. Their romantic night out was being wasted.

"Of course not." India was quick to reassure him. "I don't know what she does," she lied to protect her friend, but Gail's indiscretions were irrelevant to them, and none of Doug's business. "I'm talking about me. I'm just saying that maybe I need more in my life than just you and the children. I had a great career before I gave it up, no matter how unimportant you seem to think it was, and maybe I can retrieve some small part of it now to broaden my horizons."

"You don't have time to broaden your horizons," he said sensibly. "You're too busy with the children. Unless you want to start hiring baby-sitters constantly, or leaving them in day care. Is that what you have in mind, India? Because there's no other way for you to do it, and frankly I won't let you. You're their mother, and they need you."

"I understand that, but I managed the story in Harlem without shortchanging them. I could do others like it."

"I doubt that. And I just don't see the sense in it. You did all that, you had some fun, and you grew up. You can't go back to all that now. You're not a kid in your twenties with no responsibilities. You're a grown woman with a family and a husband."

"I don't see why one has to preclude the other, as long as I keep my priorities straight. You and the kids come first, the rest would have to work around you."

"You know, sitting here listening to you, I'm beginning to wonder about your priorities. What you're saying to me sounds incredibly selfish. All you want to do is have a good time, like your little friend, who's running around cheating on her husband because her kids bore her. Is that it? Do we bore you?" He looked highly insulted, and very angry. She had disrupted his whole evening. But he was threatening her self-esteem, and her future.

"Of course you don't bore me. And I'm not Gail."

"What the hell is she after anyway?" He was cutting his steak viciously as he asked her. "She can't be that oversexed. What is she trying to do, just embarrass her husband?"

"I don't think so. I think she's lonely and dissatisfied, and I feel sorry for her. I'm not telling you what she does is right, Doug. I think she's panicked. She's forty-eight years old, she gave up a terrific career, and she can't see anything in her future except car pools. You don't know what that's like. You have a career. You never gave up anything. You just added to it."

"Is that how you feel? The way Gail does?" He actually looked worried.

"Not really. I'm a lot happier than she is. But I think about my future too. What happens when the kids are gone? What do I do then? Run around taking pictures of kids I don't know in the playground?"

"You can figure that one out later. You'll have kids at home for the next nine years. That's plenty of time to figure out a game plan. Maybe we'll move back to the city, and you can go to museums." That was it? *All of it?* Museums? The thought of it made her shiver. She wanted a lot more than that in her future. From that standpoint, Gail was abso-

lutely right. And in nine years, India wanted
to be doing a lot more than killing time. But
in nine years it would be that much harder to
get back into a career, if Doug would even let
her. And it didn't sound like it from what he
was saying. "The kids are much too young for
you to be thinking about this now. Maybe you
could get a job in a gallery or something, once
they grow up. Why worry about it?"

"And do what? Look at the photographs
other people took, when I could have done it
better? You're right, I'm busy now. But what
about later?" In the past twenty-four hours,
the whole question had come into sharper focus for her.

"Don't borrow problems. And stop listening to that woman. I told you, she's a troublemaker. She's unhappy, and angry, and
she's just looking to cause trouble."

"She doesn't know what she's looking
for," India said sadly. "She's looking for love,
because Jeff doesn't excite her." It was probably too much to admit to him, she realized,
but since he seemed to know about her wan-
dering anyway, it didn't seem to make much
difference.

"It's ridiculous to be looking for love at
our age," Doug said sternly, taking a sip of his

wine, and glaring at his wife across the table. "What the hell is she thinking?"

"I don't think she's really wrong, I just think she's going about it the wrong way," India said calmly. "She says she's depressed about never being in love again. I guess she and Jeff aren't crazy about each other."

"Who is, after twenty years of marriage?" he said, looking annoyed again. What India had just said sounded ridiculous to him. "You can't expect to feel at forty-five or fifty the way you did at twenty."

"No, but you can feel other things. If you're lucky, maybe even more than you felt in the beginning."

"That's a lot of romantic nonsense, India, and you know it," he said firmly, as she listened to him with a growing sense of panic.

"Do you think it's nonsense to still be in love with your spouse after fifteen or twenty years?" India couldn't believe what she was hearing.

"I don't think anyone is 'in love' anymore by then. And no one with any sense expects to be either."

"What *can* you expect?" India asked in a strangled voice, as she set her glass down on the table and looked at her husband.

"Companionship, decency, respect, someone to take care of the kids. Someone you can rely on. That's about all anyone should expect from marriage."

"You can get a maid, or a dog, to provide the same things for you."

"What do you think one should expect? Hearts and flowers and valentines? You know better than that, India. Don't tell me you believe in all that. If you do, I'll know you've been spending a lot more time talking to Gail than you ever told me."

"I'm not expecting miracles, Doug. But I sure want more than just 'someone to rely on,' and you should want a lot more than just 'someone to take care of the children.' Is that all our marriage means to you?" They were rapidly getting down to specifics.

"We have something that's worked damn well for seventeen years, and it'll continue working, if you don't start rocking the boat too hard, with careers, and assignments and trips to Korea, and a lot of crap about 'being in love' after seventeen years. I don't think anyone is capable of that, and I don't think anyone has a right to expect it." She felt as though she had been slapped as she looked at him, and was horrified by what he was saying.

"As a matter of fact, Doug, I do expect it. I always have, and I had no idea you didn't. I expect you to be 'in love' with me till the day you die, or there's no point in our marriage. Just as I'm in love with you, and always have been. Why do you think I stick around? Because our life is so exciting? It isn't. It's about as mundane as it gets, as boring as it can be at times, but I stick around because I love you."

"Well, that's good to hear. I was beginning to wonder. But I don't think anyone should have a lot of crazy illusions about romance at this point. Being married to someone just isn't romantic."

"Why not?" She decided to go for broke. He had already shattered most of her dreams in one night, why not push it all the way? What difference did it make now? "It could be, couldn't it? Maybe people don't try hard enough, or spend enough time realizing how lucky they are to have each other. Maybe if Jeff spent more time doing that, maybe then Gail wouldn't be running all over the state having lunch and God knows what else with other people's husbands."

"I'm sure that has to do with her integrity and morality more than any failure on his part."

"Don't be so sure. Maybe he's just plain stupid," India snapped at him.

"No, she is, to have a lot of girlish illusions about romance and 'I love you's' at this point. India, that's bullshit, and you know it."

She was silent for a long moment and then nodded. She was afraid that if she spoke at all, she would burst into tears, or just get up and walk out, but she didn't. She sat there until they finished the meal, making small talk with him. She had heard enough that night to last her for a lifetime. In a single evening, he had challenged everything she believed, and smashed all her dreams about what marriage meant to him, and more importantly, what she did. She was someone he could rely on, who took care of his children. And all she could think of on the way home was that maybe she should call Raoul and take the assignment in Korea. But no matter how angry she was at him, or how disappointed she was by what he'd said, she wouldn't do that to her children.

"I had a nice time tonight," he said as they drove into their driveway, and she tried not to think of the knot in her stomach. "I'm glad we got the career issue behind us. I think you understand now how I feel about it. I think you should call Raoul next week and take your name off their roster." It was as though, having expressed himself, he now expected her to simply carry out his orders. The oracle had spoken. She had never known him to be like this before, but she had never challenged him on it in fourteen years either.

"I know how you feel about a lot of things," she said softly, as they sat in the car for a minute, and he turned the lights off.

"Don't be silly about that nonsense Gail filled your head with, India. It's a lot of garbage she throws around to excuse her own behavior, and if she can get you riled up about it too, all the better. Stay away from her. She just upsets you." But Gail hadn't. He had. He had said things she knew would trouble her for years, and she would never forget them. He wasn't in love with her, if he ever had been. In his opinion, love was something for fools and children. "We all have to grow up sooner or later," he said, opening the car door and looking over his shoulder at her. "The trouble is, Gail didn't."

"No, but you did," India said miserably, and just as he hadn't the night before, or that night in the restaurant, he didn't get it. In a single night, he had put their marriage on the line, tossed her career out the window like so much fluff, and essentially told her he didn't love her, or at least wasn't in love with her. And in light of that, she didn't know what to think or feel now, or how to go on as they were before, unaffected by it.

"I like the restaurant, don't you?" he asked as they walked into the house. It was quiet, and India suspected that only Jessica would still be awake. The others would be sleeping. They had spent a long time over dinner. It had taken him several hours to destroy the last, and most cherished, of her illusions. "I thought the food was better than usual," he went on, oblivious to the damage he'd done. He was like the iceberg that had hit the *Titanic.* But knowing what he'd done, she couldn't help wondering if the ship would sink now. It was hard to believe it wouldn't. Or was she simply to go on, being reliable and steadfast and a good "companion." That was what he wanted, and what he expected her to give him. It didn't leave much room for her heart, her soul, and nothing with which to feed them.

"I thought it was fine. Thank you, Doug," she said, and went upstairs to check on their children. She spent a few minutes with Jessica, who was watching TV, and as she had suspected, the others were all asleep, and after she looked into their rooms, she walked quietly into her own bedroom. Doug was getting undressed, and he glanced over at her with a curious look. There was something very strange about the way she stood there.

"You're not still upset, are you, about all that crap Gail told you?" She hesitated for a moment and then shook her head. He was so deaf, so blind, so dumb, that he had no idea what he had just done to her, or their marriage. She knew there was no point now saying more, or trying to explain it. And she knew, just as certainly, as she looked at him, that for an entire lifetime, she would never forget this moment.

Chapter 3

For the next three weeks, India moved through her life feeling like a robot. She fixed breakfast, drove the kids to school, picked them up, and went to every activity from tennis to baseball. For the first time in years, she forgot to take her camera with her, and suddenly now even that seemed pointless. She felt as though she were fatally wounded. Her spirit was dead, and it was only a matter of time before her body followed. Somehow, with what he'd said, and the illusions he'd killed, India felt as though Doug had sucked all the life out of her. It was like letting the air out of her tires. And now, everything she did seemed like an enormous effort.

She ran into Gail constantly, as she always did, and knew she was still seeing Dan Lewison. They had had lunch several more times, and she had made allusions to meeting him at a hotel somewhere. India could guess the rest, but she didn't really want to know, and she didn't ask Gail any questions.

She didn't tell her about what Doug had said, and when Gail noticed that she was depressed, she assumed it was still about the assignment she hadn't taken in Korea.

And India never did call Raoul Lopez to get off the roster. It was the last thing she wanted to do now. All she wanted to do was get away to Cape Cod, and try to forget what had happened. She thought maybe she'd feel better about him again with a little distance between them. She needed to regroup, rethink what he'd said, and try to feel better about him, if she was going to spend the rest of her life with him. But how did you feel the same again about a man who had essentially said he didn't love you, and to whom you were nothing more than a convenient companion? A man who discarded the career you had given up for him, however worthy it had been, with a single flippant gesture. Every time she looked at Doug now, she felt as though she no longer knew him. And he seemed to have no suspicion whatsoever that what he'd said to her had caused major damage. To Doug, it was business as usual. He went into the city every day on the 7:05, and came home for dinner, told her how easy or hard the day had been, and then read his papers. And when she seemed less inclined to make love to him than she had been previously, he put it down to the fact that she was either tired or busy. It never occurred to him that she no longer wanted to make love to him and had no idea what to do about it.

In the end, it was an enormous relief to her when she and the children finally left for their vacation. She had packed everything they needed in three days. They never wore anything fancy on the Cape, just shorts and jeans and bathing suits, and they left most of it there when they left at the end of the summer. But the children always came up with new things they wanted to bring with them. She managed to avoid Doug almost entirely the last week, as he was meeting with two sets of new clients, and spent two nights in the city.

And on the morning they left, he stood on the lawn waving at them, and he almost forgot to kiss her good-bye. When he did, it was hastily, and without much emotion. And for once, she didn't mind it. The kids and the dog were in the station wagon with her, and their bags were in the back, crammed in so tight it took three of them to close the door, and he shouted to her as they drove off, "Don't forget to call me!" She nodded and smiled, and drove away, feeling as though she had left a stranger behind her. He had already told her he couldn't come up the first weekend, and he had told her the night before that it looked as though he wouldn't make it up over the Fourth of July either. He had too much work to do for his new clients. He thought she was an exceptionally good sport about it, when she didn't complain, and thanked her for it. He never noticed that for the past few weeks, since their dinner at Ma Petite Amie, she had been unusually quiet.

It took them six and a half hours to drive from Westport to Harwich, and they stopped several times on the way, at McDonald's. And the children were all in good spirits. They could hardly wait to get to the beach and see their friends there. As they talked about it on the way up, and what they were going to do as soon as they arrived, only Jessica noticed that her mother was distracted. She was sitting in the front seat, next to her mother.

"Something wrong, Mom?"

India was touched that she had noticed. Doug certainly hadn't. He had been business as usual right to the last minute, and seemed almost relieved to see them go, so he could devote himself full-time to his new clients.

"No, I'm fine. Just tired. It's been pretty busy getting ready to leave." It was a plausible reason for her distraction. She didn't want to tell Jessica she was upset with her father. It was the first time she had ever felt that she and Doug had a serious problem.

"How come Daddy isn't coming up for the first two weeks?" She had noticed that her mother was quieter than usual for weeks now, and she wondered if they had had a fight or something, though usually her parents seemed to fight less than other people.

"He's busy with new clients. He'll be up for the weekend in a couple of weeks, and he's going to spend three weeks with us in August." Jessica nodded and put the earphones to her Walkman on, and for the rest of the trip India was lost in her own thoughts as she drove the familiar road to Massachusetts. She did it every summer.

She had talked to Gail the day before, and they were leaving that weekend for Paris, but Gail was as unenthused as ever. If possible, even a little more so. She'd been having a good time with Dan Lewison, and hated to leave him now, particularly knowing that it was the kind of relationship that would survive neither time nor distance. By the time she got back, he would have moved on with his life, and begun to settle into his new routine, and would have connected undoubtedly with the flock of hungry divorcées waiting to devour him. And all Gail had to offer him was the occasional clandestine afternoon in a motel, and there were plenty of others waiting to do that. She had no illusions about their importance to each other. And just listening to her talk about it depressed India still further. She wished her a good trip, and told her to call when she got back. Maybe she and the kids could come up to the Cape for a few days later in the summer while Jeff was working. And Gail said she'd love that.

It was late that afternoon when they got to the house in Harwich, and India got out and stretched her legs, and looked at the clear expanse of blue ocean with a feeling of relief. Being here was just what she needed. It was a lovely place, a comfortable old Victorian house, and she always found it blissfully peaceful. They had friends with summer-houses nearby, some from Boston, others from New York, and India was always happy to see them. Although this year, she wanted to spend a few days by herself, with the chil-dren. She needed some time to think, and re-group, and recover from the blow of what she'd felt ever since their fateful dinner. For the first time in fourteen years, once they'd settled into the house, she didn't even want to call Doug. She just couldn't. He called that night to make sure they'd arrived. He spoke to the children, and then India.

"Is everything all right?" he asked, and India assured him that everything was fine. The house had been cleaned by a service that week, and was in good order. No leaks, no broken screens or damage from the winter. She reported it all to him, and he seemed satisfied with what she told him. And then he surprised her with his next question. "Why didn't you call me when you got there? I was afraid something might have happened." Why? Since hearts and flowers were of no im-portance to him, what did it matter if she called him? What would that have meant to him? The loss of someone reliable to take care of his children? He could always hire a housekeeper if something happened to her.

"I'm sorry, Doug. We were just busy opening the house and getting settled."

"You sound tired," he said sympathetically. She had been for the past few weeks, but he had never noticed either her fatigue or her depression.

"It's a long drive, but we're all fine." Both children and caretaker were alive and well, as was the Labrador retriever.

"I wish I were there with all of you, instead of here with all my clients," he said, and sounded as though he meant it.

"You'll be here soon," she said sympathetically, anxious to get off the phone. She had nothing to say to him at the moment. She felt sapped of all her energy. She had nothing to offer him right now, in light of what he'd said to her, and he didn't seem to understand that. "We'll call you," she said easily, and a moment later they hung up. As usual, he didn't tell her that he loved her. It didn't matter anyway. It was apparently a word that, at this point in their lives, meant very little to him.

She went back to the children after that,

and helped them make their beds, since the cleaning service hadn't done it. And once they were all in bed, she slipped quietly into her darkroom. She hadn't been in it in nearly a year, but she found everything in the same meticulous order she had left it. And when she turned the light on, she saw the wall of some of her father's favorite pictures. There was one she had put up there of Doug too, and she stood and stared at it for a long moment. He had a handsome, familiar face that she knew better than any face in the world, except her children's, but she had known his for longer. And as she looked into his eyes in the photograph she saw all the coldness she had discovered there in the past three weeks, and everything that was missing in them. She wondered why she hadn't seen it sooner. Had she wanted to believe there was something else there? That he still loved her as he had in their youth? That he was still in love with her, as she had believed he was, until he told her how unimportant love was in a marriage? She could hear the words again as though he had just said them to her . . . what you need is companionship . . . decency . . . respect . . . someone you can rely on to take care of the children. She wondered now if this was really all he wanted. It was so much less than she wanted from him.

She turned away then to look at a photograph of her father. He had been tall and thin, and looked like Doug in a way, but there was laughter in his eyes as he looked at you, something happy and excited and amused about his entire demeanor. He had had a funny little tilt to his head when he talked to you, and she could imagine him being in love at any age. He had been so young when he died, only forty-two, and yet he seemed so much more alive in the photograph than Doug did. There had been something so vibrant about him. She knew her mother had suffered from his absences, and their life had been difficult for her, but she also knew how much her mother had loved him, and how much he had loved her. And how angry her mother had been at him for dying. And India could remember as though it were yesterday how devastated she had been when her mother had told her what had happened. She couldn't imagine a world without her father in it somewhere. It was hard to believe he had been gone for twenty-eight years now, it seemed like an entire lifetime to her.

There were her photographs framed on

the walls of the darkroom too, and she looked them over carefully for a moment as she stood there. They were good, very good, and captured a feeling and emotion that was almost like looking into a painting. She saw the ravaged faces of hungry children there, and a child sitting alone on a rock holding a doll, crying, while an entire village in Kenya burned behind her. There were faces of old men, and injured soldiers, and a woman laughing with sheer joy as she held her newborn baby. India had helped deliver it, and she still remembered that moment. It had been in a tiny hut somewhere outside Quito when she was in the Peace Corps. They were fragments of her life, frozen in time, and framed, so she could look at them forever. It was still hard for her to believe that all of that was gone from her life now. It had been an exchange she had made, a fair trade she always thought, only now she wondered. Had she gotten enough in return for what she'd given up? She knew she had when she thought of her children. But beyond that, what did she have now? And once the children were grown, what would she have then? Those were the questions she could no longer answer.

She checked the chemicals and the equipment, and made some notes, and then quietly turned off the light and went back to her bedroom. She took off her clothes and put her nightgown on, and then got into bed and turned off the light, and lay there for a long time, listening to the ocean. It was a peaceful sound she forgot every year, and then remembered when she came back here. It lulled her to sleep at night, and she lay listening to it when she woke in the morning. She loved the solemnity of it, the comfort it offered her. It was one of the things she loved about being here. And as she closed her eyes and drifted off to sleep, she savored the fact that she was alone here this time, with only her children, her memories, and the ocean. For now at least, it was all she wanted.

Chapter 4

The sun was brilliant when she awoke the next day in Harwich, and the ocean was shimmering as though it were trimmed in silver. The kids were already up, and helping themselves to cereal when she walked in. She was wearing a T-shirt, shorts, and sandals, with her hair piled up on her head, held by two old tortoiseshell pins, and she was unaware of it, but she looked very pretty.

"What's everybody doing today?" she asked as she put a pot of coffee on. It seemed silly to do it just for herself, but she loved sitting on the deck, with a cup of coffee and reading, glancing up occasionally to look at the ocean. It was one of her favorite Cape Cod pastimes.

"I'm going over to see the Boardmans," Jessica was quick to say. They had three older teenage sons, and a daughter her own age. Jessica had grown up with them, and loved them, and the boys were of particular interest to her now that two of them were in high school, and the third one was a freshman in college.

Jason had a friend down the street too, and had called him and made plans the night before to spend the day with him. Aimee wanted to go swimming at a friend's, and India promised to call and arrange it as soon as she had a cup of coffee, and Sam wanted to walk down the beach with her, and Crockett, the Labrador retriever. It sounded like a good plan to her, and she promised to walk with him a little later. In the meantime, he was happy playing with the toys he had left there the year before, and he was anxious to get his bike out.

By ten o'clock they were all on their way, and she and Sam walked down the steps to the beach, with the dog just behind them. Sam had brought a ball, and he kept throwing it for the dog, who fetched it devotedly, even when Sam threw it in the water. And India walked along happily, watching them, with her camera slung over her shoulder. After nearly thirty years of carrying it, it seemed like part of her body. Her children couldn't imagine seeing her without it.

They had walked almost a mile down the beach before they saw anyone they knew. It was still early in the season and people were only just beginning to arrive for the summer. The first friends they met were a couple she and Doug had known for years. They were both surgeons, from Boston. He was a little older than Doug, and she was a year or two older than he, somewhere near fifty. They had a son at Harvard Medical School, but for the past two years he hadn't come to the Cape, he was too busy, but they were both thrilled that he had decided to follow in their footsteps. They were Jenny and Dick Parker. And they smiled the moment they saw India and Sam approaching.

"I wondered when you'd get here," Jenny said with a look of delight. India had had a Christmas card from them, as usual, but they rarely spoke during the winter. They only saw each other in the summer at the Cape.

"We came up last night," India explained. "Doug won't be up for a couple of weeks though. He has too many new clients."

"That's too bad," Dick said, as he wrestled with Sam and the dog barked in excitement, running around them in circles. "We're having a party on the Fourth, I was hoping you'd come. You'll have to come without him. And bring the kids. Jenny made me hire a cook this time, after I burned all the ribs and hamburgers last year."

"The steaks were great though," India said with a smile, remembering it perfectly. The ribs had gone up in flames, while the hamburgers turned to ashes.

"Thank you for remembering." Dick grinned at her. He was happy to see her, and he had always had a special fondness for her children, as was evident the way he was playing with Sam. "I hope you will all come."

"We'd love it. Who else is here?" India asked, and Jenny went down the list of the latest arrivals. There were already a fair number of the regulars in residence, which would be nice for the children.

"And we're having friends up over the Fourth too," Jenny explained. They always had friends at the house with them, so it was nothing unusual, but this time she seemed especially eager to tell India about her guests. "Serena Smith and her husband will be here."

"The writer?" India looked momentarily startled. She was on the bestseller list constantly with her steamy novels. And India had always had the impression that she was an interesting woman.

"I went to college with her," Jenny explained. "We kind of lost touch over the years, although I knew her pretty well then. I ran into her in New York this year. She's a lot of fun, and I like her husband."

"And wait till you see his sailboat," Dick said admiringly. "They sailed around the world with it, and it's really quite something. They're going to sail it up from New York with half a dozen friends. They're planning to spend a week here. You have to bring the kids over to see it."

"Let us know when it's here," India said, and Dick laughed.

"I don't think I'll have to. You can't miss it. It's a hundred and seventy feet long, with a crew of nine. They live awfully well, but they're nice people. I think you'll like them. It's a shame Doug won't be here."

"He'll be heartbroken to miss it," India said politely. There was no need to explain to them that just looking at a boat, Doug got seasick. But she didn't, and she knew that Sam in particular would be excited to see it.

"I'm sure he knows who Paul is. He's in international banking, Paul Ward." He had been on the cover of *Time* twice in the past few years, and she'd read about him in the *Wall Street Journal.* Somehow she had never connected him with Serena Smith though. She guessed that he was somewhere in his mid-fifties.

"It'll be fun to meet them. We're getting awfully fancy here this year, aren't we? With famous authors and big yachts, and international financiers. It makes the rest of us look a little dull by comparison, doesn't it?" India smiled at them. They always seemed to have an interesting group of people around them.

"I wouldn't call you dull, my dear," Dick said with a grin, putting an arm around her shoulders. He was glad to see her. He shared her passion for photography, although he was only an amateur, but he had taken some wonderful photographs of the children. "Did you do any assignments this winter?"

"Nothing since Harlem," she said sadly, and then she told him about the job she'd turned down in Korea.

"That would have been a tough one," he said after she explained it to him.

"I couldn't leave the children for a month. Doug got mad just hearing about it. He doesn't really want me doing any work."

"That would be a real crime with a talent like yours," he said with a thoughtful look, while Jenny chatted with Sam about the sports he'd played that winter. "You should talk Doug into letting you do more work instead of less," he said seriously, which reminded her of their fateful dinner.

"Doug definitely does not share that point of view," she said with a rueful smile at their old friend. "He doesn't think work and motherhood are a good mix, I'm afraid." Something in her eyes told Dick that this was a painful subject for her.

"Let Jenny talk to him about it. I suggested she retire once, about five years ago, and she almost killed me. I just thought she was working too hard, teaching and doing surgery, and she almost divorced me. I don't think I'll try that again until she's eighty." He glanced lovingly at his wife with a whimsical expression.

"Don't even think about it then," Jenny warned him with a grin, joining their conversation. "I'm going to teach till I'm at least a hundred."

"She will too," he said, smiling at India. He was always bowled over by how beautiful India was, and how natural. She seemed completely unaware of her effect on people. She was so used to watching them through a lens, that it never dawned on her that anyone was looking at her. She told him about a new camera she'd bought then, explained it to him in detail, and promised to let him try it. She had made a point of bringing it with her. And he loved visiting her darkroom. She had even taught him how to use it. He had always been deeply impressed by her talent, far more so than Doug, who had long since come to take it for granted.

The Parkers said they had to go back to their house then to meet some friends, and she promised to come and visit with Sam in a day or two, and encouraged them to drop by any time they wanted.

"Don't forget the Fourth!" they reminded her as she and Sam started to walk on, with Crockett dancing behind them.

"We'll be there," she promised with a wave, as she and Sam walked away hand in hand, and Dick Parker told his wife how happy he was to see them.

"It's ridiculous that Doug doesn't want her to work," Jenny said as they walked down the beach, thinking about India's comment to them. "She's not just some little photographer. She did some really fantastic things before they were married."

"They have a lot of kids though," he said, trying to see both sides of the argument. He'd always suspected that was how Doug felt about it. He rarely talked about India's photographs, and didn't make much fuss about them.

"So what?" Jenny was annoyed at the excuse, it seemed an inadequate reason to her for India not to take assignments wherever she wanted. "They could get someone to help with the kids. She can't play nursemaid forever, just to soothe his ego."

"Okay, okay, Attila, I get it," he teased her. "Tell Doug, don't yell at me."

"I'm sorry." She smiled at her husband as he put an arm around her. They had been married since their Harvard days, and were crazy about each other. "I just hate it when men take positions like that. It's so damn unfair. What if she told him to quit his job and take care of the kids? He'd think she was crazy."

"No kidding. Tell me about it, Dr. Parker."

"All right, all right. So Simone de Beauvoir was my role model. So kill me."

"It's okay, you can beat me up anytime you want. I happen to love you, even if you do have strong opinions on an impressive number of subjects."

"Would you love me if I didn't?" There was still a sparkle in her eyes when she looked at him, and it was obvious how much they loved each other.

"Probably not as much, and I'd have gotten bored years ago." Being married to Jenny Parker had been anything but boring. The only thing he regretted about being married to her was not having had more children. But she had always been too involved in her work to have more than their son, and he was happy to have the one they did have. Their son, Phillip, was just like his mother, and they both thought he was going to make a great physician. For the moment, he was determined to go into pediatrics, and kids seemed to love him. They both felt it was a good decision.

And as they walked far down the beach, Sam was talking to his mother about the Parkers. He loved seeing them, and Dick's comments about the sailboat hadn't fallen on deaf ears.

"Did you hear about the sailboat their friends are bringing up on the Fourth?" India asked Sam, and he nodded. "It sounds like a really big one."

"Think they'll let us go on it?" Sam asked with interest. He loved boats and this year he was going to take a sailing class at the yacht club.

"It sounds like it. Dick said he'd take us on it." Sam's eyes were filled with excitement at the prospect, and India couldn't wait to meet Serena. She'd read two or three of her books and loved them, although she hadn't had time to read the new ones.

When they got to the end of the beach, they turned back, and walked home with their feet in the water. Sam threw the ball for the dog, and he kept retrieving it, and when they got home, the others were still out, and India made lunch, and then they took their bikes out. They rode past friends' houses, and stopped in to say hello. It felt good just being there, in a place they loved, with familiar people. It was the perfect spot for all of them. And at the last house, Sam ran into a whole group of his friends, and India agreed to let him stay for dinner. She rode back to the house alone, and when she got there, the phone was ringing. She thought it might be Doug, and hesitated for a moment before she answered. She still wasn't anxious to talk to him. But when she picked it up, it was Dick Parker.

"The Wards just called," he told her, sounding excited. "They're coming up tomorrow. Or at least he is, with a boatful of people. She's flying in for the weekend. I wanted to let you know, so you could bring Sam over. Paul says they'll be here in the morning. We'll call you."

"I'll tell Sam," India promised, and then went to the kitchen to make herself some soup. As it turned out, none of the kids came home for dinner. But at least they all called to tell her. She felt completely at ease about their independent movements. It was one of the things she liked most about being at the Cape. It was a safe community of people she knew and trusted. There were virtually no strangers, and hardly ever summer renters. The people who owned houses here loved it too much to go anywhere else. It was one of the reasons Doug never wanted to go to Europe, and in some ways she couldn't blame him, although she longed to travel with him and the children.

And when Sam came home that night she told him about the sailboat arriving in the morning. "They promised to call us as soon as it gets here."

"I hope they don't forget," Sam said, looking worried, as she tucked him into bed, and kissed him good-night, and promised him she was sure they wouldn't forget to call them.

The others came home shortly after that. She made lemonade and popcorn for them, and they sat on the deck chatting and laughing, until finally one by one they went off to bed. Doug didn't call that night, and she didn't call him either. It was a relief to have some time to herself, and after the kids were asleep, she disappeared into her darkroom. It was late when she finally went back to her bedroom, and she looked out at the full moon over the ocean. There were a million stars in the sky. It was a perfect night, in a place she loved, and for a moment she missed Doug. Maybe it would have been nice after all if he'd been there, despite their recent differences, and his depressing outlook on marriage. She didn't want to be a "reliable companion" to him, she hated the thought of it. She wanted to be the woman he loved, and still dreamed of. And it was hard to believe even now that he thought so little of that. Maybe he hadn't really meant what he said that night, she told herself hopefully, as she looked at the night sky, and began to get sleepy. He couldn't have meant it . . . could he? Was it all as cut and dried to him as he had said? She wanted to be so much more than a reliable caretaker for his children. She wanted to run down the beach with him hand in hand in the moonlight, and lie on the sand and kiss, as they had when they were young in Costa Rica. He couldn't have forgotten all that, couldn't have drifted so far from all their early dreams while she wasn't looking. What had happened to the young man he had been then, when they met, twenty years before? Their time in the Peace Corps had all been a kind of aberration for him, and twenty years had changed him into someone very different. He was not the same person he had been. He had grown up, he said. But in doing so, he had missed something . . . he had lost someone she had loved so much. Enough to give up a whole life for. And she had changed too, but not enough to forget all she had been. It was a shame, for both of them. And as she thought of it, she fell asleep, and didn't wake again until morning.

Chapter 5

It was another brilliantly sunny day when she woke up, and there was a gentle breeze rustling the curtains at her open bedroom window. She stretched and got up, and looked out, and all she could see as she looked out at the ocean was the biggest sailboat she'd ever seen. There were people running around on deck, and a series of flags flying from the mast, its hull was dark blue, and its superstructure silver. It was a spectacular sight, and she knew instantly whose it was. There was no need for the Parkers to call them. You could see the boat for miles. It was a spectacular sight as it sailed slowly past them, its mainmast towering high above the water, and she ran to get Sam to show him.

"Come on . . . get up . . . I have something to show you!" She woke him up as she came into his room, and gently pulled back the covers. "It's here!"

"What is?" He was still half asleep when he got up, and followed his mother to the window, where she pointed to the sailboat.

"Wow, Mom! Look at that! It must be the biggest sailboat in the world! Are they already leaving?" He looked worried. He was terrified he'd missed it.

"They must be going to the yacht club." They had a brightly colored spinnaker up and it was an incredible sight as they headed briskly past them. The wind had picked up just enough, and the boat was exquisitely graceful as she sailed toward the point. And then, India dashed quickly back to her bedroom and grabbed her camera. She and Sam ran out on the deck together, and she got some great pictures of the sailboat. She made a mental note to herself to give a set to Dick Parker once she developed them. The boat was absolutely lovely.

"Can we call Dick now?" Sam could hardly contain his excitement.

"Maybe we should wait a little while, Sam. It's only eight o'clock in the morning."

"But what if they go back to New York before we get a chance to see it?"

"They just got here, sweetheart, and Dick said they'd be here all week. I don't think you're going to miss it, honest. How about some pancakes first?" It was the only thing she could think of to stall him, and he agreed reluctantly. But finally, at eight-thirty, he couldn't stand it a moment longer and begged her to call them.

Jenny answered the phone, and India apologized for disturbing them so early, but explained the situation to her, and she laughed when she heard about Sam's impatience.

"They just called us from the boat, in fact. They invited us over for lunch. They're going to dock it at the yacht club."

"That's what I told Sam. It looked like that was where they were headed." Sam had gone back out to the deck, with binoculars, and the boat had disappeared around the point, and was out of sight now.

"Why don't you come to lunch with us?" Jenny suggested. "I'm sure two more won't make any difference to them. Do you think the others would like to come too? I can always call Paul, I'm sure he wouldn't mind."

"I'll ask them, and call you back. Thanks so much, Jenny. I'm not sure Sam is going to be able to stand it till lunchtime. You may have to come over and sedate him."

"Wait till he sees it!" Jenny promised, and when the others got up, India told them about the boat and asked them if they'd like to come, but they all had plans, and their friends seemed more exciting to them than a sailboat.

"Boy, are you guys dumb," Sam said to them with disgust as they ate their breakfast. India had made pancakes for everyone, and Sam was sitting at the table with them, although he'd eaten before they had. "It's the biggest sailboat in the *world*! You should see it!"

"How would you know?" Jason looked unimpressed. The Tilton children had a cousin with them from New York, and she was the cutest girl he'd ever seen. No sailboat in the world could hold a candle to her, and he wasn't about to miss an opportunity to spend the day with her, no matter how big the boat was.

"Mom and I saw it this morning. It's as big as . . . as big as . . . ." Words defied him as India smiled at his description.

Aimee was the only one of the children who got seasick like her father, and she didn't want to go on it, even if it was tied up at the dock. And Jessica had already made far more interesting plans with the Boardmans. Three teenage boys, one of them a freshman at Duke, and her best friend were far greater lures than any sailboat.

"Well, Sam and I will go to lunch," India said easily, "as long as we've been invited. Maybe they'll ask us again, and you can come then. We'll check it out, and I'll take lots of pictures." A hundred and seventy feet of sailing yacht was definitely an event not to miss, even in her book.

At noon, when she and Sam got on their bikes to go to the yacht club, he was so excited, he could hardly keep his bike straight on the way over. He almost fell twice and India had to tell him to calm down. The sailboat was not going to go anywhere without them, she assured him.

"You think they'll sail it today, Mom?"

"I don't know. Maybe. It's probably kind of a big deal to get in and out. They might not want to. But at least we'll see it."

"Be sure you take lots of pictures," he reminded her, and she laughed. It was fun to see him so happy and so excited. And sharing it with him was like seeing it through a child's eyes. She was almost as excited as he was.

They reached the yacht club easily, and rode down the dock staring at it. It was impossible to miss, as it stuck out beyond the end of the dock, its mast towering seventeen stories into the air. At first glance, it almost looked bigger than the yacht club. There were a few nice sailboats there, but nothing that even remotely compared with the one moored at the end of the dock. And much to India's relief, the Parkers were already there to greet them. It would have been embarrassing to board the yacht among strangers. But Sam wouldn't have cared if he had to crawl through pirates to get there. Nothing would have stopped him, as he ran across the gangway into the arms of Dick Parker. And India was right behind him. They had left their bikes on the dock, and she was wearing white shorts and a white T-shirt, with her hair brushed straight down her back and tied with a white ribbon. She looked more like Sam's big sister than his mother as she spotted the Parkers and smiled.

There were a number of people sitting on deck in comfortable chairs, and on two long, elegant blue canvas-covered couches, and seemingly everywhere were deckhands and crew members in navy shorts and white T-shirts. There were at least half a dozen guests, and a tall, youthful-looking gray-haired man stood out among them. As he approached, India could see that his hair had been the same color as her own, but it was woven in with white now, and the color of sand. He had intense blue eyes, and a handsome chiseled face, and he was wearing white shorts and a bright red T-shirt, over powerful shoulders and a long, lean, athletic-looking body. And within an instant, he was standing next to Dick Parker. His eyes first met India's, and then he quickly looked down at Sam with a broad smile and a hand held out to greet him.

"You must be Dick's friend Sam. What took you so long? We've been waiting for you."

"My mom rides her bike really slow. She falls off if I ride too fast," he said, by way of explanation.

"I'm very glad you both made it," their host said in a friendly, welcoming tone, as he glanced at India with laughter in his eyes. He felt an instant kinship with Sam from the mo-

ment he met him, and he was somewhat intrigued by his mother. She was a pretty
woman with an intelligent air, and a look of
good-humored amusement. She was obviously proud of the boy, and as he chatted with
him, he decided that her pride was with good
reason. He was bright and interested and
polite, and he asked a million surprisingly
knowledgeable questions. Sam even knew
that the yacht was a ketch, guessed the height
of the mainmast based on the length of the
boat correctly, and knew the names of all the
sails. He obviously had a passion for sailboats,
which endeared him instantly to his host. It
was a full five minutes before Paul Ward
could hold a hand out to India and introduce
himself to her. By then, Sam already felt as
though he owned him. They had become instant friends, and Paul disappeared with him
immediately to take him to the wheelhouse.

Dick Parker introduced India to the rest
of the guests then. He and Jenny knew all of
them, and India sat down and chatted easily
as a stewardess offered her champagne or a
Bloody Mary. She asked for tomato juice instead, and it appeared what seemed like seconds later, in a heavy crystal glass with the
name of the boat carved in the crystal. The

boat was called the *Sea Star*. It had been built especially for Paul in Italy, according to one of the guests, and it was the second boat of its kind Paul had owned. He had traveled around the world on the first one, as well as this one, and everyone commented on the fact that he was an extraordinary sailor.

"Your son will learn a lot from him," another guest explained. "He raced in the America's Cup Race as a young man, and he's been seriously involved in it ever since then. He keeps saying he's going to retire from Wall Street and just keep sailing around the world, but I don't think Serena will let him do it." Everyone laughed then.

"Does she sail everywhere with him?" India asked with interest. She was itching to start taking pictures of the boat, but she wanted to do it discreetly, and hoped she'd get the chance to later. But all of the guests laughed at her question. It appeared to be an inside joke, and one of them finally explained it.

"Serena's idea of hard sailing is from Cannes to Saint-Tropez. And Paul feels cheated unless he's sailing through a typhoon in the Indian Ocean. She manages to fly to meet him at various ports, but as infrequently as she can get away with. She keeps trying to get him to buy a plane and spend less time on the boat, but I don't think she'll win that one." A woman sitting across from India answered her, and the man sitting next to her nodded.

"My money's on Serena. She hates it when he goes away for long trips on the boat. She's a lot happier when they're tied up stern-to in Cap d'Antibes or Saint-Tropez. Serena is very definitely not a sailor." India could hardly envision a voyage on the *Sea Star* as a hardship, but maybe the famous author got seasick. But her dislike of long trips on the boat seemed to be well known among them, and inspired half a dozen stories about Serena. She sounded interesting, but not easy, as India listened to them. And as they talked, she quietly took out her camera, and began shooting. They were so busy telling stories they hardly noticed what India was doing, and after a few minutes, someone admired her camera. It was the new one she had wanted to show Dick Parker, and when she did, he loved it. It seemed natural for him to explain about India to the others.

"Her father won a Pulitzer," he said on her behalf, "and one of these days India will too, if she goes back to work. She's been to as many places in the world as Paul has, but usually with guns pointed at her, or fires raging. You should see some of her pictures," he said proudly.

"I haven't done any of that in a long time," she said modestly. "I gave it up a long time ago when I got married."

"You can still change that," Jenny said firmly, as the guests chatted easily, and it was another half hour before Sam and Paul Ward reappeared, and Sam was beaming.

Paul had shown him everything, even how the sails worked. Everything on the boat was computerized, and he could sail the huge boat single-handedly if he had to, and had often, with the crew standing by to help him. But he was truly an extraordinary sailor, and even Sam had understood that. Paul had explained it all very simply to him, and he was impressed more than ever by the child's thoughtful questions. Paul had even made some diagrams for him, to explain things more clearly to him.

"I'm afraid you have a serious sailor on your hands," Paul said to her admiringly when they returned, and Sam sat down to drink the soda a stewardess handed him with a linen napkin. "It's a serious addiction. If I were you, I'd be very worried. I bought my first sailboat at twenty, when I didn't have a dime, and practically had to sell my soul to do it."

"Can I help you sail, Paul?" Sam asked with a look of adoration, and Paul smiled as he looked down at him and ruffled his hair. He had a nice way with children, and particularly with Sam.

"I'm not sure we'll go out again today, son. How about tomorrow? We were going to take a sail out to some islands. Would you like to join us?" Sam was instantly beside himself with the sheer joy of it, and Paul glanced at India as he asked the question. "Would you like to come with us tomorrow? I think he'd really enjoy it."

"I'm sure he would." India smiled back at him. "Are you sure it wouldn't be an imposition?" She didn't want to be a nuisance. She was afraid Sam's enthusiasm would be a little overwhelming.

"He knows more about sailboats than some of my friends. I'd love to show him how it all works, if you have no objection. It isn't often I get to 'educate' a young sailor. Most of the people I have on board are more interested in the bar and the size of their cabins. I think he'd really get something out of the sailing."

"That would be terrific. Thank you." She felt strangely shy with him. He was an important man, and there was something very powerful about him, which she found a little daunting. But Sam seemed completely at ease with his new friend, and among the guests and the deckhands. Paul had made him feel entirely at home, and India was touched by what she saw. It told her something about Paul, and a few minutes later, chatting with him, she asked him if he had children. She thought he had to, to be so good with a child Sam's age. And she wasn't surprised when he nodded with a smile.

"I have one son, who has hated boats all his life," he laughed. "He'd rather be burned at the stake than spend ten minutes on a sailboat. He's a grown man now, with two children of his own, and they seem to dislike boats as much as he does. And my wife is scarcely better than my son. She tolerates life on the *Sea Star,* but barely. Serena and I have never had children. So I'm afraid the burden of my need to teach sailing to someone rests on Sam. It may prove to be a heavy responsibility for him." He accepted a glass of champagne from a silver tray the stewardess held out to him, and smiled at India, and then he noticed her camera. "Dick tells me you're a woman of extraordinary talents."

"I'm afraid not. Not anymore, at least. I just take very good photographs of my children."

"From what Dick has said, I think you're being very modest. He said your specialty was bandits, guerrillas, and war zones." She laughed at the description of her early years as a photojournalist, but he wasn't entirely wrong. She had done a lot of dangerous assignments in some very unusual places. "I've done a bit of that myself, though not with photography. I was a navy pilot when I was young, and then later, before I remarried, I was involved in airlifts to some very out-of-the-way places. I organized a group of pilots, on a volunteer basis, to do rescue missions and supply drops. We were probably in some of the same places." Just listening to him, she knew she would have liked to have photographed his adventures.

"Do you still do it?" she asked, intrigued by him. He was a man of many facets and contrasts. He obviously lived a life of luxury, but somehow managed to combine it with a life filled with danger and excitement. And she also knew of his many victories on Wall Street. He had a reputation for integrity and success that had made him a legend.

"I gave up the airlifts a few years ago. My wife had serious objections to it. She thought it was too dangerous, and she said she had no pressing desire to become a widow yet."

"That was probably sensible of her."

"We never lost a plane or a pilot," he said confidently, "but I didn't want to upset her. I still arrange funding for the project, but I don't fly the missions myself anymore. We flew a number of missions into Bosnia, to help the children while things were rough there. And of course Rwanda." Everything about him seemed both admirable and impressive, and she was fascinated by him. Just talking to him, she wanted to reach for her camera and take his picture, but she knew she couldn't. He had already been kind enough to Sam, and she didn't want to annoy him.

He chatted with some of the other guests then, and half an hour later, he walked them all into the dining room, where there was an impeccably set table, covered with exquisite china and crystal and embroidered linens. He ran his boat like a fine hotel, or a beautifully run home. Every minute detail had been seen to with perfection. His hospitality was apparently as extraordinary as his sailing.

India was surprised to find herself at Paul's right at lunch, and honored by the place he'd given her. And it enabled them to engage in a considerable amount of conversation. He was fascinating to talk to. He had an extensive knowledge of the world and the arts, a passion for politics, and a lot of strong opinions and interesting views. And at the same time, he had a gentleness, a kindness, and a wisdom that endeared him to her. And more than once, he had her laughing at stories he told on himself. He had a sense of mischief as well, and a wicked sense of humor. But no matter how many subjects they explored about the world at large, the conversation always drifted back to sailing. It was clearly the passion he lived for. And to her left, Sam was deeply engrossed in conversation with Dick Parker on the same subject. And he glanced over now and then to smile at Paul. In one brief afternoon, Paul had become Sam's hero.

"I think I'm falling desperately in love with your son," Paul confided in an undertone as the stewardesses in the dining room served them coffee in Limoges cups. "He's magical, and he knows an awful lot about sailing. He actually makes me wish I'd had more children." It was hardly too late for him, India realized. She remembered reading in *Fortune* magazine that he was fifty-seven, and Serena was roughly fifty. Given the way he felt, it surprised India that he had never had children with her. She knew from something he'd said at lunch that they had been married for eleven years, but he also talked about how intensely busy she was, writing novels, and overseeing the production of the movies made from them, in the most minute detail. She was, in fact, in L.A. doing just that at that very moment. He described her as a perfectionist, and completely driven. He said she was both talented and compulsive about her work.

Paul had told India at lunch that he had married while still in college the first time, had only the one son he'd mentioned earlier, and stayed married for fifteen years, and then waited another ten years before he married Serena. She had been thirty-nine when they were married, and for her it had been the first time.

"Actually," Paul said, explaining it to her,

"Serena has never wanted children. She's passionate about her career, and she's always been afraid that children would interfere with it." He said it without making editorial comment on her decision. But India thought that maybe since he already had a son when he married her, it hadn't mattered to him. It was, in any case, an interesting perspective for India, who had given up a career to have four children. "I don't think she's ever regretted the decision," he said honestly. "And to tell you the truth, I'm not sure she would ever have been good with kids. She's a very complex woman." India was dying to ask him what that meant, but didn't dare. And in spite of the ambiguity of what he had said, she got the feeling that he was happy with her.

It was a long, chatty lunch, and Paul and India touched on a wide variety of subjects, and eventually came back to their respectively extensive travel. He still enjoyed going to remote parts of the world, whenever possible on his sailboat. "I don't get to do it as much as I'd like to," he admitted, "but one of these days, I will. I keep telling myself I'm going to retire early, but with Serena still so involved in her work, there's no point doing that until she has more free time to be with me. And if I read the signs correctly, by the time she slows down," he smiled at India wistfully, "I'll be in a wheelchair."

"I hope not."

"Me too," he said firmly. "What about you? Are you going back to your career one of these days, or are you still too busy with your children?" He could only imagine what four young children would require of her. To Paul, it sounded more than a little overwhelming, but she sounded as though she enjoyed it. The one person she hadn't said much about was her husband, and that hadn't gone unnoticed. Paul had been quick to notice the absence of any reference to her spouse.

"I don't think I'll ever go back to work," she said thoughtfully. "My husband is violently opposed to it. He can't even imagine why I'd think about it." And not even knowing why, she told him then about the assignment in Korea, and Doug's reaction to it. It had been completely beyond him why she would even consider doing it, or be disappointed when she didn't.

"He sounds like he needs to get dragged into the twentieth century. It's a bit foolish to expect a woman to give up her career, and whatever identity and self-esteem goes with it, and not expect some kind of reaction to that kind of sacrifice and loss. Personally, I wouldn't be as brave as he is." Or as foolish, he thought, but didn't say it. Sooner or later, Paul knew, her husband was going to pay a price for it. Big time. It was inevitable. He had learned that with Serena. Even asking her to take time off to sail with him elicited nothing short of outrage from her. But then again, she was particularly compulsive about her work. "It sounds as though you miss your career, India. Am I right?" He wanted to get to know her better. There was something quiet and magnetic about her that drew her to him, and every time he watched her talk to Sam, something about the warmth of their exchange, and her gentleness with the child, touched him deeply. There were a lot of positive things he could have said about his wife, but nurturing had never been her strong suit, and *gentle* was not a word he would have used to describe her. She was exciting and passionate and opinionated and powerful and glamorous and brilliant. But she and India seemed as though they had been born on different planets and lived in different worlds. There was a softness to India, and a subtle sensuality, coupled with a sharp mind and mischie-

vous wit, which he found inordinately attractive. And her straightforwardness and honesty
were refreshing to him. His dealings with Serena were always fascinatingly convoluted.
But that was Serena. And most of all, she
loved to provoke him. India appeared to be a
far more peaceful person, although she certainly did not appear to be "weak."

And she was thoughtful before she answered his question about missing her work.
"Yes, I do miss it. The funny thing is, I didn't
for a very long time. I was too busy to even
think about it. But lately, as the kids are starting to grow up, I feel a real void in my life
where my work was. I don't know what just
yet, but I think I need something to fill it
other than children." It was that that Doug
had absolutely refused to hear when she tried
to talk to him about it. He just brushed her
off, and her feelings on the subject, dismissing
it entirely. And it was the first time she had
actually translated her thoughts into words
and told someone else about how she felt.

"I don't see why you couldn't go back
now, maybe on slightly tamer assignments,"
Paul suggested reasonably. It was more or less
what he had told his wife. She could do one
movie a year, and a book every two or three

years. She didn't have to do two movies a year, four television shows, and a six-book contract to complete in three years. But Serena didn't want to hear it, and even listening to him say the words had made her feel threatened and provoked a fight.

"I did a piece in Harlem three years ago, on child abuse," India explained. "That was perfect for me. It was close to home, not dangerous physically. It turned out very well. But I don't get assignments like that often. Whenever they do call, they seem to want me on the kind of assignments I used to do, in places where there are riots or revolutions. I guess they think that's what I'm good at. But taking assignments like that would be too hard on Doug and the kids."

"Not to mention dangerous for you." He was frowning as he said it. He wasn't sure he'd like his wife risking her neck for a story either. The worst place Serena had to be to conduct her business was at the Polo Lounge of the Beverly Hills Hotel, or in her publisher's office in New York. She was hardly in danger or at risk. "Well, you ought to figure out some kind of compromise, India. You can't deprive yourself of that kind of nourishment forever. You need it. We all do. That's why I don't retire. Much as I hate to admit it, to some extent, wielding power feeds my ego." She liked the fact that he was willing to admit it to her. It made him seem vulnerable somehow, which was not a word most people would have used to describe Paul Ward. But India sensed that clearly about him. He was vulnerable, in his feelings for his wife, in the way he talked to her, in the things he shared, even in the way he reached out to Sam. There was a great deal of moral courage to him, and sincerity, and hidden tenderness. There was a lot she liked about him. He was a very impressive man.

It was after three-thirty when they left the lunch table, and Paul volunteered to take Sam out in the little sailing dinghy they kept on board, and teach him how to sail. And Sam was ecstatic when he offered. Paul put a life jacket on the boy, and had the deckhands lower the dinghy to the water, and then they scampered down the ladder, and a moment later, India was watching them heading out toward the ocean. She was only slightly worried that they might capsize, but his friends and the crew reassured her that Paul was responsible, and also a strong swimmer. And she could tell just from his expression how happy Sam was.

She could see him laughing and smiling and looking up at Paul from where she stood, and as she watched them, she took out her camera, and got a series of great shots with her long lens. She could see both their faces clearly, and she had never seen two happier people than her son and his new friend. It was after five when they reluctantly came back to the *Sea Star,* and Sam scampered back on board.

"Wow! Mom! That was fantastic. It was so cool . . . and Paul showed me how to do it!" Sam was beaming, and Paul looked pleased too. The two had obviously formed an even greater bond in the dinghy.

"I know. I could see, sweetheart. I got lots of pictures of you," India said as Paul looked down at her with a big smile, and Sam ran off to get sodas for both of them. He felt remarkably at home on the boat thanks to Paul's hospitality, and as far as Sam was concerned, Paul was his friend for life now. India knew he would never forget the day he had just spent.

"He's a great boy, India. You should be very proud of him. He's smart and kind, and he has integrity, and a great sense of humor. Like his mother," he added. Getting to know Sam, he felt as though he knew her better. He was a kind of bridge between them that he truly enjoyed.

"You learned all that in an hour in a boat the size of a bathtub?" She was teasing, but she was touched by what he had said about her son.

"There's no better place to learn it. Sailing teaches you a lot about someone, especially in a boat that size. He was very clever about it, and very sensible and careful. You don't need to worry about him."

"I do anyway." She grinned, looking up at Paul comfortably. "It's part of my job description. I wouldn't be holding up my end of the deal if I didn't worry about him."

"He's a terrific sailor," Paul said almost proudly.

"So are you," she said simply. "I was watching the whole time."

"I'd love to see the pictures."

"I'll develop them for you, and bring them when we come tomorrow."

"I'd like that," he said, as Sam ran back to them, holding two Coca-Colas, and handed one to Paul as he grinned at his mother. It had been the best day of his life so far.

They stood for a moment, drinking their Cokes, they were tired and thirsty and happy. The breeze had come up by then, and it had been work for Paul sailing the dinghy. But it was hard to tell which of them had enjoyed it more.

They glanced over at the bar, where some of his guests were playing liar's dice. Others were sunbathing, two were reading, and one was sleeping. It had been a peaceful, easy afternoon, and India had enjoyed it. It was five-thirty when she finally told Sam they had to leave and go home to the others, and he looked crestfallen when she said it.

"You'll be back tomorrow, Sam," Paul reminded him. "Come down early if you want. We'll do some things together before we sail."

"How early?" Sam looked hopeful, and Paul and India laughed as they watched him.

"Does nine o'clock sound like the middle of the day to you?" He had a feeling Sam would be there at five, if he let him. "Make that eight-thirty." And then he glanced at India with a question in his eyes. "Is that all right with you?"

"It's fine. I'll get the other children fed

and organized before we leave. They're pretty self-sufficient. They're with their friends all day anyway. They won't miss us."

"You can bring them if you'd like to. All my guests will be off the boat for the day, it'll be just you and Sam, and me. There's plenty of room for the others, if they'd enjoy it."

"I'll ask them." It seemed a shame to miss an opportunity like this, but she had a feeling they wouldn't be tempted. They didn't want to miss a minute with their friends, and Sam was the only one of her children who had fallen in love with sailing. "Thank you for the invitation, in any case, and all your kindness." She shook his hand before they left, and she felt their eyes lock for a moment. She saw something there but she didn't know what it was . . . admiration . . . curiosity . . . friendship . . . but she felt it race through her like something indistinguishable and electric, and then the moment was gone, and she and Sam were back on their bikes, as the guests and the crew waved to them. It suddenly felt like leaving home, or a magical vacation. And like Sam, as they rode home, all she wanted to do was turn around and go back to the *Sea Star* as fast as she could.

It had been a perfect afternoon in every

way, and she couldn't help thinking of Paul as she pedaled behind Sam, trying to keep up with him without falling off her bike. There was something very rare and deep about the man she had met that afternoon. And she was sure there was more to him than what they'd seen. They didn't call him the Lion of Wall Street for nothing. There had to be a hard side to him too, perhaps even ruthless. Yet what she had seen was someone very gentle and very caring. And she knew that neither Sam nor she would ever forget the day they had just spent with him.

Chapter 6

The children were all home when Sam and India got back from their afternoon on the *Sea Star,* and everyone had had a good day, and seemed happy to see them. Sam told them all about Paul, the boat, and his adventures in the dinghy, and they listened affectionately, but without much interest. Sam felt about boats the way some small boys were about tanks or airplanes. It didn't make much sense, or hold any magic, for the others. And as they talked, India went to the kitchen to cook dinner.

She made pasta, and salad, and garlic bread, and put some frozen pizzas in the oven. She had a suspicion that additional mouths would appear eventually, and she wasn't wrong. At seven o'clock, when they sat down, four more children turned up, two of them friends of Jason's, and the other two friends of Aimee's. It was the way they lived in the summer. It was casual and relaxed, and she never cared how many kids were underfoot. That was just part of their beach life, it was expected, and she liked it.

Jessica helped her clear the kitchen afterward, while the others went to play, and as soon as they had finished loading the dishwasher, Doug called them. Sam got on the phone first and told him all about the *Sea Star*. He made it sound like the largest ocean liner in the world when he described how big it was, but he also described in great detail all the intricacies of the sails and the computer system that ran them. It was obvious that Sam had really learned a lot about sailing from Paul, and Sam had really listened to him.

And when it was finally India's turn to talk to Doug, he asked her about Sam's enthusiasm about it. "What was Sam all worked up about? Is the boat as big as he says, or was it some old tub at the yacht club?"

"It was a very nice tub." India smiled as she answered, thinking of the day they had spent on it. "The owner is a friend of Dick and Jenny's. I've read about him, and I'm sure you have too. His name is Paul Ward, and he's married to Serena Smith, the author. She's in L.A. working on a movie, and he and a bunch of friends are here for the week on his sailboat. Maybe he'll still be here when you come up."

"Spare me," Doug said, feeling seasick just thinking about it. "You know how I feel about boats, but I'd like to meet him. What's he like? Arrogant as hell and a real son of a bitch beneath the veneer?" It was what Doug expected, knowing of his power and success on Wall Street. It was inconceivable to him that anyone could have that much power and still be a decent human being too.

"No, he seems very human, actually. He was great to Sam, and even took him out in his dinghy," India said casually, annoyed that Doug automatically assumed that Paul was a bastard.

"I hear he's pretty ruthless. Maybe he was just showing off for his friends. He sounds like the kind of guy who eats his young, and anyone else's." Doug was persistent in his viewpoint, and India didn't want to argue with him.

"He didn't eat ours, at least. Sam loved

him." She was going to tell him they were going sailing with him again the next day, and then for no particular reason, thought better of it and never mentioned it to him.

"How are you?" He changed the subject then, and spared her from saying more about Paul. There wasn't much more to say anyway, other than that she thought he was terrific, and he thought she should go back to work as soon as possible. She was sure Doug would have loved to hear it.

"I'm fine. Busy with the kids. It's great here. All the same faces, old friends. Jenny and Dick have been wonderful, as usual. The kids are back with all their old pals again. Nothing new here." It was what she loved about it. The sameness and familiarity. It was like burrowing into an old cozy pillow in a favorite nightgown. "How are you?"

"Tired. Working. I haven't taken a minute off since you left. I figured I'd just buckle down and do it. I still won't make it up for the Fourth though."

"I know, you told me." Her voice was noncommittal. She was still angry at him over their conversation during the fateful dinner.

"I didn't want you or the kids to be disappointed," Doug said apologetically.

"We won't be. We're going to the Parkers for their barbecue."

"Stick to the steaks, they're the only thing Dick doesn't set fire to." She smiled at the memory, and told him that they had hired a cook this year. "I miss you guys," he said comfortably. Collectively. But not "I miss *you.*" She would have liked to hear that, but she didn't tell him she missed him either. The truth was she didn't. And she was still having conflicting feelings about him ever since their discussions before she left Westport. But somehow, she got the impression he'd forgotten all about it. He had never fully understood how deeply he had upset her, or how devastated she had felt when he talked about what he expected of their marriage. Sometimes she felt as though she didn't know who she was now, his friend, his housekeeper, his "reliable companion." She didn't want to be any of those, she wanted to be his lover. And she realized now that she wasn't. She felt like a hired hand, a slave, a convenience, an object he took for granted. Like a vehicle he had used to transport his children. She felt no more important to him than the station wagon they had used to get there. It was an empty feeling and it put a distance between them she had never felt before.

"I'll call you tomorrow," he said impersonally. "Good night, India." She waited for him to say that he loved her, or missed her, but he didn't. And she wondered, as she hung up, if this was how Gail had arrived at the place where she had been for several years now. Feeling used and bored and empty and unloved. So much so that she had to meet other men in hotels in order to feel better. It was a destination India never wanted to arrive at. She would do anything before she started meeting men in motels, or sleeping with other women's husbands. That was not what she had come this far for. But what had she come for, she asked herself as she walked into the darkroom, lost in her own thoughts.

She took out her chemicals and began developing her film as she mused over her conversation with her husband, and then as she looked at the photographs developing in the tubs, she saw him. Paul. Smiling up at her. Laughing with Sam. Ducking his head in the dinghy, against the horizon looking incredibly handsome. It was an endless string of striking portraits of him, and told the tale of a magical afternoon between a man and a boy. It was the portrait of a hero, and she stood for a long time, looking at the pictures, thinking about him, and Serena. He had used such an odd combination of words to describe her. In some ways she sounded terrifying, in others fatally enticing. She could sense easily that he was in love with her, intrigued by her, and he claimed he was happy with her. And yet, everything he said had told India instinctively that she was anything but easy. But what they seemed to share appeared to suggest excitement. It made her wonder once again what she had with Doug. What did it all mean? And more importantly, what were the essential components of a good marriage? She no longer understood them. The ingredients she thought were necessary she'd been told were unimportant, and the things Paul said about Serena, about her being difficult, obstinate, challenging, aggressive at times, seemed to make him love her. As India thought about it, she decided that deciphering relationships and what made them work was momentarily beyond her. She no longer had the answers she had been so sure of not very long ago.

She hung the pictures up to dry, and left her darkroom to check on the children. Sam had fallen asleep, on the couch, watching a video, and the others were playing tag outside the house, in the dark by flashlight, and Jessica and a friend, one of the Boardman boys, were eating cold pizza in the kitchen. Everything seemed to be in order. All was well in her safe little world.

She carried Sam to bed, and managed to undress him without waking him up. He was exhausted after all the fresh air and excitement he'd had on the *Sea Star.* And as she looked down at him, she thought of Paul and the pictures she'd taken of him.

But then she had an even stranger thought, as she turned off the light and walked slowly back to her bedroom. She wondered suddenly what it would be like to be doing this alone, if she and Doug were no longer married. How different would it be? She did it all now. She cared for the children, she was here alone. She had all the responsibility, she did all the chores, did all the nurturing and worrying and cooking and cleaning. The only thing she didn't do was support them. It was scary thinking of it, but what if Doug left her? If he died? Would her life be so different? Would she feel more alone than she did now, knowing that she was just a tool to him, a convenience? What would happen to her if she lost him? Years before, she had worried about it, when the kids were small and she felt she couldn't live for an hour without him. But that had been when she thought he was in love with her. But now that she realized he wasn't in love, and felt no need to be, what would it really mean now to be without him? She felt guilty for even thinking of it, as though she had waved a magic wand and "disappeared" him. Just thinking about it was a form of treason. But no one knew what she was thinking. She would never have dared put the thoughts into words, not to anyone, not even Gail. And certainly not to Doug.

She lay on her bed for a while, and picked up a book finally, but she found she couldn't read it. All she could hear were her own questions echoing through her head, and there were a thousand of them. And louder than all of them was the one she feared most. What did their marriage mean to her now? Now that she knew what Doug was thinking. It changed everything, like the subtle turn of a dial that changed the music from sweet melody to endless static that hurt one's eardrums. And she could no longer pretend to herself that what she heard was music. It wasn't. Hadn't been for weeks. Maybe longer than that. Maybe it never had been. That was the worst thought. Or had it been something very sweet, and had they lost it? She considered that possibility the most likely. Maybe it happened to everyone in the end. Eventually, you lost the magic . . . and wound up bitter or angry, or like Gail, trying to empty an ocean of loneliness with a teacup. It seemed hopeless to her.

She gave up on the book eventually, and went out to the deck to check on the children playing tag, and found they had settled down in the living room finally, and were talking quietly with the television on in the background. And all she could do was stand there, staring up at the stars and wondering what would happen to her life now. Probably nothing. She would drive car pools for the next nine years, until Sam was old enough to drive, or maybe three years before that when Jason could drive him and Aimee, and she would be off the hook then. And then what? More laundry, more meals until they left for college, and then waiting for them to come home for vacations. And what would happen to her and Doug then? What would they say to each other? Suddenly, it all sounded so lonely, and so empty. That was all she felt now. Empty.

Broken. Cheated. And yet she had to go on, like a piece of machinery, cranking away, producing whatever it was meant to, until it broke down completely. It didn't seem too hopeful, or too appealing. And as she thought of it, she looked out over the ocean, and saw it. The *Sea Star,* in all her glory, with all the lights lit in the main saloon and the cabins, with red lights twinkling on the mast, as they went for a night sail. It was the most beautiful thing she'd ever seen, and it looked like the perfect escape. A kind of magic carpet, to wherever you wanted it to take you. She could see why Paul sailed all over the world. What better way to explore new places? It was like taking your house with you, your own safe little world that went everywhere with you. At the moment, India couldn't imagine anything better, and for just an instant, she would have loved to hide there, and she thought Paul Ward was lucky to have it. The boat looked so lovely as it sailed past her. She was sorry that Sam was asleep and couldn't see it, but at least he'd be back on board in the morning, and she knew how much he was looking forward to it.

She got all the kids into bed by eleven, and turned out her own lights shortly after.

And in the morning, she got Sam up at seven-thirty. He was on his feet almost before she touched him, anxious to get started. She had already showered and dressed. She was wearing a sky blue T-shirt and white jeans, and pale blue espadrilles Gail had bought for her in France the previous summer, and her hair was braided and clean and tidy, as she walked into the kitchen to make breakfast.

She had promised to leave blueberry muffins and fruit salad for the others, and there were four boxes of cereal for them. They had all told her their plans the night before, including dinner with friends, and she knew they'd be fine without her. And if they had a problem, they could go to any of their neighbors. And Paul had given her the satellite number on the boat, which she left for them, so they could call her in an emergency. Everything was taken care of, and at eight-twenty she and Sam were on their bikes, heading for the yacht club again.

Paul was on deck when they got there, and the guests were just leaving. They had rented a van and were going to visit friends in Gloucester. They were staying overnight, and they waved at India and Sam as they left, and

Sam ran onto the boat with a broad grin and Paul put an arm around him.

"I'll bet you slept like a log last night after sailing that dinghy." He laughed as Sam nodded. "So did I. It's hard work, but it's fun. Today will be a lot easier. I thought we'd sail to New Seabury, stop for lunch, and then come back here after dinner. Does that work for you?" He looked up at India, and she nodded.

"That sounds lovely," India said happily, as he asked if they'd had breakfast.

"Just cereal," Sam said forlornly, as though she had starved him. And his mother smiled.

"That's no breakfast for a sailor," Paul said, looking sympathetic. "How about some waffles? They just made some in the galley. How does that sound?"

"Much better." Sam approved of the menu, and Paul told India where to leave their things in one of the guest cabins. She walked down the staircase, found the stateroom he had indicated easily, and was startled by what she saw. The room was more beautiful than any hotel room. The walls were paneled in mahogany, there were shiny brass fittings on all the drawers and closets. The room was large and airy, with several portholes, and a huge closet, and there was a fabulous white marble bathroom, with a bathtub and a shower. It was even more luxurious than what she might have expected, and even nicer than their home in Westport. And she recognized easily that the paintings all around her were by famous artists.

She put her bag down on the bed, and noticed that the blanket was cashmere with the emblem of the boat on it. And she took out the envelope of photographs she'd brought with her.

And by the time she got back to the dining room, Sam was up to his neck in waffles, with maple syrup dribbling down his chin as he and Paul engaged in a serious conversation about sailing.

"How about you, India? Waffles?"

"No, thanks," she smiled, slightly embarrassed. "You would think I never feed him."

"Sailors need to eat a big breakfast," he said, smiling at her. "How about coffee for you, India?" He loved the sound of her name, and said it often. He had asked her about it the day before, and she told him her father had been on assignment there when she was born, and Paul had told her how much he liked it. He found it very exotic.

One of the two stewardesses standing by poured India a cup of steaming coffee, in a Limoges cup with little blue stars on it. All the china and crystal had either the boat's logo or stars on it.

It was after nine when Sam finished breakfast, and Paul invited them up to the bridge. It was a gorgeous, sunny day and there was a good breeze blowing. It was perfect weather for sailing, as Paul looked up at the sky and said something to the captain. They were going to motor away from the yacht club, and then set their sails when they got a little distance from it. And Paul showed Sam everything he did, as they prepared to leave the dock, and the deckhands pulled in the fenders and released their moorings. They called to each other, and threw the ropes back on board, as the stewardesses went below to stow any movable objects. India enjoyed sitting out of the way, watching the bustling activity all around them, as Sam stood right beside Paul, while he explained everything to him. And in a few minutes, they had left the dock, and were leaving the harbor.

"Ready?" Paul asked Sam as he turned

off the motor. They lowered the keel hydraulically when they left the yacht club.

"Ready," Sam said anxiously. He could hardly wait to get sailing. Paul showed him which buttons to push, as the giant sails began to unfurl, and he set the genoa, then the staysail, followed by the huge mainsail, the fisherman staysail, and finally the mizzen at precisely the right angle. It took barely a minute for the sails to fill, and suddenly the enormous sailboat began moving. She heeled gracefully, and picked up speed immediately. It was exhilarating and extraordinary, and Sam was beaming as he looked up at Paul. It was the most beautiful sight India had ever seen as they left the shore at a good speed and headed toward New Seabury under full sail.

Paul and Sam adjusted the sails regularly, as they looked up at the huge masts, and Paul then explained all the dials to Sam again, as his mother watched them. Paul and Sam stood side by side at the wheel, and Paul let Sam hold it for a while, as he continued to stand very near him, and then finally he turned it over to the captain. Sam opted to stay with him, and Paul went to sit with India in the cockpit.

"You're going to spoil him. No other sail-boat will ever do after this. This is just fantas-tic." She was beaming at him, sailing with him was an unforgettable experience, and she loved it, almost as much as Sam.

"I'm glad you like it." He looked pleased. It was clearly the love of his life, and the place where he was the happiest and the most peaceful. At least that was what he had told her. "I love this boat. I've had a lot of good times on the *Sea Star*."

"So has everyone who's ever been here, I imagine. I loved listening to your friends' sto-ries."

"I'm sure half of them are about Serena jumping ship, and threatening to leave every time the boat moves. She's not exactly an avid sailor."

"Does she get seasick?" India was curi-ous about her.

"Not really. Only once actually. She just hates sailing, and boats."

"That must be something of a challenge, with you so crazy about them."

"It means we don't spend as much time together as we ought to. She comes up with a lot of excuses not to be here, and as busy as she is, it's hard to argue with her. I never know if she really needs to be in L.A., or see her publisher, or if she's just coming up with reasons not to be on the *Sea Star.* I used to try and talk her into it, now I just kind of let her come when she wants to."

"Does it bother you when she doesn't?" She knew it was a little presumptuous asking him that, but he made her feel so comfortable, she felt as though she could ask him. And she was curious now about what made other people's marriages work, what was their secret for success. It suddenly seemed particularly important. Perhaps she would learn something that would be useful to her.

"Sometimes it does bother me," he admitted to her, as one of the crew offered them Bloody Marys. It was nearly eleven. "It's lonely without her, but I'm used to it. You can't force someone to do something they don't want. And if you do, you pay a price for it. Sometimes a very big one. I learned that with my first wife. I did absolutely everything wrong that time, and I swore to myself that if I ever married again, it would be different. And it has been. My marriage to Serena is everything my first marriage wasn't. I waited a long time to get married again. I wanted to be sure I was making the right decision, with the right woman."

"And did you?" She asked the question so gently, he didn't feel invaded by her asking. But in an odd unexpected way, they were becoming friends.

"I think so. We're very different, Serena and I. We don't always want the same things out of life, but we always have a good time with each other. And I respect her. I'm pretty sure it's mutual. I admire her success and her tenacity, and her strength. She has a lot of courage. And sometimes she drives me absolutely crazy." He smiled as he said it.

"I'm sorry to ask so many questions. I've been asking myself a lot of the same questions these days, and I'm not sure I know the answers. I thought I did. But apparently, the correct answers weren't the ones I always thought they would be."

"That doesn't sound good," he said cautiously. And somehow, here, on the ocean, with the sails overhead, they felt as though they could say anything to each other.

"It isn't," she admitted. She hardly knew him, she realized, but she felt completely safe talking to him. "I have no idea what I'm doing anymore, or where I'm going, or where I've been for the last fourteen years. I've been married for seventeen years, and all of a sudden I wonder if the things I've done with my life make any sense, if they ever did. I thought so, but I'm not so sure now."

"Like what?" He wanted to hear what she had to say, maybe even to help her. There was something about her that made him want to reach out to her. And it had nothing to do with betraying Serena. This was entirely separate. He felt as though he and India could be friends, and speak their minds to each other.

"I gave up my job fourteen years ago. I was working for *The New York Times*. I had been for two years, ever since I came back from Asia, and Africa before that . . . Nicaragua, Costa Rica . . . Peru . . . I'd been all over." But he already knew that. "I came back because Doug told me it would be over between us if I didn't. He had waited for me in the States for more than a year, and that seemed fair. We got married a few months later, and I worked in New York for just over two years, and then I got pregnant with our oldest daughter. And that's when Doug told me I had to quit. He didn't want me running around taking pictures in ghettos and back alleys, and following gangs for a great shot once we had children. That was the deal we made when we got married. Once we had kids, I'd hang it up, and it would be all over. So I did. We moved to Connecticut. I had four kids in five years, and that's what I've been doing ever since. Car pools and diapers."

"And do you hate it?" He couldn't imagine how she wouldn't. There was too much to her to hide in a diaper pail for fourteen years, or in Connecticut driving car pools. He couldn't understand a man who was blind enough to do that to her. But evidently Doug had been.

"I hate it sometimes," she answered him honestly. "Who doesn't? It wasn't exactly what I dreamed of doing when I was in high school. And I got used to a very different life when I was on the road. But sometimes I really love it, more than I thought I would. I love my kids, and being with them, and knowing that I'm making a contribution to their lives that will really make a difference."

"And what about you? What do you get out of it?" He narrowed his eyes as he watched her, concentrating on what she was saying to him.

"I get a certain kind of satisfaction from

it. A good feeling being with my children. I like them. They're nice people."

"So are you." He smiled at her. "So what are you going to do? Drive car pools until you're too old to drive anymore, or go back to work now?"

"That's the kicker. It just came up recently. My husband is adamant about my not working. It's causing a lot of tension between us. We had a serious conversation about it recently, and he defined to me what he expects of our marriage." She looked depressed as she said it.

"And what does he?"

"Not much. That's the problem. What he described was a maid, a kind of bus driver who can cook and clean up after the kids. A companion, I think he said. 'Someone he could rely on to take care of the children.' That was about all he wanted."

"I'd say he's not one of the great romantics," Paul said drily, and she smiled. She liked talking to him, and it made her feel better. For a month now she had been stewing about what Doug had told her, and worse yet what he hadn't.

"It doesn't leave me many illusions about how he views me. And suddenly, when I look back, I realize that's all it's ever been, for a long time anyway. Maybe that's all it ever was. Just a companion with room service, and good housekeeping. And I was so damn busy, I never noticed. Maybe I could live with it if I went back to work again. But he doesn't want me to do that either. In fact," she looked at Paul intently, "he forbade me to do it."

"He's very foolish. I played that game once. And I lost. My first wife was an editor at a magazine, while I was still in college. She had a terrific job, and I wonder if I wasn't a little jealous of her. She got pregnant with our son when I graduated and got a job, and I forced her to quit. Men did things like that then. And she hated me forever. She never forgave me. She felt I had ruined her life, and condemned her to a life of running after our son. She wasn't very maternal anyway. She never wanted more kids, and eventually she didn't want me either. The marriage fell apart in ugly ways that were very painful to us. And when it was over, she went back to work. She's a senior editor of *Vogue* now. But she still hates me. It's a very dangerous thing clipping a woman's wings. The patient does not survive that kind of surgery, or at least not very often. It's why I never interfere with Serena's career. At least I learned that much. And I never forced her to have children. Mary Anne, my first wife, never should have done that either. My son, Sean, was brought up by nannies once she went back to work, went to boarding school at ten, and finally wound up with me at thirteen. And he's still not very close to his mother. At least you've done that right." He could see in Sam all the love she had lavished on him, and he was sure she had done as much with the others. "You can't force people to do what they don't want and what isn't natural to them. It just doesn't work. I think we all know that. I'm surprised your husband doesn't."

"I did want it for a long time though. I love my family. I love having the kids. And I don't want to hurt them now by going back to work full-time. I can't trek around the world like I used to. But I think they would survive it if I went now and then, a couple of times a year for a week or two, or worked on stories close to home. All of sudden I feel as though I've given up who I am, and no one gives a damn, especially not my husband. He doesn't appreciate the sacrifice I made. He just dismisses it and makes it sound like I was just out there wasting my time and having fun before we got married."

"Not from what I hear. Dick Parker says you won a hell of a lot of prizes."

"Four or five, but it meant a lot to me. All of a sudden, I just can't let go of it. And he doesn't even want to hear about it."

"So what now? What are you going to do about it? Do what he wants, or raise some hell?" It's what Serena would do, without hesitating for a minute, but it was obvious to Paul that India was very different.

"I don't know the answer to that question," she said, glancing at Sam. He was still happy as could be, standing next to the captain. He hadn't moved an inch since they started talking. "That's where I left off when I came up here. He told me to take my name off the agency roster."

"Don't do it," Paul said firmly. He didn't know her well, but he sensed easily that if she gave up that part of her completely, it would destroy something important in her. It was a form of expression for her, a form of communicating, and being and breathing. She couldn't give up taking pictures, and they both knew it. "Where is he now, by the way?"

"At home. In Westport."

"Does he realize how upset you are about what he told you?"

"I don't think so. I think he discounts it completely."

"As I said before, he's very foolish. My ex-wife came at me like a hurricane one day, after three years of taking it out on me in small, insidious ways. But once she came out of the closet with how angry she was, she went straight to the lawyers. I never knew what hit me."

"I don't think I could do that, but I don't see things the same way anymore either. In just a month, I feel like my whole life is falling apart, and I don't know what to do about it. I don't know what to say, or think, or believe. I'm not even sure I know who he is anymore . . . or worse, who I am. Two months ago, I was perfectly happy being a housewife. And now, all of a sudden, I'm standing in my darkroom all the time, crying. That reminds me," she said suddenly. "I brought you something." She had the envelope on the couch next to her and handed it to him with a shy smile. "Some of them are really terrific."

He took the photographs out of the envelope then, and looked at them carefully. He was flattered by the shots she had taken of him, and smiled at the ones of Sam, but he was struck by how good she was, and what she had achieved at a considerable distance, with no preparation and no warning. She certainly hadn't lost her touch while doing car pools in Westport.

"You're very good, India," he said quietly. "These are beautiful." He started to hand them back to her and she told him he could keep them. She had only kept one of him and Sam, and another of him alone, taken at an interesting angle. She had left it clipped up in her darkroom. "You can't go on wasting your talent."

"You must think I'm crazy telling you about all this nonsense."

"No. I think you trust me, and you're right to do that. I won't ever say anything to betray you, India. I hope you know that."

"I feel a little silly telling you all this, but I just felt as though we could talk. . . . I respect your judgment."

"I've made my own mistakes, believe me." But at least he hadn't this time, and he knew without a doubt that his marriage to Serena was solid. "I'm happy now," he said to India. "Serena is an extraordinary woman. She doesn't take a lot of guff from me, and I respect her for it. Maybe that's what you need to do now. Go back to him and tell him what *you* want. It might do him some good to hear it."

"I'm not sure he would. I tried before I came here, and he just brushed me off. He acts as though I took a job with him seventeen years ago. We made a deal, and now I have to live with it. The real problem," she said, as tears filled her eyes and she looked at him, "is that I'm not even sure he loves me."

"He probably does, and is too foolish to know it himself. But if he doesn't love you, as painful as it would be, you need to know it. You're too young and too beautiful to waste your life, and your career, for a man who doesn't love you. I think you know that, and that's what's making you so unhappy." She nodded and he touched her hand and held it for a long moment. "It's a hell of a waste, India. I hardly know you, but I can tell you, you don't deserve that."

"And then what? Leave him? That's what I keep asking myself." Just as she had done the night before, when she tried pretending that Doug wasn't coming back and she was on her own with the children. "How do I even begin to do that? I can't work full-time and take care of my children."

"Hopefully, you wouldn't have to work full-time, but only when you want to, on the stories you choose to take on. Hell, he owes you something after nearly twenty years. He has to support you." He looked outraged.

"I haven't even thought that far. I guess, in reality, I just have to get back in my traces and keep going."

"Why?" he asked her, and for a moment everything stopped inside her.

"Why not?"

"Because giving up who you are, what you do, and what you need is giving up your dreams, and if you give them up, sooner or later, it will kill you. I guarantee it. You'll shrivel up like a prune, and get bitter and angry and mean, and your insides will turn ugly. Look at the people you know, we all know them. Bitter, angry, miserable people who've been cheated in life and hate everyone for it." She wondered, with a sense of rising panic, if he could already see that in her. And at the look in her eyes, he smiled reassuringly at her. "I don't mean you. But it could happen to you, if you let it. It could happen to any of us. It started to happen to me in my first marriage. I was a bastard to everyone, because I was miserable and I knew she hated me, and I hated her eventually and was too cowardly to say it to her, or to stop being there. Thank God she ended it, or we'd have destroyed each other. At least Serena and I like each other and enjoy what she's doing. I don't like it when she doesn't come on the boat, but she hates the boat, she doesn't hate me. There's a difference." He was not only intelligent and sensitive, but he was inordinately smart about people, and India already knew that about him. "Do something, India. I'm begging you. Figure out what you want, and don't be afraid to go get it. The world is full of frightened, unhappy people. We don't need another one. And you're much too beautiful and too wonderful to become one. I won't let you." She wondered for a second how he intended to stop her. What could he do? He was someone she had met the day before, and yet she had told him her whole life story, and all the problems she had suddenly discovered in her marriage. It was the oddest experience she'd ever had, but she trusted him completely, and she loved talking to him. And she knew with every fiber of her soul that she wasn't wrong to trust him.

"I can't even imagine how one comes back from where I've been for so long. What do you do?"

"First, you call your agent, and tell him you really want to go back to work. Then you figure out the rest. It'll come, at the right time, if you let it. You don't have to force it." Just listening to him gave her a sense of freedom, and without thinking, she leaned over and kissed him on the cheek, as she would have an old friend or a brother.

"Thank you. I think you were the answer to a prayer or something. I've been feeling totally lost for the past month. And I didn't know what to do about it."

"You're not lost, India. You're just beginning to find yourself. Give it time, and be patient. It's not easy to find your way back after all this time. You're just lucky you still have your talent." But did she still have a husband? That was the question that was beginning to fill her with panic.

And then, as though on cue, Sam ran over to them. The boat was still heeling considerably, and he ran surefootedly across the deck to where they sat. They were almost in New Seabury and Sam wanted to know if they were going into the yacht club.

"We'll drop anchor and go in with the tender," Paul explained, and the child looked excited about it.

"After lunch can we come back to the boat and swim?"

"Sure. We can sail the dinghy again too, if you'd like." Sam nodded, grinning broadly. It all sounded great to him. And as she watched them, India felt grateful to Paul again, and she thought Serena was very lucky. Paul Ward was an incredible human being, and she already felt as though he had been a great friend to her. She felt as though they had known each other forever.

Two of the deckhands lowered the tender for them, and one of them stayed in it to take them to the yacht club. Paul got in first, and took India's hand as she got in, and Sam got in right behind her.

They had an easy, happy lunch, talking about a variety of things. They talked about sailing for most of it, and Sam's eyes were wide with admiration when Paul told them some of his adventures going around the world, and even about a hurricane he'd been in in the Caribbean, and a cyclone in the Indian Ocean.

After lunch, they went back to the boat,

and first Sam swam, and then he and Paul sailed the dinghy, while India took pictures of them, and around the boat. She was having a great time. Paul and Sam waved to her from time to time, and they finally came back in. Paul took the Windsurfer out then, and India took more pictures of him. It was not an easy sport, and she was impressed by his skill, and the strength with which he rode it.

And then, finally, when they headed back to Harwich, the wind had died down, and they decided to use the motors. Sam was a little disappointed, but he was tired after a full day anyway. It had been a long day, and he fell asleep as he lay quietly in the cockpit. Paul and India both smiled looking at him.

"You're lucky to have him. I'd love to meet the others," Paul said, looking at her warmly.

"I hope you will one of these days," she said as the head steward brought them each a glass of white wine. Paul had asked her to stay on board for dinner, and she had accepted.

"Maybe we'll turn them all into sailors."

"Maybe. Right now they all think that hanging out with their friends is more important."

"I remember when Sean was that age, he

nearly drove me crazy." They exchanged a
smile, as Sam stirred next to her and went on
sleeping as she stroked his hair with one hand
and held her wineglass with the other. Paul
loved watching her with him. It had been a
long time since he had seen anyone as loving.
Children hadn't been a part of his life in a
long time, and sailing with Sam that afternoon and the day before was everything he
wished he had shared with Sean, but Sean had
never taken any interest in his father's sailboats. "Will you be here all summer?" Paul
asked her then, and she nodded.

"Doug is going to stay with us for three
weeks in August. And then we'll go back to
Westport. I guess we're going to be doing a
lot of talking." Paul nodded as he thought
about it. He hoped she would come to some
decisions that would be good for her. She deserved it. "Where will you be?"

"In Europe probably. We usually spend
August in the south of France, and then I race
in Italy in September." It was a good life, and
it sounded like fun to her, and then she asked
if Serena would be going with him. "Not if she
can come up with a better idea," he laughed.

It was time for dinner then, and India

woke Sam. He looked sleepy and confused when he woke up, and he smiled at her happily. He had been dreaming of sailing the *Sea Star* and then he saw Paul, and his smile widened, and he told him what he had been dreaming.

"Sounds pretty good to me. I dream about her too, especially when I haven't been on her in a while, but that doesn't happen too often." He spent a lot of time on his boat, he had told India that afternoon, and did his business via phone and faxes.

The cook had made cold vichyssoise for them, pasta primavera and salad, and a cheeseburger for Sam, just the way India had told them he liked it, with french fries. They had peach sorbet for dessert, and delicious butter cookies that melted in your mouth. The meal was elegant and light, and they chatted as they had at lunch, and after dinner, the captain motored them in slowly to the yacht club. It was hard to believe the day was over. They had been with Paul for thirteen hours, and both India and Sam wished that they could stay forever.

"Would you like to come to the house for a drink?" India asked him as they stood on deck, all three of them looked sad that the day was ending.

"I should probably stay here. I've got some work to do, and your kids will want you to themselves after you've been gone all day. They probably think you ran away to sea, and are never coming back." It was nearly nine o'clock by then. "Come back and see me soon, Sam," Paul told him. "I'm going to miss you."

"Me too." Mother and son both felt as though they had been on a long vacation, and not just a day sail. Being on board with him had that kind of quality. It had been a wonderful day, and she was grateful for the things he had said to her. He had actually helped her, and she felt calmer than she had in weeks, and before she left, she thanked him for it.

"Just don't be afraid to do what you have to," he said gently. "You can do it."

"I hope so," she said softly. "I'll send you some pictures." He kissed her cheek then, and shook Sam's hand, and they left the boat, feeling tired and content, and knowing they had made a friend. She didn't know if she'd see him again before he left, but she knew that whether she did or not, she would never forget him. In some ways, she suspected he had changed her life forever. He had given her the gift of courage. And with courage came freedom.

Chapter 7

For the next two days, India kept busy with the kids, and she developed the photographs she'd taken on the boat with Sam. She dropped them off for Paul. He'd been off the boat somewhere with his friends, and she didn't see him. And then, much to her surprise, he called her. He said that Dick Parker had given him the number.

"How's it going?" He had a deep, resonant voice that sounded wonderfully familiar to her. They had talked for so long that she felt comfortable with him now, like an old friend, and it was good to hear him.

"Fine. Busy. Dropping the kids off to tennis, and hanging out on the beach with them. The usual. Nothing very exciting."

"I loved the pictures. Thank you." She had included a great one of Sam, and he had sat and smiled at it for a long time, remembering the day they had spent together. For the whole day afterward, he'd really missed him. "How's my friend Sam?" They both smiled when he asked her.

"He talks about you all the time. We've heard about nothing from him but the *Sea Star*."

"His brother and sisters must be ready to kill him."

"No, they just figure he made it all up. I don't think any of them really believe him."

"Maybe you should bring them down and show them." But when they talked about it, there was no time. The next day he had to go to Boston to pick up Serena. He said they had plans on the Fourth, and the day after they were sailing back to New York. And for no reason she could explain, India felt sad as she listened to him, and knew she was being foolish. He had a life, an empire he ran, a whole world he had to return to, and a wife who was an international bestselling author, and a star in her own right. There was no room in his life for a married housewife in Westport. What would he do? Drive up to have lunch with her? Like one of Gail's rendezvous in Greenwich? Just thinking of it made her shudder. Nothing about what she thought of him was anything like that.

"When do you leave for France?" she asked, sounding wistful.

"In a few weeks. I'm going to send the boat over before that. It takes them about eighteen days to get there. We usually go to the Hotel du Cap around the first of August. That's Serena's idea of hardship travel in a third world country." But he said it without malice, and they both laughed.

It was a far cry from the kind of places she and Paul had both been to in their past lives, but there was nothing wrong with Cap d'Antibes either. India knew she would have loved it. "I'll call you before we leave. It would be wonderful if you could come back to the boat, and meet Serena. Maybe for breakfast or something." He didn't tell her that Serena got up at noon, and stayed up until three or four in the morning, usually working. She said she did her best writing after midnight.

"I'd like that," India said quietly. She would have loved to see him again, and meet his wife. She would have liked a lot of things, most of them both impossible and unimportant. This was the first time she had felt this way about any man since meeting Doug twenty years before, when they were in the Peace Corps. But this time, her feelings traveled in the guise of friendship.

"Take care of yourself, and Sam," he said, in a voice that was suddenly husky. He felt oddly protective of her, and the child, and didn't know why. Maybe it was just as well Serena was coming. She had called him from L.A. to herald her arrival only that morning. "I'll call you."

She thanked him for calling then, and a moment later, after they hung up, she sat staring at the phone in silence. It was odd to think that he was so nearby, in his own world, comfortably tucked in to his life on the *Sea Star*. It was a lifetime away from her own. In truth, although they had had a sympathy of souls, their lives had nothing in common, no shared borders. Meeting him at all had been an accident of sorts, a happenstance of destiny that could just as easily have never happened. But for her sake, and Sam's, she was glad that she had met him.

She lay in bed quietly that night, thinking of him, remembering the day they had shared, the conversations about her life, and what he thought she should do with it, and she couldn't help wondering if she would ever have the courage to do what he suggested. Just telling Doug she wanted to go back to work would cause a hurricane in their marriage.

She took a long walk down the beach the next day, thinking of all of it, with the dog at her heels, wondering what to do now. It would be easiest, it seemed, to retreat back into the life she'd led for fourteen years. But she was no longer entirely sure that she could do that. It would be like going back into the womb again, an impossibility no matter how much goodwill she applied to it. And now that she knew Doug didn't recognize the sacrifices she had made, she wasn't even sure she wanted to do it. If he didn't at least give her credit for it, why bother?

The next day was the Fourth of July. The kids slept late, and that afternoon, they went, as they always did, to the Parkers. The barbecue was in full swing, and all their neighbors were there. There were huge kegs of beer, and a long buffet table covered with the food the caterer had made this year. Nothing was burned, and it all looked delicious.

All of India's children were there, and

she was talking to an old friend, when suddenly she saw Paul walk in, in white jeans, and a crisp blue shirt, with a tall, striking woman with long dark hair and a spectacular figure. She was wearing big gold hoop earrings, and India thought she had never seen anyone as beautiful as she watched her laughing. It was Serena. She was every bit as glamorous and poised and magnetic as India had thought she would be. Just watching her make her way through the crowd was mesmerizing. She was wearing a short white skirt, a white halter top, a gold necklace, and high-heeled white sandals. She looked right out of a magazine from Paris. And she had a kind of sexy elegance about her. As she approached, India could see that she was wearing a huge diamond ring, like an ice cube, on her left hand, and she stopped and said something to Paul, and he laughed. He looked happy to be with her. She was a woman you couldn't ignore or forget about, or lose in a crowd. Everyone seemed to turn and look at her, and some knew who she was. India watched her kiss Jenny and Dick, and she accepted a glass of white wine without even acknowledging the server. She looked as though she was totally accustomed to a life of luxury and service.

And as though sensing India watching her, Serena turned slowly in the crowd and looked right at her. Paul leaned over to say something to her then, and she nodded, and they made their way slowly toward her. She couldn't help wondering what Paul had said to her, how much he had told her. . . . I met this poor pathetic unhappy woman, who lives in Westport . . . she gave up her career fourteen years ago, and has had a diaper pail on her head ever since . . . be nice to her. . . . Just looking at Serena Smith, one knew that she would never be dumb enough to give up her identity or her career, or be treated as a "companion you can rely on to take care of the kids" by her husband. She was sexy and beautiful and sophisticated, she had great legs, and a fabulous figure. India felt like a total frump as Serena walked majestically toward her. And she felt breathless as Paul finally stood looking down at her, with a smile, and touched her shoulder. India could feel an electric current run through her when he did it.

"India, I'd like you to meet my wife . . . Serena Smith. . . . Darling, this is the fabulous photographer I told you about, who took all the great pictures I showed you. The mother of the young sailor." At least he had told Serena about her. But India felt even more inadequate standing beside her. She had the most perfect smile she'd ever seen, and she looked fifteen years younger than Jenny, her college roommate. But Jenny hadn't worn makeup since she was eighteen, and Serena was put together like a model.

"I've been hoping I would meet you," India said discreetly, afraid to sound like a simpering fan, but also not wanting to appear indifferent. "I read everything you wrote for a while, but my children keep me so busy I never have time to read anymore."

"I can imagine. Paul said you have hundreds of them. But I can see why. The little guy in the pictures is gorgeous, and apparently quite a sailor." She rolled her eyes then. "Whatever you do, stamp it out of him quickly. Never let him on a boat again. It's an insidious disease that rots the brain. And once it's too far gone, there's absolutely nothing you can do about it." She was funny the way she said it, and India laughed in spite of herself, feeling a little disloyal to Paul as she did so. They had had such a good time with him on the *Sea Star*. "Boats are not my thing," Serena confessed. "Paul may have told you." India wasn't sure whether to admit it, as he disappeared to get himself a beer from one of the kegs Dick was presiding over.

"I have to admit, it's a wonderful boat," India said graciously. "My little boy, Sam, just loved it."

"It's fun," Serena said blithely, "for about ten minutes." And then she looked at India strangely, who prayed she wasn't blushing. What if she guessed how much India liked her husband, and how much she had said to him about her own life. It was easy to believe that Serena wouldn't have been too pleased to hear it. And it was always hard to gauge how much a husband told his wife, or vice versa. She and Doug had kept very few secrets from each other, in her case, only Gail's indiscretions, out of loyalty to her.

"I've been wanting to ask you a favor," Serena said, looking uncharacteristically uncomfortable, and India could just guess what it was . . . . Stay away from my husband. . . . She was feeling inordinately guilty. But he was an incredibly handsome man, and she had spent a day alone with him, telling him she was unhappy with her husband. In retrospect, it was embarrassing, particularly if he had told Serena. India was suddenly feeling very foolish. "Ever since I saw your photographs," Serena went on, as India continued to dread what was coming, "I wanted to ask you a favor, if you have time. We're leaving sometime tomorrow, but I'm desperate for a new book cover photo, and I haven't had time to do anything about it. Any chance you could come over in the morning and take a few shots? I look like death in the morning, and you'll need a good retoucher. A blowtorch will do fine. Anyway, I saw how good your work was. I can never get a decent shot of Paul and you got dozens when he wasn't even looking. Usually, he makes the most godawful faces and looks like he's about to kill someone. So what do you say? I'll understand if it's not up your alley. Paul says you normally do war zones and revolutions and dead bodies." India laughed with relief at the convoluted recital. Serena didn't seem in the least upset that India had been on the boat with Sam, and taken an indecent number of photographs of her husband. India was so relieved, she wanted to kiss her. Maybe he hadn't given away her secrets after all, at least she hoped not. Or maybe Serena felt too sorry for her to even care.

"Actually, I haven't done 'war zones' in

seventeen years, and all I do now is Sam's soccer team, and newborn babies for my neighbors. I'd love to do it. And I'm very flattered that you asked me. I'm actually not that great at portraits. I was a news photographer, and now I'm just a mother."

"I've never been either, and I'm impressed by both. If you want to come over about nine tomorrow, I'll try and drag myself out of bed and not spill my coffee all over my shirt before you arrive. I think just something simple in a white shirt and jeans will do it. I'm sick and tired of glamour shots. I want something more 'real.' "

"I'm incredibly flattered that you asked me," India said again. "I just hope I can come up with something useful." But she was sure to be an easy subject. She was so beautiful, and had such wonderful bone structure and lovely skin, it was hard to imagine having trouble taking her picture. India didn't even think it would need much retouching. She could hardly wait to do it, and she was happy to be going back to the *Sea Star* again. It was a chance to see Paul, even if Serena was with him. She was his wife, after all, and very much part of the picture.

The two women chatted for a little while,

about the movie Serena was working on, her latest book, and their trip to the south of France in a few weeks, and even India's children.

"I don't know how you do it," Serena said with admiration. "I never could imagine juggling children and a career, and I always thought I'd have been a dreadful mother. Even when I was twenty. I was never tempted once to have a baby. Paul wanted another child when he married me, but I was thirty-nine, and I was even less inclined to do it then. I just couldn't handle the responsibility, and the constant demands it must put on you, and the confusion."

"I have to admit, I love it," India said quietly, thinking of her children. Two of them were playing volleyball nearby while she talked to Serena. India respected her honesty, but she also realized that they couldn't have been more different. Everything Serena was, she wasn't, and vice versa. India was far more down to earth and direct and without any kind of artifice or pretense. Serena was far more artful and manipulative, and in her own way more aggressive. But much to her own surprise, India liked her. She had somehow hoped she wouldn't. But she could see now why Paul loved her. Serena was so powerful that being with her was like riding a Thoroughbred stallion. She was anything but easygoing, and it didn't bother her in the least to be called difficult. She loved it. The only similarity they shared was that they were both very feminine, but in entirely different ways.

India was soft in all the places Serena was hard, and strong in all the ways Serena wasn't. But the shadings in India's character were far more subtle, and that had intrigued Paul. There was very little mystery to Serena, she was all about strength and power and control. India was all about softness and kindness, and far more compassionate and humane. It had struck Paul when they sat and talked for hours on the boat.

Paul came back to talk to them eventually, and he stood for a moment, admiring their contrasts. It was almost like seeing the two extremes that women came in, and if he had dared, he would have admitted that both of them fascinated him in very different ways, and for a variety of reasons.

He was almost relieved when Sam came up to them, and India introduced him to Serena. He shook her hand politely, but he looked uncomfortable while he was talking to her, and it was obvious that Serena had no idea how to talk to children. She spoke to him as though he were a very short man, and the jokes she made in front of him fell on deaf ears. He had no idea whatsoever of their meaning.

"He's awfully cute," she said when he went back to his friends. "You must be very proud of him."

"I am," India said, smiling.

"If he ever disappears, you'll know where to find him, India. Paul will be sailing to Brazil with him in the dinghy."

"He'd love that," India said, laughing.

"The trouble is, they both would. But at Paul's age, it's pathetic. Men are such children, aren't they? They're all babies. At best, they grow up to be teenagers, and whenever they don't get their way, they get bratty." Listening to her made her think of Doug, but not Paul. There was nothing "bratty" about him. He seemed incredibly mature and very wise to her, and she had been very grateful for the advice he'd given her when they last spoke.

They talked for a few more minutes, and confirmed their plans for the next morning, and then Serena wandered off to talk to Jenny for a few minutes before they left, and

India went to check on her children, who seemed to be having a great time.

It was late when India and the children got home that night, and everyone was happy and tired. She told Sam then that she was going to meet the Wards at the boat the next morning and asked if he wanted to come with her.

"Will Paul be there?" he asked sleepily with a yawn, and when she said he would, Sam said he was coming. She invited the others to join them too, but they said they'd rather sleep in. The *Sea Star* was Sam's passion, and they were satisfied to leave it to him. She was only disappointed that the others hadn't seen it, and she knew that if they ever did, they would love it.

She woke Sam up, as she had before, early the next morning, and gave him cereal and toast before they left so he didn't have to bike to the yacht club on an empty stomach. But as soon as they got to the yacht, Paul was waiting for them, and offered them both pancakes. Serena was still in the dining room, drinking coffee. And she looked up when they walked in. Contrary to her warning the day before, India thought she looked fabulous, even at breakfast. She was wearing a starched white shirt, and immaculately pressed jeans, with rubber-soled loafers, and her hair was combed to perfection. She wore it straight and long, and had pulled it back with an elastic. She had a good, clean look, with just enough makeup to enhance her looks but not overwhelm them.

"Ready for action?" she asked India when she saw her.

"Yes, ma'am." India smiled, as Sam sat down to a plate of waffles, and Paul sat down beside him.

"I'll keep Sam company," Paul volunteered. It wasn't a sacrifice for him, it was obvious just looking at him how much he liked him. "We'll go out in the dinghy or something."

"How depressing," Serena said, and meant it, as she went out on deck and India followed. And the rest of the morning flew by like minutes.

India took half a dozen rolls of film, and she was certain they had gotten some really good pictures. She was pleased to find that Serena was an easy subject.

Serena chatted amiably, and told funny stories about things that had happened on her movie sets in Hollywood and famous authors she knew and the outrageous things they had done. India enjoyed hearing about them. And when they were finished, Serena invited her to stay for lunch, with Sam of course. They had decided not to leave for New York that day, and were planning to leave the following morning.

They ate sandwiches on deck, which Serena said she preferred to the dining room, which she found pretentious and claustrophobic. India had found it anything but, but it was also pleasant eating in the open air, and Paul and Sam came back with the dinghy when the women were almost finished.

"Did you save anything for us?" Paul asked as they joined them on deck. "We're starving!" And they looked it.

"Just crusts," Serena said cheerfully, but one of the stewards was quick to take Paul's order. He ordered club sandwiches for himself and Sam, with potato chips, and pickles, he added, remembering Sam's fondness for them.

He said they'd had a good sail, and Sam seconded the opinion with a huge grin. He didn't tell his mother that they'd both fallen in, and Paul had righted the little boat again very quickly, but she had seen it, and also that Paul had resolved the problem very swiftly.

After they finished their sandwiches, India said they had to get home to see what her family was doing. And she wanted to get to work on Serena's pictures in the darkroom.

"I'll send you proofs in a few days," she promised Serena as she stood up. "You can see what you think of them," she said modestly.

"I'm sure I'll love them. If you make me look half as good as you did Paul, I'm going to use them as wallpaper in our apartment. And hell, I'm better-looking than he is." She chuckled and India laughed with her. She was a character, and it was easy to see why he liked her. She certainly wasn't boring. She was full of spice and vinegar, and wicked little stories about famous people. Who had said what and done what to whom. Listening to her all morning had been like listening to a gossip column about celebrities. And aside from that, she was not only beautiful, but incredibly sexy. India really liked her, and couldn't help but be impressed by her.

India thanked Serena then for the opportunity to take pictures of her, and Paul for taking such good care of Sam while they were busy.

"He took care of me," Paul said with a smile, and then he bent to give Sam a hug, and the boy returned it with vigor. "I'll miss you," Paul said, feeling sad to see him go, but not half as sad as Sam was. He would never forget his days on the *Sea Star.* "One of these days, you'll have to take a little trip with me," he promised him, "if your mom will let you. Would you like that, Sam?"

"Are you kidding?" He beamed. "I'll be there!"

"That's a deal then." And then Paul turned and hugged India. He felt as though he were losing old friends as they walked down the gangway to the dock, and the entire crew waved at Sam as they left. He had won everyone's hearts in the short time he'd been there. They all loved him.

On the way home, India was lost in her own thoughts, and fell off her bike, as she often did when she didn't pay attention.

"Mom, what happened?" Sam looked mildly exasperated as he helped her up. She always did that, but she hadn't gotten hurt and she was smiling at her own awkwardness, and feeling silly as Sam grinned at her. Being on the boat together and sharing its magic had suddenly made them even closer.

"I'm going to have to get one of those geriatric bikes with three wheels for next year," she said, dusting herself off.

"Yeah, I guess so." He laughed, and then, as they rode off again, they were both quiet on the way home. They were both thinking about the boat, and the people they had met there. They were impressed with Paul, but India saw him differently now that she knew Serena. Seeing them together brought things back into perspective, about how married he was and what was important in his life.

When she got home, she went straight to her darkroom. And as she worked on the photographs, she was thrilled with what she saw. The pictures of Serena were fantastic. She looked gorgeous, and India was sure she would love them. There was even a nice one of her with Paul, when he came back from his ride in the dinghy. He was draped over the back of her chair, and they both looked very glamorous with the mast above and the ocean behind them. They made a very handsome couple. And India could hardly wait to send her the pictures.

She sent them to New York by Federal

Express the next morning, and Serena called her the minute they arrived.

"You're a genius," the throaty voice said, and for an instant India didn't know who it was. "I wish I really looked like those pictures." She knew then it was Serena, and smiled.

"You look better. Do you really like them?" India was thrilled. She was proud of them, but Serena had been an easy subject.

"I love them!" Serena confirmed with admiration.

"Did you like the one of you and Paul?"

"I didn't get it." Serena sounded momentarily puzzled, and India was disappointed.

"Damn. I must have forgotten to send it. I think I left it in the darkroom. I'll send it to you. It's terrific."

"So are you. I talked to my publisher this morning, and they'll pay you for using the photographs, and of course, a credit."

"Don't worry about it," India said shyly. "They're a present. Sam had such a good time with Paul, it's just a little thing I can do to thank you."

"Don't be ridiculous, India. This is business. What would your agent say?"

"What he doesn't know won't hurt him.

I'll tell him I did them for a friend. I don't want you to pay me."

"You're hopeless. You're never going to get your career going again if you give your work away. You spent a whole morning on it, and then you had to develop them. You're a terrible businesswoman, India. I should be your agent. I can't even decide which one to pick, they're all so good." Serena went on. She was dying to show them to Paul, who was still at the office. "I'll call you and tell you which one. I wish I could use all of them, India. Really, thank you. But I wish you'd let me pay you."

"Next time," India said confidently, hoping there would be one. And after she hung up, she meant to look for the picture of Serena and Paul and then forgot all about it when Aimee came in with a splinter, and she had to remove it.

The next few days flew by, and then finally Doug arrived for the weekend. It was nearly two weeks since she'd seen him. He seemed happy to see the kids, and he was tired after the long drive. And as he always did, he took a swim before dinner. All of the children were home for dinner that night so he could see them. But they went back out to see their friends after dinner as soon as they could. They loved to play tag on the beach in the dark, and tell ghost stories, and visit each other's houses.

The Cape was the perfect place for them, and as he watched them dash out the door, Doug smiled. He was happy to be there. It was the first time India had been alone with him since he got there. They sat in the living room, and India felt awkward suddenly. So much had gone through her mind since she last saw him. Not to mention meeting Paul Ward, and the time she and Sam had spent on the *Sea Star,* and the pictures she had taken of Serena. There should have been a lot to tell him, but for some reason, she found she didn't want to. She was less anxious than she usually was to share things with him. It was as though she needed to keep something for herself now.

"So what have you been up to?" He said it as though meeting an old friend he hadn't seen since the previous summer. There had been nothing cozy or warm about his greeting, and she realized now there never had been. It was just that now she was noticing everything she had never paid attention to before. She wondered when things had changed between them.

"Not much. The usual stuff." She had talked to him often enough to hit all the high spots. "The kids are having a good summer."

"I can't wait to come up next month and stay here," he said easily. "It's been hot as hell in Westport, and worse yet in the city."

"How are all your new clients?" It was like talking to an acquaintance.

"Time consuming. I've been staying in the office till nine and ten at night. With you and the kids gone, I don't have to run for the six o'clock train. It makes it a little easier to get my work done." She nodded, thinking it was a pathetic conversation.

After two weeks apart, they ought to be able to talk about more than his clients and the heat in the city. Not once since he'd arrived had he told her that he'd missed her or loved her. She couldn't even remember the last time he had said something like that to her. And all she could think of now was why she hadn't expected him to say it to her more often. She couldn't help wondering if Paul and Serena's reunions were as lackluster as this, and she doubted it. Serena wouldn't have tolerated it for a minute. Everything about her expressed and commanded passion. But there was nothing passionate about India's relationship with Doug now. In fact, there hadn't been in nearly twenty years. It was a depressing realization.

They waited until the kids came in, talking about nothing in particular, and Doug put the TV on. And when Jessica came home, they turned off the lights and went to bed. India took a shower, assuming he would want to make love to her, and when she came out in a nightgown she knew he liked, she found he was sleeping. He was sound asleep, snoring softly, with his face buried in the pillow. And as she looked at him, feeling lonely again, she realized it was an appropriate end to the evening. And it made a statement about their life together that nothing else could have.

She slipped into bed quietly, without disturbing him, and it took her a long time to fall asleep that night, as she cried softly in the moonlight, and wished that she were anywhere but here, beside her husband.

Chapter 8

Doug and India spent the day on the beach the next day. The kids and their friends came and went, and that night Doug took them all out to dinner. They had dinner at a funny old steak house where they went every year, usually on special occasions. And they all enjoyed it.

And afterward, when they came home, Doug made love to her finally. But even that seemed different now. It seemed businesslike to her somehow, as though he didn't care if she enjoyed it. He just wanted to get it over with, and when she turned to tell him she loved him afterward, she could hear him snoring. It had definitely not been a stellar weekend for them.

And the next morning, after the children left, he turned to her with an odd expression.

"Is something wrong, India?" he asked her pointedly as she poured him a second cup of coffee. "You've been acting funny ever since I got here." She hadn't sounded like herself on the phone before that, either.

And as she looked at him, she wasn't sure how much to tell him or what to say. "I don't know. I have some things on my mind. I'm not sure if this is the right time to discuss them." She had already decided not to broach the subject of her work with him again, until he came up to join them for his vacation. She didn't want to just drop a bomb on him, and then have him drive right back to Westport. They were going to need some time to talk it over, and she knew that.

"What's bothering you? Something about the kids? Is Jess giving you trouble again?" She had been kind of snappy to her mother that winter. It was hard to believe, even for him, that there was more to life than children.

"No, she's been fine. She's been a big help, actually. They all have. It's not about them, it's about me. I've just been doing a lot of thinking."

"Then spit it out," he said impatiently,

watching her. "You know I hate it when you do this. What's the big mystery? You're not having an affair with Dick Parker, are you?" He was only kidding. He couldn't even conceive of India cheating on him. And he was right. She wouldn't. He trusted her completely. And the fact that she found Paul Ward attractive was something he would never know, and something she didn't need to tell him. She knew her attraction to him was irrelevant and would go no further.

"I've just been thinking a lot about my life, and what I want to do now."

"What in hell does that mean? Are you planning to climb Everest, or cross the North Pole in a dogsled?" He said it as though it were inconceivable that she would ever do anything worthwhile or exciting. And for the past fourteen years at least, he'd been right, she hadn't. Except bring up his children. She had become exactly what he expected her to be, "someone he could rely on to take care of the children."

She decided to cut to the chase then. "You kind of threw me when we talked before we came up here. That night at Ma Petite Amie. I somehow never thought of myself as just a 'companion, and someone you could rely on to take care of the children.' Somehow my illusions about us were a little more romantic." It hurt to even admit it to him, but that was what had started it all, that and the fact that he was adamant about her not working, and refused to understand her feelings about it, or even hear them. But in spite of that, she found it hard to say it to him.

"Oh, for chrissake, India. Don't be so sensitive. You know what I meant. I was just trying to say that after seventeen years of marriage, or fifteen, or probably even ten, you can't expect a lot of romance."

"Why not?" She looked at him squarely, and felt as though she were seeing him for the first time. "Why can't you have some romance after seventeen years? Is it too much trouble?"

"That stuff is for kids, and you know it. It goes away after a while. It's bound to. You get busy working and supporting a family and catching the six o'clock train to come home at night and when you do, you're dead tired and you don't even want to talk to anyone, let alone your wife. How romantic is that? You tell me."

"Not very. But I'm not talking about being tired, Doug. I'm talking about feelings.

About loving someone and making them feel loved. I'm not even sure anymore if you love me." There were tears in her eyes as she said it, and he looked uncomfortable and more than a little startled.

"You know I do. That's a ridiculous thing to say. What do you expect me to do? Bring you flowers every night?" He looked irritated by what she was saying.

"No. But once a year would be nice. I can't even remember the last time you did that."

"Last year on our anniversary. I brought you roses."

"Yeah, and you didn't even take me out to dinner. You said we could do that next year."

"I took you out to dinner a few weeks ago, at Ma Petite Amie, that's what started all this. It doesn't sound like such a great idea to me if this is what it leads to."

"I'm just looking at my life, and wondering what I gave up my career for. I know I gave it up for my kids. But did I give it up for a man who loves me and appreciates what I did?" It was an honest question, and now she wanted an honest answer from him.

"Is that what this is about? You working

again? I already told you that's impossible. Who's going to take care of the kids if you go back to work? It doesn't even make sense for us financially. We'd spend more than you'd make on a housekeeper, who probably wouldn't even take decent care of them. As I recall, India, your work brought in a few prizes, and practically no money. So what kind of career is that? It's a career for a kid fresh out of the Peace Corps, with no responsibilities and no reason to find a real job. Well, you have a real job now, taking care of our children. And if that's not glamorous enough for you, and you think you need to start running halfway around the world again, you'd better take a good look at what you're doing. We made a deal when you came back to New York. We'd get married and you'd work until you had kids, and then it was all over. It was nice and clear, and you didn't seem to have any problem with it, and now, fourteen years later, you want to switch the deal on me. Well, you know what? You just can't do it." He looked as though he were about to storm out of the room, but she wouldn't let him. Suddenly her eyes were blazing. He had no right to do this to her. And he had never even told her that he really loved her. He had diverted the subject completely.

"What right do you have to tell me what I can and can't do? This is my decision too. And I lived by our 'deal' as best I could. I did it fairly, and gave you plenty of value for your money, mister. But I'm not happy with it now. I feel as though I gave up too much, and you don't even give a damn about it. To you, it was just some kind of insignificant hobby you think I was pursuing. At least that's what you say and what you act like. If I'd stayed in it, I probably would have won a Pulitzer by now. That's no small deal, Doug. It's a big deal, and *that's* what I gave up to clean up after our children."

"If that was what you really wanted, then you should have stayed wherever the hell you were, Zimbabwe or Kenya or Kalamazoo, and not come back to marry me and have four children."

"I could do both if you'd let me."

"I never will. And you'd better get that loud and clear now. Because I'm not going to keep having this discussion with you. Your career, such as it was, with or without a goddamn Pulitzer, is *over*, India. Do you get that?"

"Maybe it's not my career that's over. Maybe something else is," she said bravely. There were tears running down her face, and she was choking back sobs, but Doug wasn't budging a millimeter from his position. He didn't have to. He had a career and a life, and a family, and a wife to take care of his children. He had it all exactly the way he wanted. But what did she have?

"Are you threatening me?" he asked, looking even more furious. "I don't know who's putting these ideas into your head, India—if it's that fruitcake agent of yours, Raoul, or Gail with her whoring around, or even Jenny up here playing doctor—but whoever it is, you can tell them to forget it. As far as I'm concerned, our marriage rests on your holding up your end of the bargain. This is a deal-breaker for me."

"*I* am not your business, Doug. I am not a deal you're making with a client. I'm a human being, and I'm telling you that you're starving me emotionally, and I'm going to go crazy if I don't do more with my life than just drive Sam and Aimee and Jason to school every morning. There's more to life than just sitting on my ass in Westport, dying of boredom and waiting to serve you dinner." She was sobbing as she said it, but he appeared to be entirely unmoved by it. All he felt was anger.

"You were never bored before. What the hell has happened to you?"

"I've grown up. The kids don't need me as much anymore. You have a life. And I need one too. I need more than I have right now. I'm lonely. I'm bored. I'm beginning to feel as though I'm wasting my life. I want to do something intelligent for a change, other than waiting to be of service. I need more than that. I put my own needs aside for fourteen years. Now I need just a little something more to keep me going. Is that so much to ask?"

"I don't understand what you're saying. This is crazy."

"No, it isn't," she said desperately. "But I will be if you don't start to hear me."

"I hear you. I just don't like what I'm hearing. India, you're really barking up the wrong tree here." It was rare for them to fight, but she was completely overwrought now, and he was livid. He was not going to give an inch on this subject, and she knew it. It was hopeless.

"Why won't you at least try to let me do a

couple of assignments? Maybe it would work
out. At least give it a chance."

"Why? I already know what it would be
like. I remember what it was like before we
were married. You were always up a tree
somewhere, using field telephones and dodg-
ing snipers. Is that really what you want to do
again, for chrissake? Don't you think your
children at least have a right to their mother?
Just how selfish are you?"

"Maybe half as selfish as you are. What
kind of mother are they going to have if I
have no self-esteem and I'm pissed off all the
time because I'm so goddamn bored and
lonely?"

"If that's what you want, India, then find
a new husband."

"Do you really mean that?" She was
looking at him in utter amazement, wondering if he would dare to go that far. But he
might. He seemed to feel just that strongly
about it. But her question, and the look in her
eyes when she asked it, sobered him a little.

"I don't know. I might. I need to think
about it. If this is really what you want, if
you're willing to push it this far, then maybe
we both need to rethink our marriage."

"I can't believe you'd sacrifice us just because you're not willing to compromise, and think about my feelings for a change. I've done it your way for a hell of a long time. Maybe it's time to try mine now."

"You're not even thinking of the children."

"I am. And I have for a long time. But maybe now it's my turn."

She had never said anything even remotely like that to him. And he certainly wasn't going to tell her now that he loved her. In fact, as he listened to her, he was almost sure he didn't. How could he? She was violating the deal she'd made with him, sacrificing their children, as far as he was concerned, and jeopardizing their marriage. As far as Doug was concerned, there wasn't much to love there.

And she was desperate to make one last stab at making him understand her. "Doug, what I did wasn't just a job. It was kind of an art form. It was a part of me. It's how I express myself, what's in my mind, my heart, my soul. It's why I never stopped carrying my camera. I need it to let a kind of light shine through me. What you see with your eyes, I see with my heart. I've given that up for a long time. Now I just want a little piece of it back again, like part of me I gave up, and just found I miss too much. Maybe I need that to be who I am. I don't know. I don't understand it myself, I just know that all of a sudden I realize it's important to me." But she also realized it wasn't to him. That was the bottom line for her husband. He just couldn't understand what she was saying. He didn't get it. And he didn't want to.

"You should have thought of all that seventeen years ago when you married me. You had the choice then. I thought you made the right one, and so did you. If you don't feel that way now, then we have to face it."

"All we need to face is that I need a little more in my life. Some air, some breathing room, a way to express myself and be me again . . . a way to feel that I matter in the world too, and not just you. And even more important than that, I need to know you love me."

"I'm not going to love you, India, if you pull this kind of bullshit on me. And that's all it is, as far as I'm concerned. A load of bullshit. You're being a spoiled brat, and you're letting me and our kids down."

"I'm sorry you can't hear what I'm saying," she said, crying softly, and with that, he left the room, without saying a word to her, or reaching out to touch her or take her in his arms, or tell her he loved her. At that moment, he just didn't. And he was too angry to listen to her for another minute. Instead, he walked into their bedroom and packed his suitcase.

"What are you doing?" she asked when she saw what he was doing.

"I'm going back to Westport. And I'm not coming up next weekend. I don't need to drive for six hours in order to listen to you rant and rave about your 'career.' I think we need a breather from each other." She didn't disagree with him, but she felt abandoned by him when she saw what he was doing.

"What makes you so sure that you know what's right for us, and me, and our kids? Why do you always get to make the rules?"

"Because that's the way it is, India. It's the way it's always been. And if you don't like it, you can leave me."

"You make it sound very simple." But it wasn't, and she knew that.

"Maybe it is. Maybe it's just that simple." He stood up and looked at her, with his bag in his hand, and she couldn't believe how quickly their marriage was unraveling, after seventeen years and four children. Apparently, it had to be his way, or no way. The inequity of it was staggering, but he wasn't even willing to negotiate with her, or even bother to tell her he loved her. He didn't love her enough, in fact, to care what she felt or needed. It was all about him, and the "deal" they had made. That was the bottom line for him, and he was not willing to renegotiate the contract. "Say good-bye to the kids for me. I'll see you in two weeks. I hope you come to your senses by then." He had dug in his heels, but even if she wanted to, India wasn't sure she could change now. In the past few weeks, she had become too aware of what was missing, and what she needed.

"Why are you being so stubborn about this? Sometimes we have to make changes in life, to adjust to new ideas and new situations."

"We don't need new ideas, and neither do our kids. They just need their mother doing what she's supposed to do for them. And that's all I need from you."

"Why don't you just hire a housekeeper? Then if she doesn't toe the line, or live up to the 'deal' for you, you can just fire her?"

"Maybe I'll have to, if you decide to follow in your father's footsteps."

"I'm not that stupid. I'm not asking you to let me go to war zones. I just want to cover a couple of decent stories."

"I'm not asking you anything," he said in an ice-cold tone. "I'm telling you that at the end of the summer, when we go back to Westport, you'd better be in your right mind again, and ready to give up all this nonsense. You'd better be ready to take care of our kids, and do what you signed on for." She had never realized how insensitive he was, how totally indifferent to her feelings. As long as she played the game the way he expected her to, it was fine. But with different needs, different ideas, different anything, it was unacceptable to him. He had made himself perfectly clear to her, clearer than he'd ever been, and she hated everything she was hearing. This was a lot worse than just boring. This was vicious.

He walked to the front door then, and turned one last time to look at her, and issue a final ultimatum. "I mean it, India. Pull yourself back together again, or you'll regret it." She already did, but she didn't say a word to him as he left, and stood silently at the kitchen window watching him drive down the driveway. She couldn't believe what was happening to them, what he had said to her, and what he hadn't. She was still crying when Sam walked in. She didn't even hear him come into the kitchen behind her.

"Where's Dad?" he asked, wondering. He thought maybe he was walking on the beach with Crockett.

"He left," India said flatly, wiping her eyes as she turned to face him. She didn't want him to see her crying.

"He forgot to say good-bye," Sam said, looking surprised.

"He had to go back for a meeting."

"Oh. I'm going across the street to John's house."

"Be home in time for dinner," she said, turning to smile at him. Her eyes were still damp, but he didn't see it. He only saw her smiling, and looked no further. "I love you, Sam," she said softly, and he grinned.

"Yeah . . . I know, Mom. I love you too." And then he was gone, and the front door slammed, and she watched him walk across the street to his friend's house. He had no idea what had just happened, but India had the feeling that their lives were about to change forever.

She could have called Doug in the car, she could have told him she'd changed her mind, she could have done a lot of things, but she knew that she couldn't now. There was no turning back anymore, all she could do was go forward.

Chapter 9

Doug only called her a couple of times in the next two weeks until he came up again. And when he did, the atmosphere was strained between them. He made no reference to what had happened the last time, and neither did India. But she had done a lot of thinking about her marriage, and she'd been tempted to call Raoul, her agent, to put her name at the top of the list for local work, but she had decided to wait until the end of the summer to call him. She wanted to explore the possibilities in her mind, and the risks, and the potential impact on her children. And she needed to talk to Doug again. They had some things to work out, now more than ever. But she didn't want to do anything hasty. She still wanted to go back to work, but the stakes were high, and she wanted to be sure she knew what she was doing.

Doug didn't even try to make love to her and he scarcely spoke to her all weekend. He acted as though she had committed an unpardonable transgression against him. And on Sunday after he left, Jason looked at her with eyes full of questions. He was the closest to his father.

"Are you mad at Dad?" he asked her directly while he helped her set the table.

"No. Why?" She didn't want to say anything to the children about their earlier conversation. They didn't need to know about the chill between them. There was no point upsetting them. It had been hard enough spending the weekend with Doug virtually not speaking to each other.

"You never talked to him all weekend."

"I guess I was just tired. And he had a lot of work to finish up before he comes back for his vacation." He was coming back to stay for three weeks the following weekend, and she was no longer looking forward to it. But maybe it would do them good. She hoped so. She still couldn't believe he was willing to put their marriage on the line just because she wanted to do a few stories. It hardly seemed worth it. But she was also not willing to promise him that she wouldn't do them. That seemed too unfair to her. It all did.

Jason seemed satisfied with her answer, and went back out to meet friends on the beach, and he brought two of them home for dinner. But even their meal was quiet that night. It was as though they all sensed that something was wrong, although they didn't really know it. But children were like animals sometimes, without knowing things, they sensed them. She was lying in bed reading that night, when the phone rang. She wondered if it was Doug, calling to apologize for another lousy weekend. At least this time there had been no threats, no ultimatums, and no explosions. Only silence and depression.

She reached for the phone, expecting to hear Doug, and was startled instead to hear Paul Ward. His voice was so clear he sounded as though he were standing in her bedroom.

"Where are you?" she asked, surprised to hear him. She couldn't imagine why he was calling, unless he was coming back up to the Cape, and wanted to invite Sam to join him, as he had promised. Sam was prepared to remember that promise forever.

"I'm on the boat. It's four o'clock in the morning, and we're coming into Gibraltar. I decided to make the crossing to Europe on the *Sea Star*." It sounded very brave to her, but she knew that he had done it often and loved it. He had told Sam all about it over lunch at the New Seabury yacht club.

"That sounds pretty exciting." India smiled, hearing him. He sounded so happy on his boat, sailing across the ocean. "I assume Serena isn't with you?"

He laughed at her question. She had already known the answer to that one. "No, she's in London, meeting with her British publishers. She flew over on the Concorde. What about you? How are you?"

"I'm fine." She wondered if she should tell him the truth, about her fight with Doug, and his ultimatum two weeks before. She knew he'd be upset for her. "What's it like out there?"

"Wonderful. Peaceful. We've had great weather and an easy crossing."

"You'll have to tell Sam all about it." She still wondered why he had called her. Particularly at four in the morning his time. Maybe he was just bored, and wanted someone to talk to.

"I was thinking about you. I was wondering how you are, and how your plan to go back to work was going. Have you talked about it any more with your husband?"

"I have," she sighed, "two weeks ago. He hasn't spoken to me since then. He was just here, and we had a very chilly weekend, and I don't mean the weather." It was nice to be able to talk to him. For some reason, he felt like an old friend, although she wasn't sure why. But Gail was still in Europe and there was no one else she wanted to confide in. "He more or less said that if I go back to work, at all, he'd leave me. Or at least he hinted at it. He said it was a deal-breaker for him." She sounded discouraged as she said it.

"And what about for you, India? How do you feel about it?"

"Pretty lousy. He just doesn't want to know how I feel about it. I don't know, Paul . . . I think he means it. It's a big decision, and it may not be worth it."

"And if you give in to him? How will you feel about it?" He sounded as though he cared about what was happening to her, and she was touched by it.

"I think I'll feel kind of dead inside if I back down," she answered him. "But losing my marriage is a high price to pay for a little self-esteem and some independence."

"You have to make that decision, India. No one else can make it for you. You know what I think."

"I know what Serena would do," India said with a rueful smile. "I wish I were as gutsy as she is."

"You are in your own way. You just don't know it." But in her heart of hearts, India knew she wasn't. Serena wouldn't have put up with Doug for five minutes, but she wouldn't have married him either. India had, and now she had to live with it. But the thought of letting him threaten her depressed her. He wasn't giving her much to go on these days, no warmth, no understanding, no support and no affection. And she realized now that he hadn't in a long time. They had just been involved in the mechanics of raising their children. And suddenly that wasn't enough any longer. "How's my friend Sam?" Paul asked her then, and they both smiled as they thought of him.

"Sound asleep right this minute. He's

been having fun with his friends, and telling everyone about the *Sea Star*."

"I wish he were here with me. . . . I wish you were too," he said in an odd tone, which ran the same current of electricity through her she had felt before when talking to him. There was something powerful about him, and she wasn't sure what he was saying, or why he was calling. He wasn't making any kind of overt pass at her, and she somehow knew that he wouldn't. But she also sensed that he liked her. "You'd love the crossing. I just know it. It's so peaceful." It was one of his favorite things to do. He read and slept, and took the watch whenever he felt like it, as he had just done. It was why he had called her at that ungodly hour. But he had been thinking of her all night, as he looked out over the ocean, and finally decided to call her. "We'll be going to the south of France in a few days. But I have to do some business in Paris first. Serena is going to fly over to meet me. Paris is just her cup of tea. Mine too," he confessed. It was one of his favorite cities.

"I haven't been there in ages," India said dreamily, remembering the last time she'd been there. She'd been very young and stayed at a youth hostel. She was sure he stayed someplace like the Ritz or the Plaza Athénée or the Crillon. "Where do you stay?"

"At the Ritz. Serena loves it. I sometimes stay at the Crillon. But she prefers the Ritz. I'm not sure I can tell the difference. I don't speak French, she does, of course. I always feel like a fool trying to talk to cabdrivers and negotiate my way around Paris. Do you speak French, India?"

"Enough to get around and feed myself. But not enough to make intelligent conversation. I actually learned a lot when I spent six weeks in Morocco once, but my French friends all made fun of my accent. But at least I can get by in a taxi, or at the press club."

"Serena spent a year at the Sorbonne. She speaks amazing French." Serena was, in every possible way, a tough act to follow. More than tough. Impossible. But no one was ever going to follow in her footsteps. It was easy to see that they were crazy about each other. "When do you go back to Westport, by the way?"

"Not till the end of August." They didn't have a lot to talk about, but it was nice just listening to him, and knowing where he was, at four o'clock in the morning. "The kids have to go back to school then. And I have to get them organized." He laughed at the thought of it. He wanted something more for her, and hoped she would have the courage to reach out and take it. "How long will you be in Europe?"

"Till Labor Day. But Serena has to go back to L.A. before that. I'm not sure she minds. She builds herself outs, so she doesn't have to stay anywhere for too long. She's very independent, and she gets antsy, particularly on the boat."

"She'd hate it here then. I don't do anything but lie on the beach all day, and come up to the house at six o'clock to cook dinner."

"It sounds like the good life to me, and the kids must love it."

"They do. But life is a lot more fun on the *Sea Star,* believe me. That seems like the perfect existence."

"It is. For the right people. You have to really love that life, being on boats, sailing and being out on the ocean. I think it's either in your blood or it isn't. It's not an acquired taste for most people. You fall in love with it early, like I did. I was about Sam's age when I first realized how much I loved it."

"I never knew how wonderful it was until we sailed on your boat. It's an incredible way to start. I'm afraid you've spoiled me forever. Not to mention Sam, who'll never want anything less now."

"Oh yes, he will. He's a real sailor like me. He even loved the dinghy. That's the true test, and he passed it with flying colors."

"I think I'll stick to the big ones."

"That's probably a good decision. There'll be a lot of beautiful boats here, especially some lovely classics. One of these days, I'm going to buy one. Serena will probably divorce me when I do it. One boat is bad enough, but two boats? I don't think I'd have the guts to tell her." He laughed at the prospect.

"She probably expects it of you," India said, laughing. It was so good to hear him, and talk to him. If she closed her eyes, she could just see him standing on the deck of the *Sea Star*, with Sam beside him, or talking to her in the cockpit, while Sam chatted with the captain. They had had such a terrific day when they sailed with him.

He told her then about the races he was going to in Sardinia, and the people he was going to see, the Aga Khan among them.

"It's a shame you travel in such shabby

circles, Paul," India teased him. "It's a long way from Westport."

"So is Botswana, and you need to get back there," he pushed her. He could sense that she still needed encouragement and prodding. Maybe now more than ever, with her husband threatening her. It was so rotten of him to do that. Paul hated to think of her wasting her talent, but he suspected easily that Doug was threatened. He didn't want India to have a more interesting life than he did. It would make his life seem meaningless and boring. Paul couldn't help wondering if Doug was jealous of her.

"Sometimes I wonder if I'll see any of those places again," she said sadly. "I can't even get Doug to Europe."

"I wish you were here with us. I know you'd love it. By the way, I saw the mock-up of Serena's book cover with the picture you took on it. It looks fantastic."

"I'm glad. It was fun to do it." India smiled, thinking of the morning she had spent with her.

They talked for a few more minutes, and she thought he sounded tired. It was late for him.

"I'd better go now," he said after a few

more minutes of chatting with her. "We have a little navigating to do. We're getting closer. And the sun will be coming up soon." She could just imagine him on the boat, talking to her, as they approached Gibraltar. It sounded exquisitely exotic. And very romantic. "I suppose you'll be going to sleep now." He liked thinking of her there, in her quiet life on Cape Cod. It seemed wonderfully peaceful, and he was glad he had been there to meet her. "Think about the *Sea Star*, and hopefully, one of these days, you and Sam will be on it again."

"I can't think of anything nicer."

"I can," he said, and there was a sudden silence between them. She didn't know what to say then. She was glad she had met him, and she valued the friendship he offered her. Enough not to jeopardize it, or say anything foolish she'd regret. But he didn't say anything more to her either. They both knew better.

She thanked him for calling, and they hung up a moment later. And she did exactly as he had suggested. She lay in bed and thought of him sailing toward Gibraltar on the *Sea Star*. She imagined it all lit up as it had been when it drifted past her house that night when he'd been there, looking like a magic island filled with dreams and happy people. And now she could see him on the bridge, alone in the dark just before the dawn, heading toward Gibraltar. But she didn't dream of Paul that night, or his pleasant life on the *Sea Star*. Instead, she had nightmares about Doug, and he was shouting at her. That was her reality, and the one she had to resolve or live with. For her, the *Sea Star* was nothing more than a dream, a distant star in someone else's heaven.

Chapter 10

When Doug arrived in Harwich for his three-week vacation, there was still tension between them. The subject of her working never came up again, nor did any of the things they'd said before, but the remaining aura their words had left behind hung over them like a constant cloud of vapor. At times, India felt as though she could hardly see through it, and she felt as though she were moving through a fog, and living with a stranger. The children noticed it as well, but none of them said anything. It would have been too frightening for any of them to acknowledge the malaise that remained tangible but unspoken and unresolved between their parents. It was like a bad smell that hung in the air and couldn't be ignored. But it was only in the last few days of their stay in Harwich that India finally said something to him.

"What are we going to do about all this when we go back?" she asked cautiously. The children were out, spending final moments with their friends. There was always a kind of frenzy about the end of the vacation. Usually, they gave a barbecue, but they had decided not to this year. That in itself was a statement of sorts, but India didn't question Doug's decision when he said he didn't want to do it. Neither did she. She was tired of the pretense that everything was all right between them. For the first time in seventeen years, it wasn't. The angry seeds that had been sown in June had grown into a tree whose branches had begun to choke them. And India didn't know whether to chop it down, or hope it would wither on its own. The solution to the problem was still a mystery to her.

"What do you mean?" Doug pretended not to know what she was talking about, but it was hard to ignore the unfriendly atmosphere between them, and she wanted to do something about it before they went home, and it poisoned their daily routine. It was bad enough to have sacrificed the summer to it, but a line had to be drawn somewhere before it was too late.

"It's been a pretty lousy summer, wouldn't you say?" India said, looking across the kitchen table at him. They had just had lunch, and neither of them had said a word to each other.

"We've both been busy. Some years are like that," he said vaguely, but they both knew it was a lie. No year had ever been like this between them, and she hoped it would never be like this again.

"You've been busy, and we've both been upset and angry. I'd like to know where things stand. We can't go on like this forever. Something's got to ease up, or we'll both go nuts." It was just too lonely, never speaking to each other, never touching, each of them trapped on separate islands with no boat, no bridge to join them. She had never felt as alone as this in her entire life. She felt abandoned by him, deserted. He felt she had betrayed him, by saying the things she had, pressing him about going back to work, and asking him to give more than he ever had.

"Maybe I should ask you where you stand? That's what this is all about, isn't it? Your pushing me about going back to work. Is that what you still have in mind when we go back to Westport?" But she was no longer sure now. The price was high. Maybe too high. He had said it was a deal-breaker, and she believed him, and she wasn't prepared to break the deal they had, not yet at least, and maybe never.

"All I wanted to do was let them know that I'd be willing to do a story from time to time, preferably close to home, and nothing on a long assignment. I just want to open the door a crack."

"That crack will eventually flood our lives and drown us. You know that. In fact, I think it's what you have in mind, India, and you know it."

"You're wrong, Doug. I turned down the job in Korea. I'm not looking to destroy our lives, just save mine." But she had realized it was more than that. Even if he let her do an assignment from time to time, it didn't solve the problem of how he felt about her, how dry and dreary he felt about their life. She knew now that she was something less than the woman he loved. She was a helpmate, a convenience, a caretaker for his children. But there was no passion in what he felt for her, no excitement, no romance. She could no longer fool herself about their marriage—whether she worked or not.

"I told you very clearly," he went on, "how I felt about your working. None of that has changed. What you do about it is your choice. If you want to take that chance, go ahead."

"That's a pretty terrifying challenge, Doug," she said, with tears in her eyes. "It's like daring me to jump off the roof, without telling me if there will be a net to catch me when I fall."

"What difference does it make? You don't seem to care about that anyway, do you? You're willing to sacrifice our kids, our life, and the agreement we made, to do what you want. If that's what you want, then take the chance." It was as if he was daring her to do it.

"I'm not that stupid. But you have to realize that you're taking a chance too. If you don't care what I feel, you have to realize that sooner or later it's going to take a toll on us. In fact," she said quietly, thinking of the past few weeks, and even the month before that, "it already has."

"It sounds like we're screwed either way." He looked nonplussed. The only real emotion he still seemed to have about it was anger, and absolutely no compassion for her, or at least that was how she felt about it. "Do whatever you want, India. It sounds like you will anyway."

"Not necessarily. I don't want to be irresponsible. And I never wanted to cause a revolution," she said sadly.

"Sure you did, India. That's what this is all about. But let me just tell you clearly one more time. You can't have everything you want. You can't have me, and our family, and a career. Sooner or later, you're going to have to make a choice here." But the choice he was asking her to make would cost her her self. That was the problem for her now.

"I guess you've made that pretty clear. And if I don't go back to work? Then what? You think I'm wonderful and fabulous and devoted and you adore me and are grateful for the rest of my life?" She said it bitterly, and she suddenly remembered the things Paul had said about giving up too much, and what it would do to her in the end. She didn't want to be bitter and miserable, and feel cheated for the rest of her life, as she did now.

"I don't know what you're talking about," Doug said, looking angry. "I think you've gone completely crazy, and I wish I knew who put this crap into your head. I still think it was Gail." It had been a lot of things, a lot of people, a lot of dreams she had finally remembered, which she had given up for so long. It was something Gail had said in June, and the things Doug hadn't, and talking to Paul, and meeting Serena. And now it was all the thinking she had done for the past three months, and Doug's coldness to her. He hadn't touched her since July. She knew it was her punishment for all she'd said. And she couldn't help wondering now how long the punishment would continue.

"You act as though you expect an award for being a wife and mother. India, that's your job. I don't get an award for doing mine. They don't give Pulitzers or Nobel prizes for leading a normal life. This is what you signed on for. If you're expecting a prize for this, or if you're expecting me to kiss your feet every time you pick the kids up at school, India, don't. I don't know what's gotten into you, but if you want to be a career woman, or a photographer floating all over the world, you're going to have to pay a price to do that."

"I feel like I already have just for talking to you about it, Doug. You've been punishing me for the last two months." He didn't answer, and all she could see in his eyes was ice and anger.

"I think you've been unfair, dishonest, and you've betrayed all of us with what you're saying. You never told me you'd want to go back to work one day. You never said anything about that." It was obvious how betrayed he felt from everything he'd done to her since she first said it.

"I didn't know," she said honestly. "I never really thought I'd want to go back, and for all intents and purposes, I don't. I just want to do a story from time to time." By now, it was a familiar chorus between them.

"That's the same thing." He stood up then, and looked at her with rigid disapproval, and what looked to her like strong aversion. "We've said enough about all this. Make up your mind."

She nodded, and watched him go, and she stood in the kitchen alone for a long time. She could see her children playing on the beach as she looked out the window, and she wondered if it would really be as terrible for them as he said. Would it be such a shock, such a blow, such a betrayal? Somehow she just couldn't bring herself to believe that.

Other women worked and traveled and still managed to take care of their children, and their kids didn't all end up in jail and on drugs as a result. It was Doug who wanted her there every moment, nailed to the floor, doing the job he had hired her on for, without offering her either compassion or love. It was Doug who was forcing her to make the choice. But a choice between what and what? Did she owe him total obedience, like a galley slave, with the chance to be little more than his house-keeper and companion? Or did she owe her-self something more? She knew what Paul would have said.

And as she stood there, thinking about it again, she knew it was hopeless. He was never going to come around, or agree to what she wanted. In fact, she had no choice, unless she was willing to give him up. And for now at any rate, that still seemed too high a price to pay for just a taste of freedom.

She said nothing to him when she went into the bedroom to pack their things. She made no announcement, she never told him she'd made up her mind. She just gave up. The dreams she had came at too high a price, and she knew it.

She was very quiet that night at dinner,

which was unlike her. She told the kids to pack their things the next day, and she did everything she had to, to close the house. She didn't go to see the Parkers to say good-bye, or anyone else that year. She just did what was expected of her, what her "job" was, as Doug said, and when it was time to leave, she got in the car with the others.

They stopped at McDonald's on the way home, and she ordered for the kids and Doug, fed the dog, and ate nothing herself. And when they got home and unloaded the car, she went inside, and Jessica turned to her father.

"What's wrong with Mom? Is she sick or something?" They had all noticed it, but she was the only one who dared to ask him.

"I think she's just tired," Doug said calmly. "It's a big job closing the house." Jessica nodded, wanting to believe him, but her mother had closed the house every summer, and she had never looked like that. She looked drawn and pale and unhappy, and more than once Jessica was sure she'd seen tears in her mother's eyes when India thought no one was looking. Her parents never said a word to each other on the entire trip back to Westport.

And finally that night, India said something to Doug. She turned to look at him as they were getting ready for bed, and fought back tears as she told him. "I'm not going to take my name off the roster. But I won't take any assignments if they call."

"What's the point of that? Why not do it cleanly? If you're not going to take the jobs, why let them call?"

"Why not? Eventually they'll stop calling anyway. It's just good for my ego when they call to know they still want me." He looked at her for a long moment, and then shrugged. He wanted not only her heart, but her liver and her kidneys. It wasn't enough that she had given in to him, he wanted to drive home the point. Even though he knew he'd won. He wanted to be sure the subject would never come up again. He wanted to know he owned her. And more importantly, he wanted her to know it.

He didn't thank her, didn't praise her, didn't tell her she'd done a great thing for mankind, or for him, and that he was grateful for it. He just walked into their bathroom, closed the door, and took a shower. India was already in bed when he came out half an hour later.

He turned off the lights, slipped into bed beside her, lay there for a while, and then finally turned toward her in silence, and ran lazy fingers down her back.

"Still awake?" he whispered.

"Yes." In some remote part of her she was waiting for him to tell her he loved her, that he was sorry it had been so rough for her, that he would cherish her and make her happy for the rest of her life. Instead, he reached a hand around her in silence and touched her breast, and she could feel her whole body turn to granite. She wanted to turn around and slap him for what he had done to her, for what he hadn't said, for how little he cared about her feelings, but she said nothing to him as she lay with her back turned to him in the darkness.

He tried caressing her for a little while, and she showed no reaction, and didn't turn toward him as she always had. And after a while, he stopped.

They lay side by side in the dark, with a chasm between them the size of an ocean. It was an ocean of sorrow and pain and disappointment. He had defeated her, he had won. And she had lost a part of herself. All she had now was a job. She could cook for him, clean for him, drive for their children, and make sure they were warmly dressed in winter. She could ask him how his day had been at the office, when he wasn't too tired to answer. She could give him what she had promised him years before, for better or worse. And as far as India was concerned, this was worse. And better was far, far behind them.

Chapter 11

Gail had called India several times when they got back from Harwich, but they had missed each other. She left cheery messages on the answering machine but she was never home when India called her back. They had spoken to each other twice after Gail got back from Europe, and she had a feeling something was wrong, but India insisted everything was fine when she asked her.

Gail said the trip to Europe had been more fun than she expected. Jeff had actually been more entertaining than usual, and by some miracle, despite long hours in the car, the kids managed not to fight with each other. It had been the best trip they'd ever had.

The two women didn't actually run into

each other until the first day of school, and they finally met in the parking lot after Sam and Gail's twins had gone inside. But the moment Gail saw her, she could see that something terrible had happened to India that summer.

"My God, are you all right?" India hadn't had time to braid her hair that morning. She'd had to do double car pools for Jessica, and the other kids, and she felt frazzled and knew she looked a little wild and disheveled.

"I didn't have time to brush my hair," she said, running her hand over the blond mane with a smile. "Do I look that bad?"

"Yes," Gail said honestly, with worried eyes examining her, "but it's not your hair. You look like you've lost ten pounds."

"What's wrong with that?"

"Nothing. Except you look like someone died." She had. But she hadn't wanted to tell Gail about it. "What happened to you? Did you get sick this summer?" Gail looked genuinely worried.

"Sort of," she said vaguely, trying to avoid Gail's eyes, but as usual, she was unsuccessful. Gail had a terrier quality to her when she wanted to know something.

"Oh, Jesus. Are you pregnant?" But she

didn't look like it. She looked miserable and dead inside. There was a lot more wrong with her than morning sickness. "Have you got time for a cappuccino?"

"I guess so," India said limply. She had some things to organize at home, a stack of laundry to do, and a list of women to call to confirm her car pools.

"I'll meet you at 'Caffe Latte' in five minutes."

They both got in their cars, and Gail was already ordering for them when India got there. She knew exactly the way India liked it. Cappuccino with a splash of low-fat milk, two sugars. Five minutes later, they were at a corner table, with two chocolate-covered biscotti between them.

"You didn't say anything when I called you in Harwich. What in hell has been going on with you this summer?" Gail was upset as she looked at her. She had never seen India so miserable or so lifeless, and she only hoped she didn't have some terrible physical problem. At their age, there was always that to think of, like breast cancer. As Gail watched her, India took a sip of the cappuccino and said nothing for a moment. "Is it you and Doug?" she asked with a moment of insight.

"Maybe. Actually it's me. I don't know. . . . The ball started rolling in June and it's turned into an avalanche since then."

"What ball?" What was she talking about? But Gail just sat there and listened for a minute, while India said nothing. "Did you have an affair on the Cape?" She knew that was preposterous, but it was worth asking anyway. You never knew about people. Sometimes the quiet, loyal ones like India fell the hardest. But if she'd had an affair, it certainly didn't look like it had gone well.

"After you and I talked, before school let out," India began to explain painfully, "I started thinking about working again. It was when I turned down the job in Korea. I don't know . . . maybe that was what did it . . . I honestly don't know what did. But I started thinking that I might enjoy doing stories again once in a while, nothing big, just like the one in Harlem."

"That was pretty big, India. You should have won an award for it. It was a very important piece of journalism."

"Well, anyway, I was thinking that I could do stories around here . . . in New York . . . in the States at any rate, as long as it wasn't for too long, or too far away. . . . I thought maybe I could find someone to help with the kids if I did that."

"That's terrific." Gail looked pleased for her, but it was obvious there was more to the story. "And then what?"

"Doug went crazy. He basically threatened to leave me if I did, to put it in a nutshell. We practically haven't talked to each other all summer, or done anything else with each other, for that matter," she said darkly, and Gail was quick to get the gist of her meaning.

"It sounds like he's being an asshole," Gail said bluntly.

"You might say that. He put it in no uncertain terms. He basically forbade me to do any assignments. He said I had betrayed him, that I was breaking the 'deal' I made with him when I married him, that I'd destroy our family, and he wouldn't put up with it. Basically, my choices are that I can do some work and he'll walk out on me, or I can keep my mouth shut, keep doing what I've done for fourteen years, and stay married. It's that simple."

"What's the payoff here for you? What do you get out of it if you sacrifice your talent for him, just to soothe his ego? Because it sounds to me like he's threatened, and he's bullying the hell out of you. What's he offering you to sweeten the deal?"

"Nothing. And that's the other thing . . ." India said as tears sprang to her eyes as she put down her cappuccino. "We had sort of a dumb conversation in June when he took me out to dinner. He made it sound like I'm some kind of a workhorse he bought years ago. He 'expects' me to take care of his kids, and just be there. But to tell you the truth, Gail," the tears overflowed then and rolled down her cheeks slowly, "I'm not even sure he loves me." India's voice caught on a sob as she said it.

"He probably does." Gail looked at her sympathetically, she felt sorry for her. India looked so desperately unhappy. "He just may not know it, or how to show it. He's not that different from Jeff. He thinks I'm part of the furniture, but if he ever lost me, it would probably kill him."

"I'm not sure Doug feels that way. He made it sound like he owns me, but not like he loves me. I don't think he does. And if he does, I'm so mad at him anyway, I'm not even sure I care anymore. It's the most godawful feeling . . . I feel like my whole life fell apart this summer." Gail watched her as she listened, wondering what else had happened. She suspected there was more to it, although what she had heard was enough to upset anyone. India felt ignored, unloved, and unimportant to her husband. "Anyway, I told him I wouldn't take any assignments anymore, even the ones like Harlem. I'll keep my name on the roster, but I won't take anything they give me. I just can't do it. I think he really would leave me. We argued about it for two months, and it wrecked our whole summer. If I hold out for what I want, it'll destroy our life, and I don't want that."

"So you give up what you want?" It made Gail's blood boil, but the theory wasn't unfamiliar to her. "And what did he say? Did he *thank you*? Does he get it?"

"No. He just seemed to expect it. But the night I told him, he tried to make love to me for the first time in nearly two months. I almost hit him. And he hasn't touched me since then. What I don't know is where I go from here . . . what do I do? Suddenly all the things I did without even questioning them don't feel right anymore. I feel like I lost a part of myself this summer, and I don't know how to get it back again, or if I ever will. I feel like I gave him my heart and my insides."

Looking at her, Gail was truly worried. It was obvious that India felt destroyed over what had happened, and she wasn't sure what to say to make her feel better. To Gail, this was why women had affairs, and cheated on their husbands, to find someone who made them feel loved and cherished and important. And Gail knew, maybe even more than India did, that Doug had taken a hell of a chance with his position. He may have thought he'd won, but Gail wasn't so sure yet. India was really hurting.

"What else did you do this summer, other than cry, and fight with Doug? Did you have any fun at all, go anywhere with the kids, meet new people?" She was trying to distract her. It seemed like all she could do now. And at the question she asked, India brightened.

"I met Serena Smith," she said, wiping her eyes, and blowing her nose in the paper napkin. She looked and felt awful, which confirmed to Gail what she had thought in the first place. Doug Taylor was an asshole.

"The writer?" Gail looked interested immediately. She had read everything she'd ever written. "How'd you manage that?"

"She was a friend's college roommate, and her husband came to Harwich with his sailboat. Sam and I went out on it with him, and he was wonderful to Sam. We got to know him before Serena got there. I did a book cover shot for her, and she seemed pretty happy with it." Talking about Serena reminded India that she had brought the photograph of Serena and Paul back to Westport with her, but she still hadn't had time to send it to her.

"Who's she married to?" Gail said, finishing her cappuccino.

"Paul Ward, he's a financier of some kind," she said, looking pensive for a moment, and Gail stopped as she watched her.

"*The* Paul Ward? The Wizard of Wall Street?"

"I guess so. He's a nice man. She's very lucky."

"He's also gorgeous. He was on the cover of *Time* last year for some big deal he made. He must be worth billions."

"They have a wonderful sailboat. But she hates it." India smiled as she said it, remembering their conversations about Serena's aversion to the *Sea Star,* and the funny things Paul said about it.

"Wait a minute." Gail narrowed her eyes at her friend with increasing interest, and suspicion. "Are you telling me you went out on the boat with him, *before* she got there?"

"She was in L.A., working on a movie."

Gail was never one to mince words, and she had known India for years. There was something in her friend's eyes now that caught her attention. "India, are you in love with him? Is that part of all this?" She was more astute than India wanted to believe, or would allow herself to acknowledge, even about her own feelings.

"Don't be silly."

"Bullshit. The guy looks like Gary Cooper or Clark Gable or something. *Time* magazine called him 'indecently handsome, and ruggedly alluring.' I remember what he looks like. And you and Sam went out on his boat with him? . . . Then what?"

"We kind of made friends. We talked a lot. He's very smart about people. But he's also crazy about Serena."

"That's nice for her. What about you? Did he come on to you on the boat?"

"Of course not." Even the question was offensive. She knew Paul would never have done that. Nor would she have let him if he had. They respected each other.

"Has he called you?"

"Not really." India's eyes told a different story, and Gail saw it instantly. India was protecting something, as though she had a secret about Paul.

"Wait a minute. There is calling, and not calling. What is 'not really'? Not really is calling and getting a busy signal. Did he call you?" She was digging, but she also had India's best interests at heart, and India knew that. And nothing would have shocked Gail if it had been a different story, but it wasn't.

"Yeah. He called me. Once. From Gibraltar. He was on the boat, on his way to Europe."

"On his sailboat? It must be the size of the *QE II*." She looked impressed and India laughed at her.

"It's pretty big, and really wonderful. Sam loved it."

"And what about you? Did you love it too?"

"Yes. I loved it. And I liked him. He's a wonderful man, and I think he likes me. But he's married, and so am I, and my life is falling apart and it has nothing to do with Paul Ward, believe me."

"I understand that. But he might provide

a little relief from your miseries. Did he ask to see you?"

"Of course not. Anyway, he's in Europe."

"How do you know?" Gail was fascinated by him, and by India meeting such illustrious people.

"He said he was going to be there till after Labor Day."

"With Serena?"

"I think she was going home early."

"Did he ask you to join him?"

"Will you stop? There is nothing to this, I promise. He said he'd love to have me on the boat with my children sometime. He's a friend, that's all. Forget it. And I'm not going to have an affair with anyone. I just gave up my career, or any hope of it, forever, for my husband. If I wanted to lose my marriage, I could take an assignment, for chrissake. I don't have to have an affair to fuck my life up any further."

"It might actually help it," Gail said thoughtfully, although for once she didn't really think so. India wasn't the type to enjoy it. She was too straight-arrow to play the games Gail did, and Gail loved her for it. She had a lot of respect for her, and she was sorry to see her in such bad shape now, and she had no idea how to help her. She thought Doug was a fool, and an insensitive bastard, but if India wanted to stay married to him, there wasn't anything anyone could do about it to help her. She had to play the game his way. No matter what it cost her.

"Maybe he'll call you again sometime," Gail said hopefully, but India only shrugged. She knew he wasn't the answer to her problems.

"I don't think he'll call," India said quietly. "It's really kind of pointless. We got along wonderfully, but there's no way to continue a friendship like that. Our lives are too complicated. And I really like his wife. I might do some more pictures for her." India was completely adapted to her situation.

"Will Doug let you take pictures of her?" Those were the boundaries of her life now, and she had to live with them. Like prison walls. Or a life sentence.

"Maybe. I didn't ask him. But he might. That's pretty harmless, and all I have to do is go into the city for an afternoon. I could even do it for her, without having her give me credit."

"What a waste," Gail said sadly. "You're one of the best photographers in the country, the world maybe, and you're just flushing it right down the toilet." It really made her angry, especially seeing India so depressed about it.

"Apparently that was the 'deal' I made with Doug when we got married, although he didn't spell it out quite that clearly. I said I'd give up working, I don't think I ever said I'd burn all my bridges."

"Then don't. Don't take your name off the roster. Maybe he'll back down eventually, after he stops beating his chest over it. It's all about ego, and control, and a lot of other unattractive stuff men do to make themselves feel important. Maybe in a year or two, he'll feel differently about it."

"I doubt it." That was very clear now. She just had to put one foot in front of the other, and do just what Doug expected of her.

And with that, India stood up. She had things to do at home. She hadn't even made their bed before breakfast. Lately she felt as though she had lead in her shoes, and everything seemed to take longer than usual. Even getting dressed, and she couldn't be bothered to do her hair or wear makeup. She felt as though her life were over. It all seemed so pointless.

They walked slowly back to their cars, and Gail gave her a hug and stood facing her for a minute. "Don't rule out Paul Ward entirely, India. Sometimes guys make great friends, and I don't know why, but I get the feeling that there's more to this than you're admitting to me . . . or to yourself maybe. There's something about the way you look when you talk about it." It had been the only time her eyes had come alive or her face had been animated all morning. "Don't give it up, whatever it is. You need it."

"I know," she said softly. "I think he just feels sorry for me."

"I doubt that. You're not exactly a pathetic figure normally. You're beautiful, smart, fun to be with, funny. He's probably attracted to you, maybe he's just one of the rare ones who's faithful to his wife. That's always a possibility, depressing as that is." She grinned wickedly and India laughed at her.

"You're hopeless. What about you? Any new victims for lunch or the motel circuit?" They had no secrets between them, or they hadn't until now. India hadn't wanted to admit to her how attractive she found Paul. It was better left secret. And there really was nothing to it. It was probably all a figment of her imagination. But the call from Gibraltar hadn't been. He'd probably just been bored, or maybe lonely after the crossing. But he could have called Serena instead, and he didn't. India had turned it around in her head a number of times after he called her, wondering why he had, and finally decided it didn't matter.

"Dan Lewison has a girlfriend," Gail informed her. "And Harold and Rosalie are getting married in January, after the divorce is final. And there's no one new on the horizon."

"How boring. Maybe I should give you Paul's number," she teased, and they both laughed.

"I'd love it. Anyway, kiddo, take it easy. Don't be sad. And when Doug comes home tonight, kick him in the shins, it'll do you both good. And besides, he deserves it." India didn't disagree with her, and she waved as she got into her car and drove off to the chores that were waiting. But she felt better after seeing Gail, and unburdening herself to her. There wasn't much she could do to change her life right now. But at least talking to someone about it was something, and it had helped her.

She picked the kids up after school, as usual, and took Jason and Aimee for their tennis lessons. Sam went home with a friend and came home in time for dinner. And Jessica was all excited about being a sophomore. Two seniors had actually looked at her, and one of them had actually said something to her. And mercifully, Doug stayed in the city to have dinner with clients. India just wasn't in the mood to deal with him. And she was asleep when he came home on the last train, and slipped into bed beside her.

He was already up and in the shower when she got up the next morning, and she put on her jeans and a sweatshirt without combing her hair, and ran downstairs to let the dog out and make breakfast.

She put the *Wall Street Journal* and *The New York Times* at Doug's place, and started a pot of coffee. And while she was pouring cereal into bowls for the kids, she glanced at the paper, and saw Serena on the front page. What startled her was that it was the picture India had taken of her that summer. She was surprised to see it in *The Times*, with her name along the side in a small credit line, as she unfolded the paper, and then she gasped as the cereal spilled all over the table.

For a moment, she felt as though all the air had been squeezed out of her as she read the headline. There had been a plane crash on a flight from London to New York the night before, and the FBI suspected a bomb planted by terrorists, though as yet no one had taken responsibility for it. Serena had been on the plane, and there were no survivors.

"Oh my God," she said softly as she sat down in one of the kitchen chairs, with her hands trembling as she held the paper. The story in the newspaper said that the plane had taken off, as usual, after a slight delay due to a mechanical problem of some kind, and the plane had exploded without warning two hours out of Heathrow. There had been three hundred and seventy-six people on board, among them a congresswoman from Iowa, a British M.P., a well-known ABC newscaster returning from a special he had done the week before in Jerusalem, and Serena Smith, internationally known bestselling author and movie producer. And all India could think of, as she looked at the photograph she had taken herself, were the things Serena had said while she took pictures of her that summer. It had been almost exactly two months before, and India knew without a moment's doubt that Paul would be devastated.

She didn't know what to do, whether to write or to call, or how to reach out to him. She could only imagine how he felt, and she felt terrible for him. Serena may well have been difficult, and she may not have liked his boat, but she was an extraordinary woman and it had been obvious to Serena, as it was to everyone else, that he was crazy about her. The article said that she was fifty years old and was survived by her husband, Paul Ward, and a sister in Atlanta. India was still reading the article when Sam came down to breakfast.

"Hi, Mom, what's wrong?" There was cereal all over the table, and India looked as though she'd seen a ghost. She was as white as the empty cereal bowl sitting before her.

"I . . . it . . . I was just reading something." And then she decided to tell him. "Remember Paul, with the *Sea Star*?" She knew he did, but she had to identify him somehow. "His wife died in a plane crash."

"Wow!" Sam looked impressed. "I bet Paul is really sad. She didn't like the boat though." That was equally important to Sam, and clearly showed her as defective. But he was nonetheless sorry for Paul, as she was.

And as they were talking about it, the others came down, and Doug was with them.

"What's all the excitement about?" he asked, there was an atmosphere of hysteria in the kitchen, mostly caused by the appearance of their mother. It was obvious, just looking at her, that something terrible had happened.

"My friend Paul's wife was exploded by a bomb," Sam said dramatically, as the others talked about it with interest.

"That sounds unusual," Doug said, helping himself to a cup of coffee. "Paul who?"

"Paul Ward," India explained. "He owns the yacht we visited this summer. He was married to Serena Smith, the writer." She had told him about it, and he remembered instantly, and raised an eyebrow.

"How did she manage to get in the way of a bomb?" He looked somewhat nonplussed.

"She was on a plane that went down last night out of Heathrow." Doug only shook his head in disapproval, and picked up the *Wall Street Journal.* He had no sense of how upset his wife was. And he left, without saying another word, ten minutes later, after eating a muffin. He said nothing to India as he left, and the children were still talking about the crash when they were picked up by their car pools. She was grateful she didn't have to drive them.

And she sat in the kitchen afterward, staring at the paper, and thinking of Paul. He was all she could think of now, and how distraught he must have been. But she didn't dare call him. The phone rang as she sat there. It was Gail.

"Did you see the paper?" Gail sounded breathless.

"I just read it. I can't believe it." India sounded vague and distracted.

"You never know what's going to happen, do you? At least I guess no one suffered. They said it exploded in a blinding flash in less than a second." They had been seen by another plane flying above them.

"I can't begin to imagine how he feels. He was so much in love with her." But he had nevertheless managed to call India from his boat, Gail wanted to point out, but didn't. And when he recovered from the blow, he would be a free man, which might just create an interesting dilemma for her, or so Gail thought.

"Are you going to call him?"

"I don't think I should intrude," India said, and then she remembered the photograph she had taken. She could send it to him now. It was a beautiful picture of both of them, and he might want to have it.

"You could go to the funeral. I'm sure they'll have some kind of memorial service for her in a few days. He might like to see you," Gail said practically, ever helpful.

"Maybe." They talked about it for a few minutes, and then hung up. And India went to look for the picture. She found it in a stack of papers she'd been meaning to get to in her darkroom. She had never gotten around to sending it to Serena, as she had promised. And she stood and looked at it for a long time, looking first into Paul's eyes, and then Serena's. Just the way they sat together spoke volumes. He was draped across the back of her chair, and she was leaning her head against him, on the *Sea Star,* and she was beaming. It was hard to believe she was gone, so instantly, so totally, so quickly. It must have been even harder for Paul to absorb. And as India thought about him, she realized he was probably still in Europe, on the *Sea Star.* Or flying home by then, after they notified him. She had no idea what one did in a case like this. But it was obvious to her, as she thought about it, that it was better not to call him.

Instead she sat among the breakfast
dishes on the kitchen table, and wrote him a
letter, telling him how sorry she was, knowing
how devastated he must be. It was a short but
heartfelt note, and she enclosed it with the
photograph, and drove to the post office to
send it.

She felt as though she were moving un-
derwater all afternoon. She just couldn't get
over what had happened, and she still felt
shell-shocked when she picked up the children at school.

She managed to get dinner on the table
that night, but when Doug came home, she
still hadn't combed her hair since that morning.

"What happened to you today? You look
as though you'd been kidnapped."

"I'm just upset," she said honestly, needing to share it with him finally. "I feel so badly
about Serena Smith."

"You couldn't have known her that well.
You only met her once or twice, didn't you?"
He looked disinterested, and puzzled by her
reaction.

"I did a shoot with her, for the back of
her next book. It was the picture they ran in
The Times this morning."

"You never told me," he said, his mouth setting into a thin line.

"I must have forgotten. Her husband was crazy about her. He must be just sick over it." India looked distraught as she explained it to him.

"These things happen," Doug said blandly, and started talking to Jason, as India felt her heart sink. There was no sympathy whatsoever left between them. There was nothing, only the lingering resentment of the summer, like the acrid smell of smoke after an electrical fire. It seemed to her as though everything they had once had had been burned to ashes in the meantime.

And after the children were in bed that night, India turned on the news to see what they said about the accident. There was a major story about the plane going down, and a smaller one about Serena. There were interviews with several people about the crash, and a spokesman for the FBI. And when the anchorman mentioned Serena being on the plane again, he said arrangements were being made for a memorial service at Saint Ignatius Church in New York on Friday. And India sat there for a long time afterward, staring at the TV, as they talked about sports and the weather. But she was thinking about Gail's suggestion that she go to the service.

"Are you coming to bed?" Doug asked quietly as she sat there. She still hadn't combed her hair or showered. It seemed totally irrelevant now in the face of the crash. She was completely engrossed in what had happened to Serena.

"In a while," she said vaguely, and walked into the bathroom, closed the door, and sat down in her jeans, on the toilet. She was thinking about Paul, and about his wife, and their ruptured life, that had exploded in a million tiny shards over the Atlantic. And then, somewhere in the back of her mind, she realized she was thinking about her husband, and the fact that she no longer wanted to sleep with him. She even hated getting into the same bed with him, and that couldn't go on forever. She had no idea what to do about it. It was easier to just sit there, grieving for Paul and Serena, instead of for herself and Doug and their crippled marriage.

She took forever in the shower, and washed her hair, hoping he'd be asleep when she got out, but he was in bed reading a magazine when she got there. And he turned to look at her with a cool expression.

"Are we going to keep playing these games for much longer, India?" Nothing about the way he spoke to her made him either alluring or inviting. She viewed him now like the warden in a prison, which was hardly conducive to a seductive sex life.

"What games?"

"You know what I'm talking about. If you stayed in the shower any longer than you do these days, you'd melt and go down the drain. I get the message."

"You were the one with the message all summer." She suddenly felt angry and cornered, and tired and depressed. What had happened to them in the last three months? Their relationship had become a nightmare. "It seemed pretty clear that you had no interest in me, until I told you I wasn't going to take any more assignments, and then you decided it was okay to lay a hand on me again. That's not particularly touching. You got what you wanted, so now you think you own me. Well, you do. But maybe you need to be a little subtler about it." She had never said anything like it to him, and they both looked shocked when she said it. He recoiled from her almost as though she'd slapped him.

"It's certainly helpful to know how you view things."

"You made it pretty obvious. You decided to get laid as soon as you got what you wanted. You didn't even bother to thank me, or acknowledge the concession I made, or tell me you loved me." All she wanted was to know that he cared about her and loved her.

"That again," he said, with a look of extreme irritation. "You don't exactly create an atmosphere in our bedroom that inspires that kind of declaration."

"Well, I'm sorry," she said, her eyes blazing now. She was tired of it, all of it, and particularly his attitude about their sex life. Now that he had flipped the switch to the green light again, after two months of ignoring her, he was upset that she wasn't more willing. But he did absolutely nothing to repair the hurt he had caused her all summer. "Maybe you should have put that in our 'deal' too, sex whenever you're in the mood, and who cares when I am."

"Fine, India. I get it. Forget it." He turned off the light and left her sitting in the darkness, fuming with anger. And with that, he lay on his side, turned his back to her, and in two minutes he was snoring. Their argument didn't seem to have distressed him. And she lay there for hours, hating him, and wishing that she didn't. She knew that what she had said to him had been hurtful, but after everything he'd said and done to her, he deserved it.

She closed her eyes finally, and tried to think of Paul, sending him good thoughts of sympathy and friendship. And when she fell asleep finally, she dreamed of Serena. She was trying to tell India something, but as hard as India tried, she couldn't hear it. And somewhere in the distance, she saw Paul crying, and standing all alone. But no matter how hard India tried in the dream, she couldn't get to him.

Chapter 12

The papers were full of the crash for the next few days, and India read everything she could about it. She sat for hours in the kitchen, poring over the stories. They didn't know much more than they had at first. Several Arab groups were being accused of it, but no one had taken responsibility. Though it made little difference to the families of the victims. And India had seen nothing about Paul in the papers. In his undoubtedly grief-stricken state, he was keeping well out of sight. And India's heart ached for him.

And then finally, on Thursday, there was a notice in the paper that Serena's memorial service would be held the next day at Saint Ignatius. She sat holding the paper in her hand for a long time, and she was still debating about it that night, when she and Doug went upstairs to bed. The atmosphere between them had been strained all week. There had been no way to erase the things they had said to each other three days before, and no way to forget them. Their words, as well as their actions, had done considerable damage. But she thought she should at least talk to him. It was all they had left now.

"I'm thinking of going to Serena Smith's funeral tomorrow, in the city." She was holding a black suit in her hands as she said it. Doug had bought it for her for Christmas and it seemed the right thing to wear for the service.

"Isn't that a little silly? You hardly knew her. Why get all emotional about a stranger you met once last summer?" He just didn't understand, but he also didn't know about the bond she had with Paul, and Serena was a link to it. But she couldn't explain that to him.

"I just thought it seemed respectful, since I took her picture." It was the simplest way to explain it, and Paul had been nice to Sam. She felt as though she owed him something. She hadn't heard from him since she sent the picture, but she didn't expect to. Whatever else was happening, she was sure he had his hands full. She just hoped he had gotten it, with her letter.

"It makes you look like a stargazer." Doug looked at her irritably. "Just because she was famous doesn't mean you knew her."

"No, but I liked her."

"I like a lot of people I read about too, but I wouldn't go to their funerals. I think you should rethink it."

"I'll see how I feel about it tomorrow."

And when they woke up the next day, it was raining. It was a gray, gloomy day, with a heavy rain, and a brisk wind that made an umbrella useless. It was a perfect day for a funeral, and would make it even more depressing.

Doug never said a word about it to her when he left for work, and she was busy with the children and ran errands in the morning. But she was free that afternoon, which ultimately made the decision simpler. The service was set for three o'clock, and at noon, she showered and put on the suit. She wound her long hair into a chignon, and put on a little makeup. She put on black stockings and high heels, and the suit looked well on her. As she looked at herself in the mirror before she left, she could see vaguely why people often said she looked like Grace Kelly. But she wasn't thinking of herself as she drove to the station. She was thinking of Paul and how he must feel. Just knowing how he felt made her heart heavy.

She left her car in the parking lot, and caught the 1:15 train to New York, and an hour later she was there. If anything, it was raining harder by then, and it was difficult to find a cab. She arrived at Eighty-fifth Street and Park Avenue five minutes before the service, and the church was jammed to the rafters. There were men in dark suits, and expensively dressed women. The entire literary community was there, she learned afterward, but she didn't recognize them.

People from Hollywood had come too, and many of their friends. Every pew was filled, and there were people standing along the side aisles as the service began with a Bach sonata.

It was all very proper and beautifully done, and extremely moving. And after Serena's agent, her publisher, and a friend from Hollywood spoke, Paul Ward made his way to the altar, and gave a eulogy to his wife that had everyone sobbing. It was dignified, and respectful of her many accomplishments and enormous success, but then he talked about Serena Smith, the woman. He made them laugh and cry, and think about what her life had been about, and when he wished her farewell, there wasn't a dry eye in the church. He had somehow managed to get through it, but he was sobbing as he returned to his seat in the front pew, and India could see his shoulders shake as she watched him, and ached to reach out a hand of comfort to him.

He was the first to leave the church after the service, and no one stopped him as he disappeared into a limousine, still crying. And a moment later, India saw a younger man, whom she assumed to be his son, join him. He looked just like him. There was no receiving line, and everyone was so upset, most of them disbanded very quickly and disappeared into the rain, as India watched the limousine that carried Paul drive away, and hailed a taxi. She had never taken her eyes off of him during the entire service, and she was quite sure he had never seen her. But she had only gone there out of respect for both of them, and to give support to Paul. And maybe Doug was right, she could have done as much by thinking of him at home in her living room in

Westport, but she had wanted to be here, and she was glad she had come.

She stopped to call Doug from the station. She told him she had come to town for the service, and asked if he wanted her to wait there so she could take the train home with him. Otherwise, she was going to catch the four-thirty and get home in time to make dinner.

"I'm going to be late anyway, don't wait for me," he said curtly. "I have to meet some people for drinks at six. I won't be home till nine. Don't bother saving dinner for me. I'll eat on the way home, I'll grab a sandwich or something." He sounded distant and cool, and she suspected he was annoyed she had gone to Serena's service. She wondered if he was annoyed because he never knew her. But whatever his reasons, he was anything but warm. "Did you see lots of famous people there?" he asked a little crassly, and she sighed. He really didn't understand what she was feeling.

"I didn't expect to see people I knew there." Except maybe the Parkers, but she hadn't seen them in the crowd, although they might have been there.

"I thought that was what you went for, to

see all the stars who knew her." It was a nasty thing to say and she had to force herself not to snap back at him.

"I went to pay my respects to a woman I admired. That's all. It's over. I'd better go so I don't miss the train. I'll see you at home."

"See you later," he said, and hung up. He seemed so devoid of emotion these days, so unable to empathize with her. She wondered if he had always been like that, and she had never noticed, or if he had gotten worse after their battles over the summer. Whatever it was, it left her feeling very lonely. But not as lonely as Paul, she was sure. She couldn't get the image of him out of her mind, as he left the podium sobbing. He had looked completely destroyed, and her heart had gone out to him as she watched him.

All she could think about on the way home was Paul, and the conversations they'd had on the *Sea Star.* The rain had stopped finally when she got home, and the children were all there, and they looked happy to see her.

"Where were you, Mom?" Sam asked as she came through the door and took off her raincoat.

"At Serena Smith's funeral," she said simply. "It was very sad."

"Did you see Paul?" he asked with interest.

"Only from a distance."

"Was he crying?" Sam had the ghoulish fascination of all boys his age with tragedy, death, and drama.

"Yes, he was," India said sadly. "He looked terrible."

"Maybe I'll write him a letter," Sam said sympathetically, and his mother smiled at him, as the others listened, but didn't say much. They had never met Serena, and Paul was Sam's friend.

"I bet he'd like that."

"I'll do it after dinner," Sam said, and went back to watching TV. And half an hour later, she had dinner on the table, hamburgers again, and frozen french fries. But no one complained, and they all had a lot to say over dinner, which compensated for India's somber silence. She couldn't get Paul out of her head, or her memories of Serena.

And she was still wearing the black suit when Doug got home at nine-thirty. "You look nice," he said, with a look of surprise. She had been looking pretty shaggy lately.

She had been so depressed, she didn't seem to care what she looked like. But the suit he'd given her looked very stylish and showed off her figure.

"How was it?" he asked, about the service.

"Sad."

"That's not surprising. Do you have any food left? I never had time to pick up a sandwich. I'm starving." She had thrown the last of the cold hamburgers away hours before, and there wasn't much in the refrigerator except some cold turkey slices and frozen pizza. She was going to buy groceries in the morning. He settled for fried eggs and an English muffin. And for the first time in months, he asked what they were doing that weekend.

"Nothing. Why?" She was surprised at the question.

"I thought maybe we should have dinner or something." Things had been going from bad to worse between them, and he was getting concerned. Even Doug couldn't ignore it anymore. The point had finally been brought home to him when he realized she no longer wanted to have sex with him. As long as it had been his decision, it didn't bother him. But her lack of interest was beginning to worry him. And he thought dinner out might help them.

But India thought he made dinner with her sound like a painful obligation. "We don't have to, if you don't want to," she said simply.

"I wouldn't have suggested it, if I didn't. Do you want to go back to Ma Petite Amie?" It was the first sign of peace he had offered, but she wasn't ready for it, and she still had terrible memories of the last time they had been there.

"Not really. Why don't we go out for pizza or something?"

"How about pizza and a movie tomorrow night?" It was worth a try at least. If she was going to spend the rest of her life with him, she was going to have to make peace with him sometime. It was a far cry from the love she longed for, but this was all they had. She felt as though she were making friends with her fellow passengers on the *Titanic*. No matter how good the service was, they were still going to wind up at the bottom of the ocean. She had begun to feel that for a while now.

"That sounds fine." She had nothing to lose but time. He had already destroyed her heart and her self-confidence. Going to a movie with him couldn't do much more damage. So why not?

She took off the suit after she put the kids to bed, and eventually went to bed herself. But Doug made no advances to her tonight. After their last round, he knew better. They were going to have to start small, with pizza and a movie. And after that, they could see what happened. He figured in time, with a little bit of attention, she'd come around.

They went to sleep as they had for a long time now, without saying good-night to each other. She was almost used to it. And she lay lost in her own thoughts for a long time, listening to him snoring. If nothing else, in lieu of any tenderness between them, it was a familiar sound to India, and by now the loneliness was an equally familiar feeling.

Chapter 13

The day after the funeral, Doug took Sam to his soccer game, and India helped Jessica clean out her closets. She had more junk in them than India had ever seen, and she was carrying armloads of Jessica's outgrown clothes to give away when the phone rang.

She assumed it was for one of the children, as usual, and made no effort to answer. She dropped the clothes on the garage floor, and walked back into the kitchen while it was still ringing. And finally, sounding exasperated, she answered.

"Yes?"

"Hello?" The male voice was unfamiliar and sounded like a grown-up, although lately the boys who called Jessica were sounding a lot more like men than children.

"I'm sorry. Who is this?"

"It's Paul Ward. I was calling for Mrs. Taylor." Her heart skipped a beat as he said it, and she sat down at the kitchen table.

"Paul . . . it's me. . . . How are you?" All she could think about was his face covered in tears as he left the podium at Saint Ignatius.

"Numb, I think. Someone said you were there yesterday. I'm sorry I didn't see you." The crew of the *Sea Star* had flown back for the service, out of respect for Paul, and one of the stewardesses had told Paul she'd seen her.

"I didn't expect you to. It was a beautiful service. Paul . . . I'm so sorry. . . . I don't know what to say." She truly didn't, and she was so surprised to hear him. She hadn't expected him to call her.

"I got your letter . . . it was wonderful. And the picture." She could hear that he was crying. "I love it. How are you?" he asked, trying to regain some normalcy. He had wanted to thank her for coming, and for writing to him. But now that he was talking to her, he felt overwhelmed with emotion. He knew how kind she was, and her gentle ways, and reaching out to her somehow made him feel more vulnerable than he had in days. He still hadn't absorbed what had happened. He felt stricken.

"I'm okay," she said, sounding unconvincing.

"What does that mean? Are you going back to work?"

"No. It turned into World War III for the rest of the summer." She sighed then. "I just can't do it. He put it to me very clearly. It's not negotiable. Maybe it's not important."

"You know it is," he said gently, "it's about what you need. Don't lose your dreams, India . . . you'll lose yourself if you do. You know that." It was something Serena never would have done. She had always been true to herself, no matter what it cost her, and they both knew that. But she hadn't been married to Doug Taylor. She hadn't made a "deal" with him. And Paul would never have given her the ultimatum that Doug had.

"I gave up those dreams a long time ago," India said quietly, sitting in her kitchen. "Apparently, I don't have a right to take them back now. We're going out to dinner tonight for the first time in months. Our life has been a nightmare all summer."

"I'm sorry to hear that," he said sadly. He felt sorry for her. She was wasting herself, and she knew it. They both did. "How's my friend Sam?"

"Wonderful. He's out playing soccer this morning. He said he was going to write you."

"I'd like that," he said, but it didn't sound like the old Paul, the man she had met on the *Sea Star.* He sounded tired and sad and disillusioned. He had just lost his dream, and he had no idea how he would live without her.

"What about you?" India asked gently. "What are you going to do now?"

"I'm going back to the boat, and float around for a while. I took some time off from my work. I wouldn't be any good to them right now anyway. I'm not sure where I'll go. The boat's in Italy, and I thought I'd take it down to Yugoslavia and Turkey. I don't care where we go, just so it's far away, and all I see is water." It was what he needed now to heal him.

"Is there anything I can do?" she asked, wishing she could think of something. All she had had to offer him was one picture.

But Paul answered quickly. "Call me sometime. I'd love to hear from you." And then his voice broke again, and she could hear that he was crying. "India, I'm so lonely without her. She's only been gone for five days, and I can hardly stand it. She drove me crazy sometimes, but she was so terrific. There's no one like her." He was crying openly with her, and India wished she could reach out and touch him.

"No, there isn't anyone like her," she agreed. "But she wouldn't want you to fall apart. She'd be furious over it. You have to cry and scream and stamp your feet, and sail around on the *Sea Star,* and then you have to come back and be strong for her. You know she'd want you to do that."

"Yes." He smiled through his tears, thinking of it. "She'd have been pretty rude about it." And then they both laughed. "I'll tell you what," he said then, as he stopped crying for the moment. He had been crying on and off for five days, and he felt as though he was going to do it for a lifetime. "I'll pull myself together eventually, if you promise me you won't give up your dreams completely. India, you mustn't do that."

"I can't hang on to them, and my marriage. It's just that simple. There's no compromise here. It's all or nothing. Maybe he'll relent one day, but not now."

"Just see what happens, and keep your options open for a while." And then he sounded worried. "Did you take your name off your agent's roster?"

"No, I didn't."

"Good. Keep it that way. He has no right to blackmail you into abandoning your talent."

"He can do anything he wants to, Paul. He owns me, or at least he thinks he does."

"He doesn't, and you know it. Don't let him. You're the only one who can allow him to do that."

"I gave it all to him seventeen years ago. He says we made a 'deal,' and he expects me to stick to it."

"I won't tell you what I think of his theories," Paul said, sounding stronger again, like the man she had met and been so struck by that summer. "Or his behavior," he added. He didn't even know Doug, but Paul thought he was treating India very badly. And it was obvious that she wasn't happy with him. If she had been, Paul wasn't so sure he would be calling. But in an odd way, just as friends, they needed each other. "I thought about you a lot this week, India. About the things we talked about last summer. It's funny how one can be so sure that one has everything all sewed up forever. We're all so damn confident and sure that we know it all, and have it all, and then it gets blown to smithereens in a second and we have nothing. That's how I feel. All those lives wasted on that plane, children, babies, young people, people who deserved to live . . . just like she did. I keep thinking I wish I had gone down with her."

She didn't know what to say to him for a minute. In a way, she didn't blame him, but he hadn't and he had to go on now. "That wasn't meant to happen. You're still here, and she wouldn't want you to waste it."

"No, the terrorists did that for me. They blew my life to bits, and everyone else's."

"I know." It seemed wrong to tell him that in time he'd feel better, but he would someday. It was just the way life worked. He would never forget Serena, or stop loving her, but in time he would learn to live without her. He had no choice. "It'll do you good to be on the *Sea Star,*" she said quietly, as she saw Aimee walk across the room and out again, and she wondered when Doug and Sam would be home. But she was still alone in the kitchen.

"Promise that you'll call me?" he said, sounding desperately lonely, and she nodded.

"I will. I have the number."

"I'll call you too. Sometimes I just need someone to talk to." She wanted to be there for him, and she was touched that he had reached out to her.

"You helped me a lot this summer." And then, with a sense of her own despair, she felt as though she owed him an apology or an explanation. "I'm sorry to disappoint you."

"You're not disappointing me, India. I just don't want you to let yourself down, and regret it later. But you won't. You'll see. Sooner or later you'll get up the courage to do what you have to." And do what, she wondered. Defy her husband? If she did, she knew she'd lose him, and she didn't want to.

"I'm not there yet," she said honestly, "and maybe I never will be."

"You will be. One day. Just tuck those dreams of yours into a safe place somewhere, and remember where you left them." It was a sweet thing to say, and she was touched by the entire conversation.

"I'm glad you called, Paul," she said gently.

"So am I." He sounded as though he meant it.

"When are you leaving?" She wanted to

know where he was now, so she could imagine him, and reach out to him if she had to.

"Tonight. I'm flying to Paris, and then switching planes and going on to Nice. The boat is going to pick me up there." The crew had already flown back that morning, and it was a short distance from Portofino to Nice. He knew they'd be there for him. And then he sighed, as he looked around the room where he was sitting. It was filled with pictures of Serena, and the treasures she had collected during the years of their marriage. He couldn't bear to be there. "I guess I should sell the apartment eventually. I can't stand being here. Maybe they can do it while I'm gone, and put everything in storage."

"Don't move too quickly," she said wisely. "Give it time, Paul. You don't know what you want to do yet."

"No, I don't. I just want to run away and turn the clock back."

"You can do that on the *Sea Star,*" she said gently, as Doug walked into the room and stood behind her. "Take good care of yourself, try to be strong," she urged him, as Doug left the room again to look for something. "And when you're not strong," she said softly, "call me. I'll be here."

"I know. Me too. I'm always here for you, India, if you need me. Don't forget that. And don't let anyone make you think they own you. They don't." They both knew he meant Doug as she listened. "You own you. Got that?"

"Yes, sir."

"Take care. . . ." She could hear tears in his voice again. He was on an agonizing roller coaster of emotion, and she felt so sorry for him.

"Take care of yourself, Paul. You're not as alone as you feel right now. Try to remember that. And in her own way, she's right there with you."

He laughed through his tears then. "This is probably the only way I could have gotten her to stay with me on the *Sea Star,* but it's a hell of a way to do it." If nothing else, it was good to hear him laughing. "Talk to you soon, India."

"Thanks for calling," she said, and they both hung up then. She sighed, and stood up to see Doug standing in the doorway, frowning at her.

"Who was that?" He looked angry as he asked her.

"Paul Ward. He called to thank me for a photograph of Serena I sent him."

"It sounds as though the grieving widower is recovering very quickly. How long has she been gone? Less than a week now?"

"That's an awful thing to say." She looked horrified at what he was implying. "He was crying on the phone."

"I'm sure he was. That's the oldest ploy in history. All he has to do is whine a little bit, make you feel sorry for him, and bingo. You fell for it like a ton of bricks, India. You sounded like you were talking to your boyfriend."

"That's disgusting. He's a nice man and a decent person, and he's heartbroken over losing her. He's just terribly upset and very lonely, and we struck up a nice friendship this summer."

"I'll bet you did. His wife wasn't there then either, was she? I remember your telling me she wasn't there the first time you told me about him. So where was she then, if she was so madly in love with him?" He was filled with venom and suspicion, and ready to accuse her.

"She was working, Doug," India said quietly. "Some women do that."

"Is she the one who filled your head with all that garbage? Was he part of that scheme?" Doug was just aching to despise him, and India was angry at him for it. Whatever she felt for Paul, she had no intention of acting on it, or even letting Paul know, let alone her husband. She wasn't even sure herself exactly what she felt for him, and whatever it was, the affection she felt for him had chosen the path of friendship. And there was no reason for it ever to go any further. "I think you're a fool if you don't see what he's doing here, India. And I don't want him calling here again. You sounded like you were talking to your lover."

"I don't have a lover, Doug," she said icily, suddenly unable to stop her own rage. She hated what he had been saying to her. "If I did, I might be happier than I am now. But in any case, Paul Ward is not that person. He loved his wife, and he had a deep respect for her, and her career, something which you know nothing about. And I suspect he's going to mourn her for a long time."

"And when he stops, you'll be there for him? Is that it? Maybe you'd like being the mistress of a man with all that money."

"You make me sick, Doug," she said, and

walked back up to Jessica's room to finish her closets. She didn't even want to see Doug, and for the rest of the afternoon she avoided him completely. But the atmosphere was no better between them when they left for dinner. She didn't even want to go out with him, but she thought that if she didn't, it would cause more trouble.

If she had thought about it, she might have been flattered that he had expressed jealousy over Paul, but the way he expressed it was so offensive that it only made her angry. And what he had said to her was disgusting. Paul Ward was very certainly not her lover, and never would be. He was only a very good friend. Of that, she was certain.

The meal she and Doug shared that night was strained, in spite of his allegedly good intentions in taking her out. But what he had said to her that afternoon had doomed his efforts to failure. They scarcely said a word to each other while they ate. And the movie they went to was so depressing, India just sat and cried through the whole film, and she felt worse than ever when they got home, and Doug paid the sitter. As far as India was concerned, it was a disastrous evening, and Doug didn't think it had been much better.

He was feeling discouraged as he walked upstairs, and neither of them wanted to go to bed, so they sat in chairs and turned the TV on, and watched an old movie they had both liked. It was actually better than the one they had seen in the theater. They ended up staying up late, and they went down to the kitchen for a snack at one o'clock in the morning.

"I'm sorry about what I said today," he said suddenly, looking at her unhappily, and his unexpected remorse surprised her. "I know he's not your boyfriend."

"I should hope not," she said primly, and then she unbended a little bit. "I'm sorry about the things I said too. It sure hasn't been easy lately, has it?" Everything had been so difficult. Every conversation, every exchange, every hour, every contact.

"I guess sometimes marriage is like that," he said sadly, and then what he said next touched her. "I've missed you."

"Me too," she smiled. It had been so lonely without him. During the last few months he'd barely spoken to her, and been so angry at her for suggesting she do a few assignments, it had been as though he'd been away all summer.

They finished their snack and went upstairs. The kids were all in bed, and India gently closed the bedroom door behind them. They both got ready for bed, and Doug turned the TV off, and when she came to bed, he was awake. And this time when he reached out for her tentatively, she didn't turn away or refuse him. He took her gently in his arms, and made love to her, though there wasn't the passion she wished there had been. He seemed awkward with her after so long, and he never told her he loved her. But this was the life they shared, the "deal" they had made, and for better or worse, he was her husband. This was what she had, and what she had to make her peace with.

Chapter 14

India and Doug limped along for the next two months. They had glued things back together again, but the glue no longer seemed as firm as it once had been. But at least the kids kept her too busy to think about it. And she knew for sure that nothing was going to change now. Doug was who he was, and he had made himself clear about his expectations. All she had to do was continue to live with them. That was the hard part.

She saw a lot of Gail at Sam's soccer games, and at parent meetings and dinners at the high school. They had both those age groups in common. And as she had before, and undoubtedly would again, in October, Gail had confided to India that she was seeing a new man, and as usual, he was someone else's husband. But at least she seemed happy.

"So how's it going?" she asked India late one afternoon, as they sat freezing in the bleachers. "Has Doug finally calmed down?"

"Pretty much. He's got a lot of new clients, and he's busy. We haven't talked about any of the sensitive subjects since the summer." Their sex life wasn't what it had once been, but every now and then they made whatever attempts they could to revive it. There were parts of their relationship that just hadn't recovered from the blows it had been dealt over the summer. But India had resigned herself to what she had, rather than fighting for what she wanted.

"Has Paul Ward ever called again?"

"No, I think he's in Europe." It was the first time she had ever lied to Gail, but it was something she didn't want to share with anyone, and the information was so potentially explosive if it fell into the wrong hands that she had decided not to confide in her. But he had called, though not often.

He had called her in September again, and twice in October so far. He always called at odd hours, usually when she was home alone, around dinnertime for him, and when he correctly assumed Doug would be at the office. He never said anything inappropriate, and so far he had always sounded desperately lonely. He had even sounded a little drunk once, but Serena hadn't even been gone for two months, and India knew better than anyone how hard it was for him. The boat had been in Yugoslavia the last time he had called her, and he didn't sound as though he was having much fun, but he wasn't ready to come home yet either.

He never said anything about seeing her, or about when he'd be back, though she wondered if he would return to the States around the holidays to see his son and grandchildren. Or maybe that would just be too painful. He had told her before that he and Serena had usually gone skiing in Switzerland for Christmas, and he had already vowed never to go to Saint Moritz again. He never wanted to see again the places he had been with her, never wanted to tread the same paths, or remember the dreams he had shared with her.

"That rules out a lot of places," India had teased him, and he had laughed a little. He was having a very hard time readjusting. He always asked how things were going for her, and she was honest with him. She had made her peace with her situation, although she was no longer very happy. But she still refused to try rocking the boat again. She was satisfied, she claimed, taking pictures of her children, and Paul scolded her for it. He thought she should allow herself to be braver, but she wasn't. She was very different from Serena. But he seemed to love talking to her, and derived a lot of comfort from it.

India never asked what he was going to do next, if he was going to go back to work, she never asked him for anything, or pressed him in any way. She was just there when he called, with her soothing voice and gentle ways, and it was exactly what he wanted. There was no promise that they would meet again, no allusions to an affair. He was extremely circumspect with her, but always warm, always kind, always interested in what she was doing, and whenever she explained her feelings to him, unlike Doug, he always got it. He was a gift in her life in many ways, and she no longer told Doug when he called her. She didn't want to deal with his accusations that Paul wanted to be, or was, her boyfriend. She was not Gail. She was an entirely other kind of woman, and Paul knew that. She was honorable in every way, and had a great deal of integrity, more so, in his eyes, than her husband, who had blackmailed her into what he wanted.

India hadn't heard from Paul in two weeks when the phone rang one afternoon, shortly after noon, in her kitchen. She thought Paul was back in Italy by then, and it would have been six o'clock at night for him, which was usually when he called her.

She answered the phone with a smile, expecting to hear his voice, and was surprised instead to hear Raoul Lopez's. She hadn't heard from him in six months, since she'd turned down the job in Korea.

"What are you up to these days, India? Are you getting tired of your kids yet?"

"Nope," she said firmly, feeling stupid now for leaving her name on their roster. It was just going to make him mad at her when she refused another assignment. Doug was right. She should have taken herself off it.

"I was hoping for a different answer. I have a proposition for you," he said, sounding excited. The call had just come in, and she'd been the first one he'd thought of. It was perfect for her.

"I'm not sure I should even let you tell

me, Raoul. My husband was pretty upset about Korea."

"What about Korea? You didn't do it." He was right, of course, but in the end it had provoked three months of discussions and a near revolution. And she didn't want that to happen now, no matter how good the offer. "Just listen to me for a minute."

"There's a royal wedding in England. Dignified, safe, all the crowned heads of Europe will be there. The magazine that called us on this wants someone who knows how to behave. They don't want one of their sloppy staffers. As they put it to me ten minutes ago, 'they want a real lady' to just blend in with all the fancy people. It's in London, you wouldn't be risking your life for once. And while you're there, I have another story for you. It's some kind of underground prostitution ring, somewhere in the West End, involving ten- to fourteen-year-olds. It's an acute form of child abuse. And you'd be working with the police there. Whatever you get on it will run in all the international press, syndicated obviously. It could be a fabulous story. And you could wrap up the whole thing in a week, both the wedding and the kiddies."

"Oh shit," she said, as she listened to

him, she had to admit it sounded tempting. Maybe she could sell it to Doug on the wedding. But the story that excited her was the one about ten-year-old prostitutes, it was an outrage, and she would have loved to expose it. "Why do you call me with these things, Raoul? You're going to destroy my marriage." She sighed as she said it.

"I call you because I love you, and you're the best there is. Look what you did in Harlem."

"That was different, it was an hour away on the train, and I could get home in time to fix my kids dinner."

"I'll hire a cook for you while you're gone. I'll cook for them myself, but India, please don't say no to me again. You've *got* to do this." He was desperate for her and she could hear it, and she was excited about the stories.

"When is it?" she asked, sounding worried. Maybe if she had a little time she could talk Doug into it, or plead with him, or promise to shine his shoes forever if he'd let her do it. She was dying to do the story and she didn't want to turn Raoul down again.

"It's in three weeks," he said, pretending to sound vague, as she calculated.

"Three weeks?" She worked the dates out again, and frowned as she came out at the same place she had the first time. "That's Thanksgiving."

"More or less," he said, still praying she'd do it.

"What do you mean 'more or less'? Is it Thanksgiving, or isn't it?"

"All right, all right. It's the Thanksgiving weekend, but you'd have to be there on Thursday. There are two huge events right before the wedding, and all the heads of state will be there, including the President and the First Lady. You could have turkey with them, or better yet, take one with you."

"I hate you. This is not funny. Doug is going to kill you."

"I'm going to kill him if he doesn't let you do it. India, you have to. Look, do me a favor and think about it. Call me back tomorrow."

"Tomorrow? Are you crazy? You're giving me one night to tell my husband that I'm leaving him and my children for Thanksgiving? What are you trying to do to me?"

"I'm trying to save you from a boring life, and a husband who doesn't appreciate your talent. Not to mention a bunch of kids, however cute they may be, who don't deserve to

have the use of one of the most talented photographers in the world as their personal cook
and chauffeur. Give me a break here, India. I
need it. So do you. Just do this one for me."

"I'll see what I can do," she said som-
berly. "I'll call you tomorrow . . . or the day
after. If I'm still alive then."

"I love you." He was beaming, and praying she would do it. She would be perfect for
both jobs. "Thanks, India. I'll talk to you tomorrow."

"Just remember to feel guilty when they
find my body dumped in the shopping mall in
Westport."

"Tell him to grow up and realize who he
married. He can't keep you locked up forever."

"No, but he's trying. I'll call you." She
stood in the kitchen for a long minute when
she hung up, and realized she was actually
shaking. She was terrified to say anything to
Doug, but she was as excited about the assignments as Raoul was, particularly the tough
one. But the wedding would be fun too. She
was dying to do it. But how was she ever going
to tell Doug? She sat down on a stool to think
about it, and then headed out to the market.

She bought all the foods he liked best,

and was going to make him a fabulous dinner that night. Even a little caviar. She was going to make all her specialties and his favorites, and serve him wine, and then they would talk . . . and he'd kill her. But at least she could try it.

Doug was thrilled when he came home that night, and saw what she was making. She had bought a chateaubriand, and she was making his favorite peppercorn-and-mustard sauce, baked potatoes, French-cut string beans, stuffed mushrooms, and smoked salmon with caviar to start with. And when he sat down to dinner with her and the kids, he felt like he'd died and gone to heaven.

"Did you smash the car up today, Mom?" Jason asked her casually, ladling sour cream into his baked potato.

"Of course not," she said, looking startled by the question. "Why would you ask that?"

"It sure is a great dinner. I figured you'd done something that would make Dad mad. *Really* mad," he corrected, glancing at the caviar.

"Don't be silly." But he was very clever, more so than his father, who had no suspicions whatsoever. He was sitting comfortably in his favorite chair, looking lazy and sated after dinner. She had made chocolate mousse for dessert, with Mexican Wedding Cookies, his favorite. It was anything but subtle.

"What a dinner!" He smiled as she came to sit next to him in the living room after cleaning up. The kids were all upstairs doing homework. "What did I ever do to deserve that?"

"You married me," she said, sitting on a little stool near his feet, and praying that the gods would be kind to her on this one. Just this once. Just one time. She was prepared to beg him. She was dying to go to London, even if it was over Thanksgiving.

"I guess I just got lucky," he said, leaning back in the chair and rubbing his stomach.

"So did I," she said sweetly. It was the friendliest exchange they'd had since the summer. But not without an ulterior motive this time. "Doug . . ." She looked up at him then, and in an instant he knew that it was a setup. There was blood lust in her eyes, and he couldn't help wondering what it would take to satisfy it.

"Uh-oh," he laughed, still amused by it. "Was Jason right? Did you smash up the car, or someone else's?"

"My driving record is intact, your insurance is unchallenged, and the car is in perfect order. You can check it."

"Get arrested for shoplifting, maybe?"

"Now, there's a thought." She decided to get it over with. She had to. And she had to call Raoul tomorrow, or the next day. "I got a call today," she confessed.

"From whom?" He knitted his brows as he listened. It was like asking her father if she could go on a date at fourteen, only ten times harder and more scary. A hundred times maybe. She knew only too well how Doug felt about this.

"Raoul," she said simply.

"Not that again." He sat up in his chair and glared down at her on the footstool.

"Just listen. It's the most civilized job they have ever offered me, and they wanted a 'lady' to do it." She had already decided not to tell him about the prostitution ring in the West End. He would never let her do that, even if it was in London. But maybe the wedding . . . "Someone terribly important is marrying into the British Royal Family, and they want someone to cover it. All the heads of state will be there, and the crowned heads of Europe, and the President and First Lady. . . ."

"And you won't be," he said firmly. "They can get any photographer to do that."

"But they want me, or Raoul does. Doug . . . please . . . I'd love to do it."

"I thought we already went through this. How often are we going to have to fight this battle, India? This is why I told you to get your name off his roster. He's just going to keep calling. Stop torturing me over it, and yourself. You have kids . . . you have re-sponsibilities . . . you just can't run out the door and forget about that."

"Doug, we are talking about a week. One week. That's all. The kids are not going to commit suicide because I'm not here on Thanksgiving." And with that, she looked panicked as she said it. She hadn't meant to tell him that part until later. But it was all out now, at least as much as she was going to tell him.

"I can't believe this. You're asking me if you can leave us for Thanksgiving? What do you expect me to do, cook the turkey?"

"Take them to a restaurant. I'll make a real Thanksgiving dinner before I leave, the

day before. They'll never know the difference."

"Even if they don't, I will. You know what
our agreement is. We went through all that
this summer."

"I know. But this is important to me. I
need to do it."

"Then maybe you don't *need* to be married, or have children. I'm not going to put up
with a wife who isn't here for Thanksgiving.
You might as well go to a war zone if you're
going to do that."

"At least I'll be safe at the wedding."

"Unless terrorists bomb it, like they did
your friend's plane. Now, there's a thought.
Are you willing to take that risk?" He was
willing to push every button he had to.

"I could just stay home in bed for the rest
of my life too. Why not do that? I mean, hell,
Doug, the Russians could bomb Westport, if
they ever get their shit together."

"Why not just get your shit together, India, and grow up finally? All that crap is behind you, or at least it should be."

"Well, it isn't. It's still part of me, and it
always will be. You have to understand that."

"I don't have to do anything," he said,
sounding angry as he stood up, and left her

sitting on the footstool. "I'm not going to agree to this. If you want to go anyway, that's your business. But don't expect to stay married to me, if you do it."

"Thanks, Doug, for making the choices so clear to me," she said, standing up and looking at him squarely. "You know what? I'm not going to let you bully me anymore, or blackmail me. This is who I am, who you married. You can lay down all the rules you want, but you can't threaten me," she said calmly, with no idea where the words had come from. But suddenly she knew exactly what she was doing, and where she was going. To London. "I'm going to go over there and do this story. I'm going to stay for a week, and then I'm going to come back and take care of our kids, just like I always do, and you, for that matter. And you know what? We'll survive it. You can't tell me what to do anymore, Doug. It's not fair. And I won't let you."

He listened to her without saying a word, and she was shaking as she faced him. And then he turned and walked up the stairs and she heard the bedroom door slam. But she had done it. She had dared to reach out and grab what she wanted. She had never done it before, not with him, and she was terrified, and she felt fantastic. She realized now that he had been doing this to her for years. It was his ultimatum that had brought her back from Asia seventeen years before, to marry him. He had told her in no uncertain terms that if she didn't, she'd lose him. And because she'd lost her father when she was young, she thought that the worst thing that could happen to her was to lose Doug. But what she'd discovered seventeen years later was that it was actually worse losing herself, and she had almost done that. She didn't believe she'd lose him now, and if she did, she'd face it. But she hoped not.

She waited awhile to go upstairs, and when she did, he was in bed, with the lights off. But she couldn't hear him snoring.

"Are you awake?" she whispered, and there was no answer, but she could sense that he was, and she found she was right as she approached him. She stood at the foot of the bed in the dark, and saw him stir, but he still said nothing. "I'm sorry it had to be this way, Doug. I would have liked it better if you agreed to let me go. I love you very much . . . but I have to do this . . . for myself. It's hard to explain that." It wasn't, actually, but it was impossible for him to understand it. He wanted to lay down the law and threaten her over it. That had always been his power over her, that and the terror that she'd lose him. But she couldn't stay frightened forever. "I love you, Doug," she said again, as though to reassure him and herself. But there was no answer. And a moment later, she went into the bathroom to take a shower. And she stood there with the warm water running down her back and a smile on her face, seemingly forever. She had done it!

Chapter 15

She made Thanksgiving dinner for them, just as she had promised, the night before Thanksgiving. It was the perfect meal, and they looked like the perfect family, except that Doug scowled most of the way through dinner. It was no secret to anyone how he felt about her leaving.

She had told the children herself, and after the initial shock, they were all excited for her, especially the girls, who thought covering the wedding sounded terrific. Neither of the boys cared much. But none of them had the reaction that Doug had thought they would about it. None of them felt abandoned or angry, or as though she was never coming back, as she had when her father went to Vietnam for six months, or equally terrifying places before that. This was pretty tame, and they all understood that. They were disappointed she wouldn't be there for Thanksgiving with them, but once they knew she was going to make a real Thanksgiving dinner for them, they were perfectly happy, contrary to Doug's predictions.

She was leaving for London on the morning of Thanksgiving, and Doug and the children were going to have yet another Thanksgiving dinner with friends in Greenwich, since neither Doug nor India still had living parents. She realized now too that it was why she was so dependent on him, and his approval. Other than the children, she had no one else.

The children devoured everything in sight, and Jason said it was the best dinner she'd ever made, and she thanked him. And afterward, they all sat in the living room and watched movies, as India and Jessica cleaned up the kitchen. And she sent Jessica to join the others when Doug came in to talk to her. He was looking angrier by the minute.

"Aren't you embarrassed to turn them into orphans for the holidays?" he asked pointedly, still trying to make her feel guilty.

"They're not orphans, Doug. They have a

mother who works occasionally, and they seem to understand it a lot better than you do."

"Tell me that when they start flunking out of school, as a way of expressing their displeasure."

"I don't think that is going to happen," India said firmly.

Gail had promised to pick up her car pools for her, and the sitter she used most frequently was coming to the house every day from three o'clock until after dinner, and Jessica had promised to help her with the cooking. Everything was in order, and she had left six pages of neat instructions. The only problem was her husband. But India had never felt stronger about anything in her life. Paul had called her that week and had told her he was proud of her, and she had promised to call him from London. The *Sea Star* was in Turkey. And he said he would be anxious to hear from her.

"You're going to have to reckon with me when you get back, India." Doug threatened her again, as he had for weeks. He seemed to have no hesitation, and no shame, about doing that to her. But she refused to listen. She wasn't even sure what had finally changed, but she knew she couldn't live in a box any-more, the one he had built for her fourteen years before allowed her no wingspread. She knew better than anyone that she had to do this. No matter what it cost her. Not doing it would cost her even more. And now she un-derstood that. And Raoul had been ecstatic when she called him. They were paying her a decent sum, though nothing fabulous, and she was going to use it to do something nice with the children, maybe take a trip somewhere, or go skiing after Christmas. And of course she wanted Doug to join them, if he was willing. So far he said he wasn't.

She let the children stay up late, since it was a holiday, and in the morning, before she left, she went into each of their bedrooms. They were all asleep, but they stirred as she leaned down to kiss them, and the general consensus was "Have a good time, Mom," as she promised to call them. She had given each of them the name of her hotel, and her num-ber. And it was pinned up in the kitchen. She had left everything organized to perfection. And she was startled at how easy it all was, and how smoothly it had gone. The only prob-lem was her husband.

She walked back into their bedroom to

say good-bye to him, and he glared at her. He had been awake since she got up, but pretended he wasn't. But now he just sat there, and they both knew he had lost some of his power to terrify her and make her do what he wanted. It was not a change he welcomed.

"I'll call you as often as I can, I promise," she said as though to a child, he looked like one as he sat there and watched her, and made no move to come toward her.

"Don't bother," he said curtly. "I have nothing to say to you until you get back." He looked as though he meant it.

"And then what? You throw me out in the snow? Come on, Doug, be a good sport about it. Please? Wish me luck. I haven't done this in years . . . it's exciting for me." But he wasn't happy for her. He looked irreversibly angry. And he wanted her to be frightened of the repercussions.

She still was, but not enough to turn down the assignment. He had finally pushed her too far. "I love you, Doug," she said simply, as she walked out of the room. She did love him, but she wondered if he loved her. He didn't answer her, and she walked down the stairs with her camera equipment neatly packed in a bag over her shoulder. The bag had been her father's. And she picked up her suitcase and went out to the shuttle waiting to take her to the airport.

It was a short ride, they stopped to pick several people up, and for the first time in years she felt independent. It was the first time she had gone anywhere without her children, and the feeling of freedom was overwhelming.

After she checked in at the airport, she walked around the terminal and bought some magazines, and then she called Raoul to see if he had any last instructions. He told her he'd fax her if he had any new information about the second story, but other than that, he had nothing. And then she boarded the plane, and headed for London. She was due in at nine o'clock that night, and she was going to be picked up and taken to a ball the Queen was giving for the couple in the Painted Hall at the Royal Naval Academy in Greenwich. She had brought a long velvet skirt, a velvet blouse, and a string of pearls, and she was going to change in the limousine on the way in from the airport. It was more than a little different from her old assignments, but she could hardly wait to get there.

She read and slept on the flight, and ate a

little dinner, and she looked out the window for a while, thinking about the children she had left, who had been the boundaries of her life for so long. She knew she'd miss them, but she knew that they'd be fine for the short time she'd be gone. And then she thought about Doug, and the things he had said to her, the power he had wielded over her for so long, and the reasons he'd done it. It seemed so unfair, and so unnecessary, and now when she thought about it, she wasn't angry, but sad. If he had let her go graciously, or let her grow over the years, it would have been so much kinder. But all Doug wanted was to control her, to make her do what he wanted. And thinking about it was depressing.

She was dozing when they landed at Heathrow, and then the excitement began in earnest, along with the realization that she had spread her wings at last and done something she wanted, not because it was good for someone else, or she was expected to, but because it was what *she* wanted to do. She almost crowed with delight as they landed. She hadn't been in London in years, and she could hardly wait to see it. And what better way to do it?

The driver they had promised her was

waiting just outside Customs, and he drove into town as quickly as he could, while she changed her clothes in the backseat and combed her hair as neatly as possible under the circumstances. She felt a little more disorganized than she wanted to, but when she looked in the mirror, she decided she would pass inspection. And she wasn't here to look beautiful, she was here to take photographs. No one was going to care what she looked like.

As they approached the Royal Naval Academy, she saw that there were cadets outside in formal uniforms, holding antique muskets and rifles, and they stood at attention as guests came in and out, and the surroundings were very impressive. The buildings framed an enormous square of lawn, and the domed chapel was built in 1779.

She took a couple of quick shots of the outside, and hurried inside to the party. And as she came up the steps, she looked up and saw the extraordinary paintings all around and on the ceiling. It was a cross between Versailles and the Sistine Chapel. And there were at least four hundred people dancing, and almost the moment she walked in, she began shooting. It was easy to spot her subjects.

Prince Charles, the queens of the Nether-
lands, Denmark, and Norway. She recognized
all of them, as well as the President of France,
several Crown Princes, and then she saw
Queen Elizabeth in the distance, surrounded
by guards, and chatting easily with the Prime
Minister, and the President and the First
Lady. She had had to show her pass when she
entered, but she slipped it into her pocket after that, and spent the next four hours gliding
discreetly from one group to the other. And
at two A.M., when the party broke up, she
knew she had gotten what she'd come for. It
was the same warm feeling she'd had years
before when she knew she got her story, although this time her subjects couldn't have
been more different.

The Queen had left hours before, and the
rest of the illustrious guests filed out deco-
rously, saying what an extraordinary party it
had been, and some of them went to see the
chapel. India took the last of her roll of film
there, and then climbed into her car, and
headed back to the city.

They had gotten her a small room at Claridge's, which had been one of the promised
perks of the job, and as she walked into the
lobby with her camera, and her bag, she sud-

denly realized she was exhausted. It was two-thirty in the morning there, which was only eight-thirty in the evening for her, but she had been working for hours, traveling and covering her story. It felt just like the old days, although her work clothes then hadn't included velvet skirts and evening shoes. She had worn combat boots and camouflage, but she knew that she would remember the sights she had seen that night forever. The Painted Hall was surely one of the grandest sights in England, and the people who had been there that night were forming the course of history in Europe.

She could hardly wait to get undressed and into bed, and she was asleep almost the minute her head hit the pillow. She didn't stir until she heard the phone ringing, and she couldn't imagine why anyone would call her at that hour. But when she opened her eyes, she saw there was daylight streaming into the room. It was ten o'clock on a cold November morning in London, and she had to be somewhere at noon. She had slept right through her alarm clock.

"Hello?" she said sleepily, stretching and looking around the room. It was small, but pretty, done in pale blue flowered chintzes.

"I thought you were supposed to be working."

"I am. Who is this?" For a minute, she thought it was Raoul, but it didn't sound anything like him. And then suddenly she knew. It was Paul, calling from the boat in Turkey. "I didn't recognize you for a minute. I was dead to the world. Thank God you woke me."

"How's it going?" He sounded happy to hear her.

"It's really fun. Last night was terrific. Everyone in the world was there, as long as they had *queen, prince,* or *king* in front of their name. And the Painted Hall is amazing."

"It is, isn't it? Serena and I went to a party there once, for a very nice man, a maritime author named Patrick O'Brian. He's one of my passions. The Painted Hall is quite something." He had been everywhere, it seemed to her. But even Paul was impressed by the people who had been there, when she told him about it.

"I think I got some really great pictures."

"How does it feel to be working again?" He smiled at the thought of her, tucked into her little room at Claridge's. He could almost see her. And knowing what it had taken to get there, he knew what a victory it was for her, and how much it meant to her. He was glad she had done it.

"It feels terrific. I love it." She had also told him about the second story, and he was concerned about her, but figured she knew what she was doing, and the police would protect her. "How are you, Paul?" He was sounding a little better these days, though she knew Thanksgiving probably hadn't been easy for him, but he had avoided the issue by staying in Turkey. "Any interest in coming to London while I'm here?" She threw it out as a possibility, but she didn't really expect him to take her up on it, and knew instinctively that he wouldn't. He was still hiding from real life on the *Sea Star*.

"I don't think so," he said honestly. "Though I'd really like to see you, India," he said with a smile. "You're probably too busy anyway to hang around with old friends." In the past five months, they had actually become that. She had shared all her terrors with him, and her disappointments with Doug, and he had cried on her shoulder more than once since he lost Serena. In a short time, and from great distances at times, they had been through a lot together. "I think I'm afraid to come back to civilization." It was still too painful for him, and she knew it.

"You don't have to yet." She knew he was handling most of his business by fax and phone, and his partners were managing the rest in his absence. It was better for him to stay on the *Sea Star*. The boat seemed like a healing place for him.

"How were the kids when you left?" He had thought a lot about her the previous morning.

"Fine. Better than Doug. We celebrated Thanksgiving the night before, and he hardly spoke to me. I don't think this is going to go down too smoothly. There are bound to be repercussions."

"Just steel yourself for them. What can he do, after all?"

"Throw me out, for starters, figuratively speaking. He could leave me," she said in a serious tone. It was obvious that she was worried about it.

"He'd be a fool if he did that." But they both knew he was, although Paul saw it more clearly than she did. "I think he's just making noise to scare you."

"Maybe." But she had come anyway. And

she was here now. "I guess I'd better get dressed, before I miss the next party."

"What is it today?" he asked with interest.

"I have to check my itinerary. I think it's the lunch given by Prince Charles at Saint James's Palace."

"That should be entertaining. Call me tonight and tell me all about it."

"I'll probably be home pretty late. I have to go to another dinner tonight, before the wedding."

"This sounds like a really tough story." He was teasing her, but he felt like her guardian angel. He had seen her come through all the agony it had taken her to get there. And now he wanted to share the victory with her. "I'll be up late. You can call me, now that we're almost in the same time zone. I think we're going to head for Sicily tomorrow. I want to hang around Italy for a while, and Corsica. Eventually, I want to wind up in Venice."

"You lead a tough life, Mr. Ward, with your little houseboat you can take everywhere with you. I really feel sorry for you."

"You should," he said, with more seriousness than he intended. But she knew how lonely he was from their previous conversations. He still missed Serena unbearably, and she suspected that he either drank or cried himself to sleep more often than he admitted. But it had only been three months since he lost her.

"I'll call you later," she said cheerily, and after they hung up, she went to stand at the window, and looked down on Brook Street below. Everything looked very tidy and very familiar and very English. She was so happy to be here. And she reminded herself that she had to buy lots of postcards for the children. She had promised to do that, and she wanted to go to Hamley's, if she had time, and buy some toys or games for Sam, Aimee, and Jason. She had to find something more grown up for Jessica than for the others. If she had time between stories, India was thinking of going to Harvey Nichols. But first she had to get to work. And she was still thinking of Paul when she sank into the enormous bathtub. She loved talking to him, and she hoped that one of these days she would see him. He was a terrific friend to her, even long distance.

And for the rest of the afternoon, she was busy taking photographs of royals again. She had a great time, and she found that she knew one of the other photographers. They had done a story together once in Kenya. It had been nearly twenty years since she'd last seen him. He was Irish and very funny. His name was John O'Malley, and he invited her for a drink in a local pub after the party.

"Where the hell have you been? I figured someone finally shot you on one of those crazy stories," he said, laughing, and obviously pleased to see her.

"No, I got married and had four kids, and I've been retired for the last fourteen years."

"So what made you come back now?" he asked with a broad grin. He had taken all the pictures he needed and was sipping Irish whiskey.

"I missed it."

"You're daft," he said with absolute conviction. "I always knew that about you. I'd like nothing better than to retire with a wife and four kids. Of course, this isn't exactly a dangerous story like our old ones, unless the royals attack us. And they could, you know. If they start a fight over the hors d'oeuvres, you could start a war here. And then, of course, there's the IRA, lovely people that they are. Sometimes I'm ashamed to admit that I'm Irish." They talked about the terrorist bombing in September then, and India told him a friend's wife had been on the plane.

"Damn shame. I hate stories like that. I always think about the children. Kill an army. Bomb a missile plant. But don't, for God's sake, kill the children. The bastards always do, though. Every damn country that gets pissed off, they kill the children." He had spent time in Bosnia, and hated what he'd seen there. Croat children beheaded by the Serbs while their mothers held them. It had been the worst he'd seen since Rwanda. "Don't worry about me, my dear. Man's inhumanity to man is one of my favorite subjects on my second whiskey. On my third, I get romantic. Watch out then!" He hadn't changed in years and it was fun talking to him, and he introduced her to another journalist who joined them at their table. He was Australian, and not nearly as sympathetic as John O'Malley, although he had a dry sense of humor as he commented on the party. He said they'd worked together years before, in Beijing, but she no longer remembered, and he didn't look familiar. By the time they left the pub, O'Malley was pretty well oiled, and she had to get back to Claridge's to change again before she went on to the next party. She was grateful it was the last one before the wedding. It was held in someone's home, a spectacular affair on Saint James's Place, with liveried footmen, a ballroom, and chandeliers that blazed with candles. And when she got home at midnight, she called the children. They were just sitting down to dinner. She spoke to each of them, and they sounded fine. They said that they'd had fun in Greenwich the day before, and they missed her, and on Saturday their father was taking them skating. But when India asked to say hello to him, he told the children to say he was busy. He was cooking dinner. He could have come to the phone easily, she always did while she was cooking. And the phone had a long cord, which would have reached. But she got the message; he had told her he had nothing more to say to her, and apparently he meant it.

She felt a little lonely when she hung up, after talking to them, and she decided to call Paul. She thought he might still be up, and he was, and she told him all about the party. It was nice being able to speak to him at any hour, and to tell him what she was doing.

They talked for a long time, and Paul knew the people who gave the party. He seemed to know everyone who was there, and he was amused at her descriptions. It had been an interesting evening, filled with aristocratic and distinguished people. She could see why they had decided not to just send a staffer, and was flattered that they had offered it to her instead.

"What time is the wedding tomorrow?" he asked finally with a yawn. He was getting sleepy, and the sea had been a little rough that night. But it never bothered him, in fact he liked it.

"Five o'clock."

"What are you going to do before that?"

"Sleep." She grinned. She hadn't stopped since she'd been there. It was just like the old days, but in high heels and long dresses. "Actually, I want to stop in and see the police. They left a message for me, and I'm going to start working on the other story on Sunday."

"You don't waste much time, do you, India?" Serena had been like that too, but he didn't say it. She was always working on something. A new book, a new script, a revision, a set of galleys. He missed it. He missed everything about her. "Call me tomorrow and tell me about the wedding." He loved her life, and being able to talk to her at any time of day or night. He couldn't do that when she was in Westport.

"I'll call you when I get back to the hotel."

"We'll be sailing tomorrow night." He particularly loved the night sails and she knew that. "I'll be on watch after midnight." But she knew he could talk to her from the wheelhouse. "It was nice talking to you tonight. You remind me of a world I keep telling myself I've forgotten." He just didn't want to be there without Serena. But hearing about it from India was amusing.

"You'll come back to it one of these days, when you want to."

"I suppose so. I can't imagine being there without her," he said sadly. "We did so many fun things. I can't imagine doing any of it on my own now. I'm too old to start again." He wasn't, but she knew he felt it. He somehow felt that losing Serena had aged him.

"You sound like me now. If I'm not too old to come back to work, you're not too old to come back to the world when you're ready." There were fourteen years between them, but neither of them ever felt it. At times they seemed like brother and sister, at other times she felt the same electricity between them she had sensed since the beginning. But he never made reference to it. He didn't want to be disloyal to Serena. And he still felt guilty for not going down on the plane with her. He could see no good reason to have survived her. His son was grown, his grandchildren had a good life. There was no one who needed him now, and he said as much to India. "I do," she said softly. "I need you."

"No, you don't. You're on your way now."

"Don't be so sure. Doug wouldn't even speak to me when I left. Wait till I get back to Westport. There will be hell to pay, and you know it."

"Maybe. Don't worry about it now. You have plenty to deal with before you have to face that." But they both knew she would in a matter of days. She was going home on Friday. She wanted to be with her children for the weekend.

"I'll talk to you tomorrow," she said, and then they said good-night, and she hung up. It was odd how comfortable they were with each other. As she sat and thought about him it was as though she had known Paul all her life, instead of just since the summer. They had both come a long way, over some hard places, since then. He more than she had. But her road hadn't been easy either.

She was lying in bed in the dark, drifting off to sleep, when the phone rang again. She thought it might be the kids, or Doug, but it was Paul again, and she was surprised to hear his voice.

"Were you asleep?" he asked cautiously, in a whisper.

"No. I was just lying here in the dark, thinking about you."

"Me too. I just wanted to tell you how much I admire what you've done, India . . . and how proud I am of you. . . ." He had called her just to say that.

"Thank you . . . that means a lot to me." As he did.

"You're a wonderful person." And then he added, with tears in his eyes, "I couldn't get through this without you."

"Me too." She whispered. "That was what I was thinking when you called me."

"We'll get together one of these days. Somewhere. Sometime. I'll be back. I just don't know when yet."

"Don't worry. Do what you have to."

"Good night," he said softly, and after she hung up, she closed her eyes and fell asleep, and as she did, she was smiling, and thinking about him.

Chapter 16

The wedding the next day was a grandiose affair, filled with pomp and ceremony. And India knew without even developing them that she had gotten fabulous pictures of it. The bride looked incredible in a Dior gown. She was delicate and petite, and the train seemed to reach for miles behind her. And her mother-in-law had given her an exquisite little tiara. Everything about the wedding was perfection. It was held in Saint Paul's Cathedral and there were fourteen bridesmaids. It looked like a fairy tale, and India couldn't wait to show her children the pictures. At least then they could see what she'd been doing in London.

The reception was at Buckingham Palace,

and she was home early this time. She called
Paul at ten-fifteen, and she had called the
children just before that. They had just come
back from skating and were drinking hot
chocolate in the kitchen. And this time, when
she asked for Doug, they said he was out, but
she wasn't sure if she believed them. It was
unlikely they'd be home without him. But she
didn't want to press the issue. And as soon as
she hung up, she called Paul. He said he was
sitting in the main salon and reading. He
wasn't going on watch till midnight.

"How was it?" he asked, curious about
what she was doing. He liked hearing about it.

"Unbelievable. A fairy tale. It must have
cost a million dollars."

"Probably." And then he laughed, he
sounded as though he were in good spirits.
"Serena and I got married at city hall. And
afterward, we bought chili dogs on the street,
and spent the night at the Plaza. It was a little
unorthodox, but actually very romantic. But
Serena was so determined not to marry me,
that I figured when I got her to say yes, I'd
better nail her down without waiting another
minute. She spent our entire wedding night
telling me what she wasn't going to do for me,
and how she was never going to be a proper

wife, and telling me I would never own her. She lived up to most of it, but I think eventually she forgot to make me live up to all the things I agreed to." He still talked about her constantly, but one of the many things he liked about India was that she didn't seem to mind it.

"Looking at that bride today, knowing what we do about life, you can't help wondering if it will work out, or if they'll be disappointed. It must be a little embarrassing after a wedding like that if it doesn't."

"I don't think that makes much difference. We did okay with our chili dogs and our night at the Plaza."

"You probably did better than most," India said sadly. Weddings always made her nostalgic. Especially lately.

"You did all right," Paul said quietly. He was feeling relaxed. He had been drinking a glass of wine and reading when she called. He loved to sit and read for hours.

"How was the sailing today?" she asked with a smile, knowing how much he loved it, the rougher the better.

"Pretty good." And then he changed the subject. "Did you go to the police about your assignment?"

"I spent two hours with them before the wedding. That is a nasty little investigation. They're using kids as young as eight as prostitutes. It's hard to believe they would do that."

"It sounds like an ugly story."

"It will be." But it was more up her alley than the wedding, although it had pained her to see the photographs of the children they were using. They were planning a raid in two days, and they had invited her to be there when they did it.

"Will it be dangerous for you?"

"It could be," she said honestly, although she wouldn't have admitted it to her husband. He didn't even know about the story, and she was not going to tell him.

"I hope it won't be dangerous for you," Paul said cautiously. He didn't want to interfere in her work, or her life, in any way. But he didn't like to think about her getting injured.

"They'll have to be careful because of the children. But the guys who run it are a tough group. The police think some of the girls were sold into slavery by their parents."

"God, that's awful." She nodded as if he could see her, and they went on to talk of pleasanter subjects.

He told her about the book he was reading then, and his plans in Sicily. And he was excited about going to Venice. He had never taken the boat there.

"I can't think of anything more beautiful than being in Venice on the *Sea Star,*" she said dreamily, thinking of it.

"It's a shame you and Sam won't be with me."

"He would love that."

"So would you."

They chatted for a while, and then he said he had to adjust some sails, and check the radar, but he said he'd call her the following night. They had talked about Annabelle's, and Harry's Bar, and Mark's Club, and all his favorite hangouts in London. But he also knew it would be a long time before he went back there.

And from the next morning on, her days of elegance in London would end. From then on, she would be working with police, hanging out in smoky rooms in blue jeans, drinking cold coffee.

She read some of the material the police had given her that night, to give her further background on the story, and the men who were running the operation. They sounded like monsters, and just thinking about children Aimee's age being used as prostitutes and slaves turned her stomach. It was a world her children would never know and could never have imagined. Even as an adult, she found it unthinkable, just as Paul had.

She went back to meet with the police the next day at noon, and at eight o'clock at night, she was still with them. After they finished their plans for the raid the next day, two of the inspectors took her to dinner at a pub nearby, and it was interesting talking to them. They drank a lot and gave her a wealth of inside information. And when she got back to Claridge's, there was a message from the children. They sent their love and had all gone to a movie. There was another one from Paul, but when she called him back, he was busy. But he called again as she was getting ready to leave the next morning.

"Sorry about last night. We hit a storm. The wind was fifty knots," but it was obvious, from what he said, that he loved it.

She told him what she'd learned from the police then, and that they would be conducting the raid that night at midnight.

"I'll be thinking of you. Be careful," he said soberly.

"I will," she promised, thinking how odd it was talking to him. There was never any talk of romance between them, and yet he talked to her sometimes like a husband. It was probably out of habit, she assumed, and because he missed Serena. He had never given India any real reason to think he was interested in her in that way, except for the fact that he kept calling. But their conversations were more like the meanderings of old friends than the bonding of two lovers.

"I don't know what time I'll be through. Probably at some ungodly hour of the morning."

"I hope not." He was getting an increasing sense of the danger she would be in. The men who ran the prostitution ring were not going to walk away from it with their hands in their pockets, and Paul was suddenly afraid that they might come out with guns blazing, and India could get hurt, or worse, in the process. "Don't take any chances, India. Screw the awards, and even the story, if you have to. It's not worth it." But it always was to her, and always had been, though she didn't say that to him. But now she had her children to think of, it wasn't like the old days. She was aware of that, and intended to be careful.

"Call me when it's over, no matter what time it is. I want to know you're safe. I'm going to be very worried."

"Don't be. I'll be with about fifteen cops, and probably the equivalent of a SWAT team."

"Tell them to protect you."

"I will."

After she hung up, she ran to Hamley's as quickly as she could, to get some things for the children, mostly souvenirs, and she bought a great pair of shoes and a funny hat for Jessica at Harvey Nichols, and was back with the police by noon, just as she had promised.

And for hours after that, she did nothing but listen to them, take notes, and take pictures. And at midnight, when they struck, she was as ready as they were. She went in right behind the first team, with a bullet-proof vest they'd given her, and her camera poised for action. And what they saw in the house on Wilton Crescent in the West End was heartbreaking and beyond pathetic. Little girls of eight and nine and ten, chained to walls and tied to beds, whipped and abused, and drugged, and being raped by men of every age and description. And much to the police's disgust, they rounded up two well-known M.P.s along with them. But more importantly, they had caught all the men, and one woman, who ran it. India had taken hundreds of photographs of them, and the children. Most of the little girls didn't even speak English. They had been brought from the Middle East and other places, and had been sold by their parents.

They were sent off to children's shelters and hospitals to be checked and healed and tended to. There had been more than thirty of them. And India knew it was going to make an incredible story, although it broke her heart to see them. She had carried one child out herself, a little girl of about Sam's age, with cigarette burns and whip marks all over her body. And she had cried piteously as India held her, and carried her to the ambulance. A huge, fat, ugly man somewhere in his sixties had just finished having sex with her when India took her. She had wanted to hit him with her camera, but the police had warned her not to touch him.

"Are you okay?" Paul asked anxiously when he heard her. True to her word, she called him the minute she got in, at six o'clock in the morning. He had stayed up all night, worrying about her.

"I am. Physically. Mentally, I'm not so sure. Paul, I can't even begin to describe to you what I saw tonight. I know I'll never forget it."

"Neither will the world, after they see your pictures. It must have been just awful."

"It was unspeakable." She told him a few of the things she'd seen and he felt sick listening to her. He was sorry she had had to see it. But he supposed she'd seen worse in her younger days, but nothing more heart-wrenching than the little girls they'd rescued. There had been a few boys too, but not nearly as many.

"Do you suppose you can get some sleep now?" he asked, even more worried. But at least she hadn't been injured.

"I don't think so," she said honestly. "I just want to walk, or take a bath, or do something. If I lie down, I'm going to go crazy."

"I'm so sorry."

"Don't be. Someone had to do it. And it might as well be me." She told him about the little girl she'd carried to the ambulance, and the cigarette burns all over her tiny, emaciated body.

"It's hard to imagine any man doing

things like that to children." And then he asked, "Are you finished with the story?" He hoped so, but she wasn't. She had to go back for the next few days, to wrap it up. But she said she'd be through by Thursday. And then she was flying back to New York on Friday. He had almost wanted to ask her if she wanted to fly to Sicily to meet him on the boat for a couple of days, but he knew she couldn't. And he wasn't sure yet if he was ready to see her. In fact, he was almost sure he wasn't. But he would have, if it would have helped her to forget the story. It was certainly a universe apart from the wedding.

They stayed on the phone with each other for a long time, and the sun came up over London as they talked. He felt as though he were there with her, and she was glad she had him to talk to. Doug would never have understood what she was feeling.

Finally, he told her to get into a hot bath, try and get some sleep, and call him later. And after they spoke, he walked out on deck and looked out to sea, thinking of her. She was so different from Serena in every way, and yet there was something so innately powerful about her, something so clean and strong and wonderful that it terrified him. He had no idea what would become of them, or what he was doing. And he didn't even want to think about it.

All he knew was that he needed to talk to her, more and more frequently. He couldn't imagine not talking to her every day now. And India was thinking exactly the same thing as she lay in the bathtub, and wondered where it was going. And what was she going to do when she got back to Westport? She couldn't call him constantly. Doug would see it on the bill, and wonder what she was doing.

She had no idea what she was doing with Paul, or why. And yet she knew she needed him now. He was like a drug she had become addicted to, without realizing how it had happened. But it had. They needed each other. More than either of them were willing to admit, or knew. But little by little, over time, and from a great distance, they were moving slowly toward each other. And then what, she asked herself, as she closed her eyes. What in God's name were they doing? But as she opened them again, she realized it was just one more question to which she had no answer.

And on the *Sea Star*, thinking about her,

and realizing how relieved he was that she was all right, Paul put his hands in his pockets with a thoughtful expression, and walked slowly back to his cabin.

Chapter 17

India continued to work with the police that week, filling in the details of the story. She took more photographs of the perpetrators, and some heartbreaking ones of the children. In the end, there were thirty-nine children involved, and most of them were in hospitals and shelters and foster homes. Only one, who had been kidnapped two years before, had been returned to her parents. The others had all been abandoned, or sold, or given away, or even bartered. They were truly the lost children, and India couldn't imagine, after what they'd been through, how they would ever recover.

Every night she poured out the horror stories she'd seen to Paul, and that led to talk of other things, their values, their fears, their childhoods. Like her, his parents were both gone, and he was an only child. His father had been a moderate success, but in most ways nothing like him. Paul had been driven to succeed, by demons of his own, to achieve in excess of everyone around him. And when India talked of her father and his work, it was obvious to Paul that she thought him a hero. But she was also well aware of what his constant absences had cost her. They had never been a real family, because he was always gone, which made her own family life now seem all that much more important. It was the hold that Doug had on her, she now realized, and why she didn't want to lose him. It was why she did everything he said, and followed all his orders, met all his expectations. She didn't want her children to have a life without their father. And although her own mother had worked, her job had never been important to her. It was her father who had been the central figure of their life, and whose absence, when he died, had nearly destroyed them. But she also recognized that the strain his lifestyle and his work had put on them had challenged her parents' marriage. Her mother had never thought him quite the hero that she did, and a lot of the time she was very angry at him. And India knew that his long absences had caused her mother a lot of heartache. It was why she was so nervous now about following in his footsteps, and why she had allowed Doug to force her to abandon a life, and a career, that meant so much to her. But just as her father had never been able to give up the drug of his work, and the passion he had for it, although she herself had sublimated it for so long, she had come back to it, and discovered all too easily in the past few days, how much she loved it. And she knew, as she took photographs of the children's ravaged faces and eyes and lives, that somehow she was making a difference. In exposing their pain to the world, through her camera and her own eyes, she was making sure that it could not so easily happen again. She was making people feel the agony of those children. It was precisely what her father had done with his work, and why he had won the Pulitzer. He deserved it.

It was her last night in London. She had finally finished the story, and she was leaving in the morning. She hadn't seen Paul while she'd been there, but in a way, she felt as though they'd spent the week together. They had discovered things about each other she had never said before, or dreamed about herself, or remotely guessed about him. He had been astonishingly open with her, about his dreams, his most private thoughts, and his years with Serena. And the portrait he painted of her taught India a great deal, not only about her, but about Paul, and what his needs were.

Serena had been powerful in so many ways, she had pushed and driven him further toward his immense success, and supported him when he had doubts about it. She had been a driving force, always right behind him. But she had rarely leaned on him herself, was leery of needing him too much, and although she'd been his closest friend, she was afraid of being too close to him or anyone, though Paul didn't seem to mind it. They had been partners, but she had never nurtured him or anyone the way India did with everyone around her. Paul had discovered in his new friend a never-ending source of warmth and tenderness and comfort. And the gentle hand she held out to him was one he trusted. In every possible way, the two women couldn't have been more different. And India's kindness to him was what seemed to keep him afloat now, just as his ever-present strength for her seemed to have become essential to her survival. The question was, for both of them, where did they go now?

He called late the night before she left, and he sounded lonelier than usual. "Will you call me when you go back?" Paul asked. She never had before. It had always been Paul who called her. But even he realized that it would be awkward to call her regularly in Westport.

"I'm not sure I can," she said honestly, thinking about it, as she lay comfortably on her bed, in her cozy room at Claridge's. "I'm not sure Doug would understand it. I'm not even sure I do." She smiled, wishing he would clarify it for her. But he couldn't. He was still far too steeped in his memories of his wife, to know what he wanted from India, if anything. What they both cherished from each other was their friendship. And even if Paul no longer was, India was after all still married.

"Can I call you there? Often, I mean . . . like now . . . ?" he asked. They had both come to rely on their daily phone calls. After speaking to the children every night, she looked forward to their long conversations. But back in Westport, it would be different.

"I think so. You can call me during the day." The time difference would work well for them, as long as he was still in Europe. And then she sighed, thinking of Doug, and what she owed him. "I guess I should feel guilty about talking to you. I wouldn't want Doug doing the same thing . . . talking to some woman. . . ."

"But you wouldn't treat him the way he's treated you either, would you?" In fact, they both knew she hadn't. She had always been loving, supportive, kind, reasonable, and understanding. She had more than lived up to her half of the bargain, the "deal" Doug constantly spoke of. It was Doug who had let her down, by refusing to meet her needs or understand her feelings, and giving her so little warmth and comfort.

"He's not a bad man, Paul. . . . I was very happy for a long time. Maybe I just grew up or something. We were so busy for so long, with all the kids, or at least I was, I guess I stopped paying attention to what he was giving me, or wasn't. It never occurred to me to say, 'Hey . . . wait . . . I need more than this . . .' or ask him if he loved me. And now, it feels like it's too late. He's gotten away with giving me so little for so long, that he doesn't understand that I want more, for myself, and from him. He thinks I'm crazy."

"You're not crazy, India. Far from it," Paul reassured her. "Do you think you can get it back, to get what you want out of it again?"

"I don't know." It was what she had asked herself over and over. "I just don't know. I don't think he hears me."

"He's a fool if he doesn't." Paul knew that very clearly. She was a woman well worth keeping.

"Did you and Serena ever have problems like this?" He said funny things about her sometimes, about how demanding and difficult she had been, but he didn't seem to mind it.

"Not really. She didn't put up with much. When I stepped on her toes, she let me have it. And when I didn't give her enough, she told me. Serena made her needs very clear, and her expectations, and she set very clear limits. I guess that made it easy. I always knew where I stood with her. She taught me a lot about relationships. I made a real mess of it the first time. Kind of like Doug, probably even a little worse. I was so busy establishing myself and making money, I let the relationship go right down the tubes and never saw it.

And I walked all over my wife while I did it. I told you, she still hates me. And I'm not so sure I blame her." And then he laughed into the phone, thinking about it. "I think Serena trained me. I was pretty dumb before that."

But if he had been, he no longer was. India knew by then that he was not only extremely sensitive, but also unusually perceptive and able to express his perceptions. And no matter what she explained to him, he always seemed to "get it."

"The only trouble is," he went on, "I can't imagine doing all that again, without Serena. It wasn't generic. It worked because of her, because of who she was, her powers and her magic. I don't think I could ever love another woman." They were hard words to hear, but India believed him. "There will never be another person in my life like her." Nor would he try to find one. He had decided that on the *Sea Star*.

"That may be true right now," India said cautiously, thinking of him as he lay in his cabin, "but you don't know what the future will bring. You're not old enough to give all that up. Maybe in time, you'll feel differently and someone will come along who is important to you." She wasn't pleading her own case, so much as pleading for him. It was impossible to think that, at fifty-seven, that aspect of his life was over. He was too young, too vital, too decent, and at the moment much too lonely.

"I know I couldn't do it," he said firmly. But she knew that time might tell a different story.

"You don't have to think about that now," India said gently. It was too soon for him to even think about another woman. And yet he was calling India every day, and they had become fast friends. And always somewhere, in the time they spent talking to each other, there was a hint of something else, something more, and despite the neutrality they claimed, they nonetheless reacted to each other as man and woman. But Paul insisted to himself, when he thought about it, that he wasn't in love with India, or pursuing her as a woman. They were friends, and he wanted to help her out of a difficult situation. He never said it quite so bluntly to her, but he thought her marriage was a disaster, and Doug a bastard. She was being exploited and ignored and used, and he was convinced that Doug didn't even care about her. If he did, he would have let her pursue her career, even helped her to do it. He would have cherished her, and supported her, and at least told her he loved her. Instead, he blackmailed and threatened her, and locked her up in an airless little box, for his own convenience. Paul had nothing but contempt for him. But in spite of that, he didn't want to put India in jeopardy when she went back, and he promised to be cautious when he called her.

"Can't you just tell him we're friends? That I'm sort of an adopted, self-appointed older brother?" She laughed at the suggestion, and Paul's naïveté. What man would understand that? And she knew that Doug viewed her as his possession. He didn't want another man using what was his, even if only for conversation and comfort.

"I know he wouldn't understand it." And neither did she, because the undercurrent of what she felt from Paul was not what she knew she would have felt from a brother. There was far more to it than that, and she knew it. But Paul was in no way ready to face that. If nothing else, out of loyalty to Serena.

He had told her that week that he'd been having dreams about his wife, about being on the plane with her, crashing with her, and saving himself. And she was accusing him, in the dreams, of not trying to help her, and surviving when she hadn't. She blamed him, he said, for not going down with her. The psychological implications of the dreams were easy to decipher.

"Is that how you feel?" India had asked him. "That it's your fault she died?"

"I blame myself for not dying with her," he said in a choked voice, and India knew he was crying.

"It's not your fault, Paul. You know that. It wasn't meant to happen." He had a massive case of survivor guilt, for outliving her, which was part of why he was hiding on the *Sea Star*. But India knew, as he did, that sooner or later Paul would have to face it. Sooner or later, he'd have to go back to the world. But it was still too soon. She had only been gone for three months, and he just wasn't ready. But eventually he'd have to go back. He couldn't hide forever. "Give it time," she always said gently.

"I'm never going to get over this, India," he said stubbornly. "I know it."

"You will, if you want to. What do you think Serena would say?"

"She'd kick my ass." He laughed as he said it. "If she were in my shoes, she'd have sold the boat by now, bought a flat in London, a house in Paris, and be giving parties. She always told me not to count on her playing the grieving widow, if I died, so not to bother having a heart attack because I worked too hard. She said she would find it incredibly boring. I know she didn't mean all that, but she would have handled this much better than I have. I think she was probably stronger than I am."

But India knew he was strong too, he was just deeply attached to his wife, and the bonds were not easy to sever, not that he had to. She kept trying to tell him to take Serena with him, the good parts of her, the memories, the joys, the wit, the wisdom, the excitement they had shared, the happiness she'd given him. But he had not yet found a way to do that. And in the meantime, with India, he could find a warm place to hide, a hand to hold, and a gentle soul to give him comfort. In the past week alone, he had come to need her more than he would have admitted. And the thought of not being able to call her whenever he wanted to now was beginning to upset him. And knowing she was in enemy territory, he was going to be worried about her. But the enemy he feared for her was, in fact, her husband. And Paul was nothing. A voice on the phone. A man she had met a few times the previous summer. He was in no way prepared to be more than that to her. But whatever it was they had, or had found together, he wanted.

"I'll call you at lunchtime every day," he promised. But that left a void over the weekends.

"I'll call you on the weekends," she said, feeling faintly guilty. "Maybe I can get to a pay phone, when I take Sam to soccer or something." There was something sneaky about it that disturbed her. But she didn't want her calls to him via the Satcom on their phone bill. And innocent as it was, she knew she couldn't explain this to her husband. It was the first secret pact she had made with anyone, the first clandestine thing she'd ever done, and yet when she questioned herself about it, she knew that it was different than Gail meeting men in motels. This was different.

They talked longer than usual that night, and they both sounded lonely when they finally ended the conversation. She felt as though she had spent her last evening in London with him. The inspectors she had worked with all week had invited her out, but she said she was too tired to go, and she was. She was happy staying in her hotel room and talking to Paul on the phone.

And she was surprised the next morning when he called just before she left the hotel. She had just finished closing her suitcase.

"I just wanted to say good-bye, and wish you a safe trip home," he said, sounding a little sheepish. Sometimes, when he called her, he felt like a kid again, and in spite of himself, he liked it. "Say hi to Sam for me when you see him." And then he wondered if she could do that, or if he would say something to his father. Theirs was certainly an odd situation. They were phone pals.

"Take care of yourself, Paul," she said again. "And thank you . . ." He had given her so much support while she did her stories. He was the champion of her cause to go back to work, and it was thanks to his encouragement that she had finally done it.

"Don't forget to send me the pictures. I'll tell you where to send them." He had addresses here and there to get his mail, and contracts and business papers sent to him from his office. "I can't wait to see them."

They chatted for a few more minutes,

and there was suddenly an odd moment of silence, as she looked out the window over the rooftops of London. "I'll miss you," she said, so softly he almost didn't hear her. It was nice being in the same part of the world with him, even if she hadn't seen him. In Westport, she felt like she was on another planet. But at least she could call him.

"I miss you already," he said, forgetting himself, and Serena. "Don't let anyone upset you." They both knew who he meant, and she nodded.

"Don't be too hard on yourself . . . take it easy. . . ."

"I will. You too. I'll call you on Monday." It was Friday, and they had a whole weekend to get through, unless she called him from a pay phone. And she suddenly wondered if they could do it. After spending so much time on the phone every day while she was there, she couldn't help wondering what it would be like not to talk to him for a few days. It made her feel lonely just thinking about it.

She had to run to catch her plane then, and they hung up. And she thought about him all the way to the airport, and on the plane. She sat staring out the window for a long time, thinking about him, and the things he had said, about himself, and Serena. He was so sure that he would never love anyone again, and a part of her didn't believe that. Another part of her wondered if he was in love with her. But that was foolish. They were only friends. It was what she kept telling herself all the way back to the States. It didn't matter what she felt. It was exactly what he said and nothing more. A friendship.

Chapter 18

When India walked into the house at five-fifteen on Friday night, the kids were all in the kitchen, eating snacks, and playing and teasing each other, and the dog was barking. And just looking at them made it feel as though she had never left them. It made London seem like a dream, and the stories she'd covered unreal, and her friendship with Paul nonexistent. This was her life, her reality, her existence.

And the moment they saw her, Aimee let out a squeal, and Jason and Sam both ran toward her, as Jessica waved to her with a broad grin while holding the phone and chatting to one of her buddies. And suddenly she had her arms full of children, and she realized how much she'd missed them. Her life had seemed so grown-up for a week, so independent, so free, and it had been exciting. But this was even better.

"Wow! I missed you guys!" she said as she held them close to her, and then they broke free, and told her all at once what had happened all week. Sam had scored the winning goal at soccer, twice, Aimee had lost two more teeth, Jason had had his braces off, and according to them, Jessica had a new boyfriend. It was business as usual as she listened to them, and after ten minutes of celebrating her return, everyone went upstairs to do homework, call friends, or watch TV. By six o'clock it was as though she had never left them.

She took her suitcase upstairs and sat on the bed, looking around her bedroom. Nothing had changed. It was the same safe little world, and her children had survived her absence. So had she. In an odd way, it made the trip seem completely unreal, and like a figment of her imagination.

The only time it became a reality was when she saw Doug's face when he came home at seven. He looked like a storm cloud, and he barely managed to say hello to her before they sat down to dinner. The babysitter had stayed to help her, and had left before Doug came in. They were having steak and mashed potatoes and string beans, and even the kitchen looked tidy, as India went to kiss him. She was still wearing her traveling clothes, black wool pants and a warm sweater so she wouldn't be cold on the plane. And he turned away as she tried to kiss him. She hadn't talked to him since she left eight days before, the morning of Thanksgiving. Every time she had called, the kids had said he was out or busy, and he had never called her.

"How was your trip?" he asked formally as he sat down, and the children noticed the chill between them.

"It was great," India said easily, and then she told them all about the wedding. The girls were particularly hungry for the details. But even Jason and Sam were impressed when she told them about the Kings and Queens and Prime Ministers, and that the President and First Lady had been there.

"Did you say hi from me?" Sam asked with a giggle.

"Of course I did," India smiled at him, "and the President said, 'Say hi to my friend Sam.'" But Sam laughed as she said it. They were all in good spirits, except Doug, who continued to look angry all through dinner.

And the dam finally broke when they got upstairs to their bedroom. "You seem to have enjoyed yourself," he said accusingly. He could detect no remorse in her whatsoever. Worse yet, he could see no fear of the displeasure she had caused him, or the consequences it might lead to. But that had been Paul's gift to her. She felt more at ease in her own skin than she had in years, and even proud of what she'd accomplished. But watching Doug as he sat down and glared at her, she finally felt a little tremor.

"I did some good work over there," she said quietly, but without apology. She was mostly sorry that he couldn't share the good feelings with her. "The children seem fine." It was their common bond, the one thing they seemed to have left to cling to, since they no longer seemed to have each other. He still hadn't touched her, or put an arm around her, or kissed her. He was obviously much too angry.

"No thanks to you," he said, referring to her comment about the children. "It's interesting that you're willing to do the same thing to them your father did to you. Have you thought of that at all this week?" He was trying to make her feel guilty, but thus far not succeeding.

"London for a week is not Da Nang for six months, or Cambodia for a year. That's very different."

"Eventually, you'll work up to that, India. It's only a matter of time, I'm sure." He was being incredibly nasty to her.

"No, it isn't. I'm very clear on what I'm willing to do."

"Really, and what is that? Maybe you should tell me."

"Just an occasional assignment like this," she said simply.

"It's all about your vanity, isn't it? And your ego. It's not enough to be here and take care of your children. You need to go out in the world and show off." He made it sound like she was a stripper.

"I love what I do, Doug. And I love you, and the children. They're not mutually exclusive."

"They might be. That's not entirely clear yet." There was an obvious threat in what he was saying, and the way he said it made her angry. She was tired from her trip. It was two o'clock in the morning for her, and Doug had been rotten to her from the moment he saw her.

"What does that mean? Are you threatening me?" She was getting angry too as she listened to him.

"You knew the potential risk when you walked out on us on Thanksgiving."

"I didn't 'walk out on you,' Doug. I made Thanksgiving dinner the night before I left, and the kids were fine with it."

"Well, I wasn't, and you knew that."

"It's not always about you, Doug." That was what had changed between them. At least some of it had to be about her now. "Why can't you just let this go? I did it. The kids are fine. We survived it. It was a week out of our lives, and it was good for me. Can't you see that?" She was still struggling to make him hear her. But even if he heard, her happiness was of no interest to him.

"What I see is a lifestyle that doesn't suit me. That's the problem, India." She saw, as she listened to him, that it was about controlling her. He was angry at what he saw as her insubordination and treason. But she didn't want to be controlled by him. She wanted him to love her. And she was beginning to think he didn't. She had thought that for a while now.

"I'm sorry you have to make this such a big deal. It doesn't have to be. Why not just live with it for a while and see what happens? If it gets too complicated, if it's too hard on the kids, if we really can't live with it, then let's talk about it." She tried to reason with him but he didn't answer. What she had suggested was rational, but he wasn't. Without saying another word to her, he picked up a magazine and started reading, and that was the end of the conversation. She had been dismissed. As far as Doug was concerned, it wasn't even worth discussing it with her.

She unpacked her suitcase, went to bed, and wished she could have called Paul. But there was no way she could, and by then it was five o'clock in the morning for him, wherever he was, in Sicily, or Corsica, or beginning to make his way to Venice. He seemed part of another lifetime, a distant dream that would never be a reality for her. He was a voice on the phone. And Doug was what she had to contend with, and live with.

She took Sam to soccer the next day, and she and Doug successfully avoided speaking to each other for the rest of the weekend. She saw Gail, who talked about her Christmas shopping. And after India dropped Sam off, she took her film to Raoul Lopez in the city. They went to lunch and she filled him in on all the details. He was particularly excited about her second story, and knew it was explosive material. And on her way back from the city at four o'clock, she pulled out of the traffic and stopped at a gas station. She knew the Satcom number by heart, and had purchased twenty dollars in quarters at the airport the day before, for an opportunity like this one.

A British voice answered briskly at the other end. "Good evening, *Sea Star*." She recognized him now as the chief steward, said hello to him, and asked for Paul. It was ten o'clock at night, and she suspected he was probably in his cabin, reading.

Paul came on the line very quickly, and sounded happy to hear her. "Hi, India. Where are you?"

She laughed before she answered as she looked around her. "Freezing to death in a pay phone at a gas station, on my way back to Westport. I had to drop off my film in the city." It had just started snowing.

"Is everything all right?" He sounded worried.

"More or less. The kids are fine. I don't think they even missed me." But it was so different for them than it had been for her as a child. She had been all alone with her mother. They had each other, and a happy stable life that she had carefully provided for them. "Doug hasn't spoken to me since I got home, except to tell me how rotten I was for going. Not much has changed here." Nor would it, she was realizing. This barren landscape was her life now.

"How are the pictures?" He was always excited about her work, particularly about the stories she'd just done in London.

"I don't know yet. They didn't want me to develop them myself. Big magazines do their own lab work and editing. I'm out of the loop now."

"When will they be out?"

"The wedding in a few days. Raoul has sold the prostitution ring photos to an international syndicate so it will be later in the month. How are you?" Her feet were getting numb in the cold, and her hand felt as though it were frozen to the phone, but she didn't care. She was happy to hear him. It was a warm, friendly voice in the darkness of her life at the moment.

"I'm fine. I was beginning to think you weren't going to call, and I was getting worried." He had fantasized a warm, romantic reunion with her husband when she got home, and he was a little startled to realize that the thought of it unnerved him.

"I haven't stopped since I got back. I took Sam to soccer this morning, and I had to go into the city. Tonight, I'm taking the kids to the movies." It was something to do while Doug ignored her. It would have been so much nicer to have dinner with him and tell him all about London, but there was no chance of that now. Instead she was calling Paul from a phone booth, just to have a sympathetic adult to talk to. "Where are you?"

"We just left Corsica, and we're heading south to the Straits of Messina, on our way back up to Venice."

"I wish I were there with you," she said, and meant it, and then wondered how it sounded. But it sounded good to him too. They would have talked all night, and played liar's dice, listened to music, and sailed all day. It was a lovely fantasy for both of them, but there were parts of it neither of them had come to terms with.

"I wish you were here too," he said, sounding husky.

"Did you sleep all right last night?" Knowing of his trouble with that now, it was a question she always asked him, and it touched him.

"More or less."

"Bad dreams again?" His survivor guilt haunted him, and his visions of Serena.

"Yeah, sort of."

"Try warm milk."

"I'd rather try sleeping pills, if I had some." It was beginning to upset him. His nights had become one long restless battle, particularly lately.

"Don't do that. Try a warm bath, or go up on the bridge and sail for a while."

"Yes, ma'am," he teased her, happier than he wanted to be to hear her. "Are you freezing, India?" His voice sounded sexy and gentle.

"Yes," she laughed, "but it's worth it." There was something very odd about doing something so clandestine, and she hated to be so sneaky. But it was great to hear him, and she reminded herself as she listened to him, that their conversations were harmless. "It's snowing. I can't even think about the fact that Christmas is in four weeks. I haven't done anything about it." And as soon as she said it, she was sorry. She knew Christmas would be an agony for him this year. He wasn't going to Saint Moritz, as he had every year with Serena.

"I'll bet Sam loves it," he said calmly. "Does he still believe in Santa Claus?"

"More or less. I think he kind of doesn't, but he's afraid to take a chance, so he pretends he does, just to be on the safe side." They both laughed, and then the operator came on the line and asked for more of her quarters. "I've got to go, I'm out of money," she said regretfully.

"Call me whenever you want to. And I'll call you on Monday," he confirmed. "And India?" He seemed about to say something important, and she felt her heart skip a beat. There were times when she thought they were dancing close to the line now, and she didn't know what to do once they got there, or worse yet, crossed it.

"Yes?" she said bravely.

"Keep your chin up." She smiled at what he'd said to her, both relieved and disappointed. They were still in safe territory, but she wondered if they would stay there forever. Sometimes it was more than a little confusing sorting out her feelings. She was married to a man who didn't seem to care about her, and calling a man thousands of miles away from a phone booth, and worried about how he was sleeping. In a weird, inexplicable way, it was like being married to two men, and having a real relationship with neither.

"I'll talk to you soon," she said, as plumes of frosty steam curled into the frigid air in the phone booth.

"Thanks for calling," he said warmly.

They both hung up and stood rooted to the spot for a long moment, she thinking of what she was doing now, going to these lengths to speak to him, and he encouraging her to do it. And as they both walked away from their phones, they were equally confused, and equally happy to have spoken to each other.

When she got back to Westport, everyone was waiting for her to start dinner, and they were arguing over what movie to go to. Doug was working on some papers he'd brought home, and didn't say a word to her, or ask her where she'd gone to. And looking at him, as he sat down to dinner next to her, she felt a shiver of guilt run through her. How would she have liked it, she asked herself, if Doug was calling women from pay phones? But it wasn't like that, she reassured herself. Paul was a friend, a confidant, a mentor. And the real issue, she realized, was not what Paul was providing in her life, but what Doug wasn't.

In the end, after grousing about it, Doug decided to come to the movies with them, and they went to one of those huge complexes, which showed nine different movies, and he and the boys went to something suitably violent, while she and the girls saw the latest Julia Roberts movie. And when they got home, everyone was happy and in good spirits.

All in all, despite the strain between her and Doug, it was a passably good weekend, as good as it ever was now. In order to survive the loneliness of her life, India found she had to apply different standards. As long as they didn't have any major fights, and he didn't threaten to leave her, it qualified as a decent weekend. Hardly a standard of perfection. And, as promised, Paul called her on Monday.

She told him about the movie she'd seen,

Raoul's call that morning to tell her the magazines were ecstatic about her photographs, and she asked him how his dreams were. He said he had slept well the night before, and then told her Serena's new book would be out soon, the one with India's photograph of her on the back cover. And it made him sad to think about it. It was as though she were still there, when in fact she wasn't. And India nodded as she listened.

And after a while, she and Paul hung up, after covering a variety of subjects. She picked up the kids that afternoon, and did some Christmas shopping. And for the next two weeks, Paul called every few days, to hear her news, and tell her where he was, and what he was thinking. He was beginning to dread Christmas, and he was talking more about Serena.

India's whole focus was on him when they talked, and on the children when she was with them. And she dealt with Doug as best she could, though he hadn't warmed up to her again since before Thanksgiving, and there might as well have been a glass wall between them in their bedroom. They saw each other, but never touched, or even approached each other. They had become nothing more than roommates.

India was still hoping to make the marriage work, but she had no idea how to do it. She was willing to make whatever concessions she had to, within reason. "Reason" for her now no longer included turning down all possible assignments. But maybe, with luck, they'd get through a peaceful Christmas. She hoped so, for the children.

She mentioned it to Gail once or twice, and looked as depressed about it as she felt. But other than an affair to boost India's spirits and spice things up, Gail couldn't think of anything to suggest to help them. And India still hadn't told her about her conversations with Paul. She had kept that as her darkest secret. Only she and Paul knew about it. It made them conspirators and allies.

She had just talked to him, in fact, on the day that Doug stormed into the house from a late train and asked her to come upstairs to their bedroom. She had no idea what had happened to make him so furious, as he set his briefcase on the bed, snapped it open viciously, and threw a magazine at her feet with a single brutal gesture.

"You lied to me!" he raged, as she stared

at him uncomprehendingly. All she could think of were her calls to Paul, and she hadn't in fact lied. She just hadn't told him. But it was not her calls to Paul that had upset him. He knew nothing about him. "You told me you were going to London to cover a *wedding!*" He pointed to the magazine lying at her feet, and she saw that he was shaking with rage over what he'd seen there.

"I did cover a wedding," she said, looking surprised, and a little frightened. She had never seen him as furious in all the years she'd known him. "I showed you the pictures." The story had come out the week before, and the photographs had been terrific. The children had loved them, but Doug had refused to even look at them.

"Then what's this?" he asked, picking the magazine up off the floor and waving it in her face, as she realized what had happened. The second story must have broken. She took the magazine from him, and looked at it, and nodded slowly.

"I did another story while I was there," she said quietly, but her hands were shaking. They had broken the story earlier than she expected. She had been meaning to say something to him, but the right moment had never come, and now he was livid. It was obvious that he had gone right over the edge because of it, and not only because she did a story without telling him, but he was outraged by the subject.

"It's total smut. The worst garbage I've ever seen. How could you even take pictures like that and put your name on them? It's sheer pornography, absolute filth, and you know it! It's disgusting!"

"It is disgusting. It was terrible . . . but there was nothing pornographic about the pictures. It's a story about abused children. I wanted people to feel exactly what you do, about what happened to them. I wanted people to feel sick and outraged. That's the whole point of what I was doing." He had in fact proven that she'd done a good job with it, but he was not outraged at the perpetrators, he was incensed at her for covering the story. His point of view was more than a little twisted.

"I think you're twisted to have had any part of it, India. Think of your own children, how will they feel when they know you covered this? They're going to be as ashamed of you as I am." She had never realized how narrow he was, how limited, and how archaic. It was depressing to hear him say it.

"I hope not," she said quietly. "I hope they understand, if you don't, that I wanted to help, to stop a terrible crime from happening again. That's what my work is about, not just taking pretty pictures at weddings. In fact, this is a lot more up my alley than covering a wedding."

"I think you're a very sick person," he said coldly.

"I think our marriage is much sicker than I am, Doug. I don't understand your reaction."

"You deceived me. I would never have let you go over there to do this, which is undoubtedly why you didn't tell me. India, you were deceitful."

"For chrissake, Doug. Grow up. There's a real world out there full of dangers and tragedies and terrible people. If no one exposes them, what's going to stop those people from hurting me, or you, or our children? Don't you understand that?"

"All I understand is that you lied to me in order to take photographs of a lot of filth and teenage prostitutes and revolting old men. If that's what you want in your life, India, fine, go for it. But I want no part of it, or of you, if this is the world you want to live in."

"I've been getting that message loud and clear from you," she said, looking at him with disbelief. There was no pride, no praise, no recognition of what she might have accomplished with her story. She hadn't even seen it, but she knew that if it had elicited this reaction from him, it must have been as powerful as she had intended. "I thought you'd get over it, maybe even 'forgive' me for wanting to have a little more in my life than just picking Sam up at soccer, but I'm beginning to think it is going to go on forever like this, with you punishing me for what you perceive as my many offenses."

"You're not the woman I married, India," he accused, as she looked at him with sorrow.

"Yes, I am, Doug. That's exactly who I am. I haven't been that person in a long time. I've only been the person you wanted me to become. And I tried. God knows I tried. But I think I could be both people, the one you want, and the one I've always been, the one I was before I was your wife. But you won't let me. All you want to do is kill that person. All you want is what you can make me."

"I want what you owe me," he said. And for the first time in seventeen years, after what he'd just said to her, she felt she owed him nothing.

"I don't owe you anything, Doug, any more than you owe me. All we *owe* each other is to be good to our children, and make each other happy. Neither of us *owes* the other a life of misery, or of forcing each other into being something we can't be, or worse yet, depriving each other of something that makes us feel better, as human beings. What kind of a 'deal' is that? Not a very good one." She said it with a look of grief, and everything about the way she stood there and looked at him said she felt defeated.

"I'm getting out of here," he said, looking at her furiously. He was enraged by everything she had said to him, as well as the article she'd done in London. She had been making him miserable for the last six months, and he was sick and tired of it. As far as he was concerned, she had broken every contract she had ever made with him when they married. "I've had it up to here with your bullshit," he said, as he pulled a suitcase out of the top of his closet, threw it on the bed, and started throwing things in it. He wasn't even looking at what he was packing, he was just throwing in handfuls of ties, loose socks, and whatever underwear he found in his drawers without caring what it looked like.

"Are you divorcing me?" she asked miserably. It was a hell of a time of year to do it. But there never was a good one.

"I don't know yet," he said, as he snapped his suitcase shut. "I'm going to stay in a hotel in the city. At least I won't have to do that goddamn commute every day, and then come home to listen to you bitch about your career and how unfair I'm being to you. Why did you even bother to get married?"

With a handful of words he had cast aside the years she had devoted tirelessly to him and their children. With a single gesture he was willing to throw away seventeen years of their marriage. But she had no idea what to do now to stop him, or change things. She just couldn't give up everything to please him. In the end, it would do just as much harm as what he was doing now. And she didn't entirely disagree with him. The last six months had been a nightmare.

He stomped down the stairs and out the front door without saying a word to her, or the children watching TV in the living room. And he slammed the door as hard as he could behind him. India looked out the window and saw him drive away, and she could see it had started snowing. Tears rolled slowly down her cheeks as she picked up the magazine he had left on the floor. She sat down heavily in a chair, and looked at it, and realized as she did, that it was the best thing she'd ever done, and made the Harlem child abuse story look like a fairy tale in comparison. This one was brutal. And everything those children had been through showed in their eyes and on their faces. And as she went from page to page, all India could think was that she was glad she'd done it. No matter what Doug thought.

It was a long, lonely night for her, thinking of Doug, and wondering where he was. He had never called to tell her what hotel he had decided to stay in. She lay awake, and thought about him all night, and everything that had happened since June. It was beginning to look like a mountain the size of Everest that stood between them, and she had no idea how to scale it.

At three o'clock, she rolled over and looked at the clock again, and realized that it was already nine in the morning in Venice. And with a rock still sitting on her heart, she dialed and asked for Paul, and was relieved when she heard him.

"Are you okay?" he asked, sounding worried. "You sound awful. Are you sick, India?"

"Sort of." She started to cry as soon as she said it. It was odd calling him about Doug, but she needed a shoulder to cry on. And she could hardly call Gail at three o'clock in the morning in Westport. "Doug walked out on me tonight. On us. He's staying at a hotel in the city."

"What happened?"

"That story on the kids in London broke. It's beautiful. The best thing I ever did. He thought it was disgusting, he called it pornography, and said I was sick to cover something like that, and he wants no part of me as a result. He said I lied to him about doing the story. I did," she sighed, "but if I had told him the truth, he wouldn't have let me do it. And Paul, it's terrific. Even after all this, I'm glad I did it."

"I'll go to one of the hotels here today to get it." It was in an international publication and he was sure he could find it. "I want to see it." And then he addressed her immediate problem. "What are you going to do about your husband?"

"I don't know. Wait. See what he does. I don't know what to tell the kids. If he calms down, it seems stupid to upset them. If he doesn't, they'll have to know sooner or later." And then she started crying again. "It's only nine days till Christmas. . . . Why did he have to do this now? It's going to ruin their Christmas."

"He did it because he's a son of a bitch," Paul said in a voice India had never heard him use before, "and he's been hurting you ever since the day I met you. I don't know what it was like before, India. But I'd be willing to bet that the only reason it worked for so long is because you made all the concessions." She had only recently begun to see that. "He's been a total shit to you ever since last summer, from what you said. And just what I've heard in the last few months should be enough to make you walk out on him, never mind what he wants." He was absolutely furious at what she'd told him. "You did something very important with that story and you know it. You're an incredible human being, a great mother, and I'm sure you've been a good wife to him. He has no right to be such a bastard to you. You're a decent, talented, nice person, and he doesn't deserve you."

India felt as though she'd watched an express train roar by as she listened. Paul was livid. "I'm tired of listening to you tell me stories about how he hurts you. He has no right to do that. Maybe he did the right thing today. Maybe in the long run, it will be a blessing for you and the children." But she wasn't sure yet. She was still feeling the shock and the loss and the shame of what Doug had told her. She would never forget the look on his face as he stormed out of their bedroom.

"India," Paul went on then, "I want you to hear me. You're going to be okay. You're going to be just fine. You have your kids, and your work. And he'll have to support you. You're not going to be abandoned. This is *not* like when your father died. This is very different." He knew from her that her father hadn't left them a dime when he died, he had nothing, and her mother had had to take extra jobs to make ends meet. She never complained, but they had been frightened for a long time about literally starving.

"You're not going to starve. Your kids are going to be okay, and so are you, and you have each other." But if Doug left, she would no longer have a husband. And for nearly twenty years now, her identity had been entirely tied up with him. She felt as though a part of her had just been torn away, and she was left with a gaping wound now, no matter how unhappy he had made her. This wasn't going to be easy either. It might even have been easier to give up her career, and shrivel up and die inside, doing what he told her, she told herself. But even she knew she didn't believe that. She was just scared now. But Paul was helping. Even his anger at Doug put things into sharper focus for her.

It also made her wonder for a moment if Paul was going to be there for her. But he had said nothing about that. They talked to each other almost every day, about everything that crossed their minds, and shared their most hidden secrets, but nothing had ever been said between them about the future. And this hardly seemed the time to ask him.

"Do you know where he is?" Paul asked, as she blew her nose.

"I have no idea. He never called to tell me."

"He will eventually. Maybe this is for the best. I think you should call a lawyer." But she didn't feel ready to do that. There was still a chance that Doug would calm down and come back, and they could still limp hand in hand into the future. "Can you get some sleep?" he asked sympathetically. He wished he were there to comfort her. She sounded like a frightened child as he listened to her.

"I don't think so." It was already four o'clock in the morning.

"Try, before the kids get up. I'll call you in the morning."

"Thanks, Paul," she said, as tears filled her eyes again. She was still feeling overwhelmed by everything that had happened, but he understood that.

"Everything's going to be all right," he told her, sounding confident. He had the confidence for her that he no longer had for his own life.

After they hung up, she lay in bed for a while, thinking about him, and about Doug, and everything that had happened in the past six months. And all she could think of in the dark of night was that she was going to be alone now.

And on the boat, Paul was staring unhappily out to sea, thinking of her and the constant abuse she was taking from Doug. He was sick of it on her behalf, wished he could say as much to Doug, and tell him never to come near her again. But he knew he had no right to do that.

He took the tender out after a while, and went to the Cipriani, and found the magazine her photos were in. He stood and looked at them in the lobby. They were sensational, and if Doug objected to them, as far as Paul was concerned, he was crazy. Paul couldn't have been more proud of her, and he called her at nine o'clock, her time, to tell her.

"You really like them?" she asked, sounding incredulous and pleased. Doug still hadn't called, and she was standing barefoot in her nightgown in the kitchen, making coffee. The kids were still sleeping.

"I've never seen anything so moving or so impressive. You made me cry when I read it."

"Me too," she admitted. But all Doug had seen was the sleaziness of the prostitution ring and somehow associated India with it.

"Did you get any sleep?" he asked, still sounding worried.

"Not much. About an hour. I fell asleep around seven."

"Try and take a nap today. And give yourself a big pat on the back from me, for this story."

"Thank you," she said. They talked for a

few more minutes, and then hung up. Raoul called her a little later, and said essentially the same thing Paul had about the story.

"If you don't win a Pulitzer for this, India, I'll invent a new prize for you myself. This is the most powerful thing I've ever seen in pictures."

"Thank you."

"What did your husband say?" he asked, sure that this would finally convince him to let her do the work she was so good at, and that meant so much to her.

"He left me."

There was a long pause as Raoul listened. "You're kidding, right?"

"No, I'm not. He walked out last night. I told you, he means business."

"He's crazy. He should be carrying you around on his shoulders."

"Not exactly."

"I'm sorry, India." He sounded as though he meant it. He had always liked her, and never had understood her husband's position about her working.

"Me too," she said sadly.

"Maybe he'll come back after he calms down."

"I hope so," she said, but she no longer

knew what she did hope. And Paul was slowly becoming part of an ever more tangled picture. She no longer knew if she wanted to fix it with Doug, or dare to believe that somehow, somewhere, she and Paul would manage to crawl through their respective griefs and manage to find each other. The hope of that, slim as it was, was becoming increasingly appealing. But he had never made any indication to her that that was even a remote possibility, and most of the time, she was fairly sure it wasn't. She couldn't leave a seventeen-year marriage for a vague fantasy she had about a man who swore he would never again have a woman in his life, and was determined to spend the rest of his life hiding on a sailboat. Whatever it was she had with Paul meant a great deal to her, but it was only a slim reed to hang on to. And in truth, it was more friendship than romance.

After she talked to Raoul, she and the children managed to get through the day, and she told them that Doug had had to go out of town on business to see clients. She never heard from him all weekend or from Paul again, and on Monday morning, she called Doug at the office.

"How are you?" she asked bleakly.

"I still feel the same way, if that's what you're asking," he said tersely. "Nothing's going to change, India, unless you do." And they were both beginning to realize that was unlikely.

"Where does that leave us?"

"In pretty deep water, if you ask me," Doug said unsympathetically.

"That's a pretty tough thing to do to the kids over Christmas. Don't you think we could at least put this aside until after the holidays, and then try to resolve it?" It was a reasonable solution, if not to the problem, then at least to not ruining Christmas for the children.

"I'll think about it," he answered, and then told her he had to meet with clients. He had told her the hotel where he was staying, and she didn't hear from him for the next two days. And on Wednesday he called her, and agreed to come back, at least through Christmas. "For the kids' sake." But he made no apology to her, and held out no olive branch, and she guessed correctly that his return to the house would be extremely stressful.

She talked to Paul every day that week. He called her most of the time, but she called him occasionally for moral support, and on

Friday night, a week after he had left, Doug returned to Westport. It was only four days before Christmas, and the kids were beginning to wonder why he had been gone since the previous weekend. The excuse that he had to see clients had been wearing thin, and they all seemed pleased to see him.

But Doug's return complicated things for India. It made it impossible for Paul to call her again, but she went to a phone booth every day over the weekend. On Monday, it was Christmas Eve, and on her way home from the grocery store, she called Paul collect from a pay phone. He sounded as depressed as she was. He was keening for Serena. And she was miserable with Doug. He had devoted himself to making the holidays as difficult as he could for her, and she just hoped they made it through Christmas, for the children.

"We're a mess, aren't we?" Paul smiled wistfully as he talked to her. Even being on the boat no longer cheered him. He just kept sifting through his memories, and had even gone through some of the things she had left in their cabin. "I still can't believe she's gone," he said to India, sounding bereft. And she still couldn't believe she was about to lose her marriage. It was hard to understand how lives got so screwed up, how people made such a mess of things. Paul, of course, didn't have to blame himself, or feel it was his fault. But India still wondered in her own case. Doug was so willing to blame her for everything, that at times she actually believed him.

"Are you going to do anything nice over the holidays?" she asked, wishing she could think of something to cheer him. But staying on the boat, as he did, she hadn't even been able to send him a present. She had written him a silly poem, and faxed it to the boat that morning from the post office, and he'd said he loved it. But that didn't solve their larger problems. "Are you going to church?" Venice certainly seemed a good place to do that.

"God and I are having a little problem these days. I don't believe in Him, and He doesn't believe in me. For the moment, it's a standoff."

"It might just be pretty and make you feel good," she suggested, stamping her feet in the freezing cold in the outdoor phone booth.

"It's more likely to make me angry, and feel worse," he said, sounding stubborn. In his opinion, if there was a God, he wouldn't have lost Serena, and India didn't want to argue with him about religion. "What about you? Do you go to church on Christmas Eve?"

"We do. We go to midnight mass and take the children."

"Doug should be doing some serious soul searching for the way he's been treating you in the last six months." Not to mention before that. And then, out of the blue, "I miss her so much, India, I can't stand it. Sometimes I think that the sheer pain of it is going to blow me to bits, I feel like it's going to rip my chest out."

"Just keep thinking of what she would have said to you. Don't forget that. Listen to her . . . she wouldn't want you to feel like this forever." And he wouldn't, but right now was the worst. She had been gone for less than four months, and it was Christmas. India felt helpless in the face of his agony, and at this distance. If they were together, at least she might have been able to put her arms around him, and hug him. That might have been something. But Paul couldn't even find solace in India's words now.

"Serena always had more guts than I did."

"No, she didn't. You were pretty evenly matched in that way, I suspect," India said firmly. "You can take it, if you have to. You have no choice now. You just have to get through it. There's a light at the end of that tunnel somewhere," she said, trying to make him hold on for as long as he had to. She would have liked to tell him that she would be there for him, but who knew what was going to happen to them. Nothing was sure now.

"What about you? What light do you see at the end of your tunnel?" He sounded more depressed than she had ever heard him.

"I don't know yet. I'm not that far. I just hope there is one."

"There will be. You'll find what you want at some point." Would she? She was beginning to wonder, and he did not seem to want to volunteer to be there for her either. At this point, he still felt he couldn't. He was still looking back, at Serena. And then he startled India completely with what he did say. "I wish I could tell you I'd be there for you, India. I wish I could be. But I know I won't be. I'm not going to be the light at the end of the tunnel for you. I can't even be there for myself anymore, let alone for someone else." Let alone a woman fourteen years younger than he, with a whole life ahead of her, and four young children to take care of. He had thought of it more than once, and no matter how fond he was of her, or how much they needed each other now, he knew that in the long run he had nothing to give her. He had already come to that conclusion. Only that morning, in fact, as he stood looking out at Saint Mark's Square, from the *Sea Star.* "I have nothing left to give anyone," he went on. "I gave it all to Serena."

"I understand," India said quietly. "It's all right. I don't expect anything from you, Paul. All we can do is be here for each other as friends right now. Hopefully, later on, we'll both be in a better place to make it on our own." But right then, they were both acutely aware that they needed each other's hand to get over the rough places they were facing. But he had certainly made himself clear to her. He would not be at the end of the tunnel for her. He didn't want to be there. It was a taste of reality for her, and left her few illusions. It was not what she had been hoping for, whether she had faced it or not, but it was honest. Paul was always honest with her.

They talked for a little while longer, and finally she knew she had to go home. She was frozen to the bone by then anyway, and it had not been a happy conversation. And with tears in her eyes, she wished him a Merry Christmas.

"You too, India . . ." he said sadly. "I hope next year is better for both of us. We both deserve it."

And then, for no sane reason she could fathom given what he'd said to her, she wanted to tell him that she loved him, but she didn't. That would have been crazy. But it was something they both needed, and had too little of, except from each other. The words remained unsaid, but the gifts they had given each other, of time and caring and tenderness, spoke for themselves, whether or not they heard them, or chose to.

She went back home after her call, with a heavy heart. He had told her what she had been wondering for months, and didn't want to hear, but at least she couldn't fool herself now about what might happen someday, or what she meant to him. It was precisely what she had told herself it was, nothing more than an extraordinary friendship. She could not use him as a safety net into which to leap from her burning marriage. And in her heart of hearts, she knew he was right not to be that.

She and Doug went to midnight mass, as

they always did, and took all four children with them. And when they got home, she put the last presents under the tree, while Sam put out cookies for Santa, and carrots and salt for the reindeer. The others were good sports about leaving him his illusions.

And in the morning, there were squeals of delight as they opened their gifts. She had chosen them carefully and spent a lot of time on it, and even Doug was pleased with what she gave him. She gave him a new blazer, which he needed desperately, and a handsome new leather briefcase. The gifts were without fantasy, but they suited him to perfection, and genuinely pleased him. And he had given her a plain gold bracelet, which she also liked. What she didn't like was the continuing atmosphere of hostility between them.

The cease-fire between them was brief, and by that night, she could sense the tension increasing, when they retreated to their bedroom. And she was afraid that he was going to leave again now that Christmas was behind them. But when she brought the subject up, somewhat anxiously, he said he had decided to stay until after New Year's. He was taking the week off between the holidays, which she thought might help, but in fact it made things worse and they seemed to be fighting daily.

She went out to call Paul whenever she could, but she missed him a couple of times when he was off the boat, and she had told him he couldn't call her until after New Year's.

And it was just after New Year's in fact when Doug walked into the kitchen carrying an envelope, with his face as white as the paper he held, and his dark eyes blazing. He had just picked their mail up, and he stood in front of her, while she was folding towels, and waved the envelope in her face. It looked like their phone bill.

"Just exactly what is this?" he said, almost too enraged to speak as he threw it at her.

"It looks like our phone bill." She wondered if it was too high, and then suddenly she remembered with a sense of panic. She had called Paul several times from home during the week Doug had left her.

"You're damn right it is," he said, pacing around the room like a lion. "Is that what all this was about? Is that it? It had nothing to do with your 'career' did it, all this crap for all these months? How long have you been sleeping with him, India? Ever since the summer?"

She picked the bill up and looked at it. There were five calls to the *Sea Star.*

"I'm not sleeping with him, Doug. We're friends," she said quietly, but her heart was pounding. How could she ever explain it to him? It was obvious what it looked like, and she wasn't sure she blamed him. But it truly was nothing more than a friendship. Even Paul had confirmed it. "I was upset. You had walked out on me. He's called a couple of times to talk about his wife. He knows I liked her. He's desperately unhappy. That's all it is. Two unhappy people crying on each other's shoulders." It was embarrassing to admit, but in truth there wasn't a lot more to tell him.

"I don't believe you," Doug said with utter fury. "I think you've been sleeping with him since last summer."

"That's not true, and you know it. If I were, I wouldn't be as upset about us, or trying so hard to get through to you."

"Bullshit. All you've done is fight for your 'career,' so you could dump me and the kids and get out of here. Did you meet him in London?"

"Of course not," she said calmly, although she didn't feel it. She felt sad and afraid and somewhat guilty. It was as though the last shred of what was left between them had just gone up in smoke. There was nothing left to fight for. It was hopeless.

"Did he call you?"

"Yes, he did," she said honestly.

"What do you do? Have sex on the phone with him? Some kind of kinky disgusting kicks that turn you both on?" The image he painted for her made her shudder.

"No, he cries about his wife. And I cry about you. It's not exactly sexy."

"You're both sick, and you deserve each other." She wished she did, but unfortunately, that was not the case either. "I'm not going to put up with this, India. I've had it. You're of no use to me, and you'll be of no use to him either. You're a lousy wife, and a lousy lover," he threw in for good measure, though she wasn't even sure why he did it, except maybe to hurt her. "All you're interested in is your career, that's all you care about now. Well, India, you've got it." And as though to punctuate his words and the plummeting of her heart, the phone rang. She picked it up, praying it wasn't Paul, to make matters still worse, but it wasn't. It was Raoul, and he sounded excited. She told him she couldn't talk just now, but he insisted she had to, and she saw that Doug was watching, and she was afraid he would think it was Paul, so she let him tell her what he wanted.

He had an assignment for her, right here in the States. In Montana. It was about a religious cult that had cropped up and seemingly gone berserk. They were laying siege, holding hostages, and the FBI was camped around them. There were over a hundred people involved, at least half of them children.

"This is going to be a biggie, India," Raoul promised, as she listened.

"I can't do it now."

"You have to. The magazine wants you. I wouldn't call you if it wasn't important. Do you want it or not?"

"Can I call you back? I'm talking to my husband."

"Oh shit. Is he back? All right, call me back in the next two hours. I have to give them an answer."

"Tell them I can't, and I'm sorry." She was definite this time. She didn't want to add any fuel to the fire Doug had just set, using their marriage as kindling.

"Call me back," Raoul insisted.

"I'll try," was all she'd promise.

"Who was that?" Doug asked, looking suspicious.

"Raoul Lopez."

"What did he want?"

"He has an assignment, in Montana. I told him I can't take it. You heard me."

"What difference does it make now, India? It's over." He said it with such venom that this time she knew he meant it. "I've had it. I'm finished. You're not the woman I married, or the one I want. I don't want to be married to you anymore. It's as simple as that. You can tell Raoul, or Paul Ward, or anyone you want to. I'm calling my lawyer on Monday."

"You can't do that," she said, with tears in her eyes, begging for mercy.

"Yes, I can, and I'm going to. Go do your story."

"Right now that's not important."

"Yes, it is. You were willing to fuck up our marriage for that, India, now go get it. It's what you wanted."

"It shouldn't have been a choice. I could have done both."

"Not married to me, you couldn't."

But suddenly, being married to him

wasn't an option she wanted. Just looking at him, staring at her angrily, she knew he didn't love her. And as painful as it was to realize, she knew it was something she had to face now. And as she saw it in his eyes, all the fight went out of her, and she turned and left him standing alone with their laundry.

She grabbed her coat and went outside, and took a deep breath of the cold air, feeling it sear her lungs. She felt as though her heart were breaking, and yet at the same time she knew that, as terrifying as it was to her, she had to be free now. She couldn't live with his threats anymore, or her terror that he would abandon her, she couldn't live with the mantle of guilt he tried to make her wear, or the constant accusations. She just couldn't do it. She had to let him take it all from her, and leave her to stand alone naked. She had nothing but her children now, her camera, her life, her freedom. And the marriage she had cherished for so long, clung to and hung on to, and tried to fight for, was dead and gone. It was as dead as Serena. And as she had told Paul about his own life, all she had to do now was hang on, be strong, and live through it.

Chapter 19

India turned down the story in Montana after all, and instead she and Doug told the children they were separating. It was the worst day in her life, and one she hated herself for. This was something she had never wanted to do to them, just as she had never wanted to lose her father. She knew it would change their lives, as it would hers, and yet at the same time, she knew that, because she loved them, they would survive it.

"You mean you and Dad are *divorcing*?" Sam asked with a look of horror, and she wanted to rip her heart out. But Doug had done it for her.

"Yeah, stupid, what do you think they've just been saying?" Aimee said, choking on a sob, looking daggers at her parents. She hated them both for destroying the perfect life she'd had. They had destroyed all her illusions in a single instant.

Jason said nothing at all, but ran to his room and slammed the door, and when they saw him again, with red, swollen eyes, he pretended nothing had happened.

But at the end of their explanations to them, Jessica turned on her mother. "I *hate* you," she said viciously. "This is all *your* fault, with your stupid magazines and stupid pictures. I heard you fighting with Daddy about it. Why did you have to do that?" She was sobbing and childlike, and had lost all her grown-up airs in an instant.

"Because it's important to me, it's part of who I am, Jess, and I need to do it," India tried to explain. "It's not as important to me as you are, or Dad, but it meant a lot to me and I hoped that Daddy would understand it."

"I think you're stupid, both of you!" she shouted, and then ran upstairs to her own room, to lie on her bed and sob, while India wished she could explain it to her. But how did you tell a fourteen-year-old that you no longer loved her father? That he had broken your heart, and destroyed something inside you? She wasn't sure she even understood it.

And then Sam came to sit in her lap and sobbed. He cried for hours, shaking piteously as she held him.

"Will we still see Dad?" he asked, sounding heartbroken.

"Of course you will," she said, the tears on her own cheeks flowing like rivers. She would have liked to take it all back, to tell them it wasn't true, to make it never have happened. But it had. There was no turning back. Now they all had to face it.

No one wanted to eat after that, but she made them all chicken soup for dinner. And while she was cleaning up, Sam wandered back into the kitchen, looking stricken.

"Dad says you have a boyfriend. Is that true?" India looked horrified as she turned to face him.

"Of course not."

"He said it was Paul. Is that true, Mom?" He needed to know, and she understood that. It had been a vicious thing for Doug to do. But nothing surprised her.

"No, it's not true, sweetheart."

"Then why did Daddy say that?" He wanted to believe her.

"Because he's angry, and hurt. We both are. Grown-ups say stupid things sometimes when they're upset. I haven't seen Paul since you did last summer." She didn't tell him she had talked to him. He didn't need to know that. And in any case, he wasn't her boyfriend. He was never going to be an issue in Sam's life, except as a friend, and fellow sailor. "I'm sorry Daddy said that to you. Don't worry about it."

But what she said to Doug that night was a great deal stronger. She accused him of using their children to hurt her, and told him that if he ever did it again, he'd regret it.

"It's the truth, isn't it?"

"No, it's not, and you know it. It's too easy to blame this on someone else. This is our doing, we screwed this up, no one helped us. You can't blame a man I talked to on the phone, no matter how often I talked to him, or didn't. If you want to know who's responsible for this, go look in the mirror."

Doug left the house with his bags packed the next morning. He said he was going to find an apartment in the city. And he told her that once he got settled, he wanted to see the kids on the weekends. And suddenly she realized how many things they'd have to work out, how often he saw the kids, and when and where, if she got to keep the house, what he was going to pay her for child support. Suddenly she realized how totally all their lives would be affected.

She stayed home and cried for five days after he left, mourning what she had had with him, and what she had lost. And sensing the distress she was in, Paul kept a discreet distance, and didn't call her.

She finally called him a week after Doug had left, and talked to him for a long time about the children. They were still upset, and Jessica was still furious with her, but the others seemed to be adjusting. Sam was sad, but Doug had come out to visit them, and took them out for lunch and a movie on Sunday. She had asked him if he wanted to come in when he dropped them off, just to talk, but he had looked at her as though she were a stranger.

"I have nothing to say to you, India. Do you have a lawyer yet?" She had told him she hadn't. She hadn't felt ready to face that. But from everything Doug said to her, she knew it was over. Part of her wanted it to be, wanted to get away from the constant agony of it, and part of her still mourned the good years they had had together. She knew it would take her a long time to get over it, just as it was taking Paul time to get over Serena. And he understood that.

He was back in the south of France by then, in Cap d'Antibes, and he started calling every day again. And little by little through the weeks of January, she started to feel better. And Gail gave her the name of a divorce attorney. She still couldn't believe what had happened to them.

"What do you think did it?" Gail asked her one morning in early February over cappuccino.

"Everything," India said honestly. "Time. Doug wanting me not to go back to work. His refusing to hear what I was feeling. My refusing to do what he wanted. Looking back at it now, I'm surprised we lasted this long."

"I always figured you two were a sure thing forever."

"So did I," India said, smiling wistfully at her. "But those are the ones you have to watch out for. The perfect marriages we all believe in just aren't. It only worked as long as I played by his rules. As soon as I rocked the boat a little bit, and tried to add some of mine, it was all over."

"Are you sorry? Sorry that you rocked the boat, I mean?"

"Sometimes. It would have been easier not to do it, but after a while, I couldn't. I needed more than he was willing to give me. I see that now. And this is pretty scary." The kids were her responsibility now. There was no one to be there for her, to come home to her at night, to care if she got sick, or broke a leg, or died. She had no parents, no siblings, no family, other than her children. But listening to her put Gail's own marriage into question. It hadn't been good for years, but she had never seriously thought about leaving her husband, even if she liked complaining about him. The weird part was that for India, everything had seemed fine, and then all of a sudden it wasn't. And it was over.

"What are you going to do now? Will you sell the house?" Gail looked worried for her.

"Doug says I don't have to. He can afford to let me stay here. I can stay in it until the kids grow up, or go to college, and then we can sell it. Or before that, if I get married," she grinned at Gail ruefully. "I don't think that's likely, unless Dan Lewison asks me out." There wasn't a soul in Westport she wanted to go out with. And all of the men Gail was seeing on the sly were married.

"You've got a lot of courage," Gail said with admiration. "I've bitched about Jeff for years, and I'm not even sure I like him. But I don't think I could do this."

"Yes, you could, if you had to. If you knew you had more to lose if you didn't. That's what happened to me. You probably love Jeff more than you think, you just don't want to admit it."

"Listening to you talk about the kids, the house, alimony, vacations, I may go home tonight and kiss him," Gail said, with a look of terror. And India smiled at her.

"Maybe you should." But she no longer regretted what had happened. She knew it was for the best now. As scary as it was for her, and it had been, in a funny way, she knew it was what she wanted. And if nothing else, she had freedom. She had all the responsibility of the children, but she knew she could organize it so she could take some local assignments.

Raoul sent her on one in Washington in February. It was an interview with the First Lady. It wasn't as exciting as a war zone, but it was close to home, and it kept her hand in.

And then she did another story about a coal mine in Kentucky. She had no time for any social life but by then, Doug had an apartment, and according to Gail, who had heard it on the grapevine, a girlfriend. He hadn't wasted much time, and had started seeing her a month after he left home. She was divorced and had two kids, and lived in Greenwich. She had never worked, talked too much, had great legs, and was very pretty. Three of Gail's friends knew her and made a point to tell her everything so it would get back to India. They thought she should have the information.

Paul still called her every day, and he was finally beginning to sound better. He still had bad dreams, but he had regained his sense of humor, and he was starting to talk about business. And although he wouldn't admit it, India suspected that he missed it. Serena had been gone for six months by then, and although India knew he still missed her desperately, he was starting to tell some of the funnier stories about her, about the outrageous things she'd done, the people she had insulted brilliantly, and the vendettas she had engaged in. They painted her in a less saintly light than the things he had said about her before that.

And it indicated he hadn't entirely lost his perspective about her. But what also showed, each time they spoke, was how much he still loved her.

He had been a huge support to India once Doug was gone, and he always said she was better off, and when she was down, he had trouble seeing why she missed him. The fact that she had been married to Doug for longer than he had known his wife, somehow escaped him. He thought Doug was a bastard and India was well rid of him, and he was hard put to see why she was sometimes sad about it. It was hard for him to understand that she had not only lost a husband, but a life, and all the trappings that went with it, just as he had.

In early March he was still on the *Sea Star,* but she was beginning to think he sounded restless. She knew his moods by then, his quirks, his needs, his terrors, and his pet peeves. In an odd way sometimes it almost felt as though they were married. They knew so much about each other. And he knew all the same things about her. But he still insisted, when they talked about it, that he was never going to be the light at the end of the tunnel for her. He would always be there for her, he claimed, as a friend, but he kept telling her she had to find someone to go out with.

"Okay, start leaving my phone number on bathroom walls in the south of France. I haven't seen anyone in Westport."

"You're not trying," he scolded.

"You're right. They're all ugly, stupid, or married. Or alcoholics. There are a lot of those here. And I don't need one."

"Too bad. I was about to suggest AA meetings. That might be a good place to find a date," he teased.

"Be nice, or I'll start shipping divorcées to the boat for you, and believe me, that would be pretty scary." They had an easy relationship that allowed for both solace and humor, and they had been talking to each other daily for so long that neither of them could imagine living without it, though it wrought havoc on her phone bill. And the strangest part of it was that she had no idea when she would see him again, if ever. This seemed to be all they wanted. The romantic overtone between them had begun to die down, and after Doug left in January, India seemed to be less concerned about it. Paul had made himself clear to her before that, about his intentions with her, or lack of them, and whatever electricity they had once felt, seemed to have gone underground for a long time now. They were more like brother and sister.

So she felt quite comfortable telling him about a man she had met at Sam's soccer game, who was so repulsive she had actually taken a picture of him. He was fat, bald, rude, chewed gum, picked his nose, had belched in her face, and then asked her for a date on Tuesday.

"And what did you say to him?" Paul asked, sounding amused. He loved listening to her stories. In spite of all her troubles, she still had a mischievous sense of humor.

"I told him I'd meet him at the Village Grille, of course. Hell, do you think I want to be an old maid forever?" But the truth was, she did now. She really didn't want to find anyone, she was still smarting from the last one. And she got what she needed from their phone calls. In some ways, it was keeping her from getting her feet wet. And she was still trying hard not to.

"I'm sorry to hear that," Paul said, feigning disappointment.

"Why?" she teased him. "Are you jealous?"

"Obviously. But aside from that, I'm flying in to New York next week, and I thought maybe we could have lunch or something . . . or even dinner . . . but now that you're busy . . ."

"You're *what*?" She couldn't believe what he was saying. She had begun to think he would be on the *Sea Star* forever, and was merely a figment of her imagination. "Do you mean that?"

"There's a board meeting my partners say I have to attend, so I thought I'd see how New York looks after all this time, and . . . well, you know . . . even the *Sea Star* gets a little boring."

"I never thought I'd hear you say that," she said, beaming.

"Neither did I. Thank God Serena can't hear me." But he didn't sound as sad now when he talked about her.

"When are you coming?"

"Sunday night." He'd been wrestling with the idea for weeks, and hadn't said anything to her. He didn't want to get her hopes up. And he was still a little nervous about seeing her. For all his brave words, there was something about her that touched him deeply.

"Any chance you want to meet me?" He felt like a kid asking for a date as he said it.

"At the airport?"

"Well, yes, that's usual. I'm not arriving by boat this time. Would that be a nuisance, coming in from Westport?"

"I think it could be arranged." And then she wondered. "When did you decide this?" She wondered if he had decided on the spur of the moment, or if he'd planned it.

"About a week ago. I didn't say anything, because I wanted to be sure I meant it. But I bought my ticket this morning, so I guess I'm coming. It'll be good to see you, India." There was something odd about the way he said it, but she decided it was just emotional for him coming back to New York, and staying at his apartment. He had left the day after the funeral and hadn't been back since then. And she still remembered all too clearly how devastated he had looked at Saint Ignatius. But at least he'd had some time to heal in the meantime.

"I can't wait to see you," she said simply, wondering how long he was staying, but not wanting to ask him. She didn't know if he was coming home for good, or just trying it on for size. She suspected he didn't know either, and didn't want to press him. "I guess I'll have to cancel my date then. The sacrifices we make for our friends . . ."

"Keep his number. You still might need it." They chatted for a few minutes, and then hung up. He promised to give her the details of his arrival later. And in Westport, India sat looking out the window for a long time, looking for a sign of spring. But there was none. The trees were still bare, the ground was bleak. But knowing he was coming back made her feel as though something ought to be in bloom again. They had both survived such a long, lonely winter. They deserved some small reward for what they'd gone through. But life didn't always give rewards, she knew by then. There were no prizes for despair, or tragedy, or loss, or courage. There was just more of the same. And now and then, some small flower peeking through the snow, to spur you on, and give you hope, and remind you of better days. To remind you that one day, after the winter, there would be spring, and eventually summer.

But for the moment, there was still no sign of it for her. There were long, lonely days, and nothing more to hang on to but his phone calls. And now he was coming home. But as she walked slowly upstairs with a smile, she told herself it meant nothing. But in spite of that, it would be good to see him.

Chapter 20

India drove her station wagon to the airport on Sunday night, after leaving the children with a sitter. There was a light rain falling, and the traffic was bad, and it seemed to take forever. But she had given herself plenty of time for delays, and when she parked the car in the garage, she still had half an hour to spare before Paul got there.

She wandered around the terminal, looked at the shops, and checked herself in the mirror. She had worn a gray pantsuit and high heels, and she was carrying a trenchcoat. She had thought of wearing something more glamorous for him, like her black suit, but in the end, she decided it was silly. They were just friends, and they knew each other so well by now, she would have felt foolish trying to look seductive or sexy. She had worn her hair in a French twist, which was her one concession to dressing up for him, and makeup.

But now as she stood waiting for him, she began to wonder what he expected of her, and why he had asked her to meet him. She wondered if he was afraid to come back to New York, to face his memories there, and she suspected that he would be. It wouldn't be easy for him, even after all this time, especially going back to their apartment. He had hidden in a cocoon for the past six months, cloistered on the *Sea Star,* and holding her hand, for whatever comfort she could provide, from the distance. But whatever his reason for calling her, she was happy to be there.

She checked her watch repeatedly, and looked up at the board, to see if he'd arrived, wondering if he'd be delayed. And finally the notice to his flight was changed, and told her that he'd landed. But she knew it would still be a while. He had to go through Customs. It seemed interminable to her, standing there, waiting for him.

It was another half hour before passengers began to dribble out, fat grandmothers, and men in jeans, two fashion models carrying their portfolios, and a vast array of ordinary people and young children. She wasn't sure if they were from his flight, but finally she began to hear a flood of English accents, and knew this had to be the flight from London. And then suddenly, she panicked, wondering if she'd missed him. There was an enormous crowd in the terminal, and people were eddying all around her. She hadn't seen him in nearly a year, six months since the funeral, but that had been only a glimpse. The last time she'd had a good look at him was the previous summer. And what if he didn't recognize her? What if he'd forgotten what she looked like?

She was looking around for him when she heard a familiar voice right behind her.

"I wasn't expecting you to wear your hair up," was the first thing he said to her. He had been looking for her braid, and nearly missed her. And she spun around quickly to see him, and all she could remember were Gail's words when she'd come back from Cape Cod, telling her that the press had called him "indecently handsome . . . and ruggedly alluring." He was every bit of it as he smiled at her, and then pulled her to him. She had forgotten how tall he was, and how blue his eyes were.

His hair was cropped short, and he had a deep suntan from the wind and sun on the *Sea Star.* "You look terrific," he said as he hugged her close, and she felt breathless for a moment. This was the voice she had talked to for six months, her confidant, the man who knew everything about her, and had held her hand through the unraveling of her marriage. But suddenly, seeing him again, she felt shy and embarrassed.

"So do you." She smiled up at him as he pulled away from her to see her better. "You look so healthy."

"I should. I've done nothing but sit on my boat for the past six months, and get fat and lazy." But he looked neither. He looked powerful and young and athletic, better even than he had the previous summer. If anything, he was thinner.

"You've lost weight," he commented about her too, as he picked up his bags again, and they walked slowly toward the exit. He had only brought a small overnight case, and his briefcase. He had everything he needed at his apartment. "It suits you," he complimented her. He looked so pleased to see her that she was still grinning.

"I was just thinking you have too. How

was the flight?" It was the kind of conversation she would have had with Doug, if she'd
picked him up. In a way, they knew each
other so well, it was almost like being married. But she didn't delude herself, as they
walked out of the terminal, Paul was neither
her husband nor her boyfriend. He was something very different. But it was wonderful no
longer talking to a disembodied voice. He was
real and tangible and alive, as he stood next
to her, smiling. "I can't believe you're here."
She had begun to think he would be away
forever, and she'd never see him.

"Neither can I," he beamed, "and the
flight was dreadful. There must have been two
hundred screaming babies, all of whom had
been abandoned by their mothers. And the
woman next to me talked all the way from
London, about her garden. If I never hear
about another rosebush again, I'll be happy."
India laughed as she listened. They walked
toward where she had left her car, and he
tossed his bags into the backseat as soon as
they found it. "Would you like me to drive?"
he offered, but she assumed he was tired and
hesitated.

"Do you trust me?" She knew how some
men hated women drivers. Doug had.

"You drive more car pools than I do, and you haven't had three Scotches." It had been the only antidote to the crying children, he'd decided. But he looked completely sober.

They got into her car, and she turned to look at him for an instant, as her eyes grew serious and he met them with his equally blue ones. Their eyes were almost the same color. "I just wanted to thank you," she said softly.

"What for?" He seemed startled.

"For keeping me going all this time. I couldn't have gotten through it without you." But she had done the same for him, and he knew that.

"How's it going now? Is Doug still torturing you?"

"No, his lawyer's taken over for him." She smiled as she turned the key in the ignition. "But I think we've pretty much settled it." Doug had offered her enough child support and alimony to live on comfortably, as long as she took a few assignments every year to pad it out a little. He had made her a very decent offer, and she could keep the house for nine years, until Sam went to college, or she remarried. Her lawyer had told her to take it. And she'd be divorced by Christmas. She'd discussed most of the terms with Paul already on the phone, and he had told her he thought it was probably the best she could do. It wasn't extravagant, but it was acceptable, and it still left Doug enough to live on, and even remarry, if he chose to. He made fairly decent money. Not by Paul's standards, but by normal ones. And they had agreed to split their savings, which wasn't an enormous sum, but it gave her something to fall back on.

"I can't believe I'm back, India," he said, as they watched the skyline appear. She knew it had to seem strange to him, after all this time, and the places he'd been. Turkey, Yugoslavia, Corsica, Sicily . . . Venice . . . Viareggio . . . Portofino . . . Cap d'Antibes. He had chosen some pretty places to hide in, but they hadn't brought him much joy during his months of suffering. And as she had guessed, he was nervous about going to his apartment. He said as much to India on the way into town, and she smiled gently at him.

"Maybe you should stay at a hotel," she suggested sensibly. She was nervous for him. She knew about his dreams, and the trouble he had sleeping, although lately he said he was better.

It was so odd to be sitting next to him now, after all their hours on the phone, for months and months, and all the secrets they had told each other. It was odder still putting the voice and the man together. It was something for both of them to get used to. He kept combing her with his eyes, while she was driving, and he looked happy to be there.

"I was thinking about a hotel too," he confessed. "I'll see how it goes tonight. I need to organize my papers anyway. The board meeting is tomorrow." His partners had threatened his life if he failed to join them. It had been hard enough making do without him for six months, and he had already missed two board meetings, for the last two quarters. And they felt that this time he had to be there.

"Will it be a difficult meeting?" she asked easily as they sped onto the FDR Drive, next to the East River.

"I hope not. Mostly boring." And then he glanced at her seriously for a moment. "Would you like to go somewhere for dinner?"

"Now?" She looked surprised, and he laughed.

"No. I meant tomorrow. It's two o'clock in the morning for me right now, and I'm a little bleary-eyed. But I thought maybe tomorrow night we could go somewhere you'd enjoy. What's your favorite? '21'? Côte Basque? Daniel?"

She laughed at the suggestions he was offering her. He was forgetting what her life was. "Actually, I was thinking more like Jack in the Box or Denny's. You forget, I only eat out with my children these days." And Doug never used to bring her into the city for dinner. They came in a couple of times a year, to go to the theater, and they usually ate somewhere nearby. Doug was not one to take his wife to fancy restaurants, only clients. "Why don't you decide?"

"How about Daniel?" It had been one of Serena's favorite restaurants, but he liked it too. Serena thought Daniel wasn't as showy as La Grenouille and Côte Basque, which was exactly what he liked about it, and she didn't. He thought it was more elegant, and subtler than the others. And the food was terrific.

"I've never been there," she confessed. "But I've read about it. One of my friends says it's the best in New York." Going out with Paul was certainly different from her little life in Westport.

"Can you find a sitter?"

She smiled at him as they turned off the

FDR Drive on Seventy-ninth Street. "Thank you for asking." It had to have been years since he worried about things like that, but it was nice of him to consider what she had to do to get some freedom. "I'll find one. Would you like to come out and meet the kids this weekend? Sam would love to see you."

"That would be fun. We could take them to pizza and a movie." He knew this was a favorite for them and he wanted to share it with her. It was a whole new world for both of them, and India was still a little bowled over by his unexpected appearance. She had no idea what it meant yet, or how long he would be staying. And she thought it would be rude to ask him. Besides which, she was sure he had lots of other friends to see, and she had no idea how much time she'd be spending with him. Probably very little, and they'd be back to daily phone calls. But that was all she expected of him.

His apartment was on Fifth Avenue, just above Seventy-third Street, in an elegant building with a doorman, who seemed amazed to see him. "Mr. Ward!" he said, and stuck his hand out, as Paul shook it.

"Hello, Rosario. How's New York been treating you?"

"Pretty good, Mr. Ward, thank you. You been on your boat all this time?" He had heard rumors of it, and they sent his mail to his office.

"Yes, I have," Paul confirmed with a broad smile as he and India walked into the building.

Rosario wanted to tell him how sorry he was about his wife, but with a pretty blonde with him, it didn't seem appropriate. He wondered if it was his new girlfriend, and hoped so, for his sake.

India rode up in the elevator with him, and waited while he looked for his key in his briefcase, and as he fumbled with the lock, she saw that his hand was shaking. She gently touched his sleeve then, and he turned to look at her, thinking she was going to ask him something.

"It's okay," she said softly. "Go easy, Paul. . . ." He smiled at her. She knew exactly what he was thinking. She always did. And more importantly, what he was feeling. She was that way on the phone as well, and he had come to love her for it. She was a place he could always come to for comfort. And before turning the key in the lock again, he put his briefcase down and hugged her.

"Thank you. I think this is going to be even harder than I expected."

"Maybe not. Let's try it." She was right there with him, as he had been for her for the past six months. She knew she could always call him and find him, waiting for her, on the *Sea Star.* Suddenly the face she saw no longer seemed so separate from the voice she knew like a brother. It was one man, one soul, one person she had come to rely on.

And slowly, he turned the key in the lock, the door opened, and he turned the light on. No one but the cleaning woman had been there since September. The apartment looked immaculate, but seemed very empty and silent, as India looked around a spacious black and white hallway, filled with lithographs and modern sculptures. And there was one very handsome Jackson Pollock painting.

Paul didn't say anything to her, but walked straight into the living room, and turned more lights on. It was a huge, handsome room, filled with an interesting mixture of antique and modern furniture. There was a Miró, a Chagall, and a group of bright, interesting paintings by unknown artists. It was all very eclectic, and for some reason, reminded her enormously of Serena. Everything in the apartment seemed to have her stamp on it, her style, her force, her humor. There were photographs of her everywhere, from her book covers mostly, and there was a large portrait of her over the fireplace. Paul stood silently beside India, mesmerized by it.

"I had forgotten how beautiful she was," he said in a ragged whisper. "I try not to think about it." India nodded, knowing how difficult this was for him, but she also knew he had to go through it. She wondered if he was going to move the painting eventually, or leave it there forever. It had a commanding presence, as she had. And then he walked into a smaller, paneled room, where his desk was, and set down his briefcase, as India followed. She was beginning to wonder if she was intruding, and should leave him. There was no way to know, but to ask him.

"Should I leave you?" she asked quietly, and was surprised when he looked disappointed, and a little hurt, as he looked up at her.

"So soon? Can't you stay a while, India? Or do you have to go back to the children?"

"I'm fine. I just don't want to be a nuisance."

He left himself bare then, but she knew

him anyway, and he was not afraid to show her his sorrow. "I need you. Do you want a drink or something?"

"I shouldn't. I have to drive back to Westport."

"I hate having you do that," he said, falling comfortably into a velvet settee that faced a smaller marble fireplace than the one in the living room. The whole room was done in deep blue velvet, and the painting over the mantel was a Renoir. "I should get a driver for you when you come into town. Or I can drive you back myself sometimes if you'd prefer it."

"I don't mind driving." She smiled, grateful for the thoughtful gesture. He got up to make himself a drink then, a light Scotch and soda, and she accepted a Coca-Cola. "The apartment is beautiful," she said softly. But she had expected that. The *Sea Star* was no less lovely than this, and in some ways it was more so.

"Serena did it all herself," he sighed, looking at India, and seeing again how beautiful she was. She was even more striking than he remembered, with all her blondness, and classic features. She sat on the couch with her long legs crossed gracefully. It reminded him of the summer before, when they had sat for hours, talking on the *Sea Star*. "Serena had so many talents," he said, thinking of his late wife again. "I don't think there was anything she couldn't do. Sometimes it was hard to live with." He had said as much to her before, but here in the apartment, India could see it. The whole place had an easy elegance, and a kind of wit and spice that had been characteristic of her. "I don't know what I'll do with this place," he sighed. "I guess I should pack it up and sell it."

"Maybe you shouldn't," India said, sipping her Coca-Cola. "It's a wonderful apartment. Maybe you should just move things around a little."

Paul chuckled at the suggestion. "Serena would have killed me for that. She always felt that if she put something somewhere, God had told her to do it. She raised hell if I moved an ashtray. But maybe you're right. Maybe I need to make it more mine. It's still so her now. I'd forgotten until we just walked in how powerful her style was." She had never touched anything on the boat, or cared about it, that had been Paul's world, which was why it had been so easy to be on it since September. There, the reminders were fewer and more muted. Here, she resonated from the rafters.

"What about you?" he asked then. "Are you going to redo the house in Westport, and get Doug out of your hair? Did he take a lot of his things?" There had been some discussion of it, but in the end, other than his computer, and a few old souvenirs from college, he had taken very little. Neither of them had wanted to upset the children more than they had to.

"He didn't take much. And I think it would unnerve the kids if I started making changes. They already have enough to adjust to." He knew it was like her to think of that, and to suggest to him he only "move" things, rather than tell him what to get rid of. That wasn't her style anyway, but she was also well aware that it was not her place to tell him what to do with his apartment. She was, as in all things, respectful of him, and he liked that. In all the months he'd talked to her, he had never felt threatened by her. Instead, she provided a safe haven for him. And then, she wondered about something. It seemed a safe question to ask him. "Are you going to bring the boat back here now?"

He looked thoughtful as he answered. "I

haven't decided yet. It depends how long I stay, and I haven't figured that out yet. It depends how it goes." He looked at her, and she assumed he was referring to his business, and how comfortable he was in the apartment. "I was thinking I might bring it to the Caribbean for a while. Maybe in April. That's a nice time of year in that part of the world. Have you ever been there?"

"It's one of the few places I've missed," she laughed easily. "They haven't had any wars there."

"They did in Grenada," he teased.

"I missed that one."

"Maybe if I bring the boat to Antigua, you and the children could come down for a few days, or over one of their vacations."

"They'd love that," she said easily, in spite of Aimee's seasickness, but she knew she could give her medication for it. And as she spoke to him, she saw Paul glance at one of Serena's pictures with a look of discomfort. There seemed to be one on every table, and she felt sorry for him. "Are you hungry?" she asked him then, trying to provide some distraction. "Would you like me to make you something to eat? I make a great omelette, or a peanut butter sandwich."

"I love peanut butter." He grinned, aware of what she was trying to do, and grateful to her for trying. But it was hopeless, and he knew it. Being in the apartment they had shared was like breathing Serena's perfume. "I love peanut butter, with olives and bananas." He laughed at the face she made.

"That is disgusting. Don't tell Sam about it. It sounds like one of his concoctions. Do you have any here? I'll whip up something."

"I don't think there's much here, but we can look." He wasn't sure what was still in the freezer. And at least in the kitchen, he knew he wouldn't be so overwhelmed by memories. Serena never set foot in it. They ate in restaurants, hired a caterer or a chef, or Paul cooked for her. In eleven years, she had never once cooked him dinner, and had been proud of it.

India followed him through the dining room, with a huge antique table and silver everywhere, into the spartan black granite kitchen. It looked like something out of *Architectural Digest,* and she was sure that at some point they had photographed it.

But all they found were some ancient frozen hors d'oeuvres some caterer had left, and a neat row of sodas. "Looks like you'll have an interesting breakfast tomorrow."

"I didn't tell anyone I was coming, and I guess my secretary didn't think I'd stay here. She said she'd get me a reservation at the Carlyle in case I decided not to. I might try that tomorrow." He looked at India with an odd expression, and she smiled at him. It was so good to see him. "I'm sorry I don't have anything to feed you, India."

"I'm not hungry, I just thought you were," and then she glanced at her watch. "You must be exhausted."

"I'm holding up. It's nice being with you." He wasn't happy thinking about being alone in the apartment with his memories, and all the reminders of Serena. He knew that all her clothes were still in her dressing room, and he dreaded seeing them. He hadn't asked anyone to do anything about them. And later, he would have to walk through all of it to get to his own closets. He cringed inwardly, knowing what he'd see there, her slippers and her dressing gown, and her handbags and dresses, all arranged in neat rows by color and designer. She had been incredibly organized and obsessive about everything, even her wardrobe.

"Tell me when you need to go back to Westport." He didn't want her on the road too late. It was dangerous driving back alone, he knew, but he didn't want her to leave either. After all these months of talking to her, he wanted to be close to her, but he wasn't sure how to say it. And it seemed wrong here to even put an arm around her. She interpreted his correctness as a sign of the fraternal quality of their friendship, but he had no idea how to change that.

They talked about the children then, and his board meeting the next day. He explained what it was about, and told her something more about his business. And he asked her if she'd heard anything lately from Raoul. She hadn't mentioned him in a while, and he hadn't called her for any more assignments, which she said was just as well, since she didn't want to leave the children at the moment. The divorce was still too fresh a concept for them, and she wanted to be around to make sure they made the adjustment.

They talked for a long time, as they always did, and then finally he looked at his watch, and told her that he thought she should go, so she wasn't on the road too late. It was already after midnight, and she wouldn't be home till one in the morning. But as he walked her slowly to the door, he looked like a child about to lose his best friend, and for an instant, she hated to leave him.

"Will you be okay?" she asked protectively, forgetting for a moment that he'd been halfway around the world without her.

"I hope so," he said honestly, but not entirely certain that he would be.

"If you're not, call me. I don't mind what time you call. Don't be afraid to wake me."

"Thank you," he said gently, and then he seemed to hesitate, as though he wanted to say something to her, but decided not to. "It's good to be here," he said, looking at her, and not meaning the apartment.

"It's good to have you," she smiled at the man who had become her friend, and meant it.

He went down in the elevator with her, and saw her into her car, and pointed to the door locks as she nodded. She rolled down the window and thanked him again, and he said he'd call her the next day after his meeting.

"Does seven-thirty dinner tomorrow

night sound all right to you?" he asked, and she smiled and nodded.

"Sounds great. How dressy is Daniel?"

"Not too much. Nice." It was something he would have said to Serena, and India got it. The black suit, with suede pumps, and her pearl earrings. "I'll call you."

"Take care . . . get some sleep . . ." she said as she drove off with a wave, thinking of him. He didn't even have warm milk there to soothe him if he needed it, and on the way home, she worried about him. It was wonderful having him there, better even than talking to him on the phone, and if she'd let herself, she'd have allowed her thoughts to run wild about him, but she knew she couldn't do that. She turned on the radio, and hummed to herself, thinking about dinner the next day with him at Daniel.

Chapter 21

Paul called India at seven in the morning the night after he arrived, and he sounded forlorn, and exhausted the moment he spoke. He said he had had a terrible night, and was moving to the Carlyle.

"Oh Paul, I'm sorry." It had been predictable of course, there was just too much of Serena in the apartment. "You're going to be exhausted for your meeting."

"It was awful," he confessed to her, "worse than I thought. I guess I shouldn't have tried to stay here." He sounded like he'd been crying.

"Maybe eventually you can make a few changes." It was comforting talking to him on the phone, and she felt braver immediately.

This was the voice she knew. It was still a little hard to put it together with the man, who was still so new to her, and whom she had seen so seldom. But the voice had been a constant in her life for some time now.

"I'm not sure what to do, other than sell the place intact." But he wasn't ready to do that either, and she knew it. "I'll meet you at the Carlyle tonight. In the Bemelmans Bar at seven. We can have a drink there before we go across the street to Daniel."

"I'll be there. What are you doing about breakfast, by the way? You can't go to work on an empty stomach." It was the kind of thing she worried about, having kids, and it made him smile. No one had worried about that for him for years. If ever. Not even Serena. He could have starved for all she cared. Serena never ate breakfast, and thought he didn't need to either.

"I'll have something at the office. They have a whole kitchen and two chefs. I'm sure they can dig up something, at least a cup of coffee. I'm going to go in early." He would have gone anywhere, just to get out of the apartment. The closets had almost done him in the night before, and he had been crying since six o'clock that morning. "I'm not sure I can ever come back here," he said in a choked voice.

"It'll get easier," she reassured him. It had been difficult for him even on the *Sea Star* at first. Returning to the apartment he had shared with his wife was just too big a dose of reality too soon, and coming back to New York was probably emotional for him too. None of it was easy, and she knew it.

"Thanks for being there," he said, and then he heard strange banging noises and a dog barking. "Where are you, by the way? It sounds like bedlam."

"It is." She smiled. "I'm making breakfast for the kids, and the dog is going crazy." He liked the sound of it. It sounded very friendly.

"How's Sam?"

"Hungry." She grinned.

"Go feed him. I'll call you later."

She was out all afternoon, and she came back after she picked them all up at school. She had run into Gail, who told her Doug's girlfriend had spent the weekend with him with her kids. She had heard it from two women she ran into in the market. And India was surprised to realize it bothered her. He had a right to do what he wanted, but he hadn't wasted much time. They'd only been separated for two months. And she had no one. Except Paul. But that was different. And she didn't mention him to Gail. She never did. It had remained a well-guarded secret.

The sitter came at five o'clock, while India dressed, and she left for the city at six. And this time, the children complained about her leaving.

"Why are you going out again?" Sam whined at her, as she kissed him. "You went out last night."

"I have friends in town. I'll see you in the morning." She knew he was going to ask her who they were, but she beat a hasty retreat before he could do it. She wasn't going to tell him. It was none of their business. And she didn't want to worry them. She knew they were upset about Doug's girlfriend and her two children. They didn't need anyone else to worry about, even if Paul was no threat to them.

There was a lot of traffic on the way into town, and she arrived ten minutes late, in the black suit, and new shoes, with her hair in a French twist again, and her only pair of pearl earrings. This was a new experience for her, getting dressed up at night, and driving her-

self into the city for dinner. Paul had reiter-
ated his offer of a driver but being picked up
by a limousine and whisked away like Cinder-
ella would have really startled the kids, she
laughed. They would think she was going out
with a movie star, or a drug dealer. It was a
lot simpler just driving herself into the city,
and sparing herself their questions and comments.

"You look beautiful," Paul said with a
smile when he saw her, and she noticed that
he looked tired. It had been a long day for
him, especially after being away from work
for so long. Everyone wanted a piece of him,
and all of his attention, and he was still a little
jet-lagged. "How was your day?" he asked, as
she sat down. "Not as busy as mine, I hope.
I'd forgotten how exhausting work is." He
smiled, and she ordered a glass of white wine.
There was plenty of time for it to wear off
before she had to drive back to Westport.

"I just did errands, and picked up the
kids." She told him what Gail had said about
Doug, and he raised an eyebrow.

"He sure didn't waste any time." But he
was glad. It meant he wouldn't be bothering
India, and Paul was pleased to hear it.

"How was your board meeting?" India asked with interest.

"Challenging. And I talked to my son. They're having another baby. That's a hopeful sign. It's sort of a symbol of faith in the future, I always think. Maybe at their age, they're not that philosophical about it." But as India looked at him, he didn't look like a grandfather to her. He was such a handsome man, and he didn't look his age, although he claimed that night that he felt it. She assured him it was only jet lag. But he admitted that the night before had upset him.

"I think you did the right thing moving here," she said encouragingly.

"It's a bit stupid, with an apartment a few blocks away. But I couldn't have taken another night of it. I had all the same dreams again . . . of her telling me I should have gone down with her."

"She would never have said that, and you know it," India said firmly. It was a liberty saying that to him, but she would have said it on the phone, and she was getting used to seeing him in person. It was nice finding him at the end of her day, dressing for dinner, and going out with him. She hadn't done that in a

long time, and as she sipped her wine, he was
smiling at her.

"You almost sounded like Serena for a
minute." But India was very much her own
person. "She hated it when I felt sorry for
myself, and she always gave me hell. So you're
right with what you said, as usual. You're right
a lot, India. About many things." The only
thing she hadn't been right about was her
marriage. She should have put her foot down
years before, and let him leave her. But without his support, Paul knew she never could
have done it.

They left for Daniel when they finished
their drinks, and the maître d' settled them at
a cozy corner table. He made a big fuss over
Paul, and India could see he'd been there
often. And the maître d' looked obviously intrigued to see India with him.

"Everyone is wondering who you are."
Paul smiled. "You look like a model in that
suit, India. And I like your hair that way, it
suits you." But he also missed her braid and
the way she had looked when he had met her
on the *Sea Star*. She had been so perfectly at
ease on the boat with him, and they'd had
such a good time with Sam. He couldn't wait
to have them back on the boat again. And he

had decided that afternoon to bring the boat across the Atlantic to Antigua. He was going to suggest to her that they take the kids there over Easter. But first he helped her order dinner.

They ordered lobster bisque to start, then squab for her, and he ordered steak au poivre, endive salad, and soufflé for dessert. It was a sumptuous dinner.

And as the waiter poured them wine, Paul confirmed to her that he wanted her to come to Antigua over Easter with the children.

"Isn't there someone you'd rather have?" she asked modestly. "There are an awful lot of us. And the children will drive you crazy."

"Not if they're like Sam. We can put all four of them in two cabins, and still have other guests if we want. I just thought it might be fun to have them on board. I thought I might invite Sean, but he's a very timid sailor, and with his wife pregnant, I don't think they'll come. But I can ask. Your kids might enjoy his children, although they're still pretty young. And Sam and I can sail the boat, while the rest of you play liar's dice, or watch videos, or something." He looked hopeful that they would come, and India was very touched. It was an irresistible invitation, and Doug had already said he had other plans for the vacation. He and his new friend were going to Disney World with her children, and his own children had been hurt not to be included in the invitation. But as Gail had said, that was the way divorces were. A lot of fathers lost interest in their kids once they found a girlfriend.

"Are you serious about Antigua, Paul?" India asked cautiously over their soup. "You don't have to do that."

"No, but I want to. And if you get nervous about it, India, you can stay in your cabin and call me in the wheelhouse on the phone. And then you'll remember who I am." He was teasing her, but he was not unaware of the adjustment she was making. There were a lot of adjustments these days for both of them. He had come nose to nose with his own the night before in the apartment. But India laughed at his suggestion.

"That might work pretty well, actually. Maybe I should go out now and call you from the phone booth."

"I wouldn't answer," he said seriously.

"Why not?" She seemed surprised, as he looked at her with an odd expression.

"I'm on a date. First one I've had in years. I have a lot to relearn, I'm afraid. I'm not sure I remember how you do this." There was something very vulnerable in his eyes as he said it, and when she answered, it was barely more than a whisper.

"Is this a date? I thought we were friends." He had completely confused her.

"Can't we be both?" He looked at her honestly. He had come to New York for more than just business, although he hadn't said it to her. After talking to her for the last six months, he wanted to see her.

"I suppose we could," she said, suddenly looking nervous.

"You're spilling your soup," he pointed out to her, and she grinned. She had been completely taken aback by his question. "If you're going to go out to dinner with me, India, you can't spill your soup all over the table." He sat back and looked at her, as she put her spoon down.

"I'm not sure I understand what you're saying." She didn't want to. She didn't want him to change anything. He had already told her they were only friends, at Christmas, before Doug left her. She had been standing in a phone booth, freezing, when Paul told her that he didn't want to be the light at the end of the tunnel for her. And if that were true, how could this be a date? What did he mean? And why had he changed it? "I think you're scaring the pants off me, if that's an appropriate thing to say in this case."

He couldn't help smiling at her. She looked very beautiful and very young, and naive. She hadn't dated even longer than he hadn't. It had been more than twenty years since she met Doug in the Peace Corps. "Am I really scaring you, India?" He looked suddenly worried. "I don't want to frighten you. Do you mean that?"

"A little. I thought we were just friends. That was what you said . . . at Christmas. . . ."

"Did I? That was a long time ago." Then he did remember. And he had meant it. But three months had gone by. The agony of Serena's memory had dimmed a little bit. And Doug had left her. "I'm not sure what I said, but I was probably being very stupid." She could feel her heart pound as he said it. "I think it was an extremely tasteless remark about not being a light at the end of the tunnel." She didn't understand what had happened to change it. He sighed as he looked at her, and took her hand carefully in his own, and held it across the table. "I get scared sometimes . . . and sad . . . I miss Serena . . . and I say things I probably shouldn't." Did he mean now? Or then? India could feel tears fill her eyes as she watched him. She didn't want to do anything to jeopardize what they had. She didn't want to lose him. And if this went too far, he might regret it, and run off to the safety of the boat again. Maybe this time forever.

"I don't think you know what you're doing," she said, as he gently wiped her eyes with his napkin.

"You may be right. But why don't you let me figure it out, and not worry about it so much. Just trust me, India. Let's figure it out together." She closed her eyes for a minute, enjoying the moment, and then nodded. And when she looked at him again, he was smiling. He liked what was happening to them, and what he was feeling for her. Instead of mourning the end, he was savoring the tenderness of the beginning.

Their mood lightened again after that, and he told her funny things that had happened on the boat, people who had gotten drunk or misbehaved, and a woman who had

had an affair with his captain, and another woman who had left the portholes in her cabin open and nearly sank the boat. India shuddered at that story as she listened to him.

"I'll remember not to do that."

"I'll remind you. It's so embarrassing when we sink, and very hard on the carpets." Her eyes grew wide as she listened. She knew less about sailboats than Sam did, and Paul was taking full advantage of it, although the story about the portholes was true, and they had little reminders in the cabins now, in case anyone forgot it. "You know," he went on, looking calmly at her, "it's remarkable. The *Sea Star* is so well built, we've only capsized once." Her mouth opened, as she looked at him with terror, and then realized what he was doing to her.

"I hate you," she said, sounding just like Sam, and he laughed at her.

"I'm not frightening you, am I? I thought you'd be impressed. She actually does very well when we capsize, spins right around, and comes right back up again. All we have to do is dry the sails off. I'll show you."

"Forget Antigua," she said firmly. But by then, she knew what he was doing. He was just having a little fun with her. "Tell those stories to Sam. At least he won't believe them."

"He might." Paul's eyes danced. He was enjoying her company, the dinner, and the wine. It was the most fun he'd had in a long time, longer than he wanted to think of. "I'm very convincing."

"Yes, you are," she said with a shy smile. She liked his sense of humor, and his style, and she was as at ease with him now as she'd been on the phone. They had had a wonderful evening. And after dinner, they walked slowly back to the Carlyle. It was still early, and he asked her if she'd like to come up for a few minutes before she drove back to Westport. She still had time. She really didn't have to start back until later. And the sitter had agreed to stay over in case India came home too late, which meant she had all the time she wanted.

"My suite isn't too bad, but it's not exactly Versailles," he apologized. "I think it's someone's apartment. They lease them for months at a time." He didn't offer to take her back to the bar, and they went up in the elevator as he told her about the *Sea Star*, and told her what to expect in Antigua. He said they could visit a number of other islands. In fact, they could do anything she wanted.

The elevator stopped at nine, and he let her into a large, comfortable room that was handsomely decorated, though nothing like his apartment. It was predictably impersonal, but there were flowers everywhere, and a bar with everything they could have wanted. He poured her some wine, but she didn't drink, since she still had to drive back to Westport. There were fruit and pastries as well, provided by the hotel, but neither of them was hungry after the huge meal they'd just eaten at Daniel.

India sat down on the couch, and Paul sat down next to her. He was still talking about the boat, and then he stopped and looked at her, and she felt the same electricity course through her that she had felt when she first met him. Aside from his obvious good looks, there was something irresistibly attractive about him.

"I can't believe we're sitting here," he said. "I keep expecting to wake up on the boat, and have someone tell me you're calling."

"It is funny, isn't it?" She smiled, remembering all the times they'd talked, and all the things they'd said, for so many months, the times she had called him from freezing pay phones before Doug left her. She laughed when she thought about it. "I thought I was going to get frostbite." She had carried rolls of quarters for months, so she could call him whenever she wanted.

"We've been through some hard times, you and I," he said quietly, but thinking only of her now, and not the people they had lost, or been at other times. All he could see were her eyes, the gentleness in them, and all he felt was what had grown between them in his months on the *Sea Star*.

He said nothing more to her then, but leaned over very quietly, took her in his arms, and kissed her. And as she felt his lips on hers, she had the answers to all her questions. It was a long time before they spoke again, and when they did, his voice was soft and hoarse with passion. "I think I've fallen in love with you, India," he whispered. It was not in any way what he had expected, or what she had thought would happen between them when she saw him. She had long since told herself that this would never happen.

"I tried so hard not to tell you, not to

even let myself feel it," she said, feeling all the same things he did.

"So did I," he said quietly, holding her close to him, with an arm around her shoulders. "I knew it a long time ago, but I was always afraid it wasn't what you wanted."

"I thought . . . I was afraid . . ." She had been so certain that there was no way she could measure up to Serena in his eyes. She hadn't dared to hope, but she didn't say that to him now. He kissed her again, and he held her with such strength that she felt breathless. And then without a word, he stood up and walked her slowly to his bedroom, and then stopped in the doorway.

"I'll do whatever you want," he said with a look of sorrow in his eyes. He knew that with that single gesture, he was leaving one life and entering another, if that was what she wanted. He loved her more than he had ever thought possible, and he knew it with perfect clarity at that moment. "If you want to go back to Westport, it's all right. . . . I'll understand." But she shook her head as she looked at him. She didn't want to go anywhere now without him. Like him, she had known this for a long time. She had fought it valiantly, she had been there for him, and called him from ice-cold phone booths. But now that was all behind them.

"I love you, Paul," she said softly.

He turned the lights out then, and lay her on the bed, and lay next to her, holding her and touching her, and reveling in all her warmth and softness and glory. He peeled the black suit away, and everything he found beneath it, and they clung to each other with a hunger neither of them had realized they had for each other. And when she lay naked next to him, he looked down at her with all the love and tenderness he felt for her.

"You're so beautiful, India," he whispered, as she reached up to him with the smile he had remembered for so long and the arms he had been starving for, and gently she brought him to her.

They met and held and danced in the skies, as together they found what they had been looking for, in the arms of someone whom they not only loved, but who loved them. It was everything neither of them had had before, and only discovered now, with each other. It was like being born again, for both of them, as they clung to life and hope and the dreams they each had forgotten, and long since ceased to believe in. And as she moaned softly in his arms, he brought her to places she had never known, and had only dimly realized she longed for. And when it was over, it was not an end, but a beginning.

They lay quietly side by side for a long time, and then he kissed her again, and after a while she fell asleep beside him. He watched her sleep for a long time, and then he closed his eyes and slept as he hadn't in months, with her love to bring him home again from his agonizing journey to lonely places.

The sun was coming up when they woke, and he made love to her again, and she lay in his arms afterward and sighed and told him she had never known it could be like that.

"It can't," he said with a smile, still somewhat in awe of her, and what had come to them. She was everything he had so desperately wanted and never allowed himself to realize in all the months he'd called her. "I'm never going to let you go again," he said happily. "You're going to have to go everywhere with me . . . work . . . the boat . . . I can't live without this."

"You're going to have to," she smiled up at him mischievously, "I have to drive back to

Westport." He groaned at the prospect of losing her, even until that evening.

"Can you come back tonight?" he asked, before he let her move from him. He wanted to make love to her again, but they both needed time to recover.

She knew it would be hard to leave the children again for the third night, and she looked at him hopefully. "Can you come out to Westport?"

"What about the children?"

"We'll think of something. . . . You can sleep with Sam."

"That would be interesting." He laughed, and she giggled, and slowly she unwound her body from his, still overwhelmed by everything that had happened.

He watched her walk across the room, and he didn't tell her this time that she was the most beautiful woman he'd ever seen. Saying it seemed somehow a disrespect to Serena. But he had found with India something he'd never even had with her. The fascination of Serena had been that she had never given herself to anyone completely, not even him after all those years. She always kept a piece of herself apart, as though to prove to him that he would never own her. The difference between them was that India gave herself to him completely. She opened herself to him, in all her warmth and vulnerability, and he felt as though he could disappear for a thousand years into all she gave him. He felt safe with her, and together they shared an ecstasy that satisfied him completely.

He stood in the shower with her, and then watched her dress, and then he put his own clothes on, as she looked at him, and smiled mysteriously. She was thinking that whoever had said it about him had been right . . . he was indecently handsome.

He rode down in the elevator with her, thinking of what she meant to him, and when she got in her car, he looked at her, wanting to remember this moment for a lifetime.

"Be careful. . . . I love you, India." She leaned out of the car to kiss him, with her long blond hair streaming past her shoulders. He touched it and it felt like silk to him, as she smiled up at him, all innocence and trust and hope and dreams, with the glow of what had happened still in her eyes, as she looked at him with a peaceful expression.

"I love you too. Call me, I'll give you directions."

He watched her as she drove away, with all the power of his love for her. And then as he walked back into the hotel, he felt a knife of remorse slice through his soul, as he remembered Serena.

Chapter 22

Paul drove to Westport that night, and had dinner with them. It was the first time he had met India's other children. And he thought they were very sweet, and very funny.

Sam entertained them all through the meal. And Paul and Jason had a very grown-up conversation about sailing. Aimee cautiously flirted with him, trying out her skills; she was very pretty and looked a great deal like her mother. And only Jessica seemed to have reservations about him, and immediately after dinner, she went upstairs to do her homework.

"You passed inspection," India said with a smile, as she sat down in the living room with him afterward, once they'd all gone upstairs to call their friends and watch TV. "Jason said you were cool. Aimee thought you were okay. And you already know Sam loves you."

"And Jessica hates me," he said matter-of-factly.

"No. She didn't say anything, which means she *doesn't* hate you. If she did, she'd tell you."

"That's comforting," he said with a look of amusement. They were good kids, and he could see she had done her job well. They were bright and secure, and happy. And the conversation at the table had been lively.

They went upstairs eventually, on tiptoe, after they knew the kids were in bed. She locked her door, and they made love as quietly as they could, although Paul was a little nervous about it.

"Are you sure this is all right?" he whispered afterward. On the wings of passion, he hadn't bothered to ask her, but she nodded as they lay in the dark and whispered.

"The door is locked, and they're all sound sleepers."

"The innocence of children," he whispered. "We're not going to be able to fool

them for long. I can't spend the night, can I?"
He already knew the answer to his question.

"Not yet. We need to give them time.
They're already upset about Doug's girlfriend. They spend their weekends with her."
Paul thought to himself about the bad luck of
arriving on the scene second. The prospect of
driving back to New York at four in the morning didn't thrill him.

In the end, he stayed till six, and slept
fitfully, and although he dreamt of airplanes,
he didn't dream about Serena. India tiptoed
downstairs with him, and promised to come
into the city that night to see him. But as he
drove back to town, he realized that this
wasn't going to be easy. If nothing else, the
distance and lack of sleep were going to kill
him. But she was worth it.

He was seeing Sean on Thursday night,
and on the weekend the kids were going to
their father's, and India was going to come to
the city and stay at the Carlyle with him. So
far, they had it all organized, but the prospect
of commuting to Westport on alternate
nights, and hiding from the kids, seemed
somewhat complicated to him. And all he
could think of was the perversity of
God's sense of humor. At his age, the pros-

pect of a woman with four children and a dog, and a house in Connecticut, was going to provide an interesting challenge. But she was also the most exciting woman he had ever slept with. That made up for something. The dog maybe.

But at four o'clock that afternoon when he left the office for a massage and a nap, he was exhausted. And he only looked slightly better when he took her to dinner that night at Gino's.

"How were the kids?" he asked with a look of concern. "Did they say anything? Did they hear me leave this morning?"

"Of course not." She smiled at him. With the flexibility spawned by fourteen years of motherhood, she looked undaunted. But then again she was fourteen years younger than he was, though he had already proven to both of them that in some areas at least, it was not going to be a problem.

But that night when they got back to the hotel, they were both so tired they fell asleep watching TV, and she didn't wake up until seven the next morning.

"Oh my God!" she shrieked when she saw what time it was. "The sitter's going to kill me! I told her I'd be home at midnight." India grabbed the phone, leaning a breast enticingly over him, and told a complicated tale about a friend who'd had an accident, and having been in the ICU with her all night. And then she called Gail and asked her to take her car pool. The entire situation was resolved in a matter of minutes, and they settled back into his bed again, and made up for what they hadn't done the night before, with extraordinary vigor.

And then Paul ordered room service for both of them, and she sat across from him wearing only his shirt, and looking gloriously sexy.

"Have you ever thought of an apartment in the city?" he asked cautiously, as she read the *Wall Street Journal.* She had always read it after Doug left in the morning, and she had continued his subscription after he left her.

"Doug said we'd move back after Sam went to college."

"I may not live that long," he said vaguely, and she looked at him cautiously over the paper.

"This must be hard for you," she said sympathetically. He had only been home for three days, and it wasn't hard yet, but he could see the potential.

"Not yet. But it will be. And you can't keep running back and forth to Westport." He didn't like to think of her on the road at four o'clock in the morning, or himself either. At least it wasn't snowing. But eventually, it would be.

"There are only three more months of school," she said practically. But neither of them wanted to face reality at this point. Their relationship had leapt full blown from birth to manhood. It was something to think about, realizing he hadn't fully considered the logistics of her situation, with everything from sitters to car pools. It had been a long time since he'd had to deal with that with Sean, who was thirty-one. And he also remembered that Sean hadn't done much for his love life. He had systematically hated everyone his father dated. Paul hadn't met Serena till Sean was in college. And Sean hadn't liked her then either. It had taken him years to form any kind of friendship with her. And by then, he himself was married. Thinking of him then reminded Paul that he was taking him to dinner that night. It meant he had a night off from the commute to Westport, and on Friday, India was spending the weekend with him in the city.

They finished breakfast and got dressed, and she left with him, when he left the hotel to go to the office. And he smiled at her as she got into her car again and looked up at him in all her devastating blond beauty.

"I think I'm a little crazy, but I love you," he said, and meant it. And as he watched her drive away, he forced himself not to think of Serena. It was always hardest for him when he left India. When he was with her, he didn't let himself think about Serena. This was still a major adjustment. But he had jumped into it with both feet, and he wasn't sorry.

He mentioned India to Sean that night, and told him about them, and he was surprised when Sean was less than enthused, and almost paternally cautious.

"Isn't it a little soon, Dad?"

"To be dating?" Paul was surprised by his reaction. Even once they made friends, Sean had never been that crazy about Serena. He always thought she was too flashy. And India was anything but that, she was quiet and discreet, and distinguished and unassuming. But Sean hadn't met her, so he didn't know it.

"Maybe," Sean said, in answer to his question. "It's only been six months, and you were so much in love with Serena."

"I was, and am. But don't you think I have a right to be with someone?" It was an honest question, and deserved a fair answer.

"Why? At your age, you don't need to get remarried."

"Who said anything about marriage?" He flinched at his son's words and extrasensory perception. He had been thinking about it only that morning, when contemplating the commute to Westport. There was no way they could do that forever.

"Well, if you don't want to get married, why date? Besides, you have the *Sea Star*." It seemed like a reasonable trade-off to him. And Paul was less than amused to realize that, at fifty-seven, his son thought he was too old to be dating.

"Since when are you so interested in yachting? Besides, I just thought you'd be interested in what I'm doing. One of these days, I'd like you to meet her."

"If you're not going to marry her, Dad, I don't need to meet her," Sean said bluntly, instantly creating an impossible situation. If Paul introduced India to him now it meant they were getting married. And to provide a little distraction, he told him instead about her work and her enormous talent.

"Great," Sean said without much interest. "Does she have kids?" Another psychic stroke of genius on his part. Paul nodded vaguely, as Sean honed in on him further. "How many?"

"A few." Paul said it with a feeling of rising panic, and Sean sensed it.

"How many?" he repeated.

"Four."

"Young ones?"

"Nine to fourteen." He decided he might as well tell him. Why hide it?

"Are you kidding?"

"No."

"Are you crazy?"

"Maybe." He was beginning to wonder.

"You can't even stand my kids for more than ten minutes."

"Yours are younger. And they cry all the time. Hers don't."

"Wait. They'll go to jail. They'll get drunk. They'll get into drugs. They'll get pregnant, or maybe she will. Dad, you'll love it."

"Don't be such a pain in the ass at your age. You didn't."

"You don't know half the stuff I did. Besides, you didn't let me. Dad, look, at your age, you don't need a woman with four kids. Why can't you find someone a little older?"

"How about Georgia O'Keeffe? Is that old enough for you? She must be in her nineties."

"I think she's dead," Sean said without humor. "Come on, be serious. Go back to the boat and relax. I think you're having a midlife crisis."

"Thank you for your optimism," Paul said drily, but in spite of what he was saying to his son, Sean had shaken him a little. It was hard to sell a woman with four children. "If I'm having a midlife crisis, by the way, that means you expect me to live to a hundred and fourteen. I'll do my best to oblige you. And no, I'm not senile. She's a good friend, and a nice woman, and I like her. I just thought you'd want to know, that's all. Forget it."

"No," Sean said sternly, getting even for all the lectures Paul had given him before, during, and since college, "*you* forget it." And with that, they moved on to other subjects, but it was obvious as they left '21' that Sean was still worried. He said he'd call his father on the weekend about seeing the kids, and Paul didn't have the heart to tell him he was busy. He just said he'd call him if he didn't go away for the weekend. But Sean knew instantly what that meant. And when he went home to his wife, racked with morning sickness and looking green, he told her his father had lost his marbles. But to her credit, she had the same reaction as her father-in-law, and told her husband not to be so stuffy. His father had a perfect right to do what he wanted, and Sean told her in no uncertain terms to mind her own business.

But the dreams Paul had that night were far worse than anything Sean could have wished on him. He dreamt of Serena all night, and airplanes exploding in midair. Twice he woke and heard her screaming at him about what he'd done, and then he heard her sobbing because he'd been unfaithful to her. And Paul felt ninety when he woke up in the morning. And one thing Sean had said had stuck in his mind like a cactus. What if India got pregnant? The thought of it made him nauseous. And when she called him in the office that afternoon and left the message that she'd be at the hotel to meet him at five-thirty, he had his secretary call back to say he'd be there.

But the moment he saw her, he forgot his nightmares and Sean's warnings. The instant he kissed her, he melted. They wound up in bed before dinnertime, and finally sent for room service at midnight. She was the most bewitching woman he'd ever known, and in spite of how many children she had, he knew he loved her. Worse than that. He was crazy about her. And the weekend they spent together was pure magic.

They walked in Central Park and held hands, went to the Metropolitan, and the movies. They saw a love story that ended badly, and they both cried. They bought books together, and read, and listened to music. They loved all the same things, and she talked with great anticipation about their cruise together on the *Sea Star*. She shared all her dreams with him, and her fears, as she had on the phone, and by Sunday afternoon, he hated the idea of her leaving, but she had to pick up the children after dinner. And when she drove away again, he couldn't stand the prospect of a night without her.

And Sunday night was worse than Thursday had been. He dreamed that he lay in Serena's arms all night, and she begged him not to let her die, she wanted to stay with him forever. He woke up at three A.M. and sobbed for an hour, racked with guilt over what he was doing. He never went back to sleep, and

in the morning he knew he should never have
survived her. He couldn't bear to live through
it. And when he called India, she sounded so
sweet, and she was obviously concerned about
him.

He felt like a dead man himself when he
left the hotel for the office. He had promised
to go to Westport that night, but at six o'clock
he called her and told her he couldn't. He just
couldn't face her. He needed another night to
himself, just to think about Serena, and what
he was doing. He thought he'd probably feel
better in the morning, and India had promised to drive into the city. She had a sitter who
could stay overnight, and she had told the
children she was visiting a sick friend, and had
to stay over with her. But how often could she
do that?

And when she got to the hotel that night,
Paul was waiting for her. He looked gray, and
India was instantly worried. She asked him
what he'd eaten, and if he had a fever, and he
told her calmly that he didn't.

"You don't look well, sweetheart," she
said gently. And he felt like a serial killer.
After the months they'd shared on the phone,
he knew her too well, knew how she thought
and what she felt, and everything that she be-

lieved in. She believed in hope and dreams and honesty and loyalty and all the best of human emotions. She also believed in happy endings, and this one wasn't. It couldn't be. He had realized in the two days he hadn't spent with her that he was still in love with Serena, and felt sure now that he always would be.

He sat down next to India on the couch and looked at her, and she felt her heart sliding slowly to her feet. All he could see was the golden hair, the huge blue eyes growing bigger by the minute, and her face getting so pale it scared him.

"I think you know what I'm going to say," he said miserably.

"I don't want to hear it," she said hoarsely. "What happened?"

"I woke up, India. I came to my senses."

"No, you didn't," she said, fighting back tears, "you went crazy." She knew the words before he said them, and her heart was pounding so hard she thought it was going to leap out of her chest. She was terrified to lose him. She had waited a lifetime for him.

"I was crazy when I told you I loved you. I didn't. I was excited by you. . . . I wanted it to be everything I thought it was. You're the most wonderful woman I've ever known. But I'm in love with Serena. I always will be. I know it. I can't do this."

"You're scared. That's all it is. You panicked," she said, beginning to sound desperate.

"I'm panicking now," he said honestly, looking at her. He didn't want the responsibility of her. He couldn't do it. He knew it. Sean was right. He was senile. "India, you have four kids. You have a house in Westport."

"What's that got to do with it? I'll put them up for adoption." She was half kidding, but her eyes filled with tears instantly. She could see he meant it. She was fighting for her life and he didn't want to hear it. "I love you."

"You don't even know me. All I am is a voice on the phone. A dream. An illusion."

"I know you," she said desperately. "And you know me. This isn't fair." She started to cry openly and he took her in his arms and held her. He felt like a murderer, but he knew he had to escape her. For his own survival.

"It's better now. It would be worse later," he said sensibly. "We'll just get attached to each other, and then what? I can't do this. Serena won't let me."

"She's gone, Paul." She said it gently,

through her tears, even then not wanting to hurt him, while he hurt her. "She wouldn't want you to be unhappy."

"Yes she would. She would never want me to be with another woman."

"She was smarter than that. And she loved you. I can't believe you're doing this." It had been a week. Seven days, and she had given herself to him completely, and now he was telling her it was over. A week ago, two days ago, he had told her how much he loved her. He wanted her to move to the city. He liked her children. He hated the commute, but who didn't? "Can't you give this a chance?"

"No, I can't. I won't. For your sake as well as mine. I'm going back to the boat. My son is right, I'm too old for this. You need someone younger. I can't take on four kids. I can't. When he was that age, Sean almost drove me crazy. I'd forgotten it, now I remember. And that was twenty years ago. I was thirty-seven. Now I'm a hundred. No, India," he said sternly, looking at her as she cried, but he was doing it for Serena. He owed it to her, he had let her die alone on an airplane. That never should have happened. He should have gone with her. "You've got to go now." He stood up and pulled India to her feet as she stood in front of him and sobbed. She had never expected this of him, and she hadn't been prepared for it. She had never suspected this would happen. He loved her. She knew it.

"What about Antigua?" she asked through her tears, as though it still mattered. But it was something to hang on to. And then he took that from her too. He wanted it all back now. His heart, his life, their future.

"Forget it," he said coldly. "Go somewhere else. With a nice guy. I'm not that person. The best of me died with Serena."

"No, it didn't. I love the best and the worst of you," she said, and meant it, but he didn't want to hear that either. He wanted nothing more from her. It was over. And then she looked up at him with eyes that tore his heart out.

"What'll I tell the children?"

"Tell them what a bastard I am. They'll believe you."

"No, they won't. And I don't either. You're just scared. You're scared of being happy." It was truer than she knew, and truer than he wanted her to see now.

"Go home, India," he said, and opened

the door for her. "Go back to your kids. They need you."

"So do you," she said, believing it, and knowing him better than he did. "More than they do." She stood in the doorway, looking at him for a long time then, sobbing pitifully, and her last words to him were "I love you."

And as she walked away, he closed the door quietly behind her, and walked into his bedroom. He lay on the bed he had lain on with her, and sobbed as he thought of her. He wanted her back, he wanted her to be part of him, but he knew he couldn't. It was too late for him. He was gone. Serena had taken him with her. And he owed her this now. He knew it. For not dying with her. For letting her down. He had betrayed her, and he couldn't do it again. He had no right to what India wanted to give him.

And as he lay on his bed and cried, India drove back to Westport, blinded by tears, hysterical. She couldn't believe what had happened. She couldn't believe what he had done to her. It was worse than anything Doug had done. But the difference was she loved him, and she knew he loved her. As she drove home, she was so distraught, so racked with pain, that she never saw the car next to her move out of its lane and cut in front of her. She didn't even have time to think before it hit her. She bounced off the divider, and back again into another lane, as the car spun wildly around her and she hit her head on the steering wheel, and the car stopped finally. There was a salty taste in her mouth and there was blood everywhere, as someone opened the door, and she looked at them, and fainted.

Chapter 23

It was after midnight when India called Gail. She had fourteen stitches in her head, a broken arm, a concussion, and whiplash. And her car was totaled. But she was alive, and it could have been worse. She had hit two other cars, but fortunately no one else was injured. She was at the hospital in Westport. India cried when she explained her injuries to Gail. She had thought of calling Paul first, but even in her confused state, she decided not to. She didn't want him to feel sorry for her, or guilty. It was her own fault. There was no point blaming him now.

She was sobbing incoherently when she called Gail and asked if she could come and get her. Gail sounded panicked, and arrived half an hour later, in Nikes, with a coat over her nightgown. She had left Jeff with the children.

"My God, India, what happened?"

"Nothing. I'm okay." But she was still sobbing, and badly shaken.

"You look like shit," Gail said bluntly, and she saw then that India was going to have a black eye to go with the rest. It was the first accident she'd ever had, and it was a doozy. "Were you drinking?" She whispered so no one could hear her. The police had already come and gone, but there were nurses all around them in the trauma unit.

"No. I wasn't," India answered, trying to stand up, but she threw up two minutes later. The hospital had said she could go home, but Gail thought she should stay there. "I can't. I have to go home to the kids. They'll worry about me."

"They're going to worry more if they see you," Gail said honestly. But India insisted. She just wanted to go home, and die quietly, in her own bed, with her head under the covers.

They left the hospital ten minutes later, with India wearing a blanket over her blood-soaked clothes, and holding a metal bowl in case she threw up, which she did four times on the way home, as she continued to cry softly.

"Did something happen? Did you have a fight with Doug or something?" Gail could see in her eyes that something terrible had happened.

"No, I'm fine," India kept repeating. "I'm fine. I'm sorry."

"Don't be sorry, for God's sake." Gail was worried sick about her. She half carried her up the stairs, put her to bed, and stayed nearby so she could hear her. She tried to give her a cup of tea, but India didn't want it. She just lay there crying until she finally fell asleep at six o'clock in the morning. And when they got up, Gail explained to the children that their mother had had a little accident, but she was fine. She had bumped her head, and had a headache.

"Where's the car?" Sam asked, looking puzzled, and surprised to see Gail making them breakfast in her nightgown instead of their mother. The sitter had left before that.

"The car is gone," Gail explained as she made pancakes for them. She had been up all night, watching India, and she looked it. "Forever," she added, and Jason whistled.

"Wow! It must have been a bad one."

"It was, but she was very lucky."

"Can I see her?" Aimee wanted to know, looking worried.

"I think we should let her sleep. You can see her later," Gail said firmly.

They ate their breakfast quietly, sensing that the accident had been more serious than Gail had said, and when they left for school, Gail went back up to see her. India was still sleeping. She left her a note, and went home to change, and promised to come back later.

India woke up at noon, and begging herself not to, she dialed Paul anyway. She just wanted to hear his voice. She wasn't even sure he'd take it, and she wasn't going to tell him about the accident. She was surprised when he got on the line very quickly.

"Are you all right?" he asked, sounding worried. He had been up all night, but it was better than his nightmares. He had been worried sick about her.

"Sure, I'm fine." She sounded weak and sleepy, but she tried to make herself sound normal, for his sake.

"Did you get home okay last night?"

"Yeah. It was fine," she lied, as tears slid down her cheeks. He could hear that she was lying, and all he could remember was the look of devastation in her eyes when she had left him.

"I was afraid you were too upset to drive. I thought about it as soon as you left. But I didn't want to call and wake the children."

"They were fine. I'm fine. How are you?" She sounded a little wonky, but he assumed she had slept as little as he had.

"Not so great," he said, sounding grim. And then he told her, "I'm leaving for the boat tonight. They're still in Gibraltar. And then I'm going to make the crossing to Antigua. Or go somewhere else. I haven't figured it out yet."

"Oh," she said, feeling slightly sicker. She had been hoping he had changed his mind again. Anything was possible, she hoped. But apparently, it wasn't.

"And India," he delivered the coup de grâce with one swift blow. It was better that way. Straight to the heart. But cleanly. "Don't call me."

"Why not?"

"We'll just drive each other crazy. We have to let this go now. I was wrong, terribly, terribly wrong. And I'm sorry."

"Me too," she said sadly. Her headache

was nothing compared to the rest of what she was feeling.

"I'm older than you are. I should have known better. You'll get over it. We both will." But he would never get over Serena. He knew that now. And he had killed India to please Serena. Wherever Serena was, he hoped that she was happy. And he hoped that the misery he felt now repaid some of the debt he owed her for not dying with her. "Take care of yourself," he said, as India nodded, crying too hard to speak for a minute, while he waited.

"I love you. I just want you to know that. If you get sane again, call me."

"I am sane. Finally. And I won't call you. I want you to know that." He didn't want to hold any hope out to her. That would have been even crueler. He knew now that Serena owned his soul forever. The rest wasn't worth having. "Good-bye," he said softly then, and hung up without waiting for her to answer. She heard the dial tone in her ear, and set the phone down gently. And then she closed her eyes and sobbed, wishing she had died in the car crash. It would have been so much simpler.

Gail came back to check on her that afternoon, when she picked the kids up from school for her, and she thought India looked worse when she sat down next to her bed. She hadn't eaten all day, but she insisted she didn't want to.

"You have to, baby. You're going to get even sicker." Gail made her a cup of tea and begged her to drink it, and as India finally put it to her lips, all she could do was think of Paul and she choked on it. She couldn't even swallow. And then, just looking at her, Gail knew. She didn't know who, but she knew what had happened. "It's about a guy, isn't it?" she asked gently, and India said nothing. "Don't let him do this to you, India. You don't deserve it. Not again." Doug had been bad enough, she didn't need a worse one. "You'll be okay. I promise, whoever he is, he's not worth it."

"Yes, he is." India started to cry all over again as she set the tea down. She hadn't even touched it. "He is worth it . . . that's the trouble." Gail didn't dare ask her who the guy was, but she had an odd feeling. India had never said anything about him. Not since the previous summer. And there was no reason to suspect. But as their eyes met, Gail had a sixth sense. The man in question had to be

Paul Ward. How they had met and what they'd done remained a mystery. Gail thought India had said he was in Europe. But he had come back. Gail was certain. And he had done this to her. She had never seen India look like that before. She had only seen one other woman look this devastated, her own sister when she was twenty. She had committed suicide over the boy next door, and Gail had found her. It had been the tragedy of her life, and she would never forget it. And as she looked at India now she was terrified, wondering if she had wanted to die the night before. If she had let the accident happen. But even India herself didn't know. She just lay in her bed again, and closed her eyes, and all she could think of was Paul, as Gail watched her and cried for her.

Chapter 24

For the rest of the month, India recovered slowly. The stitches on her head had left a scar that followed the edge of her hairline alongside her left temple for several inches. Within three weeks of the accident, it was still bright red, but they promised that within six months no one would see it, and it could have been worse. Much worse. She could have been brain damaged or dead, and she had been very lucky. There had been a plastic surgeon on duty in the trauma unit that night, and he had stitched her head up for her. He was pleased with his handiwork when he checked her three weeks later. And the broken arm only took four weeks, and was her left arm, so she wasn't totally handicapped by it. The injury that gave her the most trouble was the whiplash, and she was still wearing a collar for it when Raoul called her in April. He had a story for her in the city. A magazine was doing a story of the victim of a rape. It promised to be a sensational trial, and they needed photographs of it. She hesitated for two days, and then decided to take the story. She needed the distraction, and when India met her, she liked the woman. She was twenty-five years old and had been a famous fashion model, but the rapist had slashed her face and ended her career on a grassy knoll on a night in Central Park, where he had taken her at gunpoint when she got out of a cab on Fifth Avenue.

The story took two days, and the only thing she didn't like about it was that they met at the Carlyle, and it reminded her of Paul, but other than that it went very well. And the pictures made a big splash when they were published a week later. She hadn't heard from Paul in a month by then, and she hadn't called him. She had no idea where he was, and she tried not to think about it. She still felt like she was in a daze a month after he had left her. It had been like getting everything she'd ever dreamed of, and then losing it. The only difference was that the model was visibly destroyed. The scars that India carried with her now were just as deep, but could not be seen. Only she could feel them.

She still found it hard to believe she would never hear from him again, but by May, she had no choice but to accept it. He had left her life, with his agonies and his own scars, and his memories of Serena. And he had left something inside her broken, which she knew would never repair. She had to live with it now, along with her lost marriage. And for some reason, it hurt her more than losing Doug. It had hurt her more than anything ever had before, except losing her father. It was the death of hope at a time when she was already vulnerable and disappointed. But she knew this would heal in time. It was just a question of how long it would take her. Maybe her entire lifetime. But she had no choice now, she knew. The dream was gone. He had taken it with him, along with her heart and the love she had given him. And all she had left was the knowledge that he had loved her. No matter what he had said to her in the end, she still knew it was true. He had loved her, for a time, no matter how much he now denied it.

She had lunch with Gail in early May on her birthday. India took Gail out for her birthday every year. It was a tradition between them. India had finally bought a new car the day before, a brand-new station wagon, and Gail was admiring it with her, when she looked at India strangely. There was a question she had wanted to ask her for two months, but she hadn't dared. And now India seemed so much better, that she felt a little braver. It was none of her business, she knew. But her curiosity had plagued her. And when they sat down to lunch, Gail asked her finally. India didn't answer for a long time, and then she sighed and looked away. And then finally, with a look of agony, she faced her. There was no point keeping the secret now. It no longer mattered.

"Yes, it was Paul. We had been talking to each other for a long time, almost since the summer. Actually, since just after Serena died. After a while, he called me every day. He was my best friend, my brother . . . my everything for a while. He was my light at the end of the tunnel," she smiled, "although he swore he never would be. And then he came back to New York and told me he was in love with me. I think I was in love with him right from the first. And he felt the same. Even when Serena was alive, although he'd never admit that, and I don't think he really knew it. There was something very powerful between us, and it frightened him. Terribly. More than he could handle. It was over in a week. He said it was because of my kids, and his age, and a lot of stupid things that didn't matter. It was really because of him. He felt too guilty toward Serena, he said he was still in love with her. Anyway, he ended it the night I had the accident." She still cried when she talked about it, as she looked at Gail, with tears streaming down her cheeks like rivers.

"Did you want to kill yourself that night?" That was what had haunted Gail since March, and the other question she had wanted to ask her. It had reminded her of her sister so much, but at least India had been saved, and she seemed more herself now.

"I think so," she said honestly. "I wanted to die. But I didn't have the courage to do it. I still don't remember how it happened. All I know is that I was crying, and I felt like my life had come to an end. And then I woke up in the hospital. And the next thing I remember is going home with you, with a terrible pain in my head. But my heart felt a lot worse than my head did."

"Have you heard from him at all?" Gail asked sadly. It was a terrible story, and had very nearly come to a worse ending.

India shook her head. "No. And I don't think I ever will again. It really is over. It's taken me a long time to get that. But I do now. I haven't called him, and I won't. I don't want to torture him any more than he is already. We've both been through enough. I guess it's time to let go." Gail nodded, hoping she really had. If he really didn't want her, she had to accept that. And it sounded as though she had, however painful it had been for her.

They had a pleasant lunch after that at Fernando's Steak House. And they talked about other things. Her kids, the story she had done about the model, and eventually Doug's girlfriend. India was bothered by it, but not terribly. She still cared about Doug, but she was relieved to be out of the marriage. Her life was much simpler now, and quieter. There was no one she wanted to go out with. She didn't think she'd be up to that for a long time, after Paul. And Gail didn't say anything more about it. India was in no condition to be dating anyone, or going on blind dates, or casual ones, or having a quick flash of flesh in a motel. That had never been her style anyway. And Gail could see easily now how wounded she was, far more than her scars or her broken arm, or still tender neck. The real wounds were deep inside, where no one could see them, or touch them. They had been left there by Paul, his final gift to her, and India was convinced they would take a lifetime to heal. She had never loved any man, as she loved him, and she couldn't imagine going through it again. One day there would be someone, Gail was sure, but he would never touch the part of India Paul Ward had.

Raoul called the day they took the cast off her arm, and he said he had a story for her. She was expecting another local assignment, like the rape trial. He knew about the accident, and she figured he'd been going easy on her.

"How good do you feel?" he asked her cautiously, and she laughed. She was actually beginning to smile again.

"Why? Do you want to take me dancing? Okay, I guess. Though I don't think I'm up to tap yet. Maybe a little slow samba. What did you have in mind?"

"How do you feel about African rhythms these days?" he asked, and she could feel something spark deep inside her. It reminded her of the old days. "How does Rwanda sound to you?"

"Very far away," she said honestly.

And he was equally honest with her. "It is. And it'll be a tough story. There's a hospital in the jungle, taking care of the orphans who have gathered there over the last few years. Some of them are badly scarred, and still very damaged. They have terrible diseases, terrible problems. And there's not much help for them there. A bunch of Americans have kind of adopted the project, along with some missionaries from France, Belgium, and New Zealand. It's still kind of a melting pot of volunteers. It would make a great story if you want to do it. I won't push you. I know you've been sick, and you've got your kids to think of. It's up to you, India. I won't push. It's your decision."

"How long would it take?" she asked thoughtfully, mulling over what he'd said.

"Honestly? About three weeks, could be four. I think you could do it in three." If she did, she had to figure out what to do with her children.

"I'd love to do it," she said, without really thinking about it. It was exactly what she had wanted when she had come back to work. And although it was a tough spot, there was no immediate danger for her there, other than the usual tropical hazards, and disease. And all her shots for that part of the world were out of date. "Can I think about it for a couple of days?"

"I have to know tomorrow."

"I'll see what I can do." She sat by the phone, thinking for a little while, and then she decided to take the bull by the horns. She had nothing to lose. All he could do was refuse her.

She called Doug at his office, and told him about the story. She wanted to know if he would take care of the children while she was away. There was a long silence at the other end and then he asked her a question she hadn't expected, but it made sense.

"Could I stay with them in Westport?" For once, there was no accusation, there were no insults, no threats. It no longer mattered to him what she did, as long as she was responsible about what she did with their children.

"Sure. I guess so. It would probably be better for them anyway."

And then the kicker. "Could Tanya come with me?" She'd been living with him for several weeks, with both her kids. India wasn't anxious to have all of them under her roof, though she had room for them too. She thought about it for a long moment, but the trip to Africa rested on that for her, and reluctantly she agreed. She wasn't thrilled that he'd asked her, but if it meant his taking over for her, it was worth it to her to let him bring Tanya and her children too, although she wasn't sure what her own children would say about it. She knew they hated Tanya, and both her kids. "It's a deal then," he said, and she smiled. It was the concept he always used, the one he most believed in.

"Thank you," she said, and meant it. "It sounds like a great story." She was excited about it now, and she couldn't wait to call Raoul to tell him.

"How soon do you leave?"

"I'll tell you as soon as I know. I suspect pretty soon."

"Sooner than that," Raoul told her. She had to get all her shots immediately. She was leaving in a week. She whistled when he told her. It didn't give her much time to get organized, but she knew what she had to do.

She called Doug right back, and told him. He saw no problem with it, and she thanked him again. They were like strangers to each other now. It was hard to believe they had been married for seventeen years. Their marriage had ended so abruptly and so completely. It made her wonder now how much he had ever cared, and how important she had really been to him. And she could only assume that Tanya was a lot better than she was at following his rules. She had never worked, India knew. Her husband was a doctor. And he had given her an enormous settlement when he divorced her to marry his nurse, so Tanya was financially independent, and wouldn't be a burden on him.

India told the children about her trip that night, and that their father would be staying with them. They were pleased about that, but they all groaned when they heard that Tanya and her children were coming with him.

"Do they *have* to?" Aimee moaned, while Jason looked horrified.

"I'm not staying here," Jessica announced grandly. She was fifteen now. But she had nowhere else to go.

"Can I stay with Gail?" Sam moaned.

"No," India said firmly. "You can all stay here, and be nice about it. Daddy is doing me a favor by staying here, so I can do the story. And if that's how it has to be, you have to live with it. It's only for three weeks."

"Three weeks!" Everybody screamed in unison. "Why?"

"Because it's a long way to go. And that's how long it will take."

They all took appropriate revenge on her by either not speaking to her, or arguing with her about everything they could think of, from what they wore to where they went to who they went with. And for the next week she was sick. The shots made her violently sick to her stomach, and gave her a fever. But she was willing to do anything she had to, to make the trip and do the story.

The night before she left, she took them all out to dinner, and they grudgingly agreed to be nice to Tanya, if they really had to. But they swore that none of them would talk to her kids.

"You have to be nice. For Daddy's sake," she reminded them.

And that night, halfway through the night, Sam crawled into her bed. He had just turned ten. And Jason thirteen. Aimee was now twelve. But the only one who still slept with her from time to time was Sam. He was going to miss her. But she knew that, with Doug there, they'd be fine. Tanya had even called to tell her she'd take over her car pools, and it made India realize for the first time that she was probably going to stick around. It was strange to realize that Doug's life had moved on so completely. The waters had closed over her, but she didn't object to Tanya as much as her children did. They said that she was "creepy," and talked to them like babies, and wore too much makeup and perfume. But from India's perspective, it could have been a lot worse. He could have wound up with some twenty-two-year-old bimbo who hated the kids, and at least Tanya didn't. She seemed to be a good sport about them.

They were moving in the day she left, and she had everything ready for them. Lists, and instructions, a week's worth of food in the refrigerator and the freezer. She would have frozen some microwave dinners too, but Doug had told her that Tanya loved to cook, and wouldn't mind cooking for the children.

And when the children left for school, India kissed all of them after making breakfast, and reminded them to be good. She had left emergency numbers, in case they needed them, but she had warned everyone that she would be hard to reach. The field hospital had a radio of some kind, and messages to her would have to be relayed through there. More than anything, she knew it would be hard on the kids not to talk to her. And on her as well. But at least she knew they were in good hands, and thanks to Doug and Tanya, they could stay home, and not have their lives disrupted.

She called Gail before she left, and asked her to keep an eye on things, and Gail wished her luck. As much as she hated to see her go, she knew it would do her good. It was only since she'd gotten the assignment in Africa that she had begun to look like herself again. It had been two months since Paul had left her. And ever since then, India had looked dead. And for all intents and purposes, she was, and felt it. Gail hoped that somehow the trip would bring her back. She would be so busy, and so far away, and so much at the opposite end of the world, that she wouldn't have anything to remind her of him.

India started the first leg of the trip with a noon flight to London. She was spending the night at an airport hotel there, and then flying on to Kampala, in Uganda, the next day. From there she had to take a small plane to Kigali, the capital of Rwanda, and after that, she had to drive to Cyangugu, at the southern end of Lake Kivu, in a jeep through the bush. She left in blue jeans and hiking boots, with a down jacket, her old camera bag slung over her shoulder, and everything she was taking in one small tote bag. And as she left the house, she stopped for a minute, looked around, patted the dog, and prayed silently that everything would be all right till she got back.

"Take care of them for me," she said to Crockett, as he looked at her and wagged his tail. And then, with a small smile of anticipation she walked out to the shuttle waiting to take her to the airport.

As it turned out, the trip was endless. And the last two legs of the trip were even worse than Raoul had said. The small plane from Kigali to Cyangugu was a tiny egg-crate that only carried two passengers, and there was hardly room for her one small bag. It bumped along terrifyingly, barely scraping over the top of the trees, and they landed in a clearing between some scrawny bushes. But the scenery was incredible, and she had already started shooting before they touched ground. The jeep they had promised her turned out to be an old Russian truck, and God only knew where they had found it, but it was obvious to her after half an hour, that wherever they had found it, it had been abandoned by its previous owners because it no longer worked. And the half-hour drive turned out to be two and a half. They had to stop every half hour to fix the truck, or push other stalled vehicles out of the mud. She was becoming an expert with spark plugs and a jerry can by the time they were halfway there.

They had assigned her a South African driver, and he had come with a New Zealander, who had been in the area for three years. He said he loved it and explained a lot to her about the tribes in the area, mainly Hutu and Tutsi, and where the children had come from who were in the field hospital where they worked.

"It'll make a hell of a story," he assured her. He was a good-looking young guy, and it depressed her to realize he was probably half her age. In this part of the world, you had to be young to be willing to put up with the hardships. At forty-four, she was practically an old lady compared to the other people on the team. But she was only staying for three weeks.

"Where do you get your supplies from?" she asked, as they bumped along. It was long after dark by then, but both he and the driver had assured her it was safe. The only thing they had to worry about, they said, was the occasional elephant or tiger. But they were both carrying guns, and had promised they were good shots.

"We get our supplies from anywhere we can," he said, answering her question, as they rattled along in the darkness.

"Hopefully not the same place you got the truck."

He laughed and told her they got a lot of supplies airlifted in from foreign countries. And some aid from the Red Cross. It was two o'clock in the morning when they arrived, and they took her straight to her tent. It was tiny and airless, and looked like ancient war surplus from an underdeveloped country, but by then she didn't care. They gave her a sleeping bag and a cot, and suggested she sleep with her shoes on, in case elephants or rhinos passed through the camp, and she had to move fast. And they warned her that there were snakes.

"Great," she said. But this was Africa, not London, and she was so tired, she would have slept standing up.

She was woken by sounds of movement in the camp the next morning, and as she came out of the tent, still in the same clothes she wore the night before, with uncombed hair and teeth that needed brushing, she saw the field hospital up ahead. It was a huge Quonset hut that a group of Australians had built two years before. And everyone seemed to be moving around with a purpose. She felt like a sloth standing there trying to get her bearings, still half asleep.

"Nice trip?" an Englishwoman asked her crisply with a bright smile, and told her where the loo was. There was a mess tent behind the hospital, and after India brushed her teeth and washed her face and whatever else she could reach, she combed her hair and braided it, and headed there.

It was a glorious morning, and it was already hot. She had left her down jacket in the tent, and she was starving. There was an odd mixture of African food for the natives, and an unappetizing assortment of frozen food and powdered eggs for everyone else. Most people opted for a piece of fruit, and all she really needed was coffee, and then she was going to look up the list of people she had to see to get her story started.

She was finishing her second cup of coffee, with a piece of dry toast, when a group of men walked in, with the New Zealander she had met the night before, and someone said they were pilots. She was looking at the back of one of them with interest. There was something vaguely familiar about him. But he was wearing a flight jacket and a baseball cap, and she couldn't see his face. And it didn't matter anyway. She didn't know anyone here. She wondered if it was someone she knew from her old days of trekking around the world. Even that was unlikely. Most of the people she had known had either retired, moved on, or been killed. There weren't too many other options in her line of work, and most people didn't keep doing this kind of thing forever. There were too many risks attached to it, and most sane people were only too happy to trade it eventually for an office and a desk.

She was still looking at them, when the New Zealander waved to her, and started walking toward her. And as he did, the three pilots followed. One of them was short and heavyset. The second one was black. And as she stared at him and gasped, she saw that the third one was Paul. He stared at her just as she stared at him, with a mixture of horror and disbelief, and by then the group had reached the table where she sat. Ian, the New Zealander, introduced them all to her, and it was impossible not to see the expression on her face as her eyes met Paul's. Her already pale face had gone sheet white as she looked right at him.

"Do you two know each other?" Ian asked uncomfortably. He could see instantly that something was very wrong. If she could have designed the one scene in her life she didn't want to live through, it was happening at that moment.

"We've met before," she managed to say politely, and shook everyone's hand. She remembered instantly the stories he had told her about organizing airlifts to areas like this before he married Serena, and having reduced his participation to funding after that. Apparently, he had gone back to a more active role. And when the others moved on, Paul managed to hang back.

He looked down at India, and was obviously as upset as she was. No one in the world could have guessed that either of them would be there. It was an accident of the worst sort, as far as India was concerned.

"I'm sorry, India," he said sincerely. He could see how distraught she was. She had come here, to the remotest part of the world, to recover and forget him, and now here he was. It was a nightmare. "I had no idea. . . ."

"Oh, yes, you did." She tried to smile at him. It was the only thing to do now. "You planned this to torture me. I just know it." He was relieved to see a smile on her face, however small.

"I wouldn't do that to you. I hope you know that."

"You might." She was only half kidding, but she knew their meeting was an accident. "Is this a scene out of the worst movie in your life? It is mine."

"I know. When did you get here?" He looked worried.

"Last night."

"We just arrived an hour ago from Cyangugu."

"So I heard. How long will you be here?" She was praying he was going to say that day only. But no such luck.

"Two months. We're going to be taking supplies in and out for them, but I'll be staying here, and using it as a base camp."

"Great," she said limply, still unable to believe this was happening to them.

"What about you? How long are you here for?" he asked cautiously.

"Three or four weeks. I guess we'll have to make the best of it, won't we?" she said, sounding strained. Just looking at him was painful. It was like digging a machete through a fresh wound. He looked better than ever, though a little thinner, and a little drawn, but still painfully handsome, and more youthful than ever. The months they'd been apart didn't seem to have left their mark on him.

"I'll try to stay out of your way," he promised. But neither of them had understood yet how closely everyone worked here. They were all together constantly all day. This was a real team, and there was nowhere for them to go to escape each other.

"Thanks." She got up and put her coffee cup on a tray, and as she turned she saw that he was watching her with a pained expression. She wasn't mean enough to ask him how his dreams had been. Hers had been terrifying nightmares, mostly about him, since March.

"How are you?" he asked softly as she started to walk away.

"How do you think?" He nodded, and he couldn't identify it at first, but there was something different about her face. And as she left, he realized with a start, that she had a fresh scar running down one side of her face. He wanted to ask her about it but she'd already walked away. And as he went back to the others, he felt a familiar knife stab. But it wasn't Serena this time. It was India, and everything he still felt for her. He hadn't expected to still feel that way.

Chapter 25

For the next two days, India and Paul did everything they could to avoid each other, but it was obvious to both of them that was impossible, and in the end more trouble than it was worth.

He sat down at the same table where she was eating dinner at the end of the second day, and looked at her in despair.

"This is hopeless, isn't it?" he said in a low voice, so no one would hear him. He would have left if he could, but they were doing important work. And he knew she was covering a big story. Neither of them could remove themselves. It was going to be a rough few weeks for her. And it was no easier for him. His heart ground to a stop every time he saw her. And she was everywhere. A dozen times a day, he found himself looking into her face. And every time he did, he felt even worse when their eyes met. There was something in her eyes, so deeply bruised and painful. Just looking at her made him want to cry, or reach out to her.

"Don't worry about it," she said in her calm, gentle way. But there was no way he couldn't. It was easy to see what he had done to her. And her lip trembled as she looked away. She didn't want to see him, didn't want to feel the things he had awoken in her, but they had been there since the first time they met, and she realized with chagrin now, that they still were and perhaps always would be. She was beginning to believe this was a wound that would remain unhealed forever. He really was the love of her life. But even lost loves could be forgotten, she told herself. She had been given a superhuman challenge, and it had to be met. Somehow.

Within minutes, the others left the table, and not knowing what else to do, he looked at her, with worry in his eyes. "What happened to you?" he asked. She hadn't had the scar when he last saw her in New York, and it was very long and very fresh. And the day before, when he had seen her in the morning, she had had an orthopedic collar around her neck. She still wore it now and then when her neck hurt. And it had after the long trip. And now he gently touched the scar and she pulled away to avoid his touch.

"It's a dueling scar," she said, trying to make light of it, but he was not amused. "I had an accident," she said simply.

"In a car?" She nodded. "When?" He wanted to know all the details, what had happened to her since he had left her. He knew that all the other scars he'd given her were buried too deeply to see, unlike the one on her face.

"A while ago," she said vaguely. But just looking at her, he knew, and he felt sick.

"Was it right afterward?" He was tormented by the thought of it, and felt even more guilty than he had at first. He knew just from looking at her that it must have been right after he ended it with her.

"That night" was all she said.

"That night?" he repeated, looking horrified. "On your way home?" She nodded. "I knew I shouldn't have let you drive. I had an awful feeling about it."

"So did I," she said, thinking of what he

had done to her. She might have died. And nearly had. And wished she had for a while anyway.

"Was it very bad?"

"Bad enough."

"Why didn't you tell me when you called the next day?"

"It wasn't your problem anymore. It was mine." He remembered then how strange she had sounded when she had called him, giddy and out of it and a little incoherent. But he had assumed she was just terribly upset, which she was.

"I feel terrible. What can I say?"

"Don't worry about it. I'm fine." But her eyes told him a different tale. She was trying to keep her distance from him physically, since she couldn't otherwise. But so far nothing had worked, and being so constantly close to him, and seeing what was in his eyes didn't help. She knew him too well, and knew his pain, just as he knew hers. And she could see too that he still felt all the same things she did. He always had. No matter what he had said to her, he hadn't stopped loving her. And she could still see it now. Somehow, that made it worse. It was all such a waste. He had wasted two lives, their happiness, their future.

She wondered if that was why he had come here too. To escape. Just as she had come here to escape her memories of him. It was bittersweet irony that they had both come to the same place. God's little sense of humor hard at work again. Or destiny perhaps.

"How are we going to do this?" she finally looked at him and asked. There was obviously no way they could stay apart here. The circumstances were impossible, and looking at him made her realize how hopeless it was.

"Maybe we just have to grit our teeth and live with it for a while," he said, searching her eyes. "I'm so sorry, India. Never in a million years did I think you'd be here."

"Neither did I. They just offered me this story a week ago. It sounded great, and Doug and his girlfriend agreed to take care of the kids."

"Both of them?" Paul looked surprised. That was new since he'd been on the scene.

"How long have you been doing this?" she asked, referring to the airlifts she knew he was organizing. She had heard from everyone in the camp what an extraordinary job he and his friends had done. Paul was the organizer, the chief pilot, and he was providing the lion's share of the funding.

"Since March," he said quietly. "When I went back to the boat, I knew I couldn't just sit there for the rest of my life."

"Where is it now?"

"In Antibes. I thought if I really got the airlifts going again, and one of the other guys to run them, I could go back by next summer. If not, I can always stay here." It was a hell of a life for him, but he was doing a wonderful thing. "Anyway, I'll stay out of your hair as much as I can for the next three weeks. We've got a couple of runs to do this week anyway. Other than that, there isn't much I can do. They need me here. And they also need you." The international press attention she was going to give them was necessary for the very survival of the project, and attracting funds. She was as important as he was. Neither of them could just leave.

"It'll be all right," she said slowly, thinking about it. There had to be a way to make it work. They were both there with good intentions, there was no reason why they should be punished for their good deeds. And then she looked up at him sadly. For six months, he had given her so much hope, and then he had taken it all away. But now she had to find that for herself, and so did he. "Maybe this will sound crazy to you, it does to me a little bit," and it hadn't been what he wanted, she knew. He had made that very clear. "But maybe we can be friends. That's where all this started, way at the beginning. Maybe that's where it has to end. It could be that's why this happened to us, that we found each other here. As though some higher power decided to make us face each other, and make amends."

"You have nothing to make amends for, India," he said fairly. "You never did anything to me."

"I scared you. That's enough. I tried to lure you into doing something you didn't want." But they both knew that wasn't true. He was the one who had told her he loved her. He had opened a door and invited her in. And then, within days, threw her out again, and slammed the door on her forever.

"I scared myself," Paul said honestly, "you didn't scare me. I was the one who hurt you. At least remember that. If anyone should feel guilty here it's me." She couldn't deny that, but in spite of that, she thought that it was simplest if they put it behind them. Whatever she still felt for him, or the hurt he had caused her, there was no room for any of that here.

"You told me long before you came home that you didn't want to be the light at the end of the tunnel for me. And you aren't. But you gave me fair warning, you made it very clear." She remembered standing in yet another freezing cold phone booth while she listened to him. His words had seemed even colder to her than the air around her. The only thing that had confused her was that, in March, he had changed his mind. But only for a few days. That brief moment was an aberration, a shattered dream, a time that would never come again. And whatever hope she had now, she knew she had to find for herself. And so did he. She could no longer give it to him. And he didn't want it from her. He wanted his memories of Serena, his hold on the past, and his terrors all around him. And he didn't want India. She knew that very clearly. "We have to put what happened behind us. This is some kind of test, for both of us. We have to meet the challenge." She smiled at him sadly, stood up, and touched his hand. But just looking at her, and listening to what she said, he was confused again. But he had understood the wisdom of what she'd said. "Can we be friends?" she asked him point-blank.

"I'm not sure I can," he said honestly. Just being close to her was impossible for him.

"We have to. For three weeks anyway." She was the one who had chosen the high road. He had preferred to close the door in her face, not to call her, or let her call him. And she had no intention of ever calling him again. But for the next three weeks, in whatever way she had to, she would be his friend. She held out her hand to shake his, but Paul refused, and kept his hand in his pocket.

"I'll see what I can do" was all he said, and then he stood up and walked away. He wasn't angry at her, but he still felt very badly, and seeing her only made it worse. He had also missed her desperately each and every day. And now, seeing her reopened all the same wounds. But he still belonged to Serena and he knew it. But he also knew that there was a lot of wisdom, and generosity of spirit, in what India had said. And now he had to absorb it, and decide how he felt about it. India already knew what she felt about him. And if they could no longer be lovers, for now, at least, she was willing to be his friend.

"Are you two arch enemies from a past

life?" Ian asked her later that evening, as they walked back to their tents.

"Sort of," she said, it was easier than saying they had been lovers, even if only for a few days. "We'll get over it. There's no better place to do it than here." But as she lay in her sleeping bag that night, on the narrow cot that felt like it was going to collapse every time she moved or breathed, all she could think about was him. She had taken a lot of great photographs that day, and gathered good background information, but the thought that kept running through her mind was that Paul didn't even want to be her friend. He couldn't even give her that much. It was yet another blow to add to the rest. But she had done her part, and it had cost her dearly. Every time she had looked at him, or spoken to him, all she wanted to do was cry. And she did that finally, alone and in silence, as she lay in her tent sobbing.

The next day he went to Kinshasa for two days, and it was easier for her not to see him at the camp, and she concentrated on her work. She visited sick children and took photographs of them, and talked to orphans. She watched the doctors treat lepers with modern medicines that Paul had paid for and flown in.

She seemed to touch everyone in the camp with her quiet presence and her gentle ways. And she saw deep into their souls, always looking at them with her camera. And by the time Paul came back, she had made a lot of friends, and seemed to feel a little better.

On Friday night, the nurses gave a party, and they encouraged everyone to come, but India decided not to, since she was sure Paul would be there. She had promised him her friendship, but he had walked away. She really couldn't face him and this was his place now, his home for the moment, she didn't need to go to a party where she was bound to see him. She was only there for three weeks. It was easier just to stay in her tent.

She was reading quietly by flashlight, propped up on one elbow on her cot, with her hair piled on top of her head in the heat, and she heard a gentle stirring outside, and a sudden sound, as she jumped. She was sure it was an animal, or worse yet, a snake. She pointed her flashlight at the doorway, ready to scream if it was an animal. And she found herself looking into Paul's face.

"Oh," she said, relieved, but still frightened, and he was squinting in the bright light she pointed at him.

"Did I scare you?" He put his arm up to shield his eyes, and she pointed the flashlight away.

"Yes. I thought you were a snake."

"I am," he said, but he wasn't smiling. "Why didn't you go to the party?"

"I was tired," she lied.

"No, you weren't. You're never tired." He knew her better than that. In fact, he knew her much too well. And she was afraid that he would see into her heart. She had told him all her confidences for a long time. He knew what she felt, and what she thought, and how she worked.

"Well, I'm tired tonight. I had some reading I needed to do."

"You said we could be friends." He sounded dismayed. "And I want to try."

"We are," she affirmed. But he knew better. And so did she.

"No, we're not. We're still circling each other like wounded lions. Friends don't do that," he said sadly, as he leaned against the pole that held up her tent, and watched her with haunted eyes.

"Sometimes they have to. Sometimes even friends endanger each other, or make each other angry."

"I'm sorry I hurt you, India," he said agonizingly, as she tried to keep him out of her heart, as she would have a lion out of her tent. But it was no easier than that would have been. "I didn't mean to. . . . I didn't want to. . . . I just couldn't help it. I was possessed."

"I know you were. I understand it," she said, putting her book down and sitting up. "It's okay." She looked at him sadly. There seemed to be no end to the pain they caused each other, even now.

"No, it's not okay. We're both still dead. Or at least I am. Nothing has helped. I've tried everything except an exorcist and voodoo. She still owns me. She always will." He was talking about Serena.

"You never owned her, Paul. She wouldn't let you. And she doesn't own you. Just give yourself time, you'll get it together again."

"Come to the party with me. As a friend, if you like. I just want to talk to you. I miss that," he said sadly, and there were tears in his eyes as he said it. Inviting her to the party was the only peace offering he could think of.

"I miss it too." They had given each other so much for six months that it had been hard to get used to not having it anymore, and never having it again. But she had. And there was no point going backward. "It's probably better if we don't push it."

"What's to push?" he smiled ruefully. "I already broke it. We might as well sit together and cry over the pieces." He stood there looking at her, forcing himself not to remember what it had been like to kiss her. He would have given anything at that moment to hold her. But he knew that was crazy. He had nothing to give her. "Come on. Get dressed. We only have three weeks here. We're stuck out in the middle of nowhere. Why should you sit in your tent reading by flashlight?"

"It builds character." She smiled at him, trying not to see the fact that he was as handsome as ever. Even in the light of her flashlight, he looked terrific.

"You'll get glaucoma. Let's go." He looked as though he would refuse to leave unless she went with him.

"I don't want to," she said stubbornly.

"I don't care." He was more so. It was like playing Ping-Pong. "Get your ass out of bed, India. Or I'll carry you on my shoulder." And with that, she laughed. He was crazy, and she knew she would always love him. And now she'd have to forget him all over again, but for three weeks, what the hell. She had already lost him. Why not enjoy a little time together? She had mourned him for two months. This wasn't a reprieve. It was just a visit, a glimpse of the past and what might have been.

She slowly got out of her sleeping bag, and he saw that she still had her clothes on, a T-shirt and jeans, and after checking her hiking boots for insects or snakes, she put them on and stood looking at him. "Okay, mister. We're buddies for the next three weeks. And after that, you're out of my life forever."

"I thought I already was," he grumbled at her, as they made their way back up the hill to the field hospital, where the nurses were giving the party.

"You sure gave a good imitation of it," India said, looking at him, careful not to touch him. "That farewell scene at the Carlyle looked real to me."

"It did to me too," he said softly, and so did the scar she was wearing, he thought, as he gave her a hand over a rough spot. It was a beautiful night, and the sounds of Africa were all around them. Rwanda had its own special sights and smells. There were blossoms everywhere, and their heavy perfume was something India knew she would always remember. And there was always the smell of charcoal fires mixed with food in the camp.

They slipped into the party quietly, and Paul went to talk to some friends, and then chatted with his two pilots. He felt better that he had gotten her out, she had a right to some fun too, but he didn't want to crowd her. He felt as though he owed her something now, and even if there was no way he could repay it, he felt better being friendly at least.

India talked to the nurses for a long time, gathering more information for her article, and she was one of the last to leave the party. Paul watched her go, but he made no attempt to follow her. He was just glad she looked like she'd had a good time. He had a lot to drink, but he was still sober when he went back to the tent he shared with the other pilots. There was no luxury for any of them here. It was about as bare bones as it could get, even more so than her life in the Peace Corps in Costa Rica. But she found it very comforting, and good for the soul, and it was so familiar to her.

The next day India was busy photographing some newly arrived orphans, and when she tried to talk to them in the little bit of Kinyarwanda dialect she'd learned, all of them laughed at her, and she laughed with them. She was slowly beginning to regain her sense of humor. She was busy all week, and on Sunday there were religious services in a nearby church that Belgian missionaries had built, and India attended with some of the others. And that afternoon, Ian, the New Zealander, invited her to go for a ride in the jeep, to show her the surrounding territory, so she could take more pictures. She hadn't run into Paul all day, and Ian told her he'd gone to the market in Cyangugu. At least they had a little space from each other, which was rare here. For the past week, they had been constantly running into each other everywhere.

And the next day, when she was getting dressed, there was a funny knock on the pole that supported her tent. She looked out the flap as she zipped up her jeans. She was standing there barefoot, just as they had told her not to do, and her hair was hanging loosely and framed her face with blond silk as she saw who was out there. It was Paul.

"Put your shoes on."

"I am."

"You're going to get stung by some-thing."

"Thanks for the warning." It was still early and she was not in the mood to see him. He could see it on her face.

"I was wondering if you wanted to go to Bujumbura for a couple of hours. We have to pick up some supplies there. You'd get some great pictures." She hesitated, looking at him. He was right. It would be good for her story. But it was also a lot of Paul. She wasn't sure which she wanted, the pictures, or time with-out him. In the end, she opted for her story.

"Okay. Thanks for asking. When are you leaving?"

"In ten minutes." He grinned. He was glad she was going with him. He even liked it when she was rude to him, it reminded him of Serena. She had always been feisty, and nor-mally India wasn't. But it chafed her in a thousand ways to be in such close quarters with him, and most of them were still very painful.

"I'll hurry. Do I have time for coffee?"

"We can wait a couple of minutes. This isn't British Air."

"Thanks. I'll meet you at the jeep."

"I'll see you there," he said, and then

walked away with his head down. She had no idea what he was thinking. Probably about the supplies they were picking up, she told herself, as she picked up her camera, and hurried to the mess tent, which was a singularly appropriate name for it in this case. The food was the same every day. She knew she wouldn't gain weight on this trip. And Paul hadn't either. They were both thinner than they had been before, but for other reasons.

She grabbed a cup of coffee and drank it quickly, and a handful of damp crackers that tasted like they'd been there forever, and ran to meet him. He was standing with the black American pilot, whose name was Randy. He was from L.A., and India liked him.

He had been in the Air Force ten years before, and had gone to UCLA film school when he got out, and he'd done some work as a director. But he'd been out of work for so long, he had decided to use up his savings to come here, and do something for humanity for a change. Like so many others, he had been there for two years. And India knew he was dating one of the nurses. There were no secrets in camp. In many ways, it was just like the Peace Corps, only considerably more grown-up.

They were flying an old military plane Paul and his friends had bought them. And they took it off the ground easily as India sat in a jump seat behind them, shooting constantly with her camera. There were herds of rhinos on the hills beneath them, and she could see banana plantations forever. She was totally intent on what she was doing, and wished she could hang out of the plane to get better shots. Paul flew as low as he could without her asking, but she knew he was doing it for her. She also knew he took a long route for better pictures and she thanked him as they finally came in for a landing at Bujumbura.

The market was swarming with people, and she got some wonderful photographs, although they didn't really relate to her story. But they were background at least, and there was always a chance she could use them. She wasn't taking any chances. She shot everything she could get. And when Paul and Randy went to pick up supplies, she took photographs of them loading the plane, with the help of several Hutu in their native dress.

Finally they were ready to leave but first they sat at the edge of the airstrip and ate some fruit they bought in the market. And every now and then an armadillo lumbered past. She grabbed her camera a couple of times, and got the shot. But after a while, even she got blasé about what they saw.

"It's incredible here, isn't it?" Randy said with a wide smile. He was a handsome guy and he looked more like a movie star than a director. But there was nothing arrogant about him. And it was obvious he liked India tremendously. By chance, he had read her piece on abuse in Harlem, and the one she'd done in London on childhood prostitution. And as he mentioned it to her, she remembered her calls to Paul then. Thinking of them made her heart twist. "You do great work, India," Randy praised her.

"So do you. Here, I mean." She smiled at him, and then thanked him. Paul had said very little to her since that morning. But at least he had invited her to come. It had been fascinating and she loved it.

They headed back to their camp after they'd finished eating. It was only a short flight, and this time she just sat back quietly and looked out the window at the sights below. Paul was sitting in front of her, flying the plane, and he didn't talk to either her or Randy. He was painfully quiet. And after they landed, and got out of the plane, she thanked him for the opportunity, and helped them unload until some of the men came to help them. And when the truck came to pick them up, she and Paul rode in it, while Randy drove the jeep home.

Paul had been looking at her strangely, and then pointed to the scar she had from her accident in March. "Does that thing hurt, India?" He was still curious about it. It was fading, but if you looked at it closely, and he had, when she wasn't watching him, it still looked very nasty.

"Not really. It stings a little sometimes. It's still healing. They said it would take a long time to fade, but supposedly it will. I don't really care." She shrugged, but she was still grateful to the plastic surgeon who had closed it up. It would have been much worse if he hadn't been there.

He wanted to tell her again how sorry he was, but it no longer seemed appropriate. They had both said it too often, and it didn't change what had happened, what he'd done, or how he felt.

She walked into camp with him, and was going to take a shower and clean up, when one of the nurses hung out a window of the field hospital and called to her.

"We got a message on the radio after you left." She hesitated for a fraction of an instant, while India's heart stopped. And she knew she wasn't wrong when she heard the message. "Your son is hurt, he got in an accident at school and broke something. I don't know what though. The message was garbled and I lost them."

"Do you know who called?" India asked, looking worried. It could have been Doug, or Gail, or the sitter, or even Tanya, for all she knew. Or even the doctor, if someone gave him the number.

"No, I don't." The young nurse shook her head.

And then India thought of something, and asked her, "Which son?" She shouted up to the window where the nurse was calling to her.

"I don't know that either. It was too garbled, and there was a lot of static. Cam, I think. I think whoever it was said your son Cam."

"Thank you!" It was Sam then, and he had broken something, and she had no idea if it was serious. But she was very worried, and felt very guilty. And as she turned, she saw that Paul was still standing there, and had been listening. She turned to him with frightened eyes and his heart went out to her, and the boy who had sailed with him on the *Sea Star*. "How do I call home from here?" She figured he'd know that. He'd been there longer than she.

"Same way they called you. It's almost impossible to hear, though. I gave up calling weeks ago. I figure if something important happens, they'll find me somehow. If nothing else, they can call the Red Cross in Cyangugu. It's a two-hour drive from here, but they're wired into a real phone line."

She decided to cash in her chips then. "Will you drive me?" she asked him with a trembling voice and he nodded.

He only hesitated for an instant. But it seemed like the only thing to do. She needed to know what had happened. "Sure. I'll tell them we're taking the jeep out again. I'll be back in a minute." He was back in what seemed like less than that, and India hopped in beside him. Five minutes after she'd heard about Sam, they were on their way to Cyangugu. And for a long time, they both said nothing, and then finally, Paul tried to reassure her.

"It's probably nothing," he said, trying to sound calmer than he felt. Even he was worried.

"I hope you're right," she said tersely, and then, looking out the window at the landscape sliding by, she spoke in a strangled voice filled with guilt and panic. "Maybe Doug is right. Maybe I have no right to do this. I'm at the other end of the world from my kids. If something happens to one of them, it'll take me two days to get home, if I'm lucky. They can't even call me easily. Maybe I owe them more than that at this point." She was feeling awful and he could see it.

"They're staying with their father, India," he reminded her. "He can handle it until you get home, if it's serious." And then, as much to distract her as out of his own curiosity, he asked her a question. "What's with the girlfriend? Is it for real?"

"I guess so. She moved in with him, with her two kids. My kids hate them, and her. They think she's stupid."

"They'd probably hate anyone who came on the scene at this point, with either of you," he said, thinking of himself and the dinner in Westport. At the time he had thought it was fun, and then afterward when he revisited it, he decided they had all hated him, and always would. In fact, it had only been Jessica who had been cool to him. The others had liked him. But he had chosen to repress that. And his son Sean's words hadn't fallen on deaf ears. The prospect of helping her raise four potential juvenile delinquents, all of whom were sure to wind up in Attica, according to Sean, had terrified him. Not to mention his casual suggestion that India might get pregnant, though apparently she hadn't. But it had all contributed to his panic. But now all he could think of was Sam, when he had stood on the bridge next to him, and helped him sail the *Sea Star* . . . and then afterward, when he lay on the couch in the cockpit, sleeping with his head in his mother's lap, while she stroked his hair, and talked about her marriage. And now they were here, in Africa, and Sam was hurt. Rather than calming her, she had succeeded in upsetting him too. And they were both anxious to get to the Red Cross in Cyangugu to call home.

In the end, with a herd of cattle crossing the road, a dead horse blocking it completely farther on, and a group of Tutsi soldiers at a makeshift checkpoint, it had taken them three hours to get there on roads that were gutted and had been washed out by the rains. And the Red Cross office was just closing when they reached it. India hopped out even before he stopped, waving frantically at the woman locking the door, and she explained what she needed from her. The woman paused and then nodded, as India offered to pay her anything she wanted for the call.

"You may not be able to get through right away," the woman warned. "Sometimes the lines are down and we have to wait for hours. But you can try it."

India picked up the precious phone with trembling hands while Paul watched with a stern expression and said nothing. The woman went back to her office and picked up some papers. She wasn't in a hurry, and had been very kind to India. And at least the lines weren't down. It seemed like an absolute miracle when she heard the phone ringing in Westport. She had decided to call the house, for lack of a better idea where to call for information. She just hoped someone would be there. But mercifully, Doug answered on the second ring, as India fought back tears as she heard the familiar voice, and wrestled with another rising wave of panic about her youngest son.

"Hi, it's me." She identified herself quickly. "How's Sam? What happened?"

"He broke his wrist in school, playing baseball," he said matter-of-factly.

"His wrist?" She looked startled. "That's all?"

"Were you hoping it was more?"

"No, I just thought since you called me here that it was serious. I had no idea what he'd broken. I was imagining something truly awful, like a fractured skull and a coma." Paul was watching her intently.

"I think this is bad enough," Doug said, sounding pompous, "he's in a lot of pain. Tanya has been taking care of him all day. And he's off the team for the rest of the season."

"Tell him I love him," was all India could muster, "and thank Tanya for me." She was going to ask to talk to Sam then but Doug had more to say to her, and it was obvious he wasn't happy with her.

"Tanya deserves a medal. He's not her son after all, and she's been wonderful to him. And if you were here to take care of him yourself, India, you could shoulder your own responsibilities and not expect us to do it for you." Same old Doug. Same old story. Same old guilt. But it no longer hit her the way it used to. She had grown up in the past year, and although she still worried about her kids, Doug's hook on her had loosened. She no longer felt as guilty, except when something like this happened. And if it had been serious, she would have been devastated. But she thanked God it wasn't.

"They're your kids too, Doug." She lobbed the ball firmly back in his court. "And look at it this way, you get three weeks with them."

"I'm glad you can brush this off so lightly," he said coldly, and her eyes blazed as she answered, and Paul watched her.

"I just drove three hours to get to a phone to call you, and I'll have another three hours to get back to camp. I don't think I'd call that 'lightly.' " She'd had enough of him by then, and she was tying up the Red Cross phone, and keeping the woman who ran it from leaving, for nothing. Sam was fine, and it wasn't a big deal fortunately. "Can I speak to him now?"

"He's sleeping," Doug said firmly. "And

I really don't think I should wake him. He was up all night with the pain, and Tanya just gave him something for it." Hearing that Sam had been suffering made her stomach turn over, particularly knowing she hadn't been there for him.

"Tell him I love him very much when he wakes up," she said, as tears filled her eyes. Suddenly she missed not only Sam, but all her children. And with a six-hour time difference, with Westport behind her by that much, she knew the others were in school and she couldn't talk to them either.

"I would have thought you'd have called him yesterday, when it happened, by the way." He threw in one last barb for good measure. And the tone of his voice made her so angry, it diminished her sense of sadness.

"I just got the message three hours ago. I told you messages would take a while to reach me. Tell him I'll sign his cast when I get home. Save me room." She decided to ignore Doug's snide accusations.

"See that you call a little more quickly next time," he said nastily, and she wanted to tell him something unprintable, but India didn't want to offend the woman from the Red Cross, who could hear them very clearly.

She hung up then and turned to face Paul with a sigh. "He's all right. It's his wrist. It could have been much worse."

"So I gather." He looked grim, and she thought he was angry at her for making him drive her so far. She didn't blame him. And, as usual, Doug had been a real bastard about it. Nothing new about that.

"I'm sorry to have made you drive all this way for nothing." She looked embarrassed, but relieved, as she looked at him. In spite of everything, she'd been glad he'd been with her.

"He's still an asshole, isn't he?" He could just imagine the other end of the conversation from the things she'd been saying.

"Yes, he is," she sighed, "and he always will be. That's just the way it is. At least now he's Tanya's problem, and not mine. He never misses a chance to get a hit in."

"I used to hate him," Paul admitted. But it didn't bother him as much anymore, or it hadn't until then. He was removed now. He just felt sorry for India and the garbage she took from him. But he'd been impressed by how well she'd handled him. Doug was no longer tormenting her, or making her feel as guilty. He just made himself look stupid with the games he played.

"I used to love him." India smiled. "Shows what I know." She went to thank the Red Cross woman then, and pay for the call. She gave her fifty U.S. dollars and was sure it would amply cover it, and even include a small donation.

And then she and Paul got in the jeep and drove home. It took them even longer on the way back, on bad roads in the darkness. It was nine o'clock when they got to camp. They had missed dinner and they were both starving.

"I'd offer to take you to La Grenouille, but it would be a bit of a trek," he said, smiling at her ruefully when they found the mess tent dark and the food cupboards locked.

"Don't worry about it. Any old frog will do," she smiled back. She was almost hungry enough to eat one.

"I'll see what I can catch." He looked exhausted, as they walked slowly out of the tent. It had been a long day for him, flying to pick up supplies, and then driving seven hours to find out that Sam had broken his wrist playing baseball.

"I'm really sorry for the wild-goose

chase," she said again. She had apologized several times on the way back, and couldn't stop from doing it again.

"I was worried about him too," Paul admitted, as they stood in the clearing in the middle of camp, wondering what to do about their dinner. There was nowhere else to go. They were miles from any kind of civilization, and then India had an idea, and she looked up at him with an air of mischief.

"They must have food in the hospital for the patients," she said, looking hopeful. "Maybe we can steal some."

"Come on, let's try it," he said, grinning, and hurrying toward the hospital with her.

They found several boxes of crackers that had grown soggy from the humidity, a box of Triscuits that had gone stale, hidden in a cupboard, a box full of grapefruits, several cartons of Wheaties that still looked pretty good and didn't have bugs in them, half a dozen huge bottles of milk, and a tray of slightly soft red Jell-O. They had crates of it, sent to them by a church group in Denver.

"Well, Scarlett . . . that looks to me like dinner," he said, imitating Rhett Butler, as she poured the Wheaties into a bowl with milk, spooned some of the Jell-O into two bowls, and he cut up two of the grapefruits. It wasn't Daniel, but they were so hungry it looked good to both of them. They would have eaten the boxes the Wheaties came in if they had to. Neither of them had eaten anything since their picnic on the airstrip.

"Stale Triscuits or soggy Saltines?" she asked, holding both boxes out to him.

"You give me the nicest choices," he said, pointing to the Triscuits.

They ate enough to curb their appetites, and they both looked more relaxed with each other than they had in a week, as they talked about Sam, and her other kids, and he told her about his conversation with his son Sean two months before, and this time he actually laughed about it.

"He said that at 'my age,' I really shouldn't need to date. And he seemed to see no reason why I shouldn't remain celibate to the end of my days, which he seemed to calculate as a hundred and fourteen." He grinned. "At least I assume that's what he meant when he called me 'middle-aged.' Kids sure seem to have some strange ideas about their parents, don't they?" But he had a few strange ones of his own too, she knew, since he intended to remain faithful to the memory of Serena forever. But she didn't remind him of it. He looked too happy eating his Triscuits and his Jell-O for her to want to spoil it for him.

It was nice feeling at ease with him again. The crisis over Sam seemed to have broken the ice between them. And she didn't expect any more from him now, but at least they actually felt like friends. Knowing that was something she still cherished. It was where it all began for them, and they had shared so many confidences that it had brought them closer than some people ever were. It had been hard for both of them to lose that.

"What about you?" he asked, slicing another grapefruit for himself. She had had enough, but he was obviously still hungry. "Have you gone out with anyone?" It was a question he had been dying to ask her, and she looked startled by it.

"No. I've been too busy licking my wounds and growing up. Finding myself, I think they call it. I've been too involved with finding me to find anyone else. Besides, I really don't want to."

"That's stupid," he said bluntly.

"Oh, really? Who are you to talk? I don't see you out there on the singles scene, having dates with New York socialites and models.

You're sitting at the top of a tree in Rwanda, slicing grapefruits and eating Jell-O." It was a funny image and he laughed at it.

"You make me sound like half-man, half-monkey."

"Yeah, maybe." And then she wondered. "Or are you dating anyone?" She suddenly realized she really had no idea what he'd been doing. For all she knew, he was having affairs with half the nurses, but no one had said so. In fact, several people had made a point of telling her he was a nice guy, but a real loner.

"No, I haven't dated anyone," he said, spooning the juice out of his second grapefruit. He looked boyish and comfortable, and as he had before, he liked being with her. She was smart and funny and easy to be with. The problem was, he knew he wasn't. Easy, at least. He had all the rest of the virtues in the universe sewed up, but certainly not that one. And then he said almost proudly, "I'm still faithful to Serena." It was sad for him, but she understood it.

"How are the nightmares these days?" she asked cautiously. It had been a long time since she could ask him that kind of question.

"Better. I think I'm just too tired here to

have them. I seem to run into trouble when I go back to civilization."

"Yeah. I remember." He had lasted exactly nine days the last time. And she had wound up with a broken heart, a broken arm, and a concussion.

"Why haven't you gone out with anyone?" he pressed her, and she sighed.

"I think the answer to that is obvious, Mr. Ward. Or at least it should be. I needed time to recover from you . . . and Doug. That was kind of a double punch for me, one disaster right after the other." But in fact, it hadn't felt like a double loss as much as one very big one. She had actually lost Doug a long time before. But losing Paul had been the loss of everything she believed in and hoped for, the loss of the last of her illusions. "Maybe it was good for me. I guess it made me stronger in some ways, and clearer about what I want and need, if I ever have the courage to try again, which right now I doubt I will have. But you never know. Maybe one of these days, things will look different."

"You're too young to give up all that." He frowned as he listened to her. She sounded more hopeless now than he did. But she sounded stronger as well. She had grown subtly since he had last seen her. He had heard it when he listened to her talking to Doug from the Red Cross. She wasn't letting him walk all over her anymore. And in a way, she wasn't letting Paul do it either. She had finally begun to set limits. She didn't seem as afraid of losing the people she had once loved, but that was because she had already lost them. Other than her children, whom she would always love, she had nothing to lose now, and in some ways it made her braver.

"I haven't seen anyone out there I want," India said honestly. Now that they were just friends, she could say things like that to him.

"And what do you want?" He was curious about her answer, and she thought about it for a long time.

"Either peace, and a quiet life by myself," she said cautiously, "or if I stick my heart out there again, I want it to be for the right guy."

"How would you describe him?" he asked with seemingly objective interest. As he had long before, he was playing the role of Father Confessor. He liked to do that with her.

"How would I describe him?" she repeated. "I'm not sure I care how he looks, although handsome is nice, but I'd much rather have nice, good, smart, kind, compassionate . . . but you know what?" She looked him squarely in the eye and decided to be honest with him. "I want him to be crazy about me. I want him to think I'm the best thing in his life, that he is so goddamn lucky to have me, he can hardly see straight. I've always been the one who's done the loving and the giving, and made all the concessions. Maybe it's time to turn the tables, and get some of what I've been giving."

She had been madly in love with him, and had wanted to give him everything she had, including her kids, and he had been madly in love with Serena. In the final analysis, it hurt to know that. She had lost him to a woman who was gone and would never come back. He had preferred to remain with her memory, than to reach out and love India, and embrace her. "This may sound a little crazy to you," she said, but not even apologizing for it this time, because she no longer owed him any explanations, nor did she have any expectations of him. "I want a man who would cross heaven and earth because he cared for me . . . come through a hurricane for me, if he had to. I guess what I'm saying," she smiled at him then, and looked surprisingly young, and incredibly pretty, "the right guy for me is a man who really loves me. Not halfway. Not maybe. Not second best to someone else, not because he'd made a 'deal' with me, like Doug. I just want a man I love with all my heart . . . and who loves me that much back. And until I find that, I'd just as soon be here, taking pictures in Rwanda, and at home with my kids, by myself. I'm not settling for second best again, I'm not apologizing for anything anymore, I'm not begging," she said, and Paul knew she didn't just mean Doug, she meant him, because he had told her he didn't really love her. He was pleased to see she still had dreams, although he wondered if she'd ever find them. But at least she knew what they were, and what she wanted. In that sense, she was a lot better off than he was.

And then she decided to turn the focus on him, and she asked him the same question. "What is it you want, Mr. Ward, since you asked me that? Now I'm asking you. Who is the perfect woman you're looking for?"

But he didn't hesitate as she had. He wanted to tell her it was her, and he was tempted to, because there were so many things he liked about her. But instead, he said a single word. "Serena." And India was silent for a minute. The word still hit her like a fist, but she half expected it. She just didn't expect him to say it quite so clearly. "Looking back, I realize she was just about perfect, for me, at least. That doesn't leave much room for improvement."

"No, but it could leave room for something, or someone, different." And then she decided to be honest with him again. Maybe he needed to hear it, for the next one.

"I always felt I could never measure up to her, that I would always have been second best, if that . . . except for that one week. That was the only time I was really sure you loved me." And he had, she knew. No matter what he had said afterward. It had been his fear that had been speaking when he told her he didn't love her.

"I did love you, India," he said clearly, "at least I thought I did . . . for a week . . . and then I got scared, by what Sean said, by you, by your kids, by the commute . . . by my nightmares and my memories of Serena. I just felt too guilty for what I was feeling."

"You would have gotten over the nightmares. People do," she said quietly, but he shook his head as he looked at her, remembering all too easily why he had loved her. She was so gentle and so loving, and so god-damn pretty.

"I would never have gotten over Serena. I never will. I know that."

"You don't want to." They were tough words, but she said them very gently.

"That's probably true." India also suspected that Serena had seemed far less perfect to him when she was alive, but she was afraid to say that to him. His memories of Serena had been tinged with angel dust and fairy wings and the magic of time and loss and distance. But the reality of Serena had been a lot harder for him to handle, and India suspected that somewhere in his heart of hearts, he knew that.

"Just for the record, too, as long as we're talking about it, don't let Sean mess up your life, Paul. He has no right to do that to you. He has his own life and family, and he's not going to take care of you, or hold your hand or make you laugh, or worry about it if you have nightmares. I think he's jealous of you, and he wants to keep you locked in a closet, by yourself, and make sure that you're not too happy. For your own sake, don't let him do that to you."

"I've been thinking about that a lot actually since I've been here. About how selfish children are, at any age, at least in what concerns their parents. They expect you to give and give and give, and always be there for them, when they want you, whether it's convenient for you or not. But when you want a little understanding from them, they kick you in the ass and tell you that you don't have a right to the same things as they do. If my daughter-in-law died, God forbid, and I told Sean he should stay alone for the rest of *his* life, he'd have me locked up and say I was crazy." There was a lot of truth to what he was saying, and they both knew it. Children at any age could be very selfish, and not particularly kind to their parents. It was just the way things were sometimes, not always, but certainly in Paul's case.

"I suspected he'd be upset about us," India said quietly, not disagreeing with a thing he'd said, "and I wondered how you'd handle it."

"The answer to that, India, is 'very badly.' Just like I handled all of it. I made a real mess of it." He knew it every time he saw her scar now, and was reminded of how it had ended between them.

"Maybe you just weren't ready," she said charitably. "It was pretty soon after . . ." It had only been six months after Serena died, which wasn't long, but he shook his head then.

"I wasn't, but I never will be." And then he looked up at her with a sad smile, they had come through a lot, the two of them, and he saw that now. But in the end, they had lost the battle. Or at least he had. "I just hope you find that guy who comes through the hurricane, my friend . . . you deserve him . . . more than anyone else I know. I hope you find him." And he meant it. All he wished her now was love and freedom from the pain he had caused her.

"So do I," she said sadly. She couldn't imagine how or where or when she'd find someone, she somehow thought it would be a long time before she did, if ever. She still had a lot of things to work out of her system. Like Paul. But at least they could talk to each other now, and have a friendly evening.

"Just make sure you're ready for him when he comes," Paul advised, "and not hiding under your bed with your eyes closed, or far away in a place like this, as far away from the world as you can get. That's no way to find the kind of person you want, India. You have to get out there." But they both knew she didn't want to, any more than he did.

"Maybe he'll find me."

"Don't count on it. You have to make a little effort, or at least wave him in. It's not easy getting through a hurricane, you know, you've got high winds and bad weather and a lot of dangerous conditions to contend with. You've got to stand out there and wave like hell, India, if you want him." They exchanged a long smile, and silently wished each other well, whatever it was they each thought they wanted.

It was nearly midnight by then, and Paul finally got up, and they cleaned up the mess they'd made. They'd touched on a lot of important subjects to them that day, and had spent a lot of good time together.

"I'm glad Sam was okay," Paul said as she put the box of Wheaties away and nodded. And then he chuckled. "And by the way, when you find that guy who's willing to come through the hurricane for you, you'd better hide your kids somewhere, or he may run right back out into the hurricane. A woman with four kids is pretty scary, no matter how terrific she is." But she no longer believed what he was saying. Her children had scared him, but they wouldn't scare everyone, and she said as much as they cleaned up from their "dinner."

"They're great kids, Paul, as kids go. And the right guy is going to want me with them. They're not a handicap to everyone, and they'll grow up eventually." Paul had made her feel like damaged goods when he sent her away, as though she wasn't good enough for him. She didn't measure up to Serena, and she had too many children. But broken down, one by one, they were nice people. And so was she. And she was even beginning to suspect, remembering things he had said to her, that there were things about her that Serena might never have measured up to. At least it was something to think of.

He walked her slowly back to her tent, and then stopped and looked at her. It had been nice spending the day together. And it had been a turning point for both of them, a kind of farewell to what they had once shared, and a welcome to their new friendship. They had brought some good things along with them, cast some bad things away, and discovered some new things about each other.

"I'll see you tomorrow," he said. "Get

some sleep." It had been a long day, and they were both tired. And then he looked at her with a shy smile, and said something that touched her deeply. "I'm glad you came here."

"So am I," she said, and then disappeared into her tent with a silent wave. She was glad their paths had crossed again. Maybe it was destiny. They had both come a long way since they met, and had come over arduous roads, and rough terrain. And she was finally beginning to see the sun coming up over the mountains. But she knew, after listening to him, that he still had a long journey ahead. And she hoped that, for his sake, one day he'd get there.

Chapter 26

The next two weeks flew by, almost too fast for India, although she missed her children. She flew a few transport missions with Paul, and she took several trips in the jeep with Randy and Ian. She photographed the children she saw endlessly, and interviewed everyone she could lay her hands on. She had bags and bags of film to show for it, and she knew she had a great story.

And she and Paul spent several long evenings chatting. Having made their peace with the past, they found they had some terrific times together. They laughed about silly things, saw the same humor in almost everything, and she found that, even without the relationship they'd once had, they still cared about each other immensely. He always seemed to be hovering somewhere nearby, protecting her, and watching over her, anxious to make things easy for her, and she was deeply concerned about him.

And they managed to spend their last night together. He talked about what he was going to do next. He was planning to leave Rwanda sometime in June, and there was another airlift he had planned in Kenya. And he still had vague plans about going back to Europe, or the States, in the summer, to spend some time on the *Sea Star*.

"Call me if you come through town," she said, and he asked if she was going to Cape Cod again. She was, in July, and for the first week in August. After that, she was leaving the house, and the kids, to Doug and Tanya.

"It sounds pretty civilized," he said, as they shared a Coca-Cola.

"It is."

"What are you going to do for the rest of August?" He knew she had nowhere else to go except back to Westport.

"Work, I hope. I asked Raoul to find something juicy for me." She had loved her time in Rwanda. It had been far more wonderful than she'd expected, and the added bonus of finding Paul had made it a time she would never forget, and would always cherish. A final piece of the puzzle had fallen into place for her. She knew she still loved him, but she was able to let him go now.

He flew her to Kigali himself the next day, instead of having to take the egg-crate she had come in when she arrived. All she had to do now was catch a plane to Kampala, and then back to London. And after that, it was easy.

She knew the kids would be waiting for her, and she could hardly wait to see them. And as they waited for her plane to arrive, Paul reminded her to give his love to Sam, and say hello to the others.

"I will if they're not in jail," she teased him. It was easier now that his old fears were no longer between them, and she no longer had any expectations of him. Her dreams did not depend on him anymore. And though they had lost something of enormous value to her, instead in Africa they had found something very small and precious.

Her plane arrived finally, and she looked at him tenderly, and then she put her arms around him and hugged him. "Take care of yourself, Paul . . . be good to yourself. You deserve it."

"So do you . . . and if I see a guy in a slicker, looking for a hurricane, I'll send him to you."

"Don't worry about it," she said with a smile, and meant it. But she knew that despite what no longer existed between them anymore, she was going to miss him.

"I'll call you sometime, if I ever get back to civilization." There was no threat to him anymore, and no promise either.

"I'd like that."

And then he took her in his arms and held her for a few final seconds. There was a lot he would have liked to say to her, but he didn't know how. More than anything, he wanted to thank her, and he wasn't even sure why. Maybe just for knowing who he was, and letting him be that person. They had somehow managed to find a kind of unconditional acceptance of each other.

There were tears in her eyes as she boarded the plane, and he stood on the tarmac and watched her for a long time. And then he stood there and watched the plane, as it took off, circled the airfield once, and headed slowly back to where she had come from.

He got back in his own plane then, and flew back to Cyangugu, and he had an odd feeling of peace as he thought about her. She didn't frighten him anymore, she didn't make him run away, and his feelings for her now, whatever they were, didn't even make him feel guilty. He just loved her, as a friend, a mother, a sister. He knew he would miss the laughter he had shared with her, and the mischief in her eyes, and the raw outrage she expressed when she thought he had said something stupid. She was no longer hurt or angry at him or afraid of him. She wasn't desperate for him to love her anymore, nor did she expect anything from him. She wasn't desperate for anything. She was a bird sailing through her own skies, and thinking of her that way made him feel strangely happy. And it was only when he got back to camp, and everyone was saying how much they would miss her, that he felt the full force of her absence. It hit him harder than he'd expected.

He walked past her tent later that day, and felt a physical ache as he realized he wouldn't see her. Suddenly, the distractions she had provided seemed more important than he'd realized. And in spite of the independence he claimed, he felt lost without her. Just being there without her caused him pain.

And that night, as he slept in the pilots' tent, he had the first nightmare he'd had in months. He dreamed that India was on a plane, and as he watched from the ground, it exploded in the air in a million pieces. And in his dream he looked everywhere for her, crying, sobbing, begging people to help him. But wherever he looked, whatever he did, no matter how much he cried, he couldn't find her.

Chapter 27

When India walked into the house in Westport, it was immaculate, the sitter was there, and the children were eating dinner. And they all screamed with delight the minute they saw her. Sam frantically waved his cast at her, wanting to show it to her, and everyone had a thousand things to tell her. From their point of view, and even from hers, it had been an endless three weeks. But in many ways, both professional and personal, she had gotten a lot accomplished.

And when she saw how well organized everything was, and how meticulous she had been, India was actually grateful to Tanya. She called her in New York that night, and thanked her for everything she'd done. She knew Doug hadn't done more than take them to an occasional movie, and come home on the 6:51 to eat dinner. And the children even grudgingly admitted that they liked Tanya. It was still a little hard for India to accept that she had been replaced so easily in Doug's eyes. It made her what she had always feared she was, or had been in the last year of their marriage, a generic wife who could be tossed out and traded for another. But she knew she didn't want to be married to Doug. And she was always shocked to realize, after seventeen years, how little she missed him.

But she was still startled when he told her on the phone that night that he and Tanya were getting married, when their divorce was final in December. There had been total silence for a minute, while India caught her breath, and then told him she hoped he'd be very happy. But when she hung up the phone, she was stunned to see that her hands were shaking.

"What's wrong, Mom?" Jessica asked as she cruised through the room, to make sure her mother was still there, and borrow a sweater.

"Nothing . . . I . . . Did you know that your father and Tanya were getting married?" She knew it was probably the wrong way to tell her, but she was so shocked herself that she didn't think about it.

"Yeah, sort of. Her kids told me."

"Are you okay with that?" India asked her, looking worried, and Jessica laughed and shrugged.

"Do I have a choice?"

"No," India said honestly, and neither did she. She had lost her options when she had refused to toe the line and do what he wanted. But maybe it was better that way. She had found something she never would have found if she stayed with him. Herself. It was a piece of her life she knew she couldn't live without now. Having found it, she couldn't give that up for anyone, and knew she never should have in the first place.

But her ego was still feeling a little bruised the next afternoon when she saw Gail at school, when she went to pick the kids up. And she was surprised to hear that Gail knew about it.

"Does everyone know but me?" she said, still asking herself why it mattered to her. But it did. Hearing that Doug was getting married had depressed her. And she was hard on herself about it.

"Come on," Gail chided her, "you were married to the guy for seventeen years. How could you not be bothered?" On top of it, Tanya was younger than she was, and jazzier, even if the children did say she was stupid. But that was obviously what Doug wanted. And India had seen firsthand evidence that Tanya was an impeccable housekeeper.

It was odd to think of it all now. In India's eyes, everyone had someone, and she didn't. Tanya and Doug had a life, and they were going to be married. India had no one. And Paul was going to spend the rest of his life roaming the world, and dreaming of Serena. Even Gail seemed happier with Jeff these days. They had rented a house for the summer in Ramatuelle, in the south of France, near Saint-Tropez, and for once she sounded excited about it. And in the fall, she said she was getting a face-lift. Suddenly, everyone else's life seemed better to her than hers, and more settled, and like Noah's Ark, they all had someone they wanted to be with. All India had was her work, and her children.

But it was more than some people had, she reminded herself finally. And more than she had had a year before, when she and Doug were battling over her career, and his definition of marriage. Remembering her misery over that, and how lonely she had been married to him, brought it back into perspective. She was alone now, but not always lonely. In fact, most of the time, she wasn't.

The children got out of school that week, and she packed their things for Cape Cod. Everyone was excited about it, as usual, except Jessica, who didn't want to leave her new boyfriend. All she had at the Cape, she said mournfully, were "the boring Boardmans."

"You'll find someone," India reassured her the night before they left, and Jessica cried as she looked at her in anguish.

"Mom, there's *no one* out there!" And the moment she heard it, India realized how much the absurdity of what Jessica had said echoed her own feelings. The funny thing was, she didn't care as much now. She was getting used to climbing the mountains alone, doing things that mattered to her, and just being with her children. And whenever an assignment came up, she had her work to give her satisfaction. But she had no man to love her, and sometimes she missed that.

"Jessica," her mother corrected her with a smile, "if there's no one out there at fifteen, there's no hope for the rest of us, believe me." But of course, Jessica couldn't imagine why there would be a man for India, at her age. India had actually forgotten that for an instant.

"Mom, you're *ancient!*"

"Thank you," she said calmly, "I needed to hear that."

Jessica viewed her mother's life as essentially over at forty-four. It was an interesting concept, and reminded India of her conversation with Paul, about not letting Sean screw his life up. She had clearly been tossed in the same bag as Paul now. Over the hill, and useless. A fossil.

They drove to Harwich the next day, and went through all the familiar rituals, opening the house, making the beds, checking the screens, and running across the street to see their friends. And that night as she lay in bed, India smiled as she listened to the ocean.

She stopped in to see the Parkers the next day, and some other friends. The Parkers invited her to their Fourth of July barbecue, as they always did, and reminded her to bring the children. And when they went, India forced herself not to dwell on the memory of Serena and Paul there the year before. Thinking about it now was pointless.

And as the weeks flew by, she realized that even alone there this year, with no husband to spend her weekends with, and no romance to look forward to, it was turning out to be the perfect summer. It was relaxed and easy and comfortable, and she loved being with her children.

She still missed Paul, in a way, but she had had a postcard from him that told her he was in Kenya, doing pretty much the same thing he had done in Rwanda. And he sounded happy. He had added a P.S. telling her he was still looking for a guy in a slicker for her, and she had smiled when she read it.

It was odd looking back a year, to when she had met him on his yacht, and she and Sam had sailed on it. It had been the beginning of a dream for her, but at least she no longer felt it had ended in a nightmare. She still felt sad remembering what she'd felt for him, but the scars on her heart were beginning to fade, like the scar on her head she'd gotten the night he left her. She had learned that you couldn't hang on to sorrow forever.

She called Raoul at the end of July, hoping to land an assignment for the time when the kids stayed at the Cape with Doug in August. But so far, Raoul had nothing.

The oddest thing of all was remembering that only a year before, she and Doug had still been together, and doing constant battle. It seemed to her now as though they had been apart forever. It made her pensive to realize how lives changed, and how different things were. A year before, she had been married to Doug, begging him to let her work again, and Serena had still been alive. So much had changed in a year for both of them. So many lives had come and gone, and unexpectedly touched them. She wondered sometimes if Paul thought about the same things as she did. How things had changed in a year for both of them.

Sam had taken sailing lessons in July, and loved them, and she had signed him up for a second session in August. He still talked with awe about the *Sea Star.* And to India, that part of her life seemed like a dream now.

The weather had been good that year too, right up until the end of July, and then suddenly it changed and they had a cold spell. It rained for two days, and got so chilly, she had to force the children to wear sweaters, which they hated.

They stayed inside and watched videos, and she took all of them, and half a dozen of their friends, to the movies. It was harder finding things for them to do in bad weather. But at least Jessica was happy, she had struck up a romance with one of the previously "boring Boardmans." Everyone was having a good time. India was only sorry that her last week at the Cape was somewhat dampened by bad weather, but the children didn't mind it as much as she did.

The weather went from bad to worse, and five days before she was due to turn the house and the kids over to Tanya and Doug, she and the children watched the news and saw that there was a hurricane coming straight for them. Sam thought that was terrific.

"Wow!" Sam said, as they all listened to the news bulletins. "Do you think it will wash the house away?" It had happened to someone they knew, years before, and Sam had always been fascinated by it.

"I hope not," India said calmly. The warnings on the news had told them what to do. Hurricane Barbara was due in two days, and judging by the weather maps, they were directly on its path of promised destruction. The first one of the year so far, Hurricane Adam, had struck the Carolinas two weeks before and caused untold damage. And she hoped that this one wouldn't do the same to them. And despite her reassurance to the children, she was actually a little worried.

Doug called them, concerned, and gave her some helpful instructions. But basically, there wasn't much they could do. If it started to look too dangerous, and they were told to evacuate, she was going to drive them back to Westport. But India was still waiting to hear if it was going to veer away and change its course just enough to spare them. She hoped so.

And in the last hours of the hurricane watch, she got her wish. Hurricane Barbara shifted just enough to unleash an incredible storm on them, but the eye of the storm was heading now toward Newport, Rhode Island. But in spite of that, the winds still managed to tear off their screens, destroy their trees, and do enough damage to the roof to cause a leak in the kitchen. She was putting buckets under it and rushing around checking windows two days before the end of her stint in the house, when she heard the phone ring. She never answered it anymore, it was always for the children. But they were all out, and she picked it up finally with a look of irritation. There was no one on the line. She would have thought it was a prank, except for the fact that they had been having trouble with the phone lines all morning. It rang again, and did the same thing, and she was sure that either some of the phone lines were down, or they were about to lose their power. And then, when she picked it up a third time, she heard a crackling on the line, and there was so much static she couldn't hear the voice on the other end clearly. All she could hear were intermittent words that meant nothing. And there was no way she could recognize the caller, or even determine if it was a man or a woman.

"I can't hear you!" she shouted, wondering if they could hear her. She thought it might be Doug again, calling to see how they were doing. He had been very upset when she told him the roof was leaking, and was already complaining about what it would cost to repair it.

The phone rang a fourth time, and she ignored it. Whoever it was would have to call back later. A storm window had just blown off her bedroom, and as she wrestled with it, wishing the kids were home to help her, the phone just went on ringing. She picked it up again, looking exasperated, and this time, along with the static, she could hear some words more clearly, but most of them were missing. Listening to what was being said was like deciphering a puzzle.

"India . . . coming . . . storm . . . coming . . ." And then something that sounded like *thicker*, and then the phone went dead in her hand. It was obviously for her, but if they were calling to warn her about the storm, they were a little late. She was beginning to feel like Dorothy in *The Wizard of Oz* as, one by one, the storm windows blew off the house and shattered. Looking at the storm raging outside, it was hard to believe the hurricane had missed them, and she felt sorry for the people in Newport.

The children were all visiting friends while she battled with the leak in the kitchen, and another one that had sprung up in the living room. She was startled suddenly to see Sam running toward the house from the beach with a friend, as she looked out the window. They were soaked to the skin, and she tried to wave him inside, but he was beckoning to her. He loved being out in the bad weather.

She stuck her head out the door, fighting the wind, and shouted at him, but he was still too far away to hear her. The sky was so dark, it looked more like night than morning. And she was trying to wave him in, but he continued to ignore her.

She grabbed his raincoat, struggled into her own, and ran outside to see him. She had her head down against the wind, but as she looked up to find Sam, she was struck suddenly by how beautiful it was. The skies were thick and dark, and the wind was so strong, she could hardly reach him. There was an irresistible feeling of excitement and exhilaration and the power of nature. She could see why Sam loved it.

"Go inside!" she shouted at him, and tried to get his coat on him, but she saw that he was so wet it was pointless. And as she held the slicker out to him, the wind blew it from her hands, and it flew away like a sheet of paper, as they watched it. But Sam was pointing out to sea, and saying something to her. And as her eyes followed the slicker floating into the sky, she saw something in the thick weather beyond it. And then she realized what Sam was saying.

"It's . . . the . . . *Sea* . . . *Star* . . ." she heard him say finally, as she looked at him and shook her head, knowing it wasn't. The *Sea Star* was still in Europe. Paul would have called her, or at least sent a postcard, if he was coming this way. But Sam was jumping up and down and pointing, as she squinted in the rain. It was a boat of some kind, but it didn't look like a sailboat.

"No, it isn't!" she shouted back. "Go . . . inside . . . you'll catch pneumonia. . . ." And then as she tried to pull him along with her, she saw what Sam did. The boat just beyond them, on pitching seas, did look like the *Sea Star,* but couldn't have been. But whoever she was, her sails were full, and she almost looked as though she were sailing through the sky, with the speed of lightning and the wind behind her. India couldn't imagine Paul doing anything that crazy, sailing in a hurricane, even if he had been there. He was far too sensible a sailor. But along with Sam, she stood there and watched the boat anyway, fascinated by it. India was sure it was a different yacht, but she looked very much like the *Sea Star.* And then finally, she got Sam inside, in spite of his protests, and his friend went in with him. But India stayed outside for another minute to watch the sailboat flying and rolling and pitching. There were huge waves pouring off her bow, and the masts were bobbing and dipping like toothpicks. The boat was still at a considerable distance from the shore, but she seemed to be heading right past them.

India wondered if the sailboat had been far out to sea when the high winds struck, and was now desperately heading for shore to find safety, and she couldn't help wondering if they were in trouble and she should call the Coast Guard.

There were rocks farther up the coast, near the point, and in a storm like this one, any vessel at all would be in danger, even a large boat like this one. And as India began to turn away, she saw Sam and his friend continuing to watch the boat from the window. She was just about to go in, and make hot chocolate for them, when the mists shifted and she saw the boat more clearly, and at that exact same second in her head, she remembered the phone call . . . coming . . . storm . . . coming. . . . Were they telling her the storm was coming, which she already knew, or were they telling her something very different? The voice had said her name, but she couldn't recognize it, it was too disrupted and too broken, and then she knew as she looked at the boat again, and felt a hand squeeze her heart imperceptibly. She didn't know if she was being crazy, or just foolish. But suddenly she knew that Sam was right. It was the *Sea Star.* No other boat looked quite like her, and she had come much closer to them in the last few minutes.

India turned to look at Sam through the window, but he had disappeared with his friend, probably to his room . . . or to watch TV . . . but she turned back again, watching the boat fighting its way through the storm, as she heard the words again . . . coming . . . coming . . . and perhaps not *thicker* . . . but *slicker*. . . . Only he would be crazy enough, and sailed well enough, to do this. And she knew suddenly with certainty that he had called her. But what was he doing?

Instead of going back inside, she walked through the raging storm toward the water. And as she watched the boat, she saw it heading toward the yacht club. She had no idea why, or how he had gotten there, but she knew that Paul was coming . . . coming . . . coming . . . coming through the storm. And he had called to tell her. She began walking at first, and then running toward the point where they were headed. She knew the children would be all right. But she knew something else now too . . . she wanted to believe it . . . but it was much too crazy. He wouldn't do this. Or would he? And what if they were dashed against the rocks . . . what if . . . why had he done this? It made no sense now . . . or did it? It had made sense once, so long ago . . . it had made sense to both of them, not only to her. And as she began running toward the yacht club, through the wind, she knew that she was crazy to think it, or hope it, or believe it. . . . He wouldn't do this, yet she knew he had as the boat stayed on a steady course, in spite of the heavy seas that fought her.

She saw him pass the rocks on the point, and as the boat continued to battle the wind and waves, India watched it. Maybe he wasn't even on board, she told herself, so she wouldn't be disappointed. Maybe it was another boat, and not the *Sea Star*. Or maybe he was as foolish as she was, to believe in something they had once had and lost, and at times she still dreamed of. She wanted it to be him now, wanted him to be there, more than she'd ever wanted anything in her life. She wanted it to be Paul who had called her. And when she reached the yacht club finally, she was breathless. She ran out to the point, and stood there watching, waiting for him.

Boats were bobbing violently at anchor, and a few of the owners had come down to secure them. She could see them working feverishly, and as she looked out to sea again, her breath caught as she saw him. He was standing on the deck in his foul-weather gear, and there were two men with him. They were close enough to see now. She assumed the men with him were crew members, and they seemed to be moving with great speed, as he pointed to things and worked with them. But there was no doubt in her mind now it was Paul. She recognized him easily, and as she watched, he suddenly turned toward her. They were very near now, and attempting a complicated maneuver to bring them safely into the harbor.

She stood as still as she could in the wind, her eyes never leaving him, and he waved at her. And as she squinted against the storm, she saw him smiling, and she lifted her arm and waved in answer. He was standing on deck, waving back at her, and in spite of her raincoat, she was soaked to the skin. But she didn't care. She didn't care if he disappointed her again, she just wanted to know now. She had to know why he had come here.

She saw the whole crew come on deck

then, and he stopped waving at her to give them more orders. They seemed to be struggling with things she couldn't see, and he furled their sails and turned on the motors. He was determined to get as close as he could, and she saw them throw out the anchor, as two of the men lowered the tender, and she wondered what he was doing. The waters weren't as rough in the harbor, but she still didn't see how he would get to the shore in the tender without capsizing. She held her breath as she watched him. But all she could remember was what she had told him in Rwanda, about wanting a man who would come through a hurricane for her, and she knew he had remembered it from his P.S. on the postcard about the slicker. She was certain now that that was what he had been saying to her on the phone . . . it was something about a slicker. But what was the rest? Was he only teasing her? But as she saw the tender approach, and saw him wrestling with it, she knew he was deadly serious about what he was doing. And she was terrified that he would capsize and drown as she watched him.

It seemed like hours as he crossed the short distance to the steps of the yacht club, but it was only minutes. And as he came closer still, she saw him watching her, as she ran down the steps to meet him. He threw the line to her and she caught and held it, as he jumped out of the tender and tied it to one of the rings. And then he took one long stride to the step where she stood, and looked at her intently. There was a look in his eyes she had seen before. It was like a voice calling to her from the distance. It was the voice of her dreams. The voice of hope. It was the bitter-sweet memory of what they had had and lost so quickly. She wanted to ask him what he was doing there, but she couldn't speak. She could only stand there looking at him, as he pulled her to him.

"It's not a hurricane. . . . but will this do?" he said, close enough to her ear for her to hear him. "I tried to call you."

"I know," she said, and he heard her. "I couldn't hear what you were saying." She looked into his eyes then, afraid of what she would find there. Afraid she was wrong, and that the dreams had never existed.

"I said I was coming. It's not a hurricane, it's just a storm." But it was a good one. "If you want a hurricane, India . . . I'll take you to Newport . . . if you want me . . ." he said, his tears mixing with the rain that washed his cheeks. "I'm here. I'm sorry it took me so long to get here." It didn't seem long as she looked at him. It didn't seem long at all. It had taken them a year to come through the storm. A lifetime to find each other. The dream had come true finally. They had found it. She touched his cheek with a trembling hand, as she saw the *Sea Star* just behind him. They had both been lost for so long. And by some miracle, through life's storms, they had found each other.

She smiled up at him in a way that told him all he needed to know. And she knew he had come home to her at last, as he pulled her into his slicker with him, and kissed her.